PRAISE FOR JUDITH MOFFETT
AND **THE RAGGED WORLD**

"[A] considerable achievement . . . Everyone who plays a role in this complicated narrative is a stubbornly self-possessed individual . . . You will be engaged and moved."
The New York Times Book Review

"A convincing near-future world . . . Moffett, winner of the 1988 John W. Campbell Award for best new SF writer, focuses on characters and emotions in presenting a provocative possible reality."
Publishers Weekly

"One of the best new writers to enter science fiction in many years, an intense and thoughtful writer of great literary gifts, and a keen insight into the depths of the human heart."
GARDNER R. DOZOIS, editor of
Isaac Asimov's Science Fiction Magazine

"A brave book, exhilarating and harrowing . . . Judith Moffett knows all the hard truths about life, death, and the human spirit, and writes of them with the sinew and clarity of a poet."
MICHAEL SWANWICK, author of *Stations of the Tide*

"Striking characterizations and intimate storytelling . . . A rewarding experience."
Amazing Stories

"Moffett handles her story and its characters with marvelous warmth and empathy. You, like me, will find her imagination a wondrous place to visit."
Analog

THE RAGGED WORLD

A Novel of the Hefn on Earth

Judith Moffett

A Del Rey Book
BALLANTINE BOOKS • NEW YORK

A Del Rey Book
Published by Ballantine Books

Grateful acknowledgment is made to reprint from "Traveling Through the Dark" copyright © 1977 by William Stafford.
The following chapters have been published elsewhere in somewhat different form.
"Remembrance of Things Future," in *Isaac Asimov's Science Fiction Magazine*, December 1989.

" 'Ti Whinny Moor Thoo Cums at Last' " ("The Hob"), in *IAsfm*, May 1988.

"Tiny Tango," in *IAsfm*, February 1989.

"Final *Tomte*," in the *Magazine of Fantasy and Science Fiction*, June 1990.

"The Ragged Rock," in *IAsfm*, December 1990.

Library of Congress Catalog Card Number: 90-48524

ISBN 0-345-37500-9

This edition published by arrangement with St. Martin's Press, Inc.

Manufactured in the United States of America

First Ballantine Books Edition: June 1992

Cover Art by Richard Hescox

For Tim, with love

Contents

Introduction

HEFN ON EARTH

23 February 2023

My name is Nancy Sandford. I'm a plant breeder, magazine editor, and sometime college botany teacher; and I've been drafted by Godfrey—the Hefn observer to the Rodale Research Center in Maxatawny, Pennsylvania, and to assorted Amish communities scattered throughout northern Ohio—to write an introductory background essay for this book.

There isn't much I wouldn't do for Godfrey. A number of years ago he intervened, at some cost to himself, to save my life. Since only Hefn intervention *could* have saved me, this pretty well compromises my objectivity about the Hefn. The irresistible pun of my title—a real groaner, I grant you—does no more than reflect that simple truth, from my (admittedly rather special) point of view.

Not that I'd go so far as to claim that the Hefn have built Jerusalem in England's green and pleasant land, or even that ultimately they'll succeed in doing that; but let's be clear. I'm "for" the takeover and the attempt, okay? That's my position. Those who think I'm acting as a tool of an alien PR effort by writing this essay are entitled to their opinion, but I couldn't do otherwise if I wanted to, and I don't.

See, it isn't only that I was dying and they saved me. It's also that for such a long time I was myself so thoroughly alienated from the human race, the human viewpoint—that for so many years the life I had to lead was other than, and less than, a truly human life. For a person with my background, adopting the Hefn point of view is actually easier in some ways than identifying with the general human point of view.

1

If we've all got that straight, we can proceed.

Godfrey has asked for a brief history of the past seventeen years, a history of the world since the beginning of the Hefn presence here. Most of you will be familiar with most or all of the story, but he wants me to summarize the main points anyway: to recount how the aliens came, left, came back to stay—not to save the life of one obscure breeder of cantaloupes but to save the world's life; and how they've nearly done it, too, though at fearful cost to many of us who lived here before they arrived.

This, then, is what happened:

The Hefn—hairy, gnomelike humanoids, or dwarfoids—first returned to Earth in the spring of 2006. They departed that same year, after collecting what evidence they could of the comrades they had left behind a very long time ago, and for whose sake they had finally come back.

Four years later, following a change of command aboard their ship, the Hefn turned up again. They arrived, as it happened, at a moment of crisis; and their first act was to demonstrate that if they wished to, they could blast the whole surface of the Earth to flinders. To most people it was almost more terrifying that they also possessed the means of examining, and of erasing, the contents of the human mind.

(Let me jump ahead of my story for a moment and point out that the Hefn used the threat of mindwipe in order to control us without being forced to destroy us, with or without destroying Earth's biosphere at the same time. It's important to remember that. I don't think there's much doubt that they could have exterminated the human race and left the rest of the ecosystem, or the part not dependent on human life, undamaged. No one knows the extent of their ability to control by the power of suggestion. If universal infertility lay within their scope, why not a universal death wish?

Some of you are thinking that for all we know they *have* as good as exterminated us, that the ban on conceiving is just another version of humanity's fate in *Childhood's End*, that we have only their say-so that the ban will ever be lifted. All right, it's customary to think in terms of what the aliens have done to us, or for us; what I'm saying is that perhaps we would all do well to remember occasionally what they might have done, even threatened to do—yet have so far refrained from doing.)

In any event, and for whatever reasons, the faction command-

2

ing the ship in 2010 claimed to be deeply interested in trying to fix what was wrong with the Earth. While the Hefn still cared intensely about the eventual fates of their mutinous crew members, marooned in Sweden and northern England back in the mid-seventeenth century, their leaders had a new and more urgent interest now as well. So there they all sat parked on the moon, bristling with implacable power and potential menace, and sent their observers—like so many imitations of the Seven Dwarves—among the people.

At the end of several months' intent hands-off observing, the Hefn requisitioned some scribes and dictated their Directive. This they conveyed to the Secretary General of the United Nations, to be translated and published in all the languages of the world.

When the document issued from the mechanical translators, cries of protest and distress rose up at once from every nation on Earth, for the measures called for by the aliens left nobody untouched by immediate hardship, and many would ultimately be ruined.

A complicated, detailed document, the Directive's essential principles boiled down to this: we Earthlings were to be given nine years to mend our ways completely. Nine years was all we would get. If by the year 2020 we still had not managed to meet the Hefn demands, the Earth would be sterilized of human life— no appeals and no exceptions. Nothing was said about *how* this would be done, but it was difficult to doubt that the aliens were capable of carrying out their threat. (It was easier, of course, for human nature to deny that the threat would ever be carried out. Denying, the Hefn tell us, is one of the things we do best.)

Humanity must cease its ecosystem-altering behavior *at once*, that was the gist of the Directive—whatever the cost, whatever suffering, famines, or economic collapses might come of this. The tenth-measures briefly taken in response to environmental concerns that had surfaced in the West around 1970—the half-measures following upon a more serious and widespread alarm raised in the late eighties—the millennial panic of the year 2000—all these paroxysms had been opposed by vested interests and had ultimately come to little. Political gains had been made, then lost as denial set in, then abandoned in despair as things worsened to the point where the problems seemed overwhelming. The laws still in effect were far too weak.

For all organisms evolved to live in a planetary system suitable to human life, the situation was acutely critical when the Hefn came—bad in 2006, worse in 2010. Nevertheless, the aliens decided to make a last-ditch effort to keep the Earth from moving at once into an entirely new phase of its own evolution, with conditions as disagreeable to Hefn physiological processes as to human ones.

Anybody who didn't like this knew what they could do about it. The aliens weren't asking, they were telling, and they weren't bothering to be polite.

Here's what the Directive said:

All fossil fuels, and all nuclear power plants, would be phased out. Only renewable fuels, wood or alcohol or oils made from plants, could be burned; only water, wind, and sunlight could be used to generate electricity, and the great hydroelectric dams would no longer be maintained. Detroit and its ilk were given nine years to perfect an automobile that would run on either photovoltaic cells or hydrogen fuel produced from water by photolysis; in nine years' time, vehicles on major highways around the world would travel on friction-reducing rails.

Old refrigerators and air conditioners containing chlorofluorocarbons would no longer be repaired when they broke down. The few countries still making and using CFCs were to cease production immediately.

No manufacturing process would be permitted to produce toxic wastes.

Plastics had to be degradable—that is, not made from petroleum. *All* plastics.

Reforestation had to be speeded up dramatically, and not one single additional square meter of the tiny bit of remaining rain forest was to be destroyed. (Some Tanzanian farmers found out fast what violating that proviso meant.)

The waterways and aquifers of the world had to be spared any further pollution from solvents, or oil-based substances, or phosphates, or nitrates.

Further dumping of trash at sea was forbidden.

Concerned people had been saying for thirty years that the practices of agribusiness were ruinous and could not continue, but they had. Not any longer: all over the planet, farmers great and small were commanded to educate themselves in the principles of sustainable agriculture and integrated pest management, for chemical fertilizers, herbicides, and pesticides were to be entirely replaced by botanicals and animal and green manures. To reduce the erosion of topsoil the Directive mandated cover crops and no-till cultivation. Monocultural farming was to end; thousand-acre fields of corn and soybeans stretching beyond the horizon would be seen no more, even in places like Kansas and the Ukraine. In keeping with this, farm machinery powered by fossil fuels would no longer be permitted to operate. And land held in production by aquifer-draining and soil-salifying irrigation could not continue to be farmed.

The shakeup of agriculture was to be complete, and the transition period an assured nightmare for farmers and consumers alike—particularly in light of the restrictions on industry and transportation, which decreed that produce could be moved over long distances only by river barge and rail. The industry would have no choice but to shift from global to local distribution of goods, and yields were certain to plummet. It seemed that the Hefn expected people in a given area to feed and provision themselves—for many, a pure and self-evident impossibility.

The Directive took no account of this. It said nothing, for instance, about how botanical pesticides or vegetable fuels were to be made or distributed under the new law. It did not explain how the catalytic converters necessary to keep wood-burning stoves from themselves becoming a major source of air pollution could be manufactured, or how the stoves and plant-oil burners were to be forged in sufficient numbers to warm the houses of the world, or how they were to be conveyed to the people who needed them. There was a great deal it didn't say. The Hefn were concerned solely with the *what* of things; the *how* they left to the humans to devise (if they could).

In fact, their Directive seemed bent on setting the clock back about three centuries. That the world's human population had been many times smaller three centuries earlier, that the global village had come into being along with a computer-controlled, computer-dependent global economy, that the changes would have immense adverse implications for all the world's people and particularly for the most heavily industrialized and the most populous nations, that much hardship and extensive loss of life seemed certain if the Directive were fully complied with, that medical research and treatment could not hope to continue at their present levels—all this appeared not to matter to the Hefn.

5

They showed little interest in human affairs: politics, for instance, or crime. Wars, apart from nuclear wars, were not outlawed, or even discouraged. Governments were left to get on with their own affairs—but these now had to be reoriented toward bringing about the necessary changes in agriculture, industry, transportation, and waste disposal in time to meet the Hefn's deadline.

There was one more thing, an oddity. The Directive called for setting up a Bureau of Temporal Physics in Washington, D.C. (the training center of the Bureau was later relocated to Santa Barbara, in order to bypass the Hefn hibernation response to cold weather). The aliens, who claimed to understand the true nature of time, had decided to share this knowledge with human scientists—a gift (they said) to compensate humanity, a little, for the staggering deprivations imposed by the Directive.

Naturally this document was widely met with outrage, with resentment, and overwhelmingly with fear. (One clause, anticipating this, stated that anyone guilty of damaging a Hefn in any way would lose his memories, not simply beyond the age of ten—as had happened to the slash-and-burn farmers in Tanzania—but entirely.)

Yet I was not the only human with reason to be glad the Hefn had come back again. A lot of people discovered, after the first shock had worn off, that what they felt was less resentment than relief, and a kind of sneaking gratitude. The planet *was* in terrible shape. Now that the aliens had in effect assumed governorship of the world, essential environmental reforms haggled over for decades might actually be carried out; and because of this there were more than a few who viewed the aliens as the potential saviors of humankind. But even these people, many of them, were afraid. Nine years seemed very little time to change back, to localize institutions and practices that had long been national or international and make them *work*, or to find solutions to the immense number of problems posed by the Directive's restrictions, even with plenty of help from the Hefn.

For the first two years after their return, therefore, the aliens were widely viewed with mixed feelings of guarded hope and open apprehension. Then, in 2012, Earth was informed that all along the Hefn had been acting on orders. Another race, called the Gafr, was actually in command of the alien ship. Hefn and Gafr coexisted in an unexplained state of symbiosis. The thirty

Hefn had been put ashore in England and Sweden so long ago as punishment for insubordination against the Gafr. The Hefn Directive was, in fact, the Gafr Directive.

Though it made no practical difference, many people were gripped afresh by anxiety, or outrage, or both, at this reminder of the extent to which matters had been taken out of their control. So the revelation cost the aliens some support.

The Directive had been silent on the subject of the size and growth rate of the world's human population, but those who felt this silence to be more ominous than reassuring were proved correct the following year, 2013, when with much advance fanfare a Hefn appeared on television to make a major announcement. The Gafr were dissatisfied with humanity's progress (he said) and out of patience with its continual international posturing and blame-casting. The goals of the Directive could not possibly be met by the 2020 deadline at the present rate of change. Apparently people weren't frightened enough, even by the threat of annihilation, to put their differences aside and work together. Perhaps the problem was denial, on a global scale. The Hefn speaker said that he personally had often been astounded at the human capacity for self-deception—for letting wishful thinking rule reason.

At any rate, the Gafr had no intention of being forced to carry out their threat. They had decided to try another way. As of that moment, the nine-year deadline was revoked. Instead, everyone watching the Broadcast—and that was just about everyone in the world—would thenceforward find him- or herself unable to engender or conceive children. Starting in nine months' time, and unless and until the goals of the Directive should be accomplished, no more human babies—or too few to be worth mentioning—would be born.

Before the Broadcast, only a few humans had been aware of the Hefn capacity for control by the power of suggestion. Afterwards, everybody knew.

That mass posthypnotic suspension of fertility is the closest encounter most people have ever had with either of the alien races. But some humans were more personally affected—people leading busy lives with absorbing problems of their own, for the most part, whose attention was somewhere else when they stumbled into intimate contact with the invaders.

7

Like me, for one.

Like a few other people I know.

This book is the record of what happened to some of us because the Hefn came.

I

REMEMBRANCE OF THINGS FUTURE

By glow of the tail-light I stumbled back of the car
and stood by the heap, a doe, a recent killing;
she had stiffened already, almost cold.
I dragged her off; she was large in the belly. . . .

—William Stafford, "Traveling Through the Dark"

1990

That day at the frayed end of October was another raw, gray
day, and I had to mark midterms. We felt that on such days our
midget wood stove more than justified all its aggravations: the
removing, insulating, and replacing of the oak paneling above
the fireplace so the local fire marshal would let us vent the stove
into the chimney, the negotiations with chiseling dealers in cord-
wood, the chronic mess of bark bits on the carpet. The installers
had sworn it was the smallest stove they had ever not only put
in, but *seen*. We had to special-order short firewood for it, but
it was phenomenally efficient and cute as a toy. Ordinarily my
husband and I took turns working on the high-backed sofa in
front of it; but whichever of us brought home a set of papers to
grade always got the stove. Not only was its coziness a comfort,
but the endless tinkerings and adjustings required to keep it
cooking along at a flue temperature of 400 degrees were a grateful distraction, broke up the strain of the chore.

So early that October morning I had laid claim to the stove.
I'd emptied the ashes, carried in split logs and kindling till the
woodbox was heaped full, cleaned the window panel, stoked
the firebox, and adjusted the catalytic unit and the baffle; and
when there was no further help for it I squared my shoulders
and settled down on the sofa with a stack of essay exams from

9

my course in contemporary American poetry, while red flames swirled cheerily behind glass a couple of feet away.

Nothing but grim self-discipline gets you through the first paper or two; after that you sink into a sort of judgmental trance and things go better. Matt left for the day. I poked the coals occasionally, put in wood, fine-tuned the two dampers, wrote things in margins and at the bottoms of last pages. The phone rang only once: a student who hadn't turned in the take-home half of the exam on Monday needed directions so he could bring it out to the house. The call was my only interruption, and when I finally stopped for a sandwich and a glass of cider I had completed five exams, a quarter of the class and an excellent long morning's work. Two more, I promised myself, and then you don't have to do any more till tonight.

But after lunch the first paper I picked up had something wrong with it.

The paper started off in the usual way to address the second of four multiple-choice questions I had given the class on Monday, but the second page veered off weirdly; I found myself skimming over references to nuclear power and some future disaster, and stopped, groaning aloud, at a statement to the effect that alien invaders alone would save us from utter destruction. Alien invaders! I looked at the name on the paper and groaned again. Terry Carpenter was the kid on his way over with the late take-home question.

That didn't give me a lot of time to figure out what to do.

Flipping back to page one I began to read closely, cursing to myself. It is far from uncommon for undergraduates at a high-pressure university—especially if they happen to be somewhat unstable to start with—to have an "episode" of some sort at the semester's midpoint, when so many written assignments come due at the same time and so many midterm exams are given. I'd known cases of suicide threats and even attempts (none successful, thank God), of depression, inability to work, inability to cope generally. It's far from uncommon, but you always hope it won't happen to anybody in one of your own classes, because midway through the semester professors are as weary as their students and longing every bit as much for the brief Thanksgiving hiatus still three weeks distant. The last thing you want just then is more work, and troubled students create work. You have to investigate, make assessments, do something. You can't ignore it, and wouldn't if you could. But you'd love to be spared the whole problem.

The question Terry had chosen to write on required him to compare and contrast Elizabeth Bishop's lovely poem "The Moose," in which a bus full of people traveling to Boston from Nova Scotia encounters a female moose in the moonlit New Brunswick woods, with William Stafford's much shorter, pithier poem "Traveling Through the Dark," about a man who finds a car-killed doe beside a road, her fawn still alive inside her. The class had studied the Bishop piece, but "Traveling Through the Dark" had been sprung on them the day of the exam. The elements common to both poems—driving at night, confrontation between vehicle and animal and human and animal, powerful human responses to the confrontations, and so on—made it natural and easy to view the two in the light of one another, while their differences of length, tone, content, form, and purpose made the qualities of each stand out in relief against those of the other. To me it had seemed at once the easiest and the most interesting of the four questions.

But something about it had disturbed Terry Carpenter mightily, that was clear: ". . . up the hill all the trees are broken, dead, sick and stunted, the deer were wiped out completely by radiation so there are none for the alien to see on that side of the lens, and when the buck came then I felt sick too to think all that power and beauty would really come to nothing no matter how hard he chases the does now, whatever fawns he makes will all be dead or theirs will be, somewhere down the line every one of them is doomed to be killed by our stupidity, every one, so that he seemed a beautiful sorrowful wasted doomed creature. . . ." For pages it went on like that, the quasi-poetical style, and punctuation by commas only, giving an odd, trance-like quality to the writing. It was not a style I would have expected a student like Terry to use, or even be capable of. My attention kept veering away from the sense of the paper—if it could be said to have a "sense," exactly—though I read it through three times. Terry certainly had failed to answer the question, but what was it he had done instead?

A glance at the stove made me jump up; while I'd been fretting over Terry's exam the needle of the round red thermometer had swung back to 275 degrees. Pulling on leather gloves I hastily poked the glowing coals into a flat bed, then threw in a fistful

11

of small sticks and splits to hot it up enough for the chunkier lengths of ash and Osage orange to catch well. Then I closed the little iron door, spun the damper wide open, and waited on my knees while the fire picked up strength, trying anxiously to remember how Terry had sounded on the phone. I hadn't been struck by anything strange in his voice, but I'd been in such a hurry to get off the line that unless the strangeness had been very evident I probably wouldn't have noticed.

Actually, beyond acknowledging his perfectly competent classroom performance, I had taken very little notice of Terry Carpenter at all. The only grade I'd recorded for him was a B on a short written poetry explication. He had never come to any office hour of mine, nor (until now) done anything to make a personal impression. At mid-semester one is impressed chiefly with the A students and the disruptive or idiotic ones; distinguishing among the Bs takes longer unless unusual looks or behavior separate them out or they make a point of coming in to confer about something. None of these things was true of Terry. I realized that in fact I knew nothing whatever about the boy.

I stopped fussing with the stove, tossed the gloves into the woodbox, and called my husband's office: not in. Then I tried the department Chair and was told by her secretary that she would be in a committee meeting all afternoon; and before I could ask the secretary to search the records for Terry Carpenter's file—in case he should happen to be an English major, with a file there in her office—I heard a car door slam outside.

Ready or not, then, here we went.

Terry and I arrived at our opposite sides of the front door at the same instant. A large, gleaming car, its engine wastefully running, bulked in the drive behind my rust-pocked ten-year-old Toyota. When I pulled the door open Terry said, ''Hi!'' brightly, thrust a manila envelope into my hand, and began at once to sidle away, saying, ''Sorry to bother you at home, and sorry this didn't get in on time.'' In spite of these apologies he was grinning in a relieved, if tired and rueful, way—like any student happy to have disburdened himself of a task. He wore jeans and an expensive corduroy coat, unbuttoned, with a dark, plush collar. His hair was mussed and he hadn't shaved, typical signs of late-paper production. In those circumstances nobody could have looked more normal.

12

Even his rush to get away was normal. I almost let him go—but I couldn't quite shrug off the strangeness of what he had written, and a few judicious questions shouldn't take us long. "Could you come in for a couple of minutes? Something I'd like to ask you about your in-class exam." I made it more of a command than a request.

"Oh—" Terry said, "okay, I guess," but his grin disappeared. "But I better go turn off the engine first. My roommate's car," he added almost with embarrassment, having probably taken note of the shabby resident Toyota. He certainly bore no resemblance that I could see to a young man on the brink of nervous collapse; for one thing, he seemed insufficiently self-absorbed.

When he came in I shut the door firmly behind him, went to the kitchen sink, and filled and plugged in the electric kettle, saying "Tea?" in a perfunctory way while Terry—seeing he was not about to escape in a hurry—took off his coat and threw it over a chair. "Thanks. Uh, is something wrong with my midterm, or what?"

"Tell you in a minute." I clattered cups and spoons and things together, filling time. When the kettle boiled I made the tea quickly, popped a cozy over the pot, and carried the laden tray into the living room, my problem trailing uncomfortably after me. "Have a seat." I dropped onto the other end of the sofa, plucked his paper from the top of the stack, and looked him in the eye. "Okay, Terry. It would be better to tell me the truth: were you high on something while you were writing this?"

"God, *no*." He sat up very straight, obviously alarmed—but again, to my practiced eye, no more so than any student might be if challenged this bluntly, without warning. "That is—just on coffee, I'd been up most of the night trying to do the take-home. Jesus. Why'd you ask me that?"

"Ever drop acid? Sorry to pry, but I need to know."

"Well—just once. In high school."

"Bad trip?"

"No, not at all. I just wanted to see what it was like, though, I never did it again."

"And no recurrences."

Thoroughly worried now, he leaned back against the sofa's padded arm, away from me, and shook his head. "Why are we

13

talking about drugs? What's all this got to do with the midterm?"

"That's what I was hoping you could tell *me*." I handed him the paper. He read quickly through the first sheet and flipped to the second; watching narrowly as his eyes ran down the page, I saw him frown and his face get whiter. He went on to the third page, threw a frightened glance at me, began to read the fourth. His breathing had become rapid and shallow.

Abruptly he looked up, letting the pages crumple in his lap. "I don't know what to say. I just don't get it."

"Do you remember writing this?"

"N-no . . . not actually *writing* it, no I don't. I felt very weird on Monday, I'd been up most of the night for two nights running and sort of felt like I might be coming down with something."

"You *did* write it, though, didn't you?" I pressed him; I had to know.

Terry said in agitation, "Well *yeah*, I *wrote* it, I mean I must have, it's my handwriting, but I don't *remember* writing it, I swear to God!"

"Well, what's your explanation then?"

He looked ready to cry. "Well . . . ," shifting in his seat, "I could've been in worse shape than I thought, I guess. I don't know, maybe I was running a fever or something."

"But you feel all right now?"

"Before I read *this* I did. I got a lot of sleep Monday night."

I thought a minute while Terry hunched tensely beside me and the tea steeped on, ignored. "Well, then. Granted that you don't remember writing this paper, do you recognize the content of it—that is, is it like anything you might have read sometime in a science fiction novel, say, or seen on the late show?"

"That's the creepiest part," he said huskily. "I sort of do recognize it. I had a . . . dream, I guess. I guess it was a dream, it must've been."

"When was that?"

"Last weekend sometime. Around then. I'd completely forgotten about it till you showed me this thing."

"Terry, this looks pretty serious to me," I said. "Maybe you've been working a little too hard lately? Or having personal problems?" He made no reply to this, but then why, after all, should he tell *me* anything? "Whatever the source of the stress, I think it would be smart to talk to somebody at Student Health

14

about it, show them this exam and say you blanked out and wrote it on automatic, if that's what you think you did."

I stopped. Terry was no longer listening; he had bent over double, elbows on knees, head gripped hard in both hands. I had to lean forward too, to hear him: "It might not've been a dream." He rocked slightly, back and forth. "Something might have happened. In the park . . . oh, Jesus, all of a sudden my head's just splitting."

"You don't mean aliens *really* invaded?"

I instantly regretted this feeble attempt at reassurance; Terry snapped that he didn't *know* what the hell he meant and rocked harder, almost whimpering. "Could you—have you got some aspirins or something? I can't think straight."

"I'll get you a couple. Can you take them with tea? Pour us both some tea, will you, it ought to be ready by now." I dashed upstairs to the medicine cabinet and down again with the Bufferin bottle, and when Terry had dosed himself and was nursing his cup, and I had emptied mine, I said "Okay, I apologize for the wisecrack. Tell me what you meant about the 'park'—what park?"

"The state park, up north of here. I'll try to explain, but I feel so *weird*—I can't remember right—I—oh, Christ," he choked, getting up frantically. "I think I'm going to—where's the bathroom?" He rushed away, following the directions I called after him.

"Something must really be wrong with me," he said when he had come slowly back downstairs. "I *never* do that. Could I have a couple more Bufferins?" He tried a wobbly smile. "Those ones weren't down long enough to do any good."

I shook two more tablets into his palm. "Drink it *slowly*. Okay. About the park, if you feel up to talking."

Terry slumped back and turned his face, handsome under its greenish cast and stubble, toward me. "Well, I went out there early Sunday morning, hoping to think of a way to do the take-home part of the midterm—I was having a terrible time deciding what to write on for some reason. I spent hours trying on Saturday, practically the whole day and way into the night. Then I passed out for a couple of hours, and when I woke up it was about five o'clock and I suddenly felt like getting out of the city—maybe a little fresh air might blow the cobwebs away, you know? So I borrowed my roommate's car—that one out there—

15

and drove out to this park. I stopped at a Dunkin' Donuts on the way and got some coffee and a bag of blueberry muffins . . . and I parked and got out and walked around for a while. It was just getting light.''

''Why so much trouble with the midterm? It wasn't that hard.''

''I'm not sure, except I had two other midterms last week and a paper due on Friday, and I might have been getting kind of burned out. Last night I just sat down and *wrote* it, no problem.''

''Wait a minute.'' I had gotten up to tend the stove; now I propped the poker in the corner, slid the paper he had brought me out of its envelope, and glanced through it: a perfectly straightforward, perfectly unexceptionable exercise. No aliens, no disasters. ''Okay. So you drove out to the park. Where'd you leave the car?''

''Down by the creek, in the Sycamore Mills lot. You know? My dad used to take me there when I was little, when we lived out here and he worked in the city. He loved that park, he loved to see the deer. It's funny, but I hadn't been there for years, not since my parents split up, but I still remembered the exact layout of the trails and how to get there from Route 1.''

Here my ears pricked up: an episode triggered by some traumatic childhood association seemed suggested by these details. I said, ''I go over there all the time myself; it's my favorite place to run. So you walked up Sycamore Mills Road along the creek, carrying your muffins and sipping your coffee. What then?''

''Well, I stayed on the road as far as it follows the creek, to the foot of the White Trail''—he looked at me and I nodded; I knew the White Trail well—''and then I just hiked up that a little ways, to those big boulder-things in the woods at the top of the hill?''—another glance; another nod—''and climbed up on one of them and . . . just sat there for a while. For quite a while, I guess, eating a muffin or three and trying to think about Robert Penn Warren's narrative poetry without getting anywhere *at* all. And then I—went back to the car and drove home,'' he finished in a rush, rubbing his hands over his face and through his dark, tousled hair, face scrunched into a mask, all teeth and tension lines. ''No I didn't! That's what I *remember* doing, but while I was reading this paper I got a jumble of—images, pictures, like dream pictures against the background of the woods up there. Jesus, my head's about to come *off*.''

16

"You'd only had a couple of hours' sleep, you said. Might you have dozed off for a few minutes?"

"Maybe, but . . . it was *cold* up there, you know? Six, seven o'clock in the morning—and anyway I don't remember writing *any* of this stuff after the first page, not a word of it, but yet these pictures kept flicking through my mind when I read it over—something *did* happen out there on Sunday, I know it did, I can feel it—" his voice squeaked up abruptly and he clutched his head again, really whimpering now in spite of himself with the apparent ferociousness of the pain in his head.

Convinced by now that the mysterious automatic writing was a symptom of something badly amiss, I said as soothingly as I could, "Why not go upstairs and lie down, try to sleep that headache off, while I call up somebody at Student Health and then maybe one of your parents. This is nothing to fool around with, Terry, believe me. You need to get some help."

At the word *parents* Terry set down the teacup he had just picked up with a *clunk* that sloshed tea into the saucer. "No!" He shook his poor head hard. "I mean, thanks a lot, really, but I don't want my parents mixing into my problems. What I want— what I'm *going* to do, in fact, is drive back out there and see if I can figure out what might have happened on Sunday."

He stood up. So did I, saying quickly, "That strikes me as a truly terrible idea! You're anxious and upset and feeling awful; you shouldn't be driving at all, let alone returning to the scene of whatever upset you so much in the first place!" When this speech didn't prevent Terry from putting on his coat I decided it was time to play the professorial heavy. "Terry, I can't possibly allow this. You're staying right here while I call Student Health, and then we'll see what's what." This technique worked better for my husband, a large, distinguished-looking man with a mustache and graying temples, than it did for me; I wished desperately that Matt weren't gone for the day. I could cow many kids, but not always the more frantic male sort, of which Terry was at that moment a prime example.

"Call whoever you want, but I'm not staying. I don't mean to be rude, I know you're trying to help and I know people have probably trampled the place all up by now, but I still have to go see if there's anything *to* see—before I get mixed up with doctors and all that and maybe *can't* go anywhere."

But he was a well-brought-up boy and disliked defying the

17

authority figure who had exerted herself to befriend him, so when I said sternly as he was walking toward the door, "Terry, it's no use arguing, I *can't* let you drive a car in the condition you're in," he hesitated. "Okay, you win," I said quickly. "You can go check out the scene to see whether it tells you anything. But I'll drive you there and come along with you, and afterwards I'll bring you back here; and *then* we'll make arrangements with Student Health, and my husband or I will drive you into town and bring your roommate back out to collect his car himself. All right?"

"It's a lot of bother for you," he said weakly.

"Less bother than scraping you up off the pavement. Come on, let's put what's left of this pot into a thermos and pick up something to eat on the way. We'll do exactly what you did on Sunday, there's just enough light left not to have to hurry. Let me just damp the stove down, here, like so . . . and away we go." Chattering thus, trying not to sound as relieved as I felt, I steered him through the door, got him to move the monstrous car (half afraid he'd try to make a break for it) while I scribbled a note for Matt and crammed a few things into a daypack, then backed the Toyota smartly into the road. This trip could be done in under two hours; by then Matt would be home, and between the two of us we could easily intimidate Terry into doing what *we* thought best.

It was not very nice weather for what, under different circumstances, could have been a pleasant outing, yet I wasn't sorry even so to get out of the house. We parked the car where Terry had left his roommate's, I zipped our bag of Dunkin' Donuts (collected en route) into my red nylon daypack and shrugged it on, and together we walked briskly along a paved road that had been closed to motorized traffic. After weeks of thick clouds but little rain the creek was low. Most of the red-brown beech and yellow tulip poplar leaves had come down but lay still crisp and vivid on the ground. Terry too seemed affected by the fresh air. The quick pace brought color back into his face, the aspirins evidently began to do their stuff, and soon he had started to look about him and to take an interest. "If we're replaying Sunday, along about here's where I dipped into the muffin bag," he said, and I slid the pack off one shoulder and doled him out a doughnut.

Joggers and cyclists passed us in both directions, whizzing or bent double to defeat the hill. One smallish runner, garbed out-landishly in knicker-style sweatpants, wore a black balaclava mask over his face, with holes for his mouth and nose. Various articles of what appeared to be extra clothing fluttered about his waist. He glared blankly at us as he passed, arms whirling, pale bare calves twinkling. Terry grinned delightedly after him and said "Talk about your alien invaders!" in a tone so cheerful that I began to congratulate myself that this excursion was the best possible antidote for the trouble he was in, even that there was probably a perfectly reasonable explanation for it. Reasonable explanations were my stock in trade.

Soon we were at the place where the White Trail intersected the road. Terry turned into it eagerly, leading the way left and steeply uphill, following blazes of white paint stenciled on trees and rocks toward where three or four huge granite outcrops lay where a glacier had left or exposed them in a time too remote to imagine. Climbing the hill we startled a group of five does, whose puffy white tails flicked and wagged nervously out of sight among the bare trees. A steep quarter of a mile or so above the road, "This one," Terry said, and scrambled up onto an immense rock to the right of the footpath, which twisted around that massive blockiness and ran on.

The top of the rock was shaped like a natural bench. I pulled from my pack its entire contents: thermos, doughnuts, Styro-foam cups, spoons, and two foam pads of polyurethane, one of which I gave to Terry to sit on. "Watch where you put your hands. I happen to know that in summer it's solid poison ivy up here," I said; and then, the elements of our mad tea party ar-ranged between us, I poured him out a cup and passed it over.

"You know something, this is kind of fun. My dad always packed along a sack lunch when he brought me up here—sand-wiches, apples, and two cans of Coke in a quilted thing for keeping a bottle of wine cold."

"Ever read Proust? No, I don't expect you would have yet. In *Remembrance of Things Past* Proust tells how a bit of cake in a spoonful of tea brought all the repressed memories of his child-hood flooding back to him." I opened up the silly-looking bag, white with large pink and brown polka dots printed on it, and held it out to him. "All *you* have to remember, my lad, is last Sunday."

Terry tore a glazed doughnut in two, dunked one half in his

19

cup, and grinned. "Here goes, then!" He bit off the soggy end, chewed tentatively, made a comical face. "Coffee's a lot better as a dunking agent, I remember *that* much about Sunday. How fast is it supposed to work? The rest of the morning is still a blank." But he looked around more thoughtfully, eating, finishing his tea. I refilled his cup but kept quiet, letting him try. The exam was folded into the outer zippered pocket of the pack, to be produced if it seemed like a good idea. What would be the effect of reading it aloud up here, I wondered, unsure of the relative merits of pushing the situation or letting it pass completely into professional hands; and while I was dithering Terry suddenly said in an odd voice, "A deer did that."

"Did what?" He pointed into the trees behind us, where a roughly circular patch of churned-up earth showed clearly against the russet clutter of fallen leaves. "Mm-hm. It's a scrape. The bucks start making them a few weeks before the onset of the real rut—along about right now, in fact. Most of the does won't be in season for another week or two but the bucks are ready *now*, so they burn off steam digging up the ground and hooking at the low branches while they do it—see where those twigs are broken off and the bark's scraped off the branches?"

"Yeah," said Terry, "only how come *I* knew a deer did it?" He put half a doughnut down on the bare rock and hugged his middle hard with his forearms. "Oh-oh, here we go again. All of a sudden I don't feel so great." A moment later his teeth were actually chattering. My view of the wisdom of his coming back up here with only me to help him underwent instant revision.

"Your father told you, I'll bet—when you were little," I suggested, trying not to sound as alarmed as I felt.

"No. No! Not when I was little and not my father—*Sunday*. I saw it! I saw him, he was charging round and round, pawing up the ground with his front feet and arching his neck, battering at the branches with his antlers, whuffing and whirling around like crazy. I *saw* him, I was sitting right here but he never noticed, he was completely involved in what he was doing. God, it was fantastic—and—*they* were as knocked out as I was—" he broke off and, as at the house, went greenish white, his breath coming in the same shallow gasps.

" 'They' who? Who else was up here that morning?"

"The . . . there were . . . two of them. A guy . . . there, up the hill, in a, like, a beekeeper's suit. And the other one—

was—" Terry screamed, sharply and so abruptly that I knocked the thermos fifteen feet to the ground, while he sprawled flat and was sick again over the far edge of the outcrop. For at least a minute he hung there head down, retching and gasping. My own heart pounded madly; I felt more than a little queasy myself and had no idea what to do.

But when he sat up again, finally, and reached for a paper Dunkin' Donuts napkin to wipe his mouth, I could see that it was all right.

"Sorry," he said, "sorry to keep doing that to you—but that's really the last time." He put the wadded napkin into his coat pocket. "See, I wasn't *supposed* to remember, that's why I'd keep throwing up every time I started to. But *that* time I think it all came back at once." There was some cold tea left in his cup; he used it to rinse his mouth and spat over the edge of the rock.

"None of this," I said unsteadily, "makes any sense to *me*. All of *what* came back—or should you save it to tell to somebody who would know how to listen better than I do? I'd have said it all came *up* at once. Again."

Terry grinned, still pale, his face still damp. "It's okay, I don't need a shrink," he said, and at that moment he really didn't look as if he did, though twice in as many hours I had seen him switch back and forth, back and forth between apparent normality and acute illness. "I'll tell you, only you won't believe me. Nobody will . . . can I have the last doughnut, by the way?"

"Only if you *swear* to keep it *down*. How you can go on trying in the face of such discouragement is beyond me."

"You're seeing the last of this one, I guarantee it. Okay, here's what happened. I came up here just like I said, and sat right here thinking Robert Penn Warren, Robert Penn Warren, and looking around at the same time, sort of abstractedly, you know? And I suddenly noticed that right over there, right up the hill next to the trail, there was a place where it was summer."

"Summer?" He nodded. "I don't follow."

"And a different time of day, too: later, maybe early afternoon. I was, like, looking through a round window with no wall around it. Blurry at the edges, but the same hillside in the center—only it was a very bright, blue, sunny day inside the circle and everything was *green*—leaves on the trees, green stuff growing on the ground, weeds and stickerbushes and things, all green.

When I first saw it, for just a second it was a green blur sort of bouncing around, but then right away it stopped bouncing and came into clear focus as I was watching, and I got the impression of looking through a giant lens of some sort, like the lens of a camera." He had been staring up the hill as he spoke, but here he glanced back to me and smiled, pleased with himself. "I was right, as it turned out."

"A giant *lens*?" Hadn't he mentioned a lens in his exam? But way up in the middle of the air?"Ah—how big would you say it was?"

"About . . . oh, say the size of a slide projector screen." Terry grimaced and shook himself. "It was overcast that morning, too, or maybe it wouldn't have been so impossible not to notice. First I was dumbfounded, then I was scared shitless. Then I started telling myself to get down off this rock and see what would happen if I tried to walk *through* the summer part, but before I'd quite got up the nerve to try *that*, two people— well, figures—in, like, *beekeeper* suits came into the green area and sort of peered through from their side into mine. That's when I was sure it wasn't just a trick of the light or whatever. I mean, the shape of the hill was the same, there were trees in both parts, it *could* have been my coffee nerves plus no sleep plus one beam of sunlight breaking through—something like that. But these . . . figures were only partly visible. I could see most of the bigger one, but in the way you see somebody who's walking around outside a house you're *inside* of, looking out. When they get too close to the house you can only see part of them, right? The window frame cuts off the rest? Well, I could see this guy's head and shoulders down to his waist or so, but nothing below. It was," Terry said simply, "just like raising a window blind and looking out into a summer day."

"You weren't—forgive my asking again, will you?—you weren't tripping that morning either?"

"I swear I wasn't," said Terry, not angrily. "I'd been trying to write that paper."

I chose to reserve judgment. "So what about the other person, the smaller figure?"

"That was the alien," he said, and a tense little silence fell between us.

Terry broke it (which is more than I felt able to do; here came

22

the alien invaders, just as the paper had said): "Hey, it might be better if I just tell what happened."

"Go ahead, I won't interrupt again."

"Well, the tall guy, the human, he saw me right away and sort of, like, froze in horror and said, 'Oh, Christ, there's somebody *over* there,' to the alien. And the alien says, 'I see him,' and then something like, 'Well, we knew it was a calculated risk, but what a pity.' He—the alien—he was wearing protective clothing too. He was shorter though, and sort of more compactly built, and his face, what I could see of it under the beekeeper's helmet, looked hairy. Like he had on a Santa Claus beard—light colored, white or maybe gray. Anyway, I'm still perched up here scared out of my wits, but when I hear them talking ordinary American English I manage to say, 'Hey, what's going on,' or something equally clever."

"Did the alien have an accent?" I couldn't stop myself from asking.

"Nope. He talked just like we do. So the other guy—he wasn't very old, by the way—he says, 'I'll explain in a minute,' and then he says, 'Listen, is it Halloween over there?' 'Not for a few days yet,' I say, naturally thinking that there are only two kinds of people who ever say that kind of thing, amnesia victims and time travelers. And I'm thinking, no matter what I do or say now, it'll be like out of some B-grade movie—great. But I have to know, so I'm like, 'I guess that means you guys are supposed to be from the future,' and the human says, 'You got it'—just like that. Then he says, 'Only we're still *in* the future. We can see you but we're not coming through, we can't, and you can't either. What time of day have you got? It's too dark to tell from here.' So I tell him, very early morning. Playing along, but not really believing it yet, you know? But still scared as hell because I couldn't figure out how they were doing it, or what was really going on."

But as Terry spoke, I began to believe *I* knew what had "really" been going on; a picture was taking shape, of a tall human and a small alien looking back together into a past they could not (re)enter. All of this, I thought privately, would be grist for the shrinks to sift; I'd better listen carefully.

"So," Terry went on, "I said, feeling like an idiot, 'Hey, I thought you weren't supposed to risk changing the past.' 'We're not,' the guy says. 'My friend will have to mindwipe you. I'm

23

really sorry. I'm not even supposed to be doing this, and we hit the wrong day anyway.' He seemed real disappointed about that. So I say, 'Not supposed to be doing what?' and he says, 'I'm a'—I think it was like technician or engineer—'in the Bureau of Temporal Physics and I talked my friend here, who's also my boss and a supervisor in the Bureau, into taking out a time terminal so I could try to make a birthday present for this terrific old cousin of mine who's turning seventy in a couple of months, right after Halloween. I had this great idea for a *present*!'' See, he wanted to film something that happened to this cousin right here in this park a long time ago, that he always used to hear about when he was a kid. He was hoping not only to see it himself but to film it, for a surprise.''

"That's as wild as some of the excuses I get for why my students' papers don't come in on time.''

Terry grinned. ''You never know, the craziest-sounding ones might be the truest! But at the time of course I'm thinking, sure, sure, tell me another one. But he just went on explaining how the terminal had to be brought physically to the site of the event they wanted to 'see,' and that he knew it was a long shot because they can only tune it to within a few days, it isn't accurate to the day, let alone the hour and minute they want. So he knew they might hit a few days early or late, but he still seemed really disappointed, because this was his only crack at it, the terminal's expensive to run, it uses a lot of energy even to see thirty years back—that's how far back they were looking.

"Anyway, this cousin always used to bring him to the park to watch the deer through binoculars, and show him this rock, and tell him that one Halloween day just as it was getting dark the cousin was sitting right here where we are, where I was then, and all at once a buck ran out of the woods and mated with a doe right beside the rock, only a few feet away. He wanted to film *that*—the actual mating! Without being seen, of course— no wonder he had a heart attack when he saw me sitting up here; he didn't want anybody to have to be mindwiped! He was a nice guy,'' Terry said. ''I really liked him a lot, all the time I thought he was trying to snow me.''

To my mind, elements in the story were continuing to fit a pattern; even the double meaning of the word *present* fit. Mostly for the sake of saying something I remarked that the device seemed unworkably awkward; suppose they switched on the lens in the middle of a church picnic? Would they mindwipe everybody? Did they *have* to bring the lens to the precise site of the event they wanted to observe? In that case I didn't see how they could control the thing enough to use it, particularly in the absence of fine tuning.

Terry frowned. "I know. It does seem . . . but they must be able to operate it better, normally. This was a sort of rough-and-ready occasion. But Lee did say that the reason—"

"The young man's name was Lee?"

"That's what the alien called him, yeah. He said they had to bring the time window to the actual place, on the principle of haunted houses—that place and time are connected. You know, like when a ghost in an eighteenth-century getup appears in the library of an old mansion, or people who've met a violent end keep wandering around re-experiencing the death in the place where it happened. That kind of thing. We," he said cheerfully, "aren't going to find that out for a while longer—not till the aliens tell us, when they get here. The time terminal is *their* gizmo. We didn't figure out that much about time before they came. *Won't* have figured it out before they *come*, I should say."

"Which will be when?"

"Pretty soon now, I'd say. Before we blow ourselves up, at least. Less than thirty years for sure, 'cause that's how far ahead of us they were. Are." He laughed. "It's hard to talk about! But they won't get here before—see, this was the point of the present—they won't get here before there's a major accident at a power plant someplace around here and the whole region gets contaminated with radioactive crap released into the atmosphere. It'll be as bad as Chernobyl, at least as bad. Most of the people will get out, but the wildlife and vegetation, and the soil—well, I noticed the trees after he told me that, the summer trees. They were mostly green, but the young ones looked all warped and distorted and quite a few were dead. And all the animals in the park, of course, all the deer. They're all going to die."

My heart squeezed shut at this for an instant, so plausibly did Terry relate this part of his tale. But I held firmly to my sense of the pattern. Naturally, within the mythic park of Terry's childhood, all the beautiful, innocent deer of the past must die because of the meltdown divorce.

I asked him if "Lee" had told him which plant would go out

25

and wasn't surprised when he frowned again and said, "I don't think so."

"If you were so scared," I suddenly thought to wonder, "why didn't you just take off? Get out of there?"

Terry made a quizzical face. "It never occurred to me, so I guess I must have been more intrigued and fascinated than scared, right from the start. Or maybe the Hefn made me want to stay, without my knowing it. He probably could have."

"The Hefn is the alien?"

"Unh-hunh. Lee said they'd left some of their people here a long while back and were going to pick 'em up again in a year or so, but they had trouble with their ship. And when they finally did get back, their people were all dead and ours had reached the post-industrial stage and the brink of space exploration. So they sized us up and some of them wanted to stick around and help us get through it—because they could tell we were heading straight to hell in a hand-basket—and just before they arrived the power plant went. So when they landed they just took over."

He glanced at me, expecting a reaction. I could think of nothing to say. This deus ex machina solution seemed the *least* original element of Terry's tale, and I thought "Hefn" a preposterous name, probably derived from "Heffalump," or maybe "Heaven." I was beginning to feel exhausted.

"Well, anyway," he finally went on, "they rigged a kind of blind for the time terminal, so the deer couldn't see them and be spooked. Then the alien got me to scrunch down back here, on the saddle between the main parts of this rock, and put me under somehow—hypnotized me—so I just crouched down there without moving for, oh, a couple of hours. Which is how come I know for sure that they really were what Lee said they were. And I saw the buck come and make the scrape; that was the high point for them, they were *thrilled*, you should've heard them—the Hefn too. They filmed that. It was the next best thing to getting what they came for. Then they got ready to shut the lens down and turn off the terminal, but first they had to mind-wipe me."

I roused myself to say, "Lee seems to have done a lot of explaining in not very much time. When did he give you all that information—while you were hypnotized?"

"No, before that, while they were setting up the blind. I got the impression the Hefn didn't really approve, but he didn't in-

26

terfere either. It seemed like Lee hadn't ever talked to anybody in the past before. After he got over being put out he seemed—kind of excited, like he might be talking too much—because really, what was the point? If they were going to make me forget it all afterwards anyway? I tried my damnedest to talk 'em out of *that*—I said, what did they think gave them the right to hypnotize people for a couple of hours without their consent and then erase their memories, all for the sake of a *birthday* present? What about my civil rights?''

''What did he say to that?''

''He said the aliens weren't real big on civil rights. He said for them, a lot of times the end justifies the means, and they were in charge of things right now, and anyway, if I knew his cousin I'd understand why *this* Hefn had let him try to make the film, even if it meant a risk for somebody like me, who happened to be around at the wrong time. He apologized about twenty times, I could see he felt bad about it. He really was a nice guy.''

I sat silent, truly sorry and sad for Terry, whose entire bizarre story of deer and cousin, birthday present and forgetfulness and guilt, seemed detail by detail a transparent, if colorfully transformed, allegory of his own situation.

''I'm sure the mindwipe would have worked,'' he added, ''if I hadn't taken that exam the very next day. All those *deer*! You know? Because in a real sense, what happened—what's going to happen—is just that Stafford poem on a broader scale. Dead does and fawns that will never be born, because of human carelessness. Technology destroying the natural world by accident. It's all the same thing, the same idea. But even then, if you'd happened to lose all those exams in a taxis or something, or had just given me an F on mine, I'd never have remembered all this again.'' He sighed and smiled, a smile of perfect guilelessness, perfect relief. ''I'm *glad* I remembered. Nobody'll ever believe it, I know that—*you* think I got all worked up about my dad and the divorce and hallucinated the whole thing, don't you?''—I started at this perceptiveness, making Terry laugh—''and of course I see why anybody might think that, at least until the Hefn get here! But I swear to God, the whole thing happened exactly like I said.''

There seemed to be no way to answer this. I covered the awkwardness of my exposed hypothesis (which was all *my* awkwardness; Terry went on smiling gratefully at me) by starting to pack up the trash and sit-upons. It was past time to leave; already it would be dark before we got back to the car.

"Anyway," he said kindly, almost teasingly, moving to help, "some parts of the plot don't really fit, do they? That old cousin with the birthday, for example; shouldn't she have been a *male* relative, like an uncle or something? If, you know, if it was just a stand-in for my father. And then why would it be the little alien who mindwipes me, if he's really just a projection *of* me? And what about the *beard*? Mine wouldn't be gray for about forty more years, even if I grew one! Besides, wouldn't you think the guy—"

But I was no longer really listening—I'd stiffened, the foam pads half rolled, my face gone numb above them. "Terry," I broke in, "this cousin was a *woman*?"

"Yeah. Didn't I say so?"

"If you did it went right by me." Then Terry's own face went slack as the freakish possibility struck him too, and we stared at each other with the same wild surmise. "I thought *today* was Halloween," I said, and at the same instant Terry said, "When's *your* birthday, anyway?"

But before either of us could reply, the crashing in the dead leaves began, the doe—foreordained, remembered—came hurtling up the slope toward the rocky outcrops at a dead gallop, an indistinct dun-colored shape in the dusk, hotly pursued by the second, larger, nobler shape which overtook, licked and nuzzled and finally lunged above her directly beneath the great boulder where we crouched, knocking her forward onto her knees with the force of the single thrust delivered so explosively that his hind feet left the ground—and off, down and away so swiftly we had scarcely moved or breathed till there were no deer anywhere on the twilit slope below.

28

2

"TI WHINNY MOOR THOO CUMS AT LAST"

1994–2007

I

Elphi was the first of them to wake that spring, which meant he was the first to catch, almost at once, the faint whiff of corruption. Feeling ghastly, as always upon just emerging from hibernation, he dragged himself out of his bunk to go and see which of the remnant of elderly hobs had died during the winter.

He tottered round the den in darkness, unable as yet to manage the coordination needed to strike a light. Nor did he really require one. Hobs were nocturnal. Besides, this group had been overwintering in the same den for nearly a hundred years.

Tarn Hole and Hasty Bank lay together, deep in sleep. Hodge Hob seemed all right . . . and Broxa . . . and Scugdale . . . Ah. Woof Howe Hob was the dead one. Elphi checked on Hart Hall, just to make sure there had been only one death, then wobbled back to his own bed to think.

They would have to get Woof Howe out of the den: he thrust that thought, and the necessity for fast action, into the forefront of his mind to blank out the yawning hollowness, the would-be grief. Every decade or two now, another of them was lost. The long exile seemed to be coming inexorably to an end, not by rescue, as they had gone on expecting for so long, but by slow attrition. Only seven were left of the fifteen stranded in this place, and soon there would be none.

Elphi rolled out again; these thoughts were unproductive, as they had ever been. He needed a drink and a meal.

The great stone that had sealed the den all winter posed a problem. By human standards the hobs were prodigiously strong

29

for their size, even in great age, but Elphi—feeble after his months-long fast—ordinarily would not have attempted to move the stone unaided. But he managed it, finally, and poked his head with due caution out into the world.

Outside it was early April on the heather moors of North Yorkshire. Weak as he was, Elphi shuddered with pleasure as the fresh moorland wind blew into his face. The wind was strong and fiercely cold, but cold had never bothered the hobs and it was not for warmth's sake that Elphi doubled back down the ladder to fetch forth something to wrap around himself, something that would deceive the eyes of any unlikely walker still on the tops in the last few hours of light. That done, he dragged the heavy stone back across the hole, sealing in the scent of death, and set off stiffly on all fours through the snow-crusted heather.

He followed a sheep track, keeping a weather eye out as he trotted along for any farmer who might be gathering his moor ewes to bring them down "inside" for lambing now. Those years when the hobs slept a bit later than usual they sometimes found their earliest forays cramped by the presence of farmers and dogs, neither of which could be easily fooled by their disguise. When that happened they were forced to be nocturnal indeed.

But the sheep Elphi saw had a week to go at least before they would be gathered in, and he began to relax. Walkers were always fairly few at this uncomfortable season, and the archeologists who had been working at the prehistoric settlement sites on Danby Rigg the previous summer were not in evidence there now. Perhaps getting rid of old Woof Howe would not be quite so difficult as he had feared—not like the year they had woken in mid-April to find Kempswithen dead and the tops acrawl with men and dogs for days. The only humans he was at all likely to encounter this late afternoon would be hauling hay up to their flocks, and since their tractors and pickups made a din that carried for miles in the open landscape he had no fear of being caught napping.

The local dogs all knew about the hobs, of course, as they knew about the grouse and hares, but they rarely came on the tops unless they were herding sheep, and when they were herding sheep they generally stuck to business. The problem dogs were those the walkers allowed to run loose, whether under good voice control or no. *They* could be really troublesome. In August and September, when the heather turned the moorland into a shag carpet of purple flowers forty miles wide and a tidal wave of tourists came pouring up to see and photograph them, the hobs never showed their noses aboveground by day at all. But it was a bother, despite their perfect ease at getting about in the dark; for except from November to April hobs didn't do a lot of sleeping, and they always had more than enough essential work to see to. Then there was the grouse shooting, which started every year on August 12 and went on till long after Elphi and his companions had gone to ground for the winter . . .

Of course, the hoard of August visitors was also a great boon. All summer the hobs picked up a stream, steady but relatively thin, of useful stuff dropped or forgotten by visitors. August brought the flood, and the year's bonanza: bandanas, wool socks, chocolate bars, granola bars, small convenient pads of paper, pencils and pens, maps, rubber bands, safety pins, lengths of nylon cord, fourteen Swiss Army knives in fifteen years, guidebooks, comic books, new batteries for the transistors (three), and the electric torches (five). Every night in summer they would all be out scavenging the courses of the long-distance footpaths, the Lyke Wake Walk and the Cleveland Way, each with a big pouch to carry home the loot in.

Earlier and later in the year, however, they were forced to spend more time hunting, and hunting a meal was Elphi's first priority now. Luckily he and his people could digest just about anything they could catch (or they would not have been able to survive here at all). They were partial to dale-dwelling rabbit and spring lamb and had no objection to road-killed ewe when they could get it; but as none of these was available at the moment, Elphi settled for a grouse he happened to start: snapped its neck, dismembered it, and ate it raw on the spot, hungrily but neatly, arranging the feathers to look like a fox kill (and counting on a real fox to come and polish off the bones he left behind).

Satisfied, his head clearer, Elphi trotted another mile to a stream, where he washed the blood off his hands and had his first drink in more than four months. He had begun to move better now. His hands and broad feet shod in sheepskin with the fleece side out settled into their long habit of brushing through

31

the old snow without leaving identifiable tracks. Still on all fours, he picked up speed.

Now then: what were they to do with Woof Howe Hob so that no human could possibly discover that he had ever existed?

Burning would be best. But fire on the moors in April was a serious thing; a fire would be noticed and investigated. The smoke could be seen a long way, and the park rangers were vigilant. Unless a convenient mist were to cover the signs . . . but the hobs almost never, on principle, risked a fire, and in any case there were far too few stored peats in the den to burn a body, even a hob's small body. Elphi suddenly *saw* Woof Howe on a heap of smouldering peats and his insides shriveled. He forced the picture away.

They would have to find someplace to bury Woof Howe where nobody would dig him up. But where? He cursed himself and all the rest, his dead friend included, for having failed to work out in advance a strategy for dealing with a problem so certain to occur. Their shrinking from it had condemned one of their number—himself, as it turned out—to solving it alone if none of the others woke up before something had to be done.

Elphi thought resentfully of the past century and a half—of the increasing complications the decades had added to his life. In the old days nobody would have fussed over a few odd-looking bones, unless they'd been human bones. In the old days people hadn't insisted on figuring everything out. People had accepted that the world was full of wonders and mysteries; but nowadays the remains of their dead comrades disappear absolutely. They'd managed it with Kempswithen, rather gruesomely, by cutting him into very small bits quite unrecognizable as humanoid and distributing these by night over four hundred square miles of open moorland. None of them would care to go through that again, unless there were positively no other way.

Elphi thought about that while he gazed out above the stream bed and the afternoon wore gradually on. The air was utterly clear. Far off to the northwest the peak of Roseberry Topping curled down like the tip of a soft ice-cream cone (Elphi knew this, having seen a drawing of one in a newspaper a hiker had thrown away); and all between Roseberry Topping and Wester-dale Moor, where he now risked standing upright for a moment to look, swept the bristly, shaggy, snowy heath, mile after mile of it, swelling and falling, a frozen sea of bleakness that was somehow at the same time achingly beautiful. White snow had powdered over an underlayer of russet—that was dead bracken at the moor's edge—and the powdered bracken lent a pinkish tint to the whole wide scene. The snow ended roughly where the patchwork fields and pastures of Danby Dale and Westerdale began, and among these, scattered down the dales, were tiny clumps of stone farm buildings.

Elphi had spent the first, best two centuries of his exile down there, on a couple of farms in Danby Dale and Great Fryup Dale. These dales, and the sweep of bleakness above them, made up the landscape of most of his extremely long life; he could scarcely remember anymore when he'd had anything else to look at. However truly he yearned for rescue with one facet of his soul, he beheld these dales with a more immediate yearning, and the moors themselves he loved with a surprising passion. All of the hobs did (or had), except Hob o' t' Hurst and Tarn Hole Hob. Woof Howe had loved them too, as much as any.

Elphi drew in the pure icy air and turned once around completely to view the whole great circle of which he was the center, noting without concern as he turned that a wall of mist had begun to drift toward him off the sea. Then he dropped down, and was again a quadruped with a big problem.

They might *expose* Woof Howe, he thought suddenly—scatter the pieces in that way. It would be risky, but possible if the right place could be found, and if the body could be hidden during the day. Elphi set off northwestward, moving very rapidly now that the kinks were out of his muscles, instinctively finding a way of least resistance between the stiff, scratchy twigs of heather. He meant to check out a place or three for suitability before getting on back to the den to see if anybody else was awake.

Jenny Shepherd, as she tramped along, watched the roke roll toward her with almost as little concern. Years ago, on her very first walking tour of Yorkshire, Jenny—under-equipped and uncertain of her route—had lost her way in a thick, dripping fog long and late enough to realize exactly how much danger she might have been in. But the footpath across Great and Little Hograh Moors was plain, though wetter than it might have been, a virtual gully cut through the slight snow and marked with cairns, and having crossed it more than once before Jenny knew exactly where she was. Getting to the hostel would not be too difficult even in the dark, and anyway, she was equipped today to deal with any sort of weather.

In order to cross a small stone bridge the path led steeply down into a stream bed. Impulsively Jenny decided to take a break there, sheltered somewhat from the wind's incessant keening, before the roke should swallow her up. She shrugged off her backpack, leaned it upright against the bridge, and pulled out one insulating pad of blue foam to sit on and another to use as a backrest, a thermos, a small packet of trail gorp, half a sandwich in a Baggie, a space blanket, and a voluminous green nylon poncho. She was dressed already in coated nylon rain pants over pile pants over soft woolen long johns, plus several thick sweaters and a parka, but the poncho would help keep out the wet and wind and add a layer of insulation.

Jenny shook out the space blanket and wrapped herself up in it, shiny side inward. Then she sat, awkward in so much bulkiness, and adjusted the foam rectangles behind and beneath her until they felt right. The thermos was still half full of tea; she unscrewed the lid and drank from it directly, replacing the lid after each swig to keep the cold out. There were ham and cheese in the sandwich and unsalted peanuts, raisins, and chunks of plain chocolate in the gorp.

Swathed in her space blanket, propped against the stone buttress of the bridge, Jenny munched and guzzled, one glove off and one glove on, in a glow of the well-being that ensues upon vigorous exercise in the cold, pleasurable fatigue, solitude, simple creature comforts, and the smug relish of being on top of a situation that would be too tough for plenty of other people (her own younger self, for one). The little beck poured noisily beneath the bridge's span and down toward the dale and the trees below; the wind blew, but not on Jenny. She sat there tucked into the landscape, in a daze of pure contentment.

The appearance overhead of the first wispy tendrils of mist merely deepened her sense of comfort, and she sat on, knowing it would very soon be time to pack up and go but reluctant to bring the charm of the moment to a close.

A sheep began to come down the stream bed above where Jenny sat, a blackface ewe, one of the mountain breeds—Swaledale, would it be? or Herdwick? No, Herdwicks were a Lake

District breed. With idle interest she watched it scramble down jerkily, at home here, not hurrying and doubtless as cozy in its poncho of dirty fleece as Jenny herself was in her Patagonia pile. She watched it lurch toward her, knocking the stones in its descent—and abruptly found herself thinking of the albino deer in the park at home in Pennsylvania: how when glimpsed it had seemed half deer, half goat, with a deer's tail that lifted and waved as it walked or leapt away and a prick-eared full-face profile exactly like the other deers'; yet it had moved awkwardly on stubby legs and was the wrong color, grayish-white with mottling on the back.

This sheep reminded her somehow of the albino deer, an almost-but-not-quite-right sort of sheep. Jenny had seen a lot of sheep, walking the English uplands. Something about this one was definitely funny. Were its legs too *thick*? Did it move oddly? With the fog swirling more densely every second it was hard to say just *what* the thing looked like. She strained forward, trying to see.

For an instant the mist thinned between them, and she perceived with a shock that the sheep was *carrying something in its mouth*.

At Jenny's startled movement the ewe swung its dead flat eyes upon her—froze—whirled and plunged back up the way it had come. As it wheeled it emitted a choked high wheeze, perhaps sheeplike, and dropped its bundle.

Jenny pushed herself to her feet, dis-cocooned herself from the space blanket, and clambered up the steep stream bed. The object the sheep had dropped had rolled into the freezing water; she thrust in her ungloved right hand—gritting her teeth—and pulled it out. The thing was a dead grouse with a broken neck.

Now Jenny Shepherd, despite her name, was extremely ignorant of the personal habits of sheep. But they were grazing animals, not carnivores—even a baby knew that. Maybe the sheep had found the dead grouse and picked it up. Sheep might very well do that sort of thing—pick up carrion and walk around with it—for all Jenny knew. But she shivered, heaved the grouse back into the water, and stuck her numb wet hand inside her coat. Maybe sheep *did* do that sort of thing; but she had the distinct impression that something creepy had happened, and her mood was spoiled.

Nervously now she looked at her watch. Better get a move

on. She slipped and slid down to the bridge and repacked her pack in haste. There were four or five miles of open moor yet to be crossed before she would strike a road, and the fog was going to slow her down some. Before heaving the pack back on Jenny unzipped one of its outside pockets and took out a flashlight.

Elphi crashed across the open moor, beside himself. How *could* he have been so careless? Failing to spot the walker was bad enough, yet if he had kept his head all would have been well; nobody can swear to what they see in a fog with twilight coming on. But dropping the grouse, that was unpardonable. For a hundred and fifty years the success of the concealment had depended on unfaltering vigilance and presence of mind, and he had demonstrated neither. That he had just woken up from the winter's sleep, that his mind was burdened with trouble and grief, that walkers on the moors were scarcer than sunshine at this month and hour—none of it excused his incredible clumsiness. Now he had not one big problem to deal with, but two.

The old fellow groaned and swung his head from side to side, but there was no help for what he had to do. He circled back along the way he'd come so as to intersect the footpath half a mile or so east of the bridge. The absence of boot tracks in the snow there had to mean that the walker was heading in this direction, toward Westerdale, and would presently pass by.

He settled himself in the heather to wait; and minutes later, when the dark shape bulked out of the roke, he stepped upright into the path and blocked it. Feeling desperately strange, for he had not spoken openly to a human being in nearly two centuries, Elphi said hoarsely: "Stop reet theear, lad, an' don't tha treea ti run," and when a loud, startled *Oh!* burst from the walker, "Ah'll deea thee nae ho't, but thoo mun cum wiv me noo." His Yorkshire dialect was as thick as clotted cream.

The walker in its flapping garment stood rigid in the path before him. "What—I don't—I can't understand what you're *saying*!"

A woman! And an American! Elphi knew an American accent when he heard one, from the wireless, but he had *never* spoken with an American in all his life—nor with *any* sort of woman, come to that. What would an American woman be *doing* up here at this time of year, all on her own? But he pulled his wits together and replied carefully, "Ah said, ye'll have to cum wiv me. Don't be frighted, an' don't try to run off. No harm will cum ti ye."

The woman, panting and obviously badly frightened despite his words, croaked, "What in God's name *are* you?"

Elphi imagined the small, naked, elderly, hair-covered figure he presented, with his large hands and feet and bulging, knobby features, the whole wrapped up in a dirty sheepskin, and said hastily, "Ah'll tell ye that, aye, but nut noo. We's got a fair piece of ground ti kivver."

Abruptly the walker unfroze. She made some frantic movements beneath her huge garment and a bulky pack dropped out onto the ground, so that she instantly appeared both much smaller and much more maneuverable. Elphi made himself ready to give chase, but instead of fleeing she asked, "Have you got a gun?"

"A *gun* saidst 'ee?" It was Elphi's turn to be startled. "Neea, but iv thoos's na—if ye won't gang on yer own feet Ah'll bring thee along masen. Myself, that's to say. But Ah'd ruther not, t'would be hard on us both. Will ye cum then?"

"This is *crazy! No*, dammit!" The woman eyed Elphi blocking the trail, then glanced down at her pack, visibly figuring the relative odds of getting past him with or without it. Suddenly, dragging the pack by one shoulder strap, she was advancing upon him. "Get out of the way!"

At this Elphi groaned and swung his head. "Mistress, tha mun cum, and theear's an end," he exclaimed desperately, and darting forward he gripped her wrist in his large, knobbly, sheepskin-padded hand. "Noo treea if tha can break loose."

But the woman refused to struggle, and in the end Elphi had no choice but to yank her off her feet and along the sloppy footpath for a hundred yards or so, ignoring the noises she made. He left her sitting in the path rubbing her wrist and went back for the pack, which he shouldered himself. Then, without any more talk, they set off together into the fog.

By the time they arrived at the abandoned jet mine that served the hobs for a winter den, Jenny's tidy mind had long since shut itself down. Fairly soon she had stopped being afraid of Elphi, but the effort of grappling with the disorienting strangeness of events was more than her brain could manage. She was hurt and

37

exhausted, and more than exhausted. Already, when Elphi in his damp fleece had reared up before her in the fog and blocked her way, she had had a long day. These additional hours of bushwhacking blindly through the tough, mist-soaked heather in the dark had drained her of all purpose and thought beyond that of surviving the march.

Toward the end, as it grew harder and harder for her to lift her peat-clogged boots clear of the heather, she had kept tripping and falling down. Whenever that happened her odd, dangerous little captor would help her up quite gently, evidently with just a tiny fraction of his superhuman strength.

Earlier she had remembered seeing circus posters in the Middlesbrough station while changing from her London train; maybe, she'd thought, the little man was a clown or a "circus freak" who had run off into the hills. But that hadn't seemed very probable; and later, when another grouse had exploded under their feet like a feathered grenade and the dwarf had pounced upon it in a flash and broken its neck—a predator that efficient—she'd given up the circus idea for a more terrifying one: maybe he was an escaped inmate of a mental hospital. Yet Elphi himself, in spite of everything, was somehow unterrifying.

But Jenny had stopped consciously noticing and deciding things about him quite a long while before they got where they were going; and when she finally heard him say "We's heear, lass," and saw him bend to ease back the stone at the entrance to the den, her knees gave way and she flopped down sideways into the vegetation.

She awoke to the muted sound of a radio.

Jenny lay on a hard surface, wrapped snugly in a sheepskin robe, smelly and heavy but marvelously warm. For some moments she basked in the comforting warmth, soothed by the normalness of the radio's voice; but quite soon she came fully awake and knew—with a sharp jolt of adrenaline—what had happened and where she must be now.

She lay in what appeared to be a small cave, feebly lit by a stubby white "emergency" candle—one of her own, in fact. The enclosure was stuffy but not terribly so, and the candle burned steadily where it stood on a rough bench or table, set in what looked to be (and was) an aluminum pie plate of the sort snack pies are sold in. The radio was nowhere in sight.

Someone had undressed her; she was wearing her sheet sleeping bag for a nightie and nothing else.

Tensely Jenny turned her head and struggled to take mental possession of the situation. The cave was lined with bunks like the one in which she lay, and in each of these she could just make out . . . forms. Seven of them, all evidently deep in sleep (or cold storage?) and, so far as she could tell, all creatures like the one that had kidnapped her. As she stared Jenny began to breathe in gasps again, and the fear that had faded during the march returned in full strength. *What was this place? What was going to happen to her? What the hell was it all about?*

The first explanation that occurred to her was also the most menacing: that she had lost her own mind, that her unfinished therapeutic business had finally caught up with her. If the little man had not escaped from an institution, then maybe she was on her way to one. In fact, Jenny's record of mental stability, while not without an average number of weak points, contained no hint of anything like hallucinations or drug-related episodes. But in the absence of a more obvious explanation her confidence on this score was just shaky enough to give weight and substance to such thoughts.

To escape them (and the panic they engendered) Jenny applied herself desperately to solving some problems both practical and pressing. It was cold in the cave; she could see her breath. Her bladder was bursting. A ladder against one wall disappeared into a hole in the ceiling, and as the cave appeared to have no other entry-way she supposed the ladder must lead to the outside world, where for several reasons she now urgently wished to be. She threw off the robe and wriggled out of the sleeping bag— catching her breath at the pain from dozens of sore muscles and bruises—and crippled across the stone floor barefoot; but the hole was black as night and airless, not open, at the top. Jenny was a prisoner, naked and in need.

Well then, find something—a bucket, a pan, anything! Poking about, in the nick of time she spotted her backpack in the shadows of the far wall. In it was a pail of soft plastic meant for carrying water, which Jenny frantically grubbed out and relieved herself into. Half full, the pail held its shape and could be stood, faintly steaming, against the wall. Shuddering violently, she then snatched bundles of clothes and food out of the pack and rushed back into bed. In point of fact there wasn't all that much in the way of extra clothing: one pair of woolen boot socks, clean underwear, slippers, a cotton turtleneck, and a spare sweater. No pants, no shoes, no outerwear; she wouldn't get far over the open moor without any of those. Still, she gratefully pulled on what she found and felt immensely better; nothing restores a sense of confidence in one's mental health, and some sense of control over one's situation, like dealing effectively with a few basic needs. Thank God her kidnapper had brought the pack along!

Next Jenny got up again and climbed to the top of the ladder; but the entrance was closed by a stone far too heavy to move.

The radio sat in a sort of doorless cupboard, a tiny transistor in a dimpled red plastic case. BOOTS THE CHEMIST was stamped on the front in gold, and a wire ran from the extended tip of its antenna along one side of the ladder, up the hole. Jenny brought it back into bed with her, taking care not to disconnect the wire.

She was undoing the twisty on her plastic bag of food when there came a scraping, thumping noise from above and a shaft of daylight shot down the hole. Then it was dark again, and legs—whitish hair-covered legs—and the back of a gray fleece came into view. Frozen where she sat, Jenny waited, heart thumping.

The figure that turned to face her at the bottom of the ladder looked by candlelight exactly like a very old, very small gnome of a man, covered with hair—crown, beard, body, and all—save for his large hands and feet in pads of fleece. But this was a superficial impression. The arms were longer and the legs shorter than they should have been; and Jenny remembered how this dwarf had ranged before her on four limbs in the fog, looking as much like a sheep in a backpack as he now looked like a man. She thought again of the albino deer.

They contemplated one another. Gradually, outlandish as he looked, Jenny's fear drained away again and her pulse rate dropped back to normal. Then the dwarf seemed to smile. "It's a bright morning, the roke's burned off completely," he said in what was almost BBC English with only the faintest trace of Yorkshire left in the vowels.

Jenny said, calmly enough, "Look: I don't understand any of this. First of all I want to know if you're going to let me go."

40

She got an impression of beaming and nodding. "Oh, yes indeed!"

"When?"

"This afternoon. Your clothes should be dry in time; I've put them out in the sun. It's a rare bit of luck, our getting a sunny morning." He unfastened the sheepskin as he spoke and hung it from a peg next to a clump of others, then slipped off his moccasins and mitts and put them on the shelf where the radio had stood. Except for his hair he wore nothing.

Abruptly Jenny's mind skittered away, resisting this strangeness. She shut her eyes, unafraid of the hairy creature but overwhelmed by the situation in which he was the central figure. "Won't you please explain to me what's going on? Who are you? Who are *they*? What is this place? Why did you make me come here? Just—what's going *on*?" Her voice went up steeply, near to breaking.

"Yes, I'll tell you all about it now, and when you've heard me out I hope you'll understand what happened yesterday—why it was necessary." He dragged a stool from under the table and perched on it, then quickly hopped up again. "Now, have you enough to eat? I'm afraid we've nothing at all to offer a guest at this time of year, apart from the grouse—but we can't make any sort of fire in this clear weather and I very much doubt you'd enjoy eating her raw. I brought her back last night in case anyone else was awake and hungry, which they're unfortunately not . . . but let me see: I've been through your pack quite thoroughly, I'm afraid, and I noticed some packets of dehydrated soup and tea and so forth; now suppose we were to light several more of these excellent candles and bunch them together, couldn't we boil a little pot of water over the flames? I expect you're feeling the cold." As he spoke the old fellow bustled about—rummaged in the pack for pot and candles, filled the pot half full of water from Jenny's canteen, lit the candles from the one already burning, and arranged supports for the pot to rest on while the water heated. He moved with a speed and economy that were so remarkable as to be almost funny, a cartoon figure whisking about the cave. "There now! You munch a few biscuits while we wait, and I'll do my best to begin to clear up the mystery."

Jenny had sat mesmerized while her abductor rattled on, all the time dashing to and fro. Now she took out tea, sugar, dried milk, two envelopes of Knorr's oxtail soup, and a packet of flat

41

objects called Garibaldis here in England but raisin biscuits in America (and squashed-fly biscuits by the children in *Swallows and Amazons*). She was famished, and gradually grew calm as the old fellow contrived to sound more and more like an Oxbridge don providing a student with fussy hospitality in his rooms in college. She had not forgotten the sensation of being dragged as by a freight train along the footpath, but was willing to set the memory aside. "What became of your accent? Last night I could barely understand you—or aren't you the same one that brought me in?"

"Oh aye, that was me. As I said, none of the others is awake." He glanced rather uneasily at the row of shadowy cots. "Though it's getting to be high time they were. Actually, what's happened is that most of the time you were sleeping, I've been swotting up on my Standard English. I used the wireless, you see. Better switch it off now, actually, if you don't mind," he added. "Our supply of batteries is very, ah, irregular, and where should *we* be now if there hadn't been any left last night, eh?" Silently Jenny clicked off the red radio and handed it to him, and he tucked it carefully back into its cubby. Then he reseated himself upon the stool, looking expectant.

Jenny swallowed half a biscuit and objected, "How can you totally change your accent and your whole style of speaking in one night, just by listening to the radio? It's not possible."

"Not for you, of course not, no, no. But we're *good* at languages, you see. Very, very good; it's the one thing in us that our masters valued most."

At this Jenny's wits reeled again, and she closed her eyes and gulped hard against nausea, certain that unless some handle on all this weirdness were not provided *right away* she might start screaming helplessly and not be able to stop. She *could not* go on chatting with this Santa's elf for another second. Jenny Shepherd was a person who was never comfortable unless she felt she understood things; to understand is, to some extent, to have control over. "Please," she pleaded, "just tell me who and what you are and what's happening here. Please."

At once the old fellow jumped up again. "If I may—" he murmured apologetically and peered again into the treasure trove of Jenny's backpack. "I couldn't help but notice that you're carrying a little book I've seen before—yes, here it is." He brought the book back to the table and the light: the Dalesman paperback guide to the Cleveland Way. Swiftly finding the page he wanted he passed the book over to Jenny, who got up eagerly from the bed, holding the robe around her, to read by candle-light:

The Cleveland area is extremely rich in folklore which goes back to Scandinavian sources and often very much further. Perhaps the hobs, those strange hairy little men who did great deeds—sometimes mischievous, sometimes helpful—were in some way a memory of those ancient folk who lingered on in parts of the moors almost into historic times. In the years between 1814 and 1823 George Calvert gathered together sto-ries still remembered by old people. He lists 23 "Hobmen that were commonly held to live hereabout," including the famous Farndale Hob, Hodge Hob of Bransdale, Hob of Tarn Hole, Dale Town Hob of Hawnby, and Hob of Hasty Bank. Even his list misses out others which are remembered, such as Hob Hole Hob of Runswick who was supposed to cure the whooping cough. Calvert also gives a list of witches. . . .

But this was no help, it made things worse! "You're telling me you're a *hob*?" she blurted, aghast. What nightmarish fantasy was this? "Hob . . . as in hobbit?" However dearly Jenny might love Tolkien's masterpiece, the idea of having spent the night down a hobbit-hole—in the company of seven dwarves!—was a completely unacceptable idea. In the real world hobbits and dwarves must be strictly metaphorical, and Jenny preferred to live in the real world all the time.

The odd creature continued to watch her. "Hob as in hobbit? Oh, very likely. Hob as in hobgoblin, most assuredly—but as to whether *we* are hobs, the answer is yes and no." He took the book from her and laid it on the table. "Sit down, my dear, and bundle up again; and shall I pour out?" for the water had begun to sizzle against the sides of the little pot.

"What did you mean, yes *and* no?" Jenny asked a bit later, sitting up in bed with a steaming Sierra cup of soup balanced in her lap and a plastic mug of tea in her hands, and thinking: This better be good.

"First, may I pour myself a cup? It's a long story," he said, "and it's best to begin at the beginning. My name is Elphi, by the way.

43

"At least the dale folk called me Elphi until I scarcely remembered my true name, and it was the same with all of us—we took the names they gave us and learnt to speak their language so well that we spoke no other even amongst ourselves.

"This is the whole truth, though you need not believe it. My friends and myself were in service aboard an exploratory vessel from another star. Hear me out," for Jenny had made an impatient movement, "I said you need not believe what I tell you. The ship called here, at Earth, chiefly for supplies but also for information. Here, of course, we knew already that only one form of life had achieved mastery over nature. Often that is the case, but on my world there were two, and one subordinate to the other. Our lords the Gafr were physically larger than we and technologically gifted as we were not, and also they did not hibernate; that gave them an advantage, though their lives were shorter (and that gave *us* one). We think the Gafr had been with us, and over us, from the first, when we both were still more animal than thinking thing. Our development, you see, went hand in hand with theirs, but their gift was mastery and ours was service—always, from our prehistory.

"And from our prehistory our lives were intertwined with theirs, for we were of great use to one another. As I've said, we Hefn are very good with languages, at speaking and writing them—and also we are stronger for our size than they, and quicker in every way, though I would have to say less clever. I've often thought that if the Neanderthal people had lived on into modern times their relations with *you* might have developed in a similar way . . . but the Gafr are far less savage than you and never viewed us as competitors, so perhaps I'm wrong. We are very much less closely related than you and the Neanderthal people."

"How come you know so much about the Neanderthalers?" Jenny interrupted to ask.

"From the wireless, my dear! The wireless keeps us up to date. We would be at a sad disadvantage without it, don't you agree?

"So the Gafr—"

"How would you spell that?"

"*G, a, f, r*. One *f*, not two, and no *e*. The Gafr designed the starships and we built them and went to work aboard them. It was our life, to be their servants and dependents. You should

44

understand that they never were cruel. Neither we nor they could imagine an existence without the other, after so many eons of relying upon one another.

"Except that aboard my ship, for no reason I can now explain, a few of us became dissatisfied and demanded that we be given responsibilities of our own. Well, you know, it was as if one day the sheepdogs hereabouts were to complain to the farmers that from now on they wanted flocks of their own to manage, with the dipping and tupping and shearing and lambing and all the rest. Our lords were as dumbfounded as these farmers would be—a talking dog, you see. When we couldn't be reasoned or scolded out of our notion and it began to interfere with the smooth functioning of the ship, the Gafr decided to put us off here for a while to think things over. They were to come back for us as soon as we'd had time to find out what running our own affairs without them would be like. That was a little more than three hundred and fifty years ago."

Jenny's mouth fell open; she had been following intently. "Three hundred and fifty of *your* years, you mean?"

"No, of yours. We live a *long* time. To human eyes we appeared to be very old men when still quite young, but now we are old indeed—and look it too, I fear.

"Well, they put fifteen of us off here, in Yorkshire, and some dozen others in Scandinavia somewhere. I often wonder if any of that group has managed to keep alive, or whether the ship came back for them but not for us—but there's no knowing.

"It was early autumn; we supposed they meant to fetch us off before winter, for they knew the coming of hard winter would put us to sleep. They left us well supplied and went away, and we all had plenty of time to find life without the Gafr as difficult—psychologically, I suppose you might say—as they could possibly have wished. Oh, yes! We waited, very chastened, for the ship to return. But the deep snows came and finally we had to go to earth, and when we awoke the following spring we were forced to face the likelihood that we were stranded here.

"A few found they could not accept a life in this alien place without the Gafr to direct their thoughts and actions; they died in the first year. But the rest of us, though nearly as despairing, preferred life to death—and we said to one another that the ship might yet return.

"When we awoke from our first winter's sleep, the year was

45

1624. In those days the high moors were much as you see them now, but almost inaccessible to the world beyond them. The villages were linked by a few muddy cart tracks and stone pannier trods across the tops. No one came up here but people that had business here, or people crossing from one dale into another: farmers, poachers, panniermen, Quakers later on . . . the farmers would come up by turf road from their own holdings to gather bracken for stock bedding, and to cut turf and peat for fuel, and ling—that's what they call the heather hereabouts, you know—for kindling and thatching. They burned off the old ling to improve the grazing and took away the burned stems for kindling. And they came after bilberries in late summer, and to bring hay to their sheep on the commons in winter, as some still do. But nobody came from outside, passing through from one distant place to another, and the local people were an ignorant, superstitious lot as the world judges such things, shut away up here. They would sit about the hearth of an evening, whole families together, and retell the old tales. And we would hang about the eaves, listening.

"All that first spring we spied out the dales farms, learnt the language and figured our chances. Some of us wanted to go to the dalesmen with our story and ask to be taken into service, for it would have comforted us to serve a good master again. But others—I was one—said such a course was as dangerous as it was useless, for we would not have been believed and the Church would have had us hunted down for devil's spawn.

"Yet we all yearned and hungered so after direction and companionship that we skulked about the farms despite the risk, watching how the men and milkmaids worked. We picked up the knack of it easily enough, of milking and churning and threshing and stacking—the language of farm labor as you might say!—and by and by we began to lend a hand, at night, when the house was sleeping—serving *in secret*, you see. We asked ourselves, would the farmers call us devil's spawn for *that*? and thought it a fair gamble. We'd thresh out the corn, and then we'd fill our pouches with barley and drink the cat's cream off the doorstep for our pay.

"At least we thought it was that cat's cream. But one night at harvest-time, one of us—Hart Hall it was—heard the farmer tell his wife, 'Mind tha leaves t'bate o' cream for t'hob. He deeas mair i' yah neet than a' t'men deea iv a day.' That's how we learnt that the people were in no doubt about who'd been helping them.

"We could scarcely believe our luck. Of course we'd heard talk of witches and fairies, very superstitious they were in those days, and now and again one would tell a tale of little men called hobmen, part elf, part goblin as it seemed, sometimes kind and sometimes tricksy. They'd put out a bowl of cream for the hob, for if they forgot, the hob would make trouble for them, and if they remembered he would use them kindly."

"That was a common practice in rural Scandinavia too—to set out a bowl of porridge for the *tomte*," Jenny put in.

"Aye? Well, well . . . no doubt the cats and foxes got the cream, before *we* came! Well, we put together every scrap we could manage to overhear about the hobmen, and the more we heard the more our way seemed plain. By great good fortune we looked the part. We *are* manlike, more or less, though we go as readily upon four feet as two and stood a good deal smaller than the ordinary human even in those days when men were not so tall as now, and that meant no great harm would come of it should we happen to be seen. That was important. There hadn't been so many rumors of hobbish helpfulness in the dales for a very long time, and as curiosity grew we were spied upon in our turn—but I'm getting ahead of my tale.

"By the time a few years had passed we'd settled ourselves all through these dales. Certain farmsteads and local spots were spoken of as being 'haunted bi t'hob'; well, one way and another we found out where they were, and one of us would go and live there and carry on according to tradition. Not all of us did that, now—some just found a farm they liked and moved in. But for instance it was believed that a certain hob, that lived in a cave at Runswick up on the coast, could cure what they called t'kink-cough, so one of us went on up there to be Hob Hole Hob, and when the mothers would bring their sick children and call to him to cure them, he'd do what he could."

"What *could* he do, though?"

"Not a great deal, but more than nothing. He could make them more comfortable, and unless a child was very ill he could make it more likely to recover."

"How? Herbs and potions?"

"No, not at all—merely the power of suggestion. But quite effective, oh aye.

47

"There was a tradition too of a hob in Farndale that was the troublesome sort, and as it seemed wisest not to neglect that mischievous side of our ledger altogether, once in a while we would send somebody over there to let out the calves and spill the milk and put a cart on the barn roof, and generally make a nuisance of himself. It kept the old beliefs alive, you see. It wouldn't have done for people to start thinking the hobs had all got good as gold, we had the sense to see that. The dalesfolk used to say, 'Gin t'hobman takes ti yan, ya'r yal reet i' t'lang run, but deea he tak agin' 'ee 'tis anither story!' We wanted them to go right on saying that.

"But we did take to them—aye, we did indeed, though the Gafr and the dalesmen were so unalike. The Yorkshire farmer of those times, for all his faults, was what they call the salt of the earth. They made us good masters, and we served them well for nigh on two hundred years."

Jenny wriggled and leaned toward Elphi, raptly attending. "Did any of you ever *talk* with humans, face to face? Did you ever have any human friends, that you finally told the truth to?"

"No, my dear. We had no friends among humans in the sense you mean, though we befriended a few in particular. Nor did we often speak with humans. We thought it vital to protect and preserve their sense of us as magical and strange—supernatural, in fact. But now and again it would happen.

"I'll tell you of one such occasion. For many and many a year my home was at Hob Garth near Great Fryup Dale, where a family called Stonehouse had the holding. There was a Thomas Stonehouse once, that lived there and kept sheep.

"Now, the time I'm speaking of would have been about 1760 or thereabouts, when Tommy was beginning to get on a bit in years. Somehow he fell out with a neighbor of his called Matthew Bland, an evil-tempered fellow he was, and one night I saw Bland creep along and break the hedge, and drive out Tommy's ewes. Tommy was out all the next day in the wet, trying to round them up, but without much luck, for he only found five out of the forty, and so I says to myself: here's a job for Hob. The next morning all forty sheep were back in the field and the hedge patched up with new posts and rails.

"Well! but that wasn't all: when I knew Tommy to be laid up with a cold, and so above suspicion himself, I nipped along and let Bland's cattle loose. A perfectly hobbish piece of work that

48

was! Old Bland, he was a full fortnight rounding them up. Of course, at the time the mischief was done Tommy had been in his bed with chills and a fever, and everybody knew it; but Bland came and broke the new fence anyway and let the sheep out again—he was that furious, he had to do something.

"As Tommy was still too ill to manage, his neighbors turned out to hunt the sheep for him. But the lot of 'em had wandered up onto the tops in a roke like the one we had yesterday evening, and none could be found at all. All the same, that night Hob rounded them up and drove them home, and repaired the fence again. Bear in mind, my dear, that such feats as the farmers deemed prodigious were simple enough for us, for we have excellent sight in the dark, and great strength in the low gravity here, and are quick on our feet, whether four or two.

"Now, four of Tommy's ewes had fallen into a quarry in the roke and broken their necks, and never came home again. When he was well enough he walked out to the field to see what was left of the flock and cut some hay for it—this was early spring, I remember, just about this time. We'd awakened sooner than usual that year, which was a bit of luck for Tommy. I saw him heading up there, and followed. And when I knew him to be grieving over the four lost ewes I accosted him in the road and said not to fret any more, that the sheep would be accounted for and then some at lambing time—for I knew that most were carrying twins, and I meant to help with the lambing as well, to see that as many as possible would live.

"He took me then for an old man, a bit barmy though kindly intentioned. But later, when things turned out the way I'd said, it was generally talked of—how there was no use Matthew Bland trying to play tricks on Tommy Stonehouse, for the hobman had befriended him, and when t'hobman taks ti yan . . . aye, it was a bit of luck for Tommy that we woke early that spring.

"But to speak directly to a farmer so, that was rare. More often the farmer took the initiative upon himself, or his wife or children or servants did, by slipping out to spy upon us at work, or by coming to beg a cure. There was talk of a hob that haunted a cave in the Mulgrave Woods, for instance. People would put their heads in and shout, 'Hob-thrush Hob! Where is thoo?' and the hob was actually meant to reply—and the dear knows how *this* tradition began—'Ah's tying' on mah lef' fuit shoe, An' Ah'll be wiv thee—noo!' Well, we didn't go as far as that, but

49

once in a while one of us might slip up there for a bit so's to be able to shout back if anyone called into the cave. Most often it was children.

"Mostly, people were frightened of t'hob. But as I've said, we thought it as well to keep the magic bright. There was one old chap, name of Gray, with a farm over in Bransdale; he married himself a new wife who couldn't or wouldn't remember to put out the jug of cream at bedtime as the old wife had always done. Well, Hodge Hob, that had helped that family for generations, he pulled out of there and never went back. And another time a family called Oughtred, that farmed over near Upleatham, lost *their* hob because he died. That was Hob Hill Hob, that missed his step and broke his neck in a mine shaft, the first of us all to go out since the very beginning. Well, Kempswithen overheard the Oughtreds discussing it—whyever had the hob gone away?—and they agreed it must have been because one of the workmen had hung his coat on the winnowing machine and forgot it, and the hobman had thought it was left there for *him*—for everyone knew you mustn't offer clothes to fairies and such or they'll take offence.

"Well! We'd been thinking another of us might go and live at Hob Hill Farm, but after that we changed our minds. And when a new milkmaid over at Hart Hall spied on Hart Hall Hob and saw him flailing away at the corn one night without a stitch on, and made him a shirt to wear, and left it in the barn, we knew he'd have to leave there too, and he did. One curious thing: the family at Hart Hall couldn't decide whether the hob had been offended because he'd been given the shirt at all, or because it had been cut from coarse cloth instead of fine linen! We know, because they fretted about it for months, and sacked the girl.

"At all events we'd make the point now and then that you mustn't offend the hob or interfere with him or get too close and crowd him, and so we made out pretty well. Still hoping for rescue, you know, but content enough on the whole. We were living all through the dales, north and south, the eleven of us who were left alive—at Runswick, Great Fryup, Commondale, Kempswithen, Hasty Bank, Scugdale, Farndale, Hawnby, Broxa . . . Woof Howe . . . and we'd visit a few in-between places that were said to be haunted by t'hob, like the Mulgrave Cave and Obtrush Rook above Farndale. It was all right.

"But after a longish time things began to change.

"This would be perhaps a hundred and fifty years ago, give or take a couple of decades. Well, I don't know just how it was, but bit by bit the people hereabouts began to be less believing somehow, less sure their grandfathers had really seen the fairies dance on Fairy Cross Plain, or that Obtrush Rook was really and truly haunted by the hobman. And by and by we began to feel that playing hob i' t'hill had ceased to be altogether safe. Even in these dales there were people now that wanted explanations for things, and that weren't above poking their noses into our affairs.

"And so, little by little we began to withdraw from the farms. For even though we were no longer afraid of being taken for Satan's imps and hunted down, concealment had been our way of getting by for such a very long time that we preferred to go on the same way. But for the first time in many a long year we often found ourselves thinking of the ship again and wishing for its return. Yet I fear the ship was lost, and I'll tell you why I think so.

"The Gafr discovered a way of looking back in time, a time window they can set up in a place, through which they can see everything that ever happened in that place, all the way back to the beginning. And whoever they see through the window can see them too, my dear. That's the point. It's costly, but not so costly to look into the recent past that they wouldn't have used the window had they ever come back. So ever since we were left here, we'd taken it in turns each day, except in winter, to pass the spot where we'd been 'put ashore,' so that one of us would be sure to see the open window and receive the message."

" 'Unavoidably delayed—hang on till 370th year of exile'?''

"No, not a telegram—a familiar face, speaking to us from the future. A face in a window.

"But the message never came, and gradually we drew back out of the dales to the high moortops, moved into the winter dens we'd been using right along, and set ourselves to learning how to live up here entirely—to catch grouse and hares, and find eggs and berries, instead of helping ourselves to the farmer's stores. Oh, we were good hunters and we loved these moors already, but still it was a hard and painful time, almost a second exile. I remember how I once milked a ewe—thinking to get some cream—only to find that it was the jug set out for me by

51

the farmer's wife that I wanted and missed, for that was a symbol of my service to a master that respected what I did for him; but a worse time was coming.

"There were mines on the moors since there were people in the land at all, but not so very long after we had pulled back up out of the dales altogether, ironstone began to be mined in Rosedale on a larger scale than ever before, and they built a railroad to carry the ore right round the heads of Rosedale and Farndale and down to Battersby Junction. I daresay you know the right of way now as a footpath, my dear, for part of it lies along the route of the Lyke Wake Walk. But in the middle of the last century men came pouring onto the high moors to build the railroad. Some even lived up here, in shacks, while the work was ongoing. And more men poured across the moors from the villages all round about, to work in the Rosedale pits, and then there was no peace at all for us, and no safety.

"That was when we first were forced to go about by day in sheepskin.

"It was Kempswithen's idea, he was a clever one! The skins weren't too difficult to get hold of, for sheep die of many natural causes, and also they are easily killed, though we never culled more than a single sheep from anyone's flock, and then always an old ewe or a lame one, of little value. It went against the grain to rob the farmers at all, but without some means of getting about by daylight we could not have managed. The ruse worked well, for nearly all the railroad workers and miners came here from outside the dales and were unobservant about the ways of sheep, and we were careful.

"But the noise and smoke and peacelessness drove us away from out old haunts and onto the bleakest part of the high moors where the fewest tracks crossed. We went out there and dug ourselves in.

"It was a dreary time. And the mines had scarcely been worked out and the railroad dismantled when the Second War began, and there were soldiers training on Rudland Rigg above Farndale, driving their tanks over Obtrusch Rook till they had knocked it to bits, and over Fylingdales Moor, where we'd gone to escape the miners and the trains."

"Fylingdales, where the Early Warning System is now?"

"Aye, that's the place. During the war a few planes made it up this far, and some of the villages were hit. We slept through a good deal of that, luckily—we'd found this den by then, you see, an old jet working that a fox had opened. But it was uneasy sleep, it did us little good. Most particularly, it was not good for us to be of no use to any master—that began to do us active harm, and we were getting old. Two of us died before the war ended, another not long after. And still the ship did not return.''

Something had been nagging at Jenny. ''Couldn't you have reproduced yourselves after you came up here? You know—formed a viable community of hobs in hiding. Kept your spirits up.''

''No, my dear. Not in this world. It wasn't possible, we knew it from the first, you see.''

''Why wasn't it possible?'' But Elphi firmly shook his head; this was plainly a subject he did not wish to pursue. Perhaps it was too painful. ''Well, so now there are only eight of you?''

''Seven,'' said Elphi. ''When I woke yesterday Woof Howe was dead. I'd been wondering what in the world to do with him when I so stupidly allowed you to see me.''

Jenny threw the shadowed bunks a startled glance, wondering which contained a corpse. But something else disturbed her more. ''You surely can't mean to say that in the past hundred and fifty years not one of you has ever been caught off guard until yesterday!''

Elphi gave the impression of smiling, though he did not really smile. ''Oh, no, my dear. One or another of us has been caught napping a dozen times or more, especially in the days since the Rosedale mines were opened. Quite a few folk have sat just where you're sitting and listened, as you've been listening, to much the same tale I've been telling *you*. Dear me, yes! Once we rescued eight people from a train stalled in a late spring snowstorm, and we've revived more than one walker in the last stages of hypothermia—that's besides the ones who took us by surprise.''

His ancient face peered up at her through scraggly white hair, and Jenny's apprehension grew. ''And none of them ever told? It's hard to believe.''

''My dear, none of them has ever remembered a thing about it afterwards! Would we take such trouble to keep ourselves hidden, only to tell the whole story to any stranger that happens by? No indeed. It passes the time and entertains our guests, but they always forget. As will you, I promise—but you'll be safe as houses. Your only problem will be accounting for the lost day."

Jenny had eaten every scrap of her emergency food and peed the plastic pail nearly full, and now she huddled under her sheepskin robe by the light of a single fresh candle, waiting for Elphi to come back. He had refused to let her climb up to empty her own slops and fetch back her own laundry. "I'm sorry, my dear, but there's no roke today—that's the difficulty. If ever you saw this place again you would remember it—and besides, you know, it's no hardship for me to do you a service." So she waited, a prisoner beneath the heavy doorway stone, desperately trying to think of a way to prevent Elphi from stealing back her memories of him.

Promising not to tell anybody, ever, had had no effect. ("They all promise, you know, but how can we afford the risk? Put yourself in my place.") She cudgeled her wits: what could she offer him in exchange for being allowed to remember all this? Nothing came. The things the hobs needed—a different social order on Earth, the return of the Gafr ship, the Yorkshire of three centuries ago—were all beyond her power to grant.

Jenny found she believed Elphi's tale entirely: that he had come to Earth from another world, that he would not harm her in any way, that he could wipe the experience of himself from her mind—as effortlessly as she might wipe a chalkboard with a wet rag—by "the power of suggestion," just as Hob Hole Hob had "cured" the whooping cough by the power of suggestion. Somewhere in the course of the telling both skepticism and terror had been neutralized by a conviction that the little creature was speaking the unvarnished truth. She had welcomed this conviction. It was preferable to the fear that she had gone stark raving mad; but above and beyond all that, she did believe him.

And all at once she had an idea that just might work. At least it seemed worth trying; she darted across the stone floor and scrabbled frantically in a pocket of her pack. There was just enough time. With only seconds to spare, she burrowed back beneath the sheepskin robe where Elphi had left her.

The old hob backed down the ladder with her pail flopping from one hand and her bundle of clothes clutched in the opposite arm, and this time he left the top of the shaft open to the light and cold and the wuthering of the wind. He had tied his sheepskin on again. "Time to suit up now, I think—we want to set you back in the path at the same place and time of day." He scanned the row of sleepers anxiously and seemed to sigh.

Jenny's pile pants and wool socks were nearly dry, her sweaters, long johns, and boots only dampish. She threw off the sheepskins and began to pull on the many layers of clothing one by one. "I was wondering," she said as she dressed, "I wanted to ask you, how could the hobs just *leave* a farm where they'd been in secret service for maybe a hundred years?"

Elphi's peculiar flat eyes peered at her mildly. "Our bond was to the serving, you see. There were always other farms where extra hands were needed. What grieved us was to leave the dales entirely."

No bond to the people they served, then; no friendship, just as he had said. But all the same . . . "Why couldn't you come out of hiding now? People all over the world would give anything to know you exist!"

Elphi seemed both amused and sad. "No, my dear. Put it out of your mind. First, because we must wait here so long as any of us is left alive, in case the ship should come. Second, because we love these moors and would not leave them. Third, because here on Earth we have always served in secret, and have got too old to care to change our ways. Fourth, because if people knew about us we would never again be given a moment's peace. Surely you know that's so."

He was right about the last part anyway; people would never leave them alone, even if the other objections could be answered. Jenny herself didn't want to leave Elphi alone. It was no use.

As she went to mount the ladder the old hob moved to grasp her arm. "I'm afraid I must ask you to wear this," he said apologetically. "You'll be able to see, but not well. Well enough to walk. Not well enough to recognize this place again." And reaching up he slipped a thing like a deathcap over her head and fastened it loosely but firmly around her neck. "The last person to wear this was a shopkeeper from Bristol. Like you, he saw more than he should have seen and was our guest for a little while one summer afternoon."

"When was that? Recently?"

"Between the wars, my dear."

Jenny stood, docile, and let him do as he liked with her. As he stepped away, "Which was the hob that died?" she asked through the loose weave of the cap.

There was a silence. "Woof Howe Hob."

"What *will* you do with him?"

Another silence, longer this time. "I don't quite know . . . I'd hoped some of the rest would wake up, but the smell . . . it's beginning to trouble me too much to wait. I don't imagine you can detect it."

"Can't you just wake them up?"

"No, they must wake in their own time, more's the pity."

Jenny drew a deep breath. "Why not let *me* help you, then, since there's no one else?"

An even longer silence ensued, and she began to hope. But "You can help me *think* if you like, as we walk along," Elphi finally said, "I don't deny I should be grateful for a useful idea or two, but I must have you on the path by late this afternoon, come what may." And he prodded his captive up the ladder.

Aboveground, conversation was instantly impossible. After the den's deep silence the incessant wind seemed deafening. This time Jenny was humping the pack herself, and with the restricted sight and breathing imposed by the cap she found just walking quite difficult enough; she was too sore (and soon too winded) to argue anymore.

After a good long while Elphi said this was far enough, that the cap could come off now and they could have a few minutes' rest. There was nothing to sit on, only heather and a patch of bilberry, so Jenny took off her pack and sat on that, wishing she hadn't eaten every last bit of her supplies. It was a beautiful day, the low sun brilliant on the shaggy, snowy landscape, the sky deep and blue, the tiers of hills crisp against one another.

Elphi ran on a little way, scouting ahead. From a short distance, with just his back and head showing above the vegetation, it was astonishing how much he really did move and look like a sheep. She said as much when he came back. "Oh, aye, it's a good and proven disguise, it's saved us many a time. Mind you, the farmers are hard to fool. They know their own stock, and they know where theirs and everyone else's ought to be—the flocks are heafed on the commons and don't stray much. 'Heafed,' that means they stick to their own bit of grazing. So we've got to wear a fleece with a blue mark on the left flank if we're going one way and a fleece with red on the shoulder if we're going another, or we'll call attention to ourselves and that's the last thing we want."

"Living *or* dead," said Jenny meaningfully.

"Aye." He gave her a sharp glance. "You've thought of something?"

"Well, all these abandoned mines and quarries, what about putting Woof Howe at the bottom of one of those, under a heap of rubble?"

Elphi said, "There's fair interest in the old iron workings. We decided against mines when we lost Kempswithen."

"What did you do with *him*? You never said."

"Nothing we should care to do again." Elphi appeared to shudder.

"Haven't I heard," said Jenny slowly, "that fire is a great danger up here in early spring? There was a notice at the station, saying that when the peat gets really alight it'll burn for weeks."

"We couldn't do that!" He seemed truly shocked. "Nay, such fires are dreadful things! Nothing at all will grow on the burned ground for fifty years and more."

"But they burn off the old heather, you told me so yourself."

"Controlled burning that is, closely watched."

"Oh." They sat silent for a bit, while Jenny thought and Elphi waited. "Well, what about this: I know a lot of bones of pre-historic animals, cave bears and Irish elk and so on—*big* animals—were found in a cave at the edge of the park somewhere, but there haven't been any finds like that on the moors because the acid in the peat completely decomposes everything. I was reading an article about it. Couldn't you bury your friend in a peat bog?"

Elphi pondered this with evident interest. "Hmm. It might be possible at that—nowadays it might. Nobody cuts the deep peat for fuel anymore, and bog's poor grazing land. Walkers don't want to muck about in a bog. About the only chaps who like a bog are the ones that come up to look at wildflowers, and it's too early for them to be about."

"Are there any bogs inside the fenced-off part of Fylingdales, the part that's closed to the public?"

Elphi groaned softly, swinging his head. "Ach, Woof Howe did hate it so, skulking in that dreary place. But still, the flowers would have pleased him."

"Weren't there some rare plants found recently inside the

57

fence, because the sheep haven't been able to graze them down in there?''

"Now, that's true," Elphi mused. "They wouldn't disturb the place where the bog rosemary grows. I've heard them going on about the bog rosemary and the marsh andromeda, over around May Moss." He glanced at the sun. "Well, I'm obliged to you, my dear. And now we'd best be off. Time's getting on. And I want you to get out your map, and put on your rain shawl now."

"My what?"

"The green hooded thing you were wearing over your other clothes when I found you."

"Oh, the poncho." She dug this out, heaved and hoisted the pack back on and belted it, then managed to haul the poncho on and down over pack and all, despite the whipping of the wind, and to snap the sides together. All this took time, and Elphi was fidgeting before she finished. She faced him, back to the wind. "Since I helped solve your problem, how about helping me with mine?"

"And what's that?"

"I want to remember all this, and come back and see you again."

This sent Elphi off into a great fit of moaning and head-swinging. Abruptly he stopped and stood, rigidly upright. "Would you force me to lie to you? What you ask cannot be given. I've told you why."

"I *swear* I wouldn't tell anybody!" But when this set off another groaning fit, Jenny gave up. "All right. Forget it. Where is it you're taking me?"

Elphi sank to all fours, trembling a little, but when he spoke his voice sounded ordinary. "To the track across Great Hograh, where we met. Just over there, do you see? The line of cairns?" And sure enough, there on the horizon was a row of tiny cones. "You walk before me now, straight as you can, till you strike the path."

Jenny, map in hand and frustration in heart, obediently started to climb toward the ridge, lifting her boots high and clear of the snow-dusted heather. The wind was now at her back. Where a sheep track went the right way she followed it until it wandered off course, then cast about for another; and in this way she climbed at last onto the narrow path. She stopped to catch her breath and admire the view, then headed east, toward the youth hostel at Westerdale Hall, with the sun behind her.

For a couple of miles after that Jenny thought of nothing at all except the strange beauty of the scenery, her general soreness and tiredness, and the hot, bad dinner she would get in Westerdale. Then, with a slight start, she wondered when the fog had cleared and why she hadn't noticed. She pulled off the flapping poncho—dry already!—rolled it up, reached behind to stuff it under the pack flap, then retrieved her map in its clear plastic cover from between her knees and consulted it. If that slope directly across the dale was Kempswithen, then she must be about *here*, and so would strike the road into Westerdale quite soon. She would be at the hostel in, oh, maybe an hour, and have a hot bath—hot wash, anyway, the hostel probably wouldn't have such a thing as a bathtub, they hardly ever did—and the biggest dinner she could buy.

"This is our off-season. You're in luck," said the hostel warden. "We were expecting you yesterday. In summer there wouldn't have been a bed in the place, but we're not fully booked tonight, so not to worry. Will you be wanting supper?"

"I booked for the fifth," said Jenny a bit severely. "I'm quite sure, because the fifth is my sister's birthday."

"Right. But the fifth was yesterday; this is the sixth." He put his square finger on a wall calendar hanging behind him. "Thursday, April the sixth. All right?"

"It's Wednesday the fifth," said Jenny patiently, wondering how this obvious flake had convinced the Youth Hostel Association to hire him for a position of responsibility. She held out her wrist so he could read the day and date.

He glanced at the watch. "As a matter of fact it says Thursday the sixth. But it's quite all right, you'll get a bed. Now what about supper, yes or no? There's people waiting to sign in."

Jenny stared at the little squares on the face of her watch and felt her own face begin to burn. "Sorry, I guess I made a mistake. Ah . . . yes, please, I definitely do want supper." A couple of teenage boys, waiting in the queue behind her, were looking at her strangely; she fumbled out of her boots, slung them into the boot rack, hoisted up her pack, and with all the

59

dignity she could summon, proceeded toward the dormitory she'd been assigned to.

Safe in the empty dorm she picked a bed and sat on it, dumping her pack on the floor beside her. "I left Cambridge on the third," she said aloud. "I stayed two nights in York. I got on the Middlesbrough train this morning, changed there for Whitby, got off at Kildale, and walked over the tops to Westerdale. How and where in tarnation did I manage to lose a day?"

On impulse she got out her seat ticket for the Inter-City train. The seat had been booked for the third. The conductor had looked at and punched the ticket. Nobody else had tried to sit in the same seat. There could be no reasonable likelihood of a mistake about the day.

Yet her watch, which two days ago had said Monday, April 3, now said Thursday, April 6. Where could the missing day have gone?

But there was no one to tell her, and the room was cold. Jenny came back to the present: she needed hot water, food, clean socks, her slippers, and (for later) several more blankets on her bed. She wrestled her pack around, opened it, and pulled out her towel and soap box; but her spare pair of boot socks was no longer clean. In fact, it had obviously been worn hard. Both socks were foot-shaped, stuck full of little twiglets of heather, and just slightly damp.

The prickly bits of heather made Jenny realize that the socks she was wearing were prickly as well. She stuck a finger down inside the prickliest sock to work the bits of heather loose, giving this small practical problem all her attention so as to hold panic at bay.

The prickle in her right sock was not heather but a small piece of paper folded up tight. Hands shaking, Jenny opened the scrap of paper and spread it flat on her thigh. It was a Lipton tea bag wrapper, scribbled over with a pen on the nonprinted side, in her own handwriting. The scribble said:

hob called ELFY (?)—caught me in fog, made me come home with him—disguised as *sheep*—lives in hole with 6 others—*hobs are aliens*—he'll make me forget but TRY TO REMEMBER—Danby High Moor?/Bransdale? Farndale?—KEEP TRYING, DON'T GIVE UP!!!

* * *

60

These words, obviously penned in frantic haste, meant nothing whatever to Jenny. What was a hob? Yet she had written this herself, no question.

Her mind did a slow cartwheel. The sixth of April. Thursday, not Wednesday.

Jenny folded up the scrap of paper and stowed it carefully in her wallet. Methodically then she went through the pack. The emergency food packet had gone, vanished. So had the flashlight and the candles. The spare shirt and underwear that ought to have been fresh were not. Her little aluminum mess kit pot, carefully soaped for easy cleaning through so many years of camping trips, had been blackened with smoke on the bottom.

Something inexplicable had happened and Jenny had forgotten what it was—been made to forget, apparently; and to judge by this message from out of the lost day, she had considered it well worth remembering.

All right then, she decided, hunched aching and grubby on a hard bed in that cold, empty room, the thing to do was to follow instructions and not give up. Trust her own judgment. Keep faith with herself, even if it took years.

It did take years, but Jenny never gave up. She returned often to the North York Moors National Park as increasingly superheated summers, semester breaks, and sabbaticals permitted, coming to know Danby High Moor, and Bransdale and Farndale and *their* moors, as well as a foreign visitor possibly could know them in every season; and each visit made her love that rugged country better. In time she became a regular guest at a farm in Danby Dale that did bed-and-breakfast for people on holiday, and never again needed to sleep in Westerdale Hall.

The wish to unriddle the mystery of the missing April 5 retained its strength and importance without, luckily, becoming obsessive, and this fact confirmed Jenny's instinctive sense that when she had scribbled that note to herself she had been afraid only of forgetting, not of the thing to be forgotten. She wanted the lost memories back, not in order to confront and exorcise them but to repossess something of value that rightfully belonged to her.

But Elphi's powers of suggestion were exceptional. Try as she might, Jenny could not recapture what had happened. Diligent research did uncover a great deal of information about hobs (including the correct spelling of Elphi's name, for he had been

61

famous in his day). And Jenny also made it her business to learn what she could about people who believed themselves to have been captured and examined by aliens (for instance, they are drawn back again and again to the scene of the close encounter). Many of these people, clearly, had been traumatized, and were afterwards tormented by their inability to remember what had happened to them. Following their example, in case it might help, Jenny eventually sat through a few sessions with a hypnotist; but whether because her participation was halfhearted or because Elphi's skills were of a superior sort, she could remember nothing.

None of her efforts, in fact, produced the results she wanted. It took the return of the Gafr ship to accomplish that.

II

The great vessel's arrival in the solar system was, of course, the event of the century if not the millennium. This time there could be no secrecy. Telescopes were tracking the ship before it had passed the orbit of Mars. Jenny was just as scared and excited as everyone else, and like everyone else she was astonished when it turned out that negotiations about approaching the Earth were carried out in excellent American English, skipping right over the stage of expressing the speed of light in binary numbers. Oddly enough, it never crossed her mind that *these* aliens—real ones, who could be absolutely nothing else—might be connected with the elusive "aliens" she had been in pursuit of for so long, who might be anything at all. The message on the tea bag wrapper had not mentioned the Gafr or the ship, and perhaps that part of Elphi's story had impressed itself upon Jenny's unconscious less deeply than his other tale of concealment and survival.

But the instant she saw, on her own viewscreen in her own living room, what stepped out of the lander at John F. Kennedy International to be greeted by the UN delegation, there was one heart-stopping instant of pure shock that first stunned her, then jerked her out of her chair. "Elphi!" she exclaimed to the screen, to the empty room, and the entire complex of lost memories dumped itself upon her like a wave, every detail complete.

Jenny's laughing/crying fit was brief, however; in minutes she was on the phone to her department, and right after that she put a call through to England. The next morning found her in the stand-by queue for London; the morning after that she was sound asleep aboard an Inter-City express train hurtling through the washed-out late-winter landscape toward York.

By that time the whole world had been told how, some three hundred and fifty years ago, the aliens had visited Earth and dropped off some friends in the Skåpane province of Sweden and some others in the north of England, and how mechanical difficulties combined with time dilation had delayed their return. The aliens expressed great regret, though little surprise, that the records made no reference to their stranded comrades, and said that of course they did not really expect to find any trace of them after so long. But naturally they wanted to see for themselves.

The Early Warning System on Fylingdales Moor made York-shire a more sensitive target than provincial Sweden, so while various officials were deciding how to handle that, the aliens were conducted to Skåne right away. From the first glimpse of the visitors, every Swede had been put in mind of the famous *tomte* paintings by John Bauer and Harald Wiberg, and this was taken as a possible sign that the exiles had been alive and known to Swedish peasants of an earlier time, even though no formal record could be found of their existence.

The aliens called themselves Hefn. They spelled it for their hosts: *H, e, f, n.* There were five Hefn in the delegation; all of them spoke beautiful American English, and all of them looked like Elphi, only less shaggy and unkempt. They had learned the language from radio transmissions intercepted far out in space, they said, adding that the Hefn are extraordinarily good at lan-guages. To prove this they were speaking quite passable Swedish in a couple of days. They never said a single word about the Gafr, parked like hawks on the moon in the great ship and doubt-less watching the proceedings from there in silence and secrecy.

Jenny couldn't have explained exactly why she needed to be in Yorkshire now. In a way it seemed self-evident, the necessary conclusion of the long, frustrating quest. In another way it was pointless, for she still had no idea how to find the winter den where she had spent her missing day. If Elphi and the others were alive they must know the ship had come—they would have heard about it on the "wireless," the red BOOTS THE CHEMIST transistor or another left behind by some weary Lyke Wake Walker. That nothing had yet been heard from them made it seem unlikely that any of the hobs were, in fact, now left alive.

The cold March wind keened along the platform at Danby village when she swung down from the rackety Esk Valley train to Whitby and was collected, bags and all, by John Dowson, the farmer whose house had come to be home base for Jenny in Yorkshire. "Good to see you again!" he shouted above the wind, and she shouted back, "Glad you could have me on such short notice!" John and his wife had been putting her up through fifteen years of hob hunting—not that they'd known that's what it was—and Jenny noticed with a slight shock that John had gotten to be quite an old man. For that matter she was well into middle age now herself. Perhaps, after this, she would not be doing this trip quite so often. The thought brought a pang; she pushed it away.

"We reckoned this just might have something to do with the space folk," John observed in his cheerful, deliberate manner, once they were in the Land Rover and driving up the dale.

"You might be right about that." Jenny stared greedily out upon a landscape she had not expected to see again for months.

"The government don't want 'em up on Fylingdales." He snorted. "Seems a bit daft. What do Whitehall think they're going to learn about our defenses that they don't already know?"

"Are the local people upset by all the fuss, John?"

"Interested, more. We're not often in the news." He slowed to guide the car through two right angles where the road bent, then straightened, around a churchyard.

"Do the people here believe there were exiles from outer space in the dales, three hundred and fifty years ago?"

John took his time replying. "Oh aye, I reckon some might do. There's not many ready to swear it couldn't be true, come to that—it was lonely country in the old days, and wild on the tops. Anything might've been up there. They used to tell of witches and fairies, and great things like monsters chasing you at night—the Gabbleratchet and the Bargast and I don't know what all." He chuckled.

"Well, does it worry you and Rita?"

John negotiated the Land Rover over a cattle grid. "Not to say worry. Don't seem to have much to do with us somehow. I don't find myself thinking about it. Mind you, there's some that does—there was a chap down in the pub last night going on about how he'd *seen* some of these little people on the tops when he was a lad. Course, folk'll say anything when they've taken a

64

few pints too many. How does he come to be telling about it now only, when he claims it happened thirty years since?"

When Jenny could trust herself to speak she said, "Who *was* the guy, do you know him?"

"Oh aye, chap called Frank Flintoft, son of a friend of ours that has a farm over in Westerdale. Young Frank, he's a dreamy sort of fellow and always was, though a good farmer like his father and his uncle before him—has a place over near Swainby, right on the edge of the Park. Went off to university, took a degree, and then came back up here. There's not so many that does that, you know—mostly, when they've left they're gone. But always a bit dreamy-like. And off-beat ideas—doesn't hold with the chemicals, fertilizers nor herbicides nor none of that, not even to spray his bracken. Makes out all right, though, I'll give him that, his Swaledale gimmer lambs take Best-of-Breed more years than not at the Danby Show. Well, here we are."

They were turning into the steep lane leading up the daleside to the house. "John," said Jenny as calmly as she could, "I believe I'd like to have a talk with this Frank What's-his-name. Think you could fix it for me?"

"Borrow the car tonight if you like—Frank'll be home, he's not the one to go out drinking above one night in the week. We'll just ring first to make sure."

Jenny's night vision was poorish; at home she drove at night only where the roads were familiar, and this was England. Nevertheless, after a dinner she was much too excited to notice the badness of and nearly too excited to eat, she found herself maneuvering Rita Dowson's little car the twenty-five steep, black, twisted miles to the village of Swainby and peering into the dark for the landmarks by which she had been told she would recognize Frank Flintoft's farm.

He answered her knock at once, a lean man about her own age with a pleasant, weathered, curiously innocent face and flyaway gray hair. Like John Dowson he had a farmer's coarsened hands and deliberate rhythms of speech, but his blue eyes were wide awake. He appeared to be alone in the house, and Jenny—relieved to be spared the effort of social pleasantries—came directly to the point. "I heard from John that you've been saying you saw some of the marooned aliens on the moors, thirty years back. Is that right?"

"It was not quite twenty-eight years but it's true enough."

"Would you be willing to tell me about it?"

"I'll be happy to, but I wish you'd tell me something first: what makes you so interested?"

"I expect you've already guessed," said Jenny, and her voice went up in a squeak. She cleared her throat. "I saw them too. Twelve years ago this spring."

Frank Flintoft looked at Jenny as if he had never been so glad to see anyone in his life—as if he could barely stop himself from throwing his arms around her. He gave her a dazzling grin instead. "Thank God for that! Look, do you want something to drink while we talk? This may take a while, and I'm afraid the house is rather cold."

The house *was* cold. Central heating had made its way to the Dowson farm, but not to this one. "Just some tea then—I can barely see to drive as it is, I won't tempt fate."

"Right. Better come into the kitchen."

The kitchen was marginally warmer than the sitting room. Frank clicked on an electric fire set in a tiled hearth and drew two chairs up before it, and while his hands began to turn taps and reach things down from shelves he launched straight into his story.

"I was down from university—it was the vacation between Lent and Summer Terms—and I'd brought a friend from Cornwall home with me. Just before we were due back in Cambridge we decided to do the Lyke Wake Walk. This was well before the route of the Walk got to looking like the landing strip of an airfield across Wheeldale Moor. The farm that used to be Bill Cowley's is only a stone's throw from here, by the way. He was the fellow that actually invented the Walk, back in 1955, and made up the rules—that you had to cross forty miles of open moorland, from Scarth Wood Moor in the west to Ravenscar in the east, in twenty-four hours on your own two feet. Well, you can imagine how that kind of thing would appeal to a lad of twenty. My friend and I let our enthusiasm carry us away—kids always think they're indestructible, but still it was inexcusably stupid of me. We set out with nothing but the clothes on our backs and a couple of sandwiches and chocolate bars, and a flask in each of our rucksacks, and about halfway across we were caught in a freak spring snowstorm.

"We struggled along, but the snow was blowing and drifting, and before long we had no idea where we were. I recall being less frightened than furious at my own folly—I'd lived up here all my life, I knew this kind of thing could happen, and Toby had trusted me. Well, we floundered along as best we could on a compass bearing—there's no shelter worth tuppence up there—and I remember at some point I'd put a bit of chocolate in my mouth that wouldn't melt. And that did scare me; that's when I knew we were in a pretty bad way.

"After *that* I don't remember much of anything until I came to and found that Toby and I were in some sort of underground den, an old mine by the look of it, and there were about a dozen of these Hefn looking us over.

"We were down there for hours. They warmed us up and gave us some stale biscuits and told us all about themselves—that they'd come from another star and been put off here in a disciplinary action by their leaders, who were meant to come back for them but never had. And they told us they were the hobmen—now that was a stunner, I'd heard tales of the hob since I was in infant school. I remember they said we were damn lucky because they'd been asleep all winter and had just waked up a couple of weeks before. They spoke a very broad Yorkshire, as I'd done myself before I was at school, but Toby had his work cut out to follow their talk.

"Finally the storm blew itself out, and the little chaps dug themselves out and blindfolded us and hauled us on a kind of sheepskin sledge over the snow—they had like snowshoes on, to keep from sinking in the drifts. They hauled us to the road, which seemed to be quite a ways from the underground cave—at least the journey took a good while. The plow had already gone through by the time we got there, so all we had to do was walk down off the moor to Castleton and telephone my parents. They were frantic of course—they'd alerted the police and the park rangers, but none of *them* could do anything till the storm decided to pack it up.

"Nobody ever could figure out how we survived. Toby and I were as mystified as the rest, because all we could remember was blacking out one day and coming to ourselves the next, trying to break a trail through deep snow to the road on Castleton Rigg. It's puzzled me all my life, and fretted me, too, in a way I couldn't explain. And then, when I switched on the telly day before yesterday, the whole thing just *fell* on me like an avalanche the instant I laid eyes on those five Hefn. Even with

American accents I knew my hobs! I didn't know *what* to do, who to tell—Toby died in a plane crash ten years back, and my parents think I'm enough of a flake as it is—but I felt so desperate to tell somebody that like a damn fool I took more than was good for me at the Duke of Wellington and sounded off to anybody that would listen."

"Just as well you did, really," said Jenny, "or I wouldn't have heard about you," and she proceeded to tell her own story. "I've been wondering why they haven't said anything about the Gafr," she concluded. "Maybe if the hobs—Hefn—are smaller and better at languages than the Gafr, then they'd, one, communicate better with us and two, seem less threatening."

This intrigued Frank. "Or maybe one aspect of serving the Gafr is to be their emissaries when the occasion calls for that, or maybe they want to avoid putting us off with the suggestion of slavery in the status of the Hefn."

"Maybe the Gafr aren't humanoid. That *would* be a major drawback! Maybe they're big blobs with faces that would stop a clock."

"Or maybe it just makes good sense to set a Hefn to catch a Hefn. Or maybe—"

"Hold it a second, Frank!" Jenny broke in. "When exactly did you say this Lyke Wake Walk caper of yours took place—what time of year?"

"Why, just at lambing time, round about the third week of April."

"Well, it was the *first* week of April that I ran into Elphi—April fifth, in fact—and he was the only one awake. They're not *awake* yet, Frank—if any of them are still alive, they're hibernating. They don't know the ship's come back for them yet!"

Frank leaned toward Jenny, blue eyes snapping. "Nor they would—and not only that, these Hefn emissaries *know* the hobmen aren't awake yet, or mightn't be at least, not here and not in Sweden either. Now why haven't they been straight with us? What would be the good of pretending?"

"I've got a harder one than that: what do you think *we'd* better do about it?"

They emptied the teapot while reviewing their options. Nuts and cranks by the hundreds must have come crawling out of the woodwork already, each claiming to have seen and spoken with the stranded aliens; that sort of thing happened after every UFO incident, as Jenny had learned from her reading. The authorities, unable to distinguish false reports of this kind from authentic ones, would almost certainly discount them all. The ones who could instantly tell the difference would be the Hefn themselves, but the Hefn were being kept neck-deep in security people, away from the general public; and anyway, mightn't it be just a bit naive to tell them "We know you're lying" without being able to guess *why* they were lying?

"What I'd really *like* to do," said Jenny, stifling a yawn, "is find Elphi and ask him what *he* thinks his pals are up to. Oh gosh, I've got to get to bed. It's four in the morning in my brain, and I haven't had a proper night's sleep since I knew the hobs and the Hefn were the same."

"Stay here if you like," Frank surprisingly said. "I've plenty of room. I don't know whether John and Rita told you—I was married, years ago, to a woman I met at Cambridge. We came up here for a time, but she didn't take to the life and I couldn't stick London, so we decided to call it off." He smiled at her shyly. "You're more than welcome to stay."

Gratified and flattered, Jenny smiled back. "I'd better not. They're expecting me, and I ought to get Rita's car back to her, anyway. Thanks, though."

At breakfast the next morning Jenny turned on the Dowsons' brand new viewscreen and watched the news while she ate her egg and bacon. The aliens, together with a small army of U.S., UN, and Swedish officials and security personnel, were in southern Sweden. No sign of their comrades had turned up on the ground, but the Swedes now seemed convinced that the image of *tomten* popularized by Bauer and Wiberg must originally have been drawn from the life. (How fascinating that the Swedish Hefn apparently had discovered and exploited the very same folkloric niche for themselves as had the ones in England!) Japan had issued a warning that they would view any official American alliance with the visitors as a hostile move on the part of both. Tokyo was huffy and nervous because the lander had put down at an American airport—UN or no UN—and irritated with the aliens for choosing to learn English instead of Japanese. British and U.S. authorities were still discussing the sensitive question of access to Fylingdales Moor. A decision could be expected in a few days.

Japan's nervous aggressiveness set Jenny off on another train of thought. It seemed to her that the aliens had showed so slight a degree of interest in *any* of Earth's peoples as to seem downright unflattering, almost rude. They were polite, but all they seemed to want was to find their friends. This was hardly the First Contact anybody had expected. Humanity in general felt an intense interest in the visitors. Carl Sagan and Co. were beside themselves with excitement; other reactions ranged from terrified to fawning, but almost nobody could feel indifferent. It was hard to be sure, but the Hefn gave the impression of genuine indifference. Of course this was not a First Contact for them—but they had said nothing, nothing at all, about the future. No offers to exchange cultural and technological information, no expressions of friendship . . . but even the hobs had felt no friendship toward the farmers they served. Excitement was still running so high that perhaps nobody had noticed yet, but Jenny doubted that the Japanese had anything to worry about. Alliance didn't seem to be on the Hefn's minds. She suspected that all they wanted was to find any traces their exiles might have left, and then get out. They were probably keeping quiet about the fact that, if alive, these exiles would still be in hibernation, in order to allow themselves a few weeks in which to give the Earth the once-over. So far they'd shown no sign of being favorably impressed.

As she was finishing her breakfast she got a phone call, a reminder that Frank's invitation last night had put that relationship on an interesting footing. "Feel like a turn on the tops this morning? I've got hold of a chap who'll see to the farm. Maybe between us we can find that bloody den."

So all that day, and for two more after that one, Jenny searched the moors with Frank. Using an Ordnance Survey map of the park with all surface features marked in detail, they poked systematically into every disused jet mine they could locate in the vicinity of Farndale, Bransdale, and Danby High Moors. Frank went in for amateur archeology and knew the ground extremely well. He and his friend Toby had been somewhere in the area between Rosedale Moor and Danby High Moor, just south and east of Castleton Rigg, when the storm struck, a spot roughly eight or ten miles from the bridge where Elphi had blundered onto Jenny in his distraction. Both felt it was fairly far from the den to where they had been "put back" (so to speak) into their proper lives, a matter of some miles of distance and hours of time, but neither had been able to see and could not swear there had been no backtracking to confuse their sense of the distances involved.

The weather held fair and they had a marvelous time together. But the three days' effort produced no results and at the end both still felt undecided about whether or how to try telling their respective governments about the existence of the Gafr. "We don't *know* they're up there," Frank pointed out. "And I'm not sure it makes much difference any road, except that I always feel the more facts you've got hold of the better off you are."

Driving down into Danby Dale on the third fruitless evening, Jenny mused, "You know, even if we'd found the den . . . I asked Elphi why he didn't wake some of the others up so they could help him decide what to do about the dead hob, and he said something like, 'They have to wake up in their own time,' as if it might be dangerous to bring them out of it prematurely."

"Um. Like helping a chick out of the egg."

"Well . . . if they bring the Hefn up here, I guess it's just barely possible you might be able to get through to one of them, or to *somebody*. Have they made up their minds about Fylingdales?"

For answer Frank turned on the car radio. Looking down over the crazy-quilt of fields and thickets still brown with winter as the car descended between tall hedges that flanked the road, Jenny listened to other news and the sports and weather, and then: "A decision is expected tomorrow as to whether the Hefn will be permitted to search for signs of their lost companions within the boundaries of the North York Moors National Park. The park is the site of the Early Warning System established jointly by the governments of the United States and Great Britain on Fylingdales Moor."

"What happens if it's no, and they insist?" Frank shook his head and reached to snap the radio off, but the announcer went on:

"Some governments, notably those of India and Japan, have expressed doubts as to the truth of what these off-world visitors have been saying. It has been suggested that the aliens are using a far-fetched tale to insinuate themselves into the innermost circles of three Western governments. The advantage, it would seem, is all to these governments and to themselves. The Japanese specifically dismiss the controversial evidence implied by

71

pictures of the Swedish *tomte*, which are thought by some to resemble the Hefn. According to Swedish tradition the *tomte* is a gnome that attaches itself to a farm and performs many helpful tasks at night while the family are asleep.''

''Christ Almighty,'' said Frank, silencing the radio.

''If they go on saying that kind of thing, by the time the hobs wake up we could be in the middle of a very big mess. And you know what? I'll bet you anything you like that the Hefn understand that perfectly well. They're deliberately letting the tension build to see what'll happen, how we'll handle it—and I still can't make up my mind what to do, and I have *got* to be on a train to London tomorrow night at the latest.'' Jenny groaned, tired and discouraged. ''What *are* we going to do? We have to decide.''

''God knows,'' said Frank wearily. ''We might try locating other people who've remembered meeting the hobs. An advert in the *Times*: 'If the word GAFR means anything to you, write P.O. Box 777, Danby, Whitby, North Yorks.' Maybe if there were enough of us we'd be able to catch somebody's attention—but I have a feeling we're running out of time in more ways than one.''

''What I don't understand is, why haven't the bloody fools noticed how profoundly *un*interested the Hefn are in forming any alliances with us?''

''Probably because it's what they'd do if *they* were the Hefn. Remember Vietnam? Lyndon Johnson might not have made such a balls-up of that if he'd been able to imagine that there actually are people in the world who don't want exactly what the average American citizen wants. Sorry if that sounds rude,'' he added.

''No, it's the plain truth. And I guess you're right. A deadly anthropomorphism. Potentially deadly.''

They drove in gloomy silence, unhappy for several reasons. After some minutes Jenny quietly began to recite:

> Midwinter nights the frost is deep,
> The stars are glistening and sparkling.
> All on the lonely farm are asleep,
> Moveless through midnight darkling.
> Silent the road where the moon glides bright,
> Snow on the boughs is gleaming white,
> White on the rooftops gleaming.
> All but the Gnome are dreaming.

* * *

Frank glanced at her inquiringly but held his peace, and Jenny
continued:

> He goes to the toolshed and dark storehouse,
> Tries all the locks and latches.
> Huge by their stanchions dream the cows,
> Moonlight gilding their patches;
> Harness and whip forgotten quite
> Prince in the stable dreams all night:
> The manger he's drooping over
> Seems heaped with sweet-scented clover. . . .

"It's from a children's book, a translation of poem about the
tomte," she explained. "Funny. It was illustrated with those Harald Wiberg pictures everybody's talking about, but *I* wouldn't have
said they look very Hefn-like myself. I'd have remembered sooner
if they did, I've got the book around the house somewhere."

Frank said, "Either the poet got it wrong or the Swedish hobs
didn't hibernate."

"They sound more like caretakers than hard workers, too.
Poetic license?"

"Maybe, or maybe the *tomtes* and the Hefn just aren't the
same."

"Tomtar," said Jenny automatically. "Listen, Frank, I believe I *do* have a sort of idea after all."

"Fine, let's hear it."

"First, tell me if you know what May Moss is."

Frank looked surprised. "A boggy spot over on Fylingdales,
inside the fence. Some of the rarest moorland plants have come
back over there, where the sheep can't get at them—bog rosemary, few-flower sedge, that sort of thing. Not much to look at,
any of them, but rare as rare. I went along with a lot of botanists
from York University one Sunday and had a look."

"Well," said Jenny, "I'm pretty sure that's where Elphi buried Woof Howe Hob."

They had arrived at the bottom of the Dowsons' lane. Frank
stopped the car. "Am I to conclude that what you have in mind
is a spot of grave robbing?"

Jenny reflected again that there were no flies on Frank. "Why
wouldn't producing a dead hob be almost as useful as producing

73

a live hob? Either one would shut Tokyo up for a minute and get *us* through to the Hefn, if anything would. Then maybe we could find out from them why the Gafr are still a well-kept secret, and *then* maybe we could decide whether or not to blow their cover. And anyway, it's my last chance.''

"There wouldn't be anything left of him, surely.''

"I told Elphi not, but I hadn't heard then about the two-thousand-year-old bog people they found in Denmark and Ireland and some other places. I thought the acid in the peat would rot the body fast—I'd actually read that somewhere—but instead it turns out that if there used to be oaks growing where the bog is now, then the tannic acid in the water *preserves* the body, like tanning leather.''

"I see.'' Frank sat quiet in the near dark, thinking. "You do know the likeliest reason we haven't been told about the Gafr, don't you?''

Jenny gave him an appraising look. "You mean—for the same reason any aggressor keeps his secret weapon secret till it's needed. Meaning that if their intentions were altogether honorable, they probably would have been straightforward with us, both about the hobs still being asleep and about the Gafr.''

"Yes.''

"So you think they're going to—what, invade? Take over? Murder us in our beds?'' Jenny laughed, a little wildly. "Why bother talking to us at all, in that case? Why not just push a button and Bob's your uncle?''

"I've no idea! I'm not a Hefn! The possibility exists, though, don't you agree?'' They sat together unhappily for a moment. Then Frank stirred and sighed. "Sorry. I'm testy, I'm afraid—trying to get you to persuade me I'm being paranoid, and cross as two sticks when your arguments fail to convince.'' He gripped the wheel and started out across John Dowson's muddy field of winter turnips. "I think, actually, that the taking-over option is likelier than the one about murdering us in our beds. And—I'm going to say something rather awful, Jenny—this whole affair makes me see that from where *I* stand, the outlook's no worse if the Gafr, whatever they are, do take charge of us, than it is if the superpowers carry on dicing over us like they've been doing and let the planet be ruined in the name of economic health. The Gafr might do better and they might do worse, but I find I honestly doubt they'd do much worse by us in the long run than we've been doing on our own. Six of one and a half-dozen of the other." He tried to smile. "I hadn't realized quite how cynical I'd become."

"Six of The Thing That Ate Chicago and half a dozen Conservative backbenchers in striped trousers? I know," Jenny said. "But suppose the Gafr were to set about making servants out of *us*? The Hefn are a servile bunch; we're not. I think it could probably be a whole *lot* worse for us, if that's what they have in mind."

Frank made an impatient noise. "Better frozen or broiled or blasted to bits than pushed about? I don't agree. Where there's life, you know. Of course, I could be wrong. But actually it's far more likely that they would leave us to our own devices as not worth saving. If you want to fret about something, fret about that." He shook his head ruefully. "You see what happens when I stop being a farmer, even for a couple of days. I learned a long time ago that life only makes sense to me on the land, and it's still true." Abruptly he half-turned in his seat to face Jenny. "All right: here's how we'll do it. The only way into the station is through the gate—I do not intend to get myself chewed on by guard dogs or shot for a spy. I'll ring my friend at York tonight and see if something can be set up for tomorrow. It'll probably be all right, they know him at the station and he can vouch for me. I don't reckon they'll have started keeping people off the tops quite yet, even if a Hefn delegation is expected shortly."

Jenny, steeling herself for a different response, was slow to react. "You mean—you'll do it?"

"Of course I shall. What else is there to do? But I warn you, if we hurt a hair on the head of a single bog rosemary plant, Dennis will eat us both for breakfast."

Tired but grinning, Frank drove up the lane the next morning through a light rain and leaned across to open the door for Jenny. "What are you looking so pleased with yourself about?" she asked rather crossly, climbing in. She had slept poorly, and packing her bags had depressed her.

"You'll be pleased too. I," he said, "have been to York and back already since breakfast."

"What on earth for?"

"To pick up a letter from Dennis that'll admit us to the sta-

75

tion, for one thing. And for another, to borrow a fancy new machine that uses X rays to see belowground.''

"Really?'' Jenny's irritation vanished. "Do *you* know how to work it?''

"After a fashion. I borrowed it from a bloke I know in Archeology, who has it on loan from the York police, and he gave me a demonstration. At least I know enough not to zap either of us with radiation, and I'm pretty sure that if something's there, I'll know it.'' Frank chuckled, clearly pleased with himself. "I had to swear a solemn oath that I'd have it back in his rooms before dark tonight *and* promise him a lavish dinner at the restaurant of his choice. Worth it, though. If the grave's fairly shallow, and always assuming the corpse hasn't decomposed completely after all, we might just find our late hobman with this thing.''

Jenny beamed at him. "You are a gifted and enterprising person, did you know that? With a superior class of friend.''

"And you're a bloody inspiration. Did you know *that*?''

Like three enormous golf balls the huge radomes of the Early Warning System lowered above the landscape, visible (between squalls of rain) for many miles in all directions in that open country, growing larger as they approached Fylingdales Moor via the A-road from Whitby. "They always remind me of the eyes of Dr. T. J. Eckleburg,'' Jenny said.

"The which?''

"Forget it. Something from an American novel.''

"Oh. *Gatsby*, isn't it? I'd forgot about those eyes,'' said Frank complacently, and Jenny beamed at him again.

The guard at the gate glanced over Frank's letter, agreed that they were expected, and told him where to leave the car. The mysterious Dennis obviously enjoyed an excellent reputation here; nobody asked where they were bound or what Frank had in the gunnysack. The rain, choosing the moment of their arrival to become heavier, pelted noisily upon their nylon-shrouded heads and shoulders. Through this downpour, beneath the oppressive presence of the three cloud-muffled radomes, Frank led the way along a path that angled off from the paved drive and rapidly out onto the moor. Thus easily had they come upon what was still, for the alien visitors, forbidden ground.

Frank stumped ahead with his farmer's gait, carrying the infernal machine over his shoulder like a spade in a burlap bag.

Jenny followed, squinting into the rain. Unexpectedly he made her laugh by launching into the Lyke Wake Dirge, intoning it in time with his own footsteps:

> "This yah neet, this yah neet,
> Ivvery neet an' all,
> Fire an' fleet an' cannle leet,
> An' Christ tak up thy saul.
> When thoo frae hence away art passed
> Ivvery neet an' all,
> Ti Whinny Moor thoo cums at last,
> An' Christ tak up thy saul.
> If ivver thoo gav owther hosen or shoon,
> Ivvery neet an' all,
> Clap thee doon, an' put 'em on,
> An' Christ tak up thy saul. . . ."

A fit theme for a moorland grave robbing! There were ten stanzas and Frank had plenty of time to sing all of them in his pleasant light baritone, accompanied by the moaning wind, and start over from the beginning before breaking off to say, "Here's May Moss. Mind your feet." The ground was sopping, the dark-stained water of the bog a lifeless-looking stretch of fibrous muck under the close gray sky. Both grave robbers were wearing rubber Wellingtons, but the black water looked too deep in most places for Jenny's, borrowed from a Dowson daughter long since married and moved away.

The machine, which Frank now unlimbered, had somewhat the look of a bulky, heavy metal detector with a backpack power pack. "What's its name?" Jenny asked.

"Search me. Andrew said, but I forgot. Corpse Finder." Awkwardly he strapped himself in and made a few experimental passes with the business end of the machine. "Right, here goes," he said, and started the motor.

"I don't think Elphi would have buried him right wherever the rare plants were growing twelve years ago," Jenny called above the racket. "He knew people were interested in those and might notice if the ground had recently been disturbed."

"Right. We'll work round the sensitive area then, and hope like hell the bog rosemary haven't spread so much they're growing right on top of him now." Frank adjusted his shoulder straps and gravely began to pace along in the wet, swinging the proboscis of the detector from side to side before him while peering through the viewfinder. Back and forth he splashed, covering the area methodically in strips, ignoring the rain.

Not strong enough to carry the equipment herself, Jenny was left with little to do but chafe at her inadequacies and think about how cold she was, how little time in Yorkshire remained to her, and how badly she minded leaving both the unsolved mystery and her new friend behind. Frank's very earnestness as he peered and paced gave him an endearingly comical look to Jenny's eye, yet his steady patience was of more use in the present enterprise than her own nervier energy, and she knew it.

After about an hour they had one exciting false alarm: a dead sheep, mired deep in the muck. It cheered them both tremendously to have proof that the machine did what it was designed to do and that Frank had got the hang of it well enough to be able to interpret what it showed him. But as the afternoon wore on without further finds Jenny's brainwave began to seem more and more pointless. Certainly she would have given up without the steadying effect of Frank's enduring patience; and certainly she was as astonished as well could be when, after five hours of searching, they actually found, two and a half feet below the surface of the water, the small, leathery, amazingly well preserved form which was all that was left of Woof Howe Hob.

Throughout the ensuing weeks of furor Jenny kept hoping that Elphi or one of the other exiles in Yorkshire or in Sweden would wake up, turn on the radio, and pop out of hiding. The little body dug out of the bog had verified the Hefn story and the building international crisis lost its head of steam. But when Jenny and Frank and the five sleek Hefn envoys—who were nowhere near as scruffy or weatherbeaten, or appealing, as Elphi at close quarters—finally were granted an hour alone together, in a debugged room with glass walls and uniformed guards at both doors, and Frank laid their cards on the table, the Hefn became still as five statues. Withholding information from one's lords (they presently explained) was all but impossible for a Hefn to imagine. When no announcement had come, the delegates had assumed that no human knew of the Gafr's existence. Why had these two said nothing? When Frank replied, "For fear some damn fool would do something rash and get us all killed," the Hefn seemed to relax.

"That was well done," said the one who seemed to be their speaker. "We'll be off the minute we find our people, or are convinced they're all dead. Keep what you know to yourselves till then, and the world will go on for you exactly as if we had never come. Spare us all a lot of trouble."

"You don't mean to maintain contact with us, then," said Jenny.

"We've been here long enough to know better. No, you'll get no information or advice from us, but neither will we do you any harm, unless we have to."

"By 'we,'" said Frank, "you mean the Gafr."

"Naturally."

"I suppose they could destroy the world by pushing a button?"

"More or less, yes."

"Could they save it? Take over governments, get rid of weapons systems, force us to pull our socks up?"

The speaker hesitated. "They could do everything you say, but they couldn't breed the violence and greed out of you—that's a product of your entire evolutionary history. And few Gafr are interested in policing other races. Those who command our ship are not, certainly."

"They want nothing to do with us then," Jenny said, not sure whether to feel rejected or relieved."

"Nothing whatsoever. Your scientists—some of them are so fascinated with us they simply cannot imagine that we might not be equally fascinated with them, or equally interested in cultural and scientific exchanges and so on. We've been stalling them off, we don't want to give offense. We don't want to raise false expectations either. But the sooner we can finish our business here and get away, the better pleased we'll be. For all our sakes, say nothing to anyone about the Gafr! You can only do your own people more harm than good by speaking out."

"Poor Carl Sagan," said Jenny later.

"Poor Sir Francis Crick," said Frank. The irascible old man, now ninety, was constantly on the viewscreen making statements about the interstellar community of the future. "Speaking for the Gafr, at least, these Hefn are right bastards. Our hobmen were a decent sort.''

''And loved the moors. Elphi called the dales farmers the salt of the earth.''

''But we're going to take their advice, aren't we,'' Frank continued in a moment. ''Because arrogant or not, they're right. It's just too likely that more harm than good would come of stirring up the hornet's nest.''

Jenny made a frustrated noise. ''I *wish* some other witnesses had come forward after May Moss, somebody else to share the responsibility—it's *too much* for just us!''

''It's way too much for the idiots in power,'' said Frank with finality. ''Better us than them, anyway, at least this time.'' And they left it at that.

Meanwhile the search for the exiled Hefn went forward. The five original envoys grew drowsy in the continuing cold—on the ship, they said, it was early summer now—and were replaced by five fresh envoys; but still no hobs or *tomtar* emerged to claim a berth. In case both groups might now be without radios, or batteries to run them, in late April loudspeaker trucks were driven over the moor roads and through the Swedish countryside, blaring out the news and urging the exiled Hefn to stand forth and be recognized.

A time window was also brought to each of the two landing sites and a message sent into the past: three hundred and fifty years past in Skåne, but only twelve in Yorkshire. As of 1994, when Jenny encountered him, Elphi and his companions had not seen the window. Very well: there was no point then in directing a message to an earlier year—and not because of the risk of changing the present. The Hefn drove the physicists of Earth crazy by blandly assuring them that time was one and unalterable, that if in the present time line a message had not been received by the hobs prior to 1994, no past now ever could exist in which a message *had* been received by them prior to that date. When and where messages had been sent and received through a time window, those events had already been incorporated into the single line of time.

Human physicists, sputtering with frustration, were interviewed on TV or quoted in the papers, all saying that this was preposterous and impossible and challenging the Hefn to explain. The aliens replied politely that an explanation would require an expert in time theory, and unfortunately there were no experts in time theory aboard the ship. They regretted that they could not allow any scientists to examine the time terminal, which in any case seemed not to be working properly.

And when all of these efforts produced no results, the envoys announced their imminent departure. They would take with them the mummified body of Woof Howe Hob, the recordings made by Jenny and Frank at their long public hearing, and nothing else, absolutely nothing. Now, at last, they openly refused to engage in any sort of exchange with the peoples of Earth or to divulge the location of their own star. They merely wanted to leave. And while government officials protested that their good will had been taken advantage of, and scientists howled, and a good many people expressed disappointment that the Hefn weren't going to stay and fix the planet's social and environmental ills, most of Earth's citizens were very well pleased to hear that the aliens were leaving and would not be back.

In this, of course, humans and Hefn alike were mistaken.

On the very day the Gafr ship left the moon, Jenny flew home, a celebrity, to finish out her term of teaching. Frank got back to his farm, too late for the spring lambing, and within a day was drowning in neglected work. "What if we were wrong?" Jenny had asked when he was seeing her off at Heathrow; but he had shaken his head firmly, more confident than she.

On a mild summer evening the following year Frank Flintoft stood in the kitchen door and called in to his wife, "What in the name of sanity possessed you to try mucking out the chicken coop all on your own?" He sounded quite cross, for him.

Jenny came into the kitchen carrying a book. "Is this a clever way of shaming me into action? You know I've had the bloody chicken coop on my conscience for weeks, but if anybody's been mucking it out it wasn't me."

"Come and see."

Frank led her through the gathering dusk, across the barnyard. There stood the coop, its floor scraped down to the wood and spread with clean straw. The hens clucked about contentedly in their yard. The manure-filled rubbish had been raked into a tidy heap for composting. Jenny stared, flabbergasted.

"Do you actually mean to say," said Frank, "that this isn't your doing?"

"It ought to be, but it's not."

They walked slowly back toward the house, arms about each other, trying to puzzle it out.

"Maybe Billy Davies dropped by after school, thinking to earn a few pounds and surprise us," Frank said. "I've paid him to muck out the pigs, and the barn, and he knows about composting . . . but it doesn't seem his style somehow."

"I suppose it could have been John, or Peter," Jenny said doubtfully. "Though why either of them would take it upon himself . . . and the only person I've actually *spoken* to about wanting to get around to the job is you. Could you have mentioned it to anybody?"

The thought struck them both at the same instant.

"You don't suppose—" said Jenny, and "Surely it's not possible—" said Frank, and suddenly both were speechless.

In a moment Frank found his voice. "Say the wireless *was* working all along—"

"—they'd know we'd married and where we're living, it was in the news for a week!"

"—and they found in the end that they couldn't bear to leave the moors—*you* couldn't!"

"*I* couldn't!"

"Who else would muck out a chicken coop without being asked, tell me that!"

They were laughing and clutching at each other. Abruptly Jenny broke away and ran up the kitchen steps. She snatched a stoneware jug down from the shelf, filled it brim-full with cream from the crock in the fridge, and set the jug on the top step, careful not to spill a drop.

3

TINY TANGO

1985–2012

I've been encouraged (read:ordered) by my friend, a Hefn called Godfrey, to make this recording. I'm not sure why. It's to be the story of my life, and frankly, a lot of my life's been kind of grim. Godfrey tells me he values the story as an object lesson, but to whom and for what purpose he's not saying. It isn't news anymore that the Hefn don't think like we do.

I made an important choice at age twenty-two. Because of that choice I'm alive right now, but I'm still wondering: was it a wise choice, given that the next twenty-five years turned out to be a kind of living death? I hoped that if I did this recording, thought it all through in one piece, I'd be able to answer that question. I need to understand my life better than I do. I'm about to be put to sleep for a long time—forever if things go badly—and I need to know . . . well, what Godfrey thinks *he* knows. What it's meant. What it's all been *for*.

I can't really say that this review has worked, because I still don't think I know. But who can tell? Maybe you listeners in the Archive will see something in it I can't see. (Godfrey's betting that you will.)

I

I recall a certain splendid June morning between the two accidents, mine and Peach Bottom's—a bright, cool morning of the kind I could remember as common in the Junes of my childhood but which the greenhouse effect had made rare in more recent years. I'd hobbled out to the patio in robe and slippers with my breakfast tray and loitered over my homegrown whole-grain honey and raisin muffins and strawberry soyshake, browsing through a new issue of *Organic Gardening* (featuring an article I'd written, on ways to discourage squirrels in the orchard and corn patch). Then, after a while, I'd taken my cane and gimped out in a leisurely way to inspect the crops. I'd broken an ankle bone that was taking its time about healing; to be forbidden my exercise routines was distressing, but also kind of a relief.

Because the kitchen garden provided my entire home supply of vegetables and fruit, my interest in it was like a gardening hobbyist's crossed with a frontier homesteader's. If a crop failed I knew I wouldn't, or needn't, starve. On the other hand, since I never, ever, bought any produce for home consumption— except once in a blue moon from the preposterously expensive and notoriously undependable organic food co-op in Media—if a crop failed it *would* almost certainly mean doing without something for a whole year. The daily tour of the kitchen garden was therefore always deeply interesting; and if the tour of the field test plots was even more so, theirs was an interestingness of a less intimate type.

Something serious had happened to the Kennebec potatoes, I noticed it at once. Yesterday at dusk the plants had been bushy and green, bent out of their beds on water-filled stalks by last week's storm of rain but healthy, thriving, beginning to put out the tiny flowers that meant I could soon steal a few small tubers from under the mulch to eat with the new peas. Now the leaves of several plants were rolled and mottled with yellow. I pulled these up right away, doubting it would do any good, sick at heart as always to see my pampered children fail, however often failure struck them down.

The biggest threat to crops in an organic garden like mine is always disease spread by insects—in this case aphids or leaf-hoppers, which had all but certainly passed this disease on to other potato plants by now. The mottling and leaf-rolling meant that the bugs—probably aphids, the flightless sort I'd been taught to call "ant cows" in grade school—had infected my Kennebecs with a virus. At least one virus, maybe more. The ants would soon have moved their dairy herd all through the patch, if they hadn't already. Plants still symptom-free would not remain so for long. When Eric showed up I would get him to spray the patch with a Rotenone solution, but it was almost certainly too late to save the crop by killing the carriers, the vector. These potatoes already had a virus, incurable and potentially lethal.

I remember thinking: Well, that makes some more of us, doesn't it.

I left the heap of infected plants for Eric to cart to the incinerator; they must be not composted but burned, and at once, or there'd be no chance at all of saving the crop and I could look forward to a potatoless year.

Destroy the infected to protect the healthy. The AIDS witch hunts of the late nineties, the vigilante groups that had broken into testing and treatment facilities all over the country in order to find out who the infected people were, had been acting from a similar principle: identify! destroy! They wanted not just the ones with the acute form of the disease but also those who'd tested positive to HIV-I, II, and/or III. I'd been lucky; workers in the Task Force office where my records were kept had managed to stand off the mob while a terrified volunteer worked frantically to erase the computer records and two others burned the paper files in the lavatory sink. The police arrived in time to save those brave people, thank God, but in other cities workers were shot and, in that one dreadful incident in St. Louis, barricaded in their building while somebody shattered the window with a firebomb.

My luck hadn't stopped there, no siree. I had the virus right enough, but not—still not, after twenty-five long years—the disease itself. (These two facts have shaped my life. I mean my adult life; I'd just turned twenty-two and was about to graduate from college in the spring of 1985 when my Western Blot came back positive and everything changed.)

Even the sporadic persecutions ended in 2001, when they got the Lowenfels vaccine. That took care of the general public; but nobody looked for a cure, or expected that a way would ever be found to eliminate the virus from the bodies of those of us who'd already been exposed to it. The best *we* could hope for was a course of treatment to improve our chances of not developing full-blown AIDS, at least not for a long, long time. The peptide vaccine that had become the standard therapy by 1994, which worked with the capsid protein in the cells of the virus, was ineffective with too many patients, as were the GMSC factor injections; and zidovudine and its cousins were just too toxic. A lot more research still needed to be done. We hoped that it would be, that we would not be forgotten; but we didn't think it a very realistic hope.

The bone punch, and especially the Green Monkey vaccine, which quickly supplanted that radical and rather painful procedure, meant the end of terror for the unsmitten; for the less fortunate it meant at least the end of persecution, as I said, and so for us too the day when the mass inoculations began was a great day. A lot of us were also suicidally depressed. Imagine how people crippled from childhood with polio must have felt when they started giving out the Salk vaccine to school kids on those little cubes of sugar, and the cripples had to stand around on their braces and crutches and try to be glad.

It didn't do to think too much about it.

The test site clinician who gave me the news steered me into a chair right afterwards and said, "When the results came in I made you an appointment for tonight with a counselor. She'll help you more than you'd ever believe, and I don't care what other commitments you've got to break: you be there." And he wrote the address and the time on a piece of paper, and I went.

The counselor was a woman in her thirties, sympathetic but tough, and she told me things that evening while I sat and was drenched in wave after icy wave of terror and dread. "We don't know why some people seem to resist the virus better than others and survive much longer, or why some of those who are HIV-positive develop the disease fairly quickly while others can have a latency period of five or six years," Elizabeth said. "We don't know for sure what triggers the development of the acute disease, if and when it does develop, nor what percentage of infected people will eventually develop it.

"But there's a lot of research going on right now into what they call 'cofactors,' variables that may influence the behavior of the virus in individual cases. Cofactors are things like general health, stress levels, life-style. We think—we're pretty sure—that it's extremely important for people like you, who've been exposed, to live as healthfully and calmly as you possibly can. The HIV-I virus is linked to the immune system. You get the flu, your immune system kicks in to fight the flu virus, the AIDS virus multiplies; so the trick is to give your immune system as little to do as possible and buy yourself some time.

"Now, what that means in practical terms is: take care of yourself. Get lots of sleep and exercise. Don't get overtired or too stressed out. Pay attention to your nutrition. Meditate. Above all, try not to fall into a despairing frame of mind! There's a good chance they'll find an effective treatment in four or five years, and if that happens and you're still symptom-free, you should be able to live a normal life with a normally functioning immune system, so long as you keep up your treatments.''

That was the gist of her talk, and some of it sank in. She was wrong about the treatment, of course. In those days everybody expected it would be the vaccine that would prove impossible to make, that a drug to control the course of infection seemed much likelier. We were better off not knowing. Even with treatments to hope for, in those days it was fairly unusual to survive as long as four or five years after infection.

Elizabeth suggested a therapy group of people like myself that I might like to join, a group that had volunteered for a research project being done by a team of psychoneuroimmunologists, though we didn't know that's what they were. They were the hope givers, that was enough. During the weeks that followed, with help from Elizabeth and the group, I began to work out a plan—to impose my own controls over my situation, in accordance with the research team's wish to explore the effects of an extraordinarily healthful life-style on symptom-free HIV-I carriers.

My undergraduate work in biology had been good enough to get me accepted into the graduate program at Cornell with a research assistantship. Until the test results came back I'd been excited by the challenge and the prospect of a change of scene; afterwards, and after a few sessions with Elizabeth and her group, I began instead to feel apprehensive about the effort it would take to learn the ropes of a new department, new university community, new city famous for its six annual months of winter. It seemed better to stick to familiar surroundings and to continue with the same counselor and therapy group. So I made a late application to my own university's graduate department and was admitted, and stayed on: my first major life decision to be altered, the first of many times I was to choose a less challenging and stressful alternative over one that in every other way looked like the more attractive choice.

I'd caught the virus from my major professor; he'd been my only lover, so there could be no doubt of that. While I was still getting up the nerve to tell him about the blood test he died in an accident on Interstate 95. I'm afraid I felt less grieved than relieved. The death let me off the hook and, more important, cleared the way for me to stay, for Bill's presence would have been a difficulty. I'd felt from the first instant that I wanted *no one*, apart from the Task Force people, to know. Not my Fundamentalist family, certainly. Not my friends, from whom I now found myself beginning to withdraw (and since, like me, most of these were graduating seniors, this was easier than it sounds). Overnight my interests had grown utterly remote from theirs. They were full of parties and career plans; I was fighting for my life, and viewed the lot of them from across the chasm of that absolute unlikeness.

I strolled, more or less, through graduate school, working competently without distinguishing myself. I wasn't in a hurry, either. Distinction and rapid progress would have meant a greater commitment and a lot more work, and these were luxuries I could no longer afford, for my first commitment, and first responsibility, now, were to keeping myself alive.

As for how I was to use this life, a picture had gradually begun to form.

First of all, it was necessary to divest myself of desire. The Yuppiedom I had only recently looked forward to with so much confidence—the dazzling two-career marriage and pair of brilliant children, the house in the suburbs, the cabin in the Poconos and the vacations in Europe—had become, item by item, as unavailable to me as a career in space exploration or ballet. Children, obviously, were out. So was marriage. So, it seemed, was sex in any form; sex had been my nemesis, scarcely discovered before it had blighted me forever. The prestigious high-pressure career in research, which my undergraduate record had made seem a reasonable ambition, had become anything but. I was not, after all, going to be one of those remarkable professional mothers, making history in the lab, putting in quality time with the kids every day, keeping the lines of communication with my husband open and clear at every level no matter what. I built up the picture of the life I had aspired to for my counselor and my group—and looked at it long and well—and said good-bye to it, as I believed, forever. All that was over.

The next step was to create an alternate picture of a life that *would* be possible. We discussed my abilities and my altered wish list. I toyed briefly with the idea of a career in AIDS research—but AIDS research in the late eighties was about as calm and unstressful a line of work as leading an assault on the North Face of the Eiger in winter, and I had no yearning for martyrdom, then or ever. Through the hours and hours of therapy it emerged that what I wanted most was simple: to survive until the other scientists working that field had found a drug that would control the virus and make a normal life possible again. It wasn't hard to work this out in group, because we all wanted the same thing: just to hang on until the day—not too far away now—when some hero in a white coat, mounted on a white charger, would come galloping up to the fort, holding a beaker of Miracle Formula high like a banner.

But *how* to hang on? For each of us the answer, if different in particulars, was also the same. We wanted to be able to support ourselves (and our families, if we had them) in reasonable comfort and to keep our antibody status secret. Achieving this, for some of us—the older ones—meant giving up practices in law or medicine, or business careers, or staying in but lowering our sights. Some of us quit struggling to save troubled marriages or get custody of children.

For me the obvious course seemed to be a teaching job in an academic backwater, preferably one in that same metropolitan area. Accordingly—at a time in my life when I'd expected to be at Cornell, cultivating a mentor, working with keen zest and keener ambition at my research, developing and pursuing a strategy for landing a classy position at a prestigious eastern university—I quietly looked into the several nearby branch campuses of the Pennsylvania State University Commonwealth Campus System and made a choice.

My personal style altered a lot during graduate school. I'd done some acting in high school and college, and that made it easier—though you mustn't suppose it was *easy*—to put my new persona over by turning down invitations ("too busy") and so on. Before long my department, which had been so delighted to keep me, had lumped me in with that breed of student that fizzles out after a promising undergraduate takeoff, and the rest of the RAs had given up on me too.

My therapy group speedily became my complete social universe. Nobody in the Bio Department could possibly have shared the intensity of common concern *we* shared within what we came to call the Company (after the thing Misery loves best).

When as time went by one or another of us would lose the battle for wellness, the rest would push aside our own fears and rally round the ailing boon Companion, doing our best to make the final months as comfortable as we could. That wasn't easy either, let me tell you. But we did it. We were like a church family, all in all to one another. Elizabeth, who had given her life to helping us and the researchers at Graduate Hospital—she was our pastor and our friend and yet, even so, a little bit of an outsider. When she asked what I meant to do for *fun*—since life could not consist entirely of the elimination of challenges and risks—I could only reply that just staying alive and well seemed like plenty of fun for the present—thinking privately that no true Companion would ever need to have *that* explained to him or her.

We never told our real names, not in a quarter of a century, and stubbornly refused all that time to evolve from a collective into an assembly of intimates, but we knew each other inside out.

But to the people in my department, who did know my name, I appeared by the age of twenty-nine to have contracted into a prematurely middle-aged schoolmarmish and spinsterish recluse, and nobody there seemed surprised when I accepted a job for which I was grossly overqualified, teaching basic biology and botany at a two-year branch of the Penn State System, fifteen miles out in the suburbs of Delaware County.

My parents in Denver were also unsurprised. Neither had known how to read between the lines of my decision to stay put rather than go to Cornell. To them all college teaching seemed equally prestigious, and equally fantastic. They liked telling their friends about their daughter the future biology professor, but they knew too little about the life I would lead for the particulars to interest them much or invite their judgment. After the first grandchild came they'd been more incurious than ever about my doings, which had seemed less and less real to them, anyway, ever since I left the church. My new church was the Company, and of this they knew nothing, ever.

My job was a dull one made duller by my refusal to be drawn into the social web. But it was tolerable work, adequately paid. I stayed in character as the reliable but lackluster biologist; I did what was necessary, capably, without zest or flair. My pretenure years were a balancing act, filled but not overfilled. I prepared and taught my classes, swam a mile or ran five every day, meditated for half an hour each morning and evening, carefully shopped for and cooked my excruciatingly wholesome and balanced meals, and took the train into the city one night a week to meet with the Company and one afternoon a month for my aptly named gag p24 treatments. Every summer for five years I would spend some leisurely hours in the lab, then sit in my pleasant apartment and compose a solid, economical, careful paper developing one aspect or another of my Ph.D. research, which had dealt with the effects of stress on the immune system in rats. One after another these papers were published in perfectly respectable scientific journals, and were more than enough to satisfy the committee that in due course awarded me tenure.

By the time they had approved me, in the fateful year 1999, my medical records had been destroyed. No document or disk anywhere in the world existed to identify me by name as a symptom-free carrier of the HIV-I virus, though no other personal fact spoke as eloquently about the drab thing I had become.

The fourteen years had thinned the ranks of Companions, but a fair number of us were still around. Just about all of us survivors had faithfully—often fanatically—followed the prescribed fitness/nutrition/stress management regimen, and it was about then that our team of doctors began to congratulate us and one another that we were beating the bejeezus out of the odds. If you're wondering about the lost Companions, whether they too hadn't stuck to the routines and rules, the answer is that they usually *said* they had; but it was easy enough for us to see (or suppose) how this or that variable made their cases different from ours.

I myself hardly ever fell ill, hardly had colds or indigestion, so extremely careful was I of myself. My habits, athletics aside, were those of a fussy old maid—Miss Dove or Eleanor Rigby or W. H. Auden's Miss Edith Gee. They were effective though. When a bug did get through my defenses despite all my care—as some inevitably did, for student populations have always harbored colds and flus of the most poisonous volatility—I would promptly put myself to bed and stay there, swallowing aspirins, liquids by the bucket, and one-gram vitamin C tablets, copious supplies of which were always kept on hand. No staggering in with a fever to teach a class through the raging snowstorm—no siree, not on your life. Not this survivor.

After tenure I bought a little house in a pleasant development of modest brick tract homes on half-acre lots near the campus, and settled in for the long haul. For years I'd subscribed to the health magazine *Prevention*, published by Rodale Press; now at last I'd be able to act on their advice to grow my own vegetables instead of buying the toxin-doused produce sold in the super-markets. I mailed off my subscription to *Organic Gardening*, had the soil tested, bought my first spade, hoe, trowel, and rake, and some organic fertilizers, spaded up a corner of the back yard, and began.

The first post-tenure summer I made a garden and wrote no paper. My mood was reflective but the reflections led nowhere much. The next year of teaching was much the same: I did my job, steered clear of controversy, kept in character. But as the following spring came on—spring of the year 2000—I became restless and vaguely uneasy. Even as I loosened the soil in my raised beds and spread over them the compost I had learned to make, I had dimly begun to know that the cards I'd been playing thus far were played out, that it was time for a new deal.

What I felt, I know now, were the perfectly ordinary first stirrings of a midlife crisis, probably initiated by the "marker event" of successfully securing my means of support for the foreseeable future. Ordinary it might have been, but it scared me badly. Uneasiness is stressful; stress is lethal.

I've stopped to read over what I've written up to this point. It all seems true and correct, but it leaves too much out, and I think what it mainly leaves out is the terror. I don't mean the obvious terror of the Terror, the riots of 1998 and 1999, when I might have been killed outright had the mob that stormed the Alternate Test Site on Walnut Street gotten its talons into my file and learned my name, when the Company met for months in church basements kept dark, when threatening phone calls woke Elizabeth night after night and she didn't dare come to meetings because the KKK was shadowing her in hopes of being led to us. I certainly don't deny that we were scared to death while the nightmare lasted, but it *was* like a nightmare, born of hysteria and short-lived. In a while, we woke up from it. I'm talking about something else.

We all know, of course, that we're going to die. Whether we're crunched by a truck tomorrow while crossing the street or expire peacefully in our sleep at ninety, we know it'll happen.

Now, as long as one fate seems no more likely than the other, most people manage to live fairly cheerfully with the awareness that one day they will meet their death for sure. But knowing that your chances of dying young, and soon, and not pleasantly, are many percentage points higher than other people's changes your viewpoint a lot. Some of the time my radically careful way of life kept the demons at bay, but some of the time I would get up and run my five miles and shower and dress and meditate and drive to school and teach my classes and buy cabbages and oranges at the market and drive home and grade quizzes and meditate and eat supper and go to bed, all in a state of anxiety so intense I could scarcely control it at all.

There were drugs that helped some, but the best were addictive so you couldn't take those too often. The only thing that made years of such profound fear endurable was the Companionship of my fellow travelers. Together we could keep our courage up, we could talk out (or scream or sob out) our helpless rage at the medical establishment as years went by without producing the miracle drugs they'd been more or less promising, the drugs that would lift this bane of uncertainty from us and make us like everybody else—mortal, but with equal chances. Now, terror and rage are extremely stressful. Stress is lethal, I had said so over and over in print, my white rats and I had demonstrated it in the lab, statistics of every sort bore out the instinctive conviction that we had more to fear from fear itself than from just about anything else; and so our very terrors terrified us worst of all. But we bore it better together than we possibly could have borne it alone.

A few of my Companions in these miseries took the obvious next step and paired off. One or two probably told each other their real names. I wasn't even tempted. But sexual denial is stressful too; so on Saturday afternoons I used to rent a pornographic video or holo. A lot of these were boring, but trial and error taught me which brands showed some imagination in concept or direction, and voyeurism in that sanitary form did turn me on, it worked, it took care of the problem. Miniaturized in two or three dimensions, the shape-shifting penises of the actors seemed merely fascinating and the spurting semen innocent. No matter that a few spurts of semen had destroyed my life, and that a penis, the only real one I'd ever had anything to do with, had been the murder weapon; these facts did not feel relevant to the moaning and slurping of the young folks—certified HIV-negatives every one—who provided my weekly turn-on.

For a very long time I was content to release my sexuality, for hygienic reasons, into its narrow run for an hour or so each weekend, like some dangerous animal at the zoo. A few of the guys in the Company were straight, and maybe even willing, but a real relationship—a business as steamy and complicated as that—would have been out of the question for me. Others might have the skills; I lacked them. How much safer and less demanding the role of voyeur in the age of electronics, able to fast-forward through the dull bits and play the best ones over!

The Company, directed by Elizabeth, seemed to understand the force of these feelings. At any rate I wasn't pushed to try to overcome them.

Well, as I was saying: the beginning of my thirty-seventh summer, one year after receiving tenure at the two-year college where I seemed doomed to spend the rest of my life, however long that proved to be, and a year after the worst of the rioting had ended—the beginning of that summer found me very jittery and depressed, and worried about being jittery and depressed. Probably I wouldn't have acted even so; but at about the same time, or a bit earlier, I'd begun to exhibit a piece of obsessive-compulsive behavior that until then I'd only heard about at Company gatherings: one morning, toweling down after my shower, I caught myself scrutinizing the skin of my thighs and calves for the distinctive purplish blotches of Kaposi's sarcoma, the form of skin cancer, previously rare, whose appearance is a diagnostic sign of the acute form of AIDS.

How long I'd been doing this half-consciously I couldn't have told you, but from that morning on I was never entirely free of the behavior. I'd reached an age when my skin had begun to have its share of natural blotches and keratoses, and I gave myself heart failure more times than I can count, thinking some innocent bruise or lesion meant *this was finally it*. After several weeks, growing desperate, I gave up shaving my legs—and shorts and skirts in consequence—and suffered through the hot weather in loose overalls, just to avoid the chronic anxiety of seeing my own skin. I nearly drove myself nuts.

The Company assaulted this symptom with shrewd concern and a certain amount of relish. Your unconscious is trying to tell you something, dummy, one or another of them would say; I used to do that when I got so freaked out in the riots . . . sloppy about doing my Yoga . . . too busy chasing the bucks . . . into a bad way after I lost my mother . . . upset because I couldn't afford to keep the house but didn't want to sell. Remember when *I* did that? they'd say. Just figure out what you're doing wrong and fix *that*, then you'll be okay. For starters, try deciding whether it's something you need to work into your life, or something you need to get rid of.

I didn't see how it could very well be the latter, since my present life had been stripped to the bare essentials already. But what they said made sense. It was this sort of counsel that made us so necessary to one another.

Elizabeth, moreover, had a concrete suggestion. On her advice I rented a condo in the Poconos near the Delaware Water Gap—almost the vacation spot of my former Yuppie dreams—for a couple of weeks. The Appalachian Trail, heavily used in summer unfortunately, passes through the Gap. I spent the two weeks of my private retreat hiking the Trail, canoeing on the river, and assessing the state of my life.

How was I doing?

Well, on the plus side, *I was still alive.* Half of the original Company of sixteen years before, when I'd just come into it, were not, most from having developed the disease, though in a few cases more than a decade after seroconverting. In the early days it had been hoped that if a person with HIV-I antibodies had not fallen ill after six or eight years or so he probably never would, but it hadn't turned out like that. So far, the longer we survived, the more of the virus we had in us; to be alive at all after such a long time was pretty remarkable. I tried to feel glad.

I'd chosen a suitable job and fixed things so I could keep it; I'd also managed my money intelligently during the years before getting tenure. My salary, while not great, was adequate for a single person who hardly went anywhere and whose expensive tastes ran to top-of-the-line exercise equipment and holographic projectors. Raises would be regular, I would be able to manage my house payments easily. I'd already bought nearly all the furniture I needed and had assembled a solid reference library of books, tapes, and disks on nutrition, fitness, stress management, and diseases (especially my own); and the gardening and preserving shelf was getting there. In short, all the details of the plan I had devised for myself sixteen years before were in place. And it had worked out: here I was.

So how come I felt so lousy?

At first, when I tried to tot up the negatives, it was hard to think of any at all. I was alive, wasn't I? Didn't that cancel out all the minuses right there?

As a matter of fact, it didn't. Once I got started the list went on and on.

As a bright college senior I had planned to make something really dazzling and grand of my life. That dream had been aborted; but I began to see that all these years I had been secretly grieving for it, as for an aborted child. However obvious this looks now, at the time the recognition was a terrific shock. Years and years had lapsed since my last conscious fantasy of knocking the Cornell Biology Department on its collective ear, and I really believed I had ritualistically said good-bye to all that, early in my therapy.

Just what was it I'd wanted to do after Cornell, apart from becoming rich and famous? I could hardly remember. But after a while (and an hour of stony trail, with magnificent views of New Jersey) I had called back into being a sense of outward directedness, of largesse bestowed upon a grateful world, that differed absolutely from the intense and cautious self-preoccupation that had governed my life from the age of twenty-two. Once I had craved to be a leader in an international scientific community of intellectual exchange. Now I thought, planned, and worked for the well-being of just one individual, myself—for what was the Company but just myself, multiplied by fifteen or eleven or nine? I'd hardly given a thought to *normal* people, people not afflicted as we were, for a long, long time, and certainly I had given them nothing else—not even a halfway decent course in botany.

It was an awful shock, remembering what it had been like to take engagement with the great world for granted. I turned aside from the Trail and its traffic to climb a gray boulder shaggy with mountain laurel, and sat staring out over the summery woods, remembering the hours I'd spent talking with Bill—my professor, the one who'd exposed me to the virus—about world population control and sustainable agriculture. No details came back; but the sheer energy and breadth of vision, the ability to imagine tackling issues of such complexity and social import, now seemed unbelievable. How had I shrunk so small?

At that moment on the mountain my triumph of continuing to live looked paltry and mean. Really, hadn't I died anyway? Wasn't this death-in-life a kind of unwitting suicide? But I knew at bottom that it was no ignoble thing to have gone on living where so many had died. My fit of self-loathing ran its course, and I climbed down from the rock and started back down the Trail toward the Water Gap, three miles below, where I'd left my car.

I pondered as I went. What was missing from my life now seemed clearer. Meaningful work, first and foremost. Engagement. Self-respect, if that wasn't asking too much—not simply for having survived, but for contributing something real to society; and perhaps even the respect of others.

And last of all I let myself remember, really remember, those springtime afternoons in Bill's sunny office with its coffee machine and little refrigerator and daybed, and added one more thing: intimacy, social and sexual. Not the Company, that bunch of neutered and clairvoyant clones, but I and Thou: intimacy with the Other.

It was a list of things necessary to a fulfilled and happy life, and it bristled like a porcupine with potential stresses.

The trail was rough and steep, and I was wiped out from both my journeys, the inner more than the outer. When I let myself back into the condo the sun had set, and I thought with a fierce rush of resentment how *nice* it would be, just for once, to microwave a box of beans and franks and open a Coke, like a normal American citizen on holiday, instead of having to boil the goddamned homemade pasta and cook the spaghetti sauce from scratch. The strength of my resentment astounded me all over again: how long had I been sitting on this powderkeg of rage *against the virus itself*?

Enlightenment came early in the first week of my retreat, so I had plenty of time left to process my insights and form conclusions.

First, about personal intimacy. Essential or not, I found that I still just didn't feel able to risk it. The potential trouble seemed

97

bigger than the potential payoff; as I've mentioned, I lacked the skills.

About engagement. More promising. The thought of connecting myself in a meaningful way to society by some means that didn't threaten my own stability appealed to me a lot. I could *teach* in a more engaged fashion, but that felt far too personal, too exposed and risky. Then I thought of something else, something actually quite perfect: I could volunteer to work with AIDS patients. This may sound uniquely stressful for someone in my position, but the prospect oddly was not. I already knew everything about the progression of the disease—I'd been through it half a dozen times with dying Companions—so could not be shocked; I didn't need to fear infection (being infected already); and I felt certain that my powers of detachment would be adequate.

Then about meaningful work. I pondered that one for the whole remaining ten days, pretty much all the time.

In the end it was a dream—the holo of the unconscious—that showed me what to do. I dreamed of Gregor Mendel, the Austrian monk who invented modern genetics while serving obscurely in a monastery. In my dream Mendel had the mild wide face with its little round-lensed spectacles of the photograph in the college biology text I used. Sweating and pink-faced in his heavy cassock, he bent tenderly over a bed of young peas, helping them find the trellis of strings and begin to climb. I stood at a little distance and watched, terribly moved to see how carefully he tucked the delicate vines around the strings. As I approached he looked up and smiled as if to say, "Ah, so *there* you are at last!"—a smile brimful of love—and handed me his notebook and pen. When I hung back, reluctant somehow to accept them, he straightened up slowly—his back was stiff—and, moving closer, drew me into an embrace so warm and protective that it seemed fatherly; yet at once I was aware of his erection where it arched against me through the folds of cloth, and of his two firm breasts pressed above my own. He kissed the top of my head. Then he was gone, striding away through the gate, and I stood alone among the peas, the pen and notebook in my hands somehow after all—in my own garden, my own back yard.

It had been a long time literally years, since I'd last cried about anything; but when I woke that dawn my soaked pillow and clogged sinuses showed that I'd been weeping in my sleep, evidently for quite a while. Not since childhood had I felt such powerful love; not since childhood had anyone loved *me*, or held me, in just that way. To be reminded broke my heart, yet there was something healing in it too, and in the luxury of crying.

I lay in my dampness and thought about Mendel—how, having failed to qualify as a teacher, he had returned to the monastery; and there, in that claustrophobic place, in that atmosphere of failure, without the approval or maybe even the knowledge of his bishop, he had planned his experiments and planted his peas.

In its way Mendel's life was as circumscribed, and presumably as monastic, as my own. Yet instead of whining and bitching he'd turned his hand to what was possible and done something uniquely fine.

Me, I'd written off further research because the campus lab facilities were so limited and so public, and applying for funding or the chance to work for a summer or two in a better-equipped lab seemed incautious. It was also true that I'd done about as much in the area of stress and the immune system as I cared to do, and that white rats got more expensive every year and the administration more grudging each spring when my requisition forms went in. But if I could change directions completely. . . .

Well, the Company had a perfect field day with that dream. You can imagine. They were all sure I'd been telling myself to do exactly that: *shift directions*, devise some experiments for my own back yard garden and publish the results. About the symbolism of the hermaphroditic monk, opinion was divided; one person thought him a fused father/mother figure, breasts and gownlike cassock muddling his obvious identity as *Father* Mendel. ("Monks are called *Brother*," a lapsed-Catholic Companion protested.) Others suggested variously that the dream message concerned repressed bisexuality, incest, plain old sexual frustration, even religious longings. They all seemed to have a clearer idea of that part of what it meant than I had myself. But I thought they were right about the other part: that I seemed to want to turn my garden to scientific account in some way, then write up the results (the pen and notebook, both anachronistic types) and disseminate them.

II

That was the year 2000, when four separate strains of HIV virus had been isolated and more than a million people had died. There was a desperate need for qualified volunteer help, for the hospital wings thrown up in haste by the recently organized National Health were bursting with AIDS patients. The great majority of new cases were addicts and the partners and infants of addicts, and most of these were poor people. Except among the poor, sexual transmission of the virus had become much less common, for a variety of reasons. So there were far fewer groups like ours being formed by then, but still plenty of old cases around—people exposed years ago who had survived a long time but whose luck had finally run out. As mine might, any day.

Perhaps I secretly believed that by caring for such people I could somehow propitiate or suborn the Fates—"magical thinking" this is called—or perhaps my bond with them, which I refused to *feel*, demanded some other expression of solidarity. I don't know. I told myself that this was my debt to society, due and payable now.

So, soon after returning from my retreat, I attended an Induction Day for volunteers at the AIDS Task Force office in the city. The experience wrung me out and set me straight. I'd vaguely pictured myself helping in the wards, carrying lunch trays and cleaning bedpans, but it was plain from what the speakers told us that I would find this sort of work more emotionally demanding than I'd expected and more than I'd be able to handle. I had already known better than to offer myself as a counselor or a "buddy" assigned to a particular patient; I'd been a buddy to too many Companions already, with more of this sure to come, and even in that collective and defended context it was hard. That left the dull but essential clerical work: getting new patients properly registered and identified within the bureaucracy of the National Health, processing and filing information, explaining procedures, taking medical histories.

I signed up for that, one afternoon a week. Compared to the burdens other volunteers were shouldering I felt like a coward, but within the Company itself I was a sort of hero, though resented also for what my action made the rest face anew: their fear. Several of the gay men who had gone to Induction Days in years past, but had felt unable to sign up for anything at all, felt

100

especially put down; but *everyone* reported a sense of being implicitly criticized. "You're, like, the teetotaler at the cocktail party," said one of the gays, making us all laugh.

We were no band of activists and saints, the nine of us left of the original Company. Nobody new had joined us for a long time. When the National Health was chartered by Congress, the mandatory anonymous universal blood tests establishing who was and who was not a carrier had brought in a few fresh faces for a time, but those just-identified HIV-positives had mostly preferred to form groups of their own. The rigors of psychoneuroimmunology didn't appeal to everybody; nor did the medical profession agree unanimously that avoiding stress should be a First Principle for the infected. But it was ours; and by making my Companions feel guilty I was guilty myself of stressing them. I understood their resentment perfectly.

At the same time I did feel a first small flush of self-respect to find that none of the others could face this work, relatively undemanding though it was, and that I could.

And almost at once I had my reward. The obsessive blotch-hunting stopped; I could again bear with composure the sight of my own skin. But a stranger and funnier reward was to follow. One day in the hospital outlet shop, on an errand for a busier volunteer, my eye fell by chance upon an object invented to make life easier for diabetic women: a hard plastic device molded to be tucked between the legs, with a spout designed to project a stream of urine forward, the more conveniently to be tested with litmus strips. In a flash a bizarre idea sprang fully developed into my head, exactly like one of those toads that lie buried in dried-up mudholes in the desert, patiently waiting out the years for the rains that tell it the time has come to emerge and mate. I bought the thing.

Back home I dug out an old electric dildo whose motor had long since burned out—a flexible rod with a "skin" of pink rubber. This I castrated, or rather circumcised. I then glued the three inches of amputated rubber foreskin snugly to the base of the plastic spout and snipped a hole in the tip.

I now had an implement capable of letting female plumbing mimic male plumbing, at least from a short distance, unless the observer were very sharp-eyed or very interested.

Inspired, my next step was to go out and buy myself a complete set of men's clothing: socks and underwear, trousers generously tailored, shirt, sweater, tie, and loosely fitting sport jacket, all of rather conservative cut and color and of good quality. I even bought a pair of men's shoes. I'm quite a tall woman—five feet ten and a half inches—with a large-boned face, a flat chest, and the muscular arms and shoulders you build up through years at the rowing machine. And I found that the proverb *Clothes make the man* is true, for my full-length bathroom mirror confirmed that I made a wholly creditable one. Last of all, into the pouch of my brand-new jockey shorts, right behind the zipper of my new slacks, I tucked the plastic-and-rubber penis. The hard thing pressed against my pubic bone, none too comfortably.

Dress rehearsals went on for a whole weekend. By Monday, based on comparisons with certain water-sports videos I had seen, I thought the effect hilariously realistic. *Where Brother Mendel leads,* I said to myself with reckless glee, *I follow!* I can tell you for sure that this entire undertaking—making my dildo, buying my disguises, learning to fish out the fake penis suavely and snug it in place and let fly—was altogether the most fun I'd had in years. The *only* fun, really, the only bursting out of bounds. The thought of beans and franks was nothing compared to this.

When I felt ready for a trial run I put on my reverse-drag costume and drove to a shopping mall in a neighboring state, where for three hours I practiced striding confidently into the men's rooms of different department stores. I would hit the swinging door with a straight arm, swagger up to a urinal, plant my feet wide apart . . . I kind of overacted the role, but I could do this much with a flourish, anyway. What I could *not* do was unclench my sphincter; I was all style and no substance in the presence of authentic (urinating) men. So I flunked that final test.

But my first purpose all along had been voyeuristic, and in this I was wildly, immediately successful. It was a mild day in early autumn. Lots of guys in shirtsleeves, with no bulky outer clothing to hinder the eager voyeur, came in and struck a pose at urinals near mine. For three hours I stole furtive glances at exposed penises from within a disguise that no one appeared even to question, let alone see through. It was *marvelous*. I drove home exhilarated quite as much by my own daring as by what I'd managed to see. To have infiltrated that bastion of male

102

privilege and gotten away with it! What a triumph! What an actor!

All that year, the year 2000, I worked by fits and starts on my role of male impersonator, adding outfits to suit the different seasons and practicing body control (roll of shoulders, length of stride) like a real actor training for a part. I cruised the men's rooms less often than I would have liked, since it seemed only prudent to avoid those near home, and I was kept fairly busy. But over time, by trial and error I gained confidence. I learned that large public men's rooms in bus and train stations, airports, interstate rest areas and the like, were best—that men visiting these were usually in a hurry and the rooms apt to be fairly crowded, so that people were least likely to take notice of me there. It was in one such place that I was at last able to perfect my role by actually relieving myself into the porcelain bowl, and after that time I could usually manage it, a fact which made me smug as a cat.

Every cock I sneaked a look at that year seemed beautiful to me. The holos were so much less interesting than this live show that I all but stopped renting them. I also made some fascinating observations. For instance, young gay men no longer rash enough to pick somebody up in a bus station or whatever would sometimes actually stand at adjacent urinals, stare at one another, and stroke themselves erect. Wow! I felt a powerful affinity with these gays, whose motives for being there were so much like my own. Alas, they also made me nervous, for my prosthesis couldn't hold up to fixed regard, and sometimes, if I lingered too long, someone would show more interest than was safe.

I also discovered a surprising amount of display among some seemingly straight men so proud of their equipment that they would guide themselves with whichever hand would permit an unobstructed view, and hold their jackets helpfully back out of the line of sight. The vibes coming off these types felt different. They just wanted to be admired. Since I did admire them, we both got what we wanted.

After a while I started to wonder if anything had ever been written about the social dynamics of public men's rooms. I even tried to research the subject, but turned nothing up and concluded it probably hadn't been done. Men were too used to them; and women, who would be powerfully struck by the difference between their own situation and one in which people routinely display their sexual organs in one another's presence, had no idea that all this interesting stuff went on.

The Company had been three-fourths gay men in the beginning, five of whom were still around, yet not one had ever said a word to the rest of us about mutual exhibitionism in public toilets; and it seemed possible that most straight men had never noticed. After sixteen years of weekly group therapy I'd have sworn that none of us could possibly have any secrets left; but perhaps the gay Companions simply preferred not to offer up this behavior to the judgment of the straights—even now, and even us. Perhaps it was humiliating for them, even a bit sordid. I could see that. This behavior of mine had its sordid side. The recreational, adventurous side outweighed that, twenty to one; but I took my cue from the gays and kept my weird new hobby to myself—learning in this way that withholding a personal secret from the Company, retaining one exotic scrap of privacy, exhilarated me nearly as much as having live penises to admire after all those dreary years of admiring them only on tape.

But if the dream image of Mendel-as-hermaphrodite was present to me through much of this experience—for I knew that in some deep way they were connected—Mendel was a still more potent icon in the garden that summer. At first thought, back yard research seemed very small beer. I knew as well as anyone that the day had long since passed when a single white-coated scientist, working alone amid the test tubes in his own basement laboratory, could do important research. Mendel himself had had a larger plot of ground at his disposal.

Yet examining the unfamiliar literature of this field, and browsing in *Biological Abstracts*, forced me to revise my view: there were some very useful experiments within the scope of even a back yard researcher. Some of the published papers that interested me most had been written by amateurs. It appeared that master gardeners, like amateur archeologists and paleontologists, had long made substantial contributions to the fields of plant breeding, pest control, cultivation practices, and the field trials of new varieties. Organic methods of gardening and farming, which were what interested me, were particularly open to contributions from gardeners and farmers, nonscientists who had taught themselves to run valid trials and keep good records. Genetic engineering and chemical warfare were clearly not the only ways to skin the cat of improved crop yields.

The more I looked into it, the more impressed, and correspondingly the more hopeful, I was. Though but a beginning gardener I was a trained scientist; if these other people could do something useful in their modest way, I certainly should be able to.

I'd lost my first two crops of melons to bacterial wilt or mosaic virus, I wasn't sure which, and both years my cucumbers had also died of wilt. (The first couple of seasons in an organic garden are tough sledding.) The striped cucumber beetle was the probable vector for both diseases. God knows I had enough of the little bastards. Now, you can grow *Cucurbita*—the vining crops, including all melons, squashes, cucumbers, and gourds—under cheesecloth or spun-bonded floating row covers, which exclude the bugs, but you have to uncover the plants when the female flowers appear so the bees can get at them, and if the bees can, so can the beetles. Besides, half the fun of gardening is watching the crops develop, and how can you do that if they're shrouded under a white web of Ultramay?

No, the thing was to produce a cultivar with resistance, or at least tolerance, to one or more of the insect-borne diseases. After reading everything I could get my hands on about bacterial wilt and cucumber mosaic virus I concluded that a project of trying to breed a really flavorful variety of muskmelon strongly resistant to bacterial wilt would make the most sense. Wilt was a bigger problem in our area, and some hybridization for wilt resistance in muskmelons had already been done. But I was much more powerfully attracted to the mosaic problem. It took the Company about half a minute to point out, once they'd understood the question, that cucumber mosaic is caused by a *virus*. There's no cure for mosaic; once it infects a plant the plant declines, leaf by leaf and vine by vine, until it dies. (Just like you know who.)

There's no cure for bacterial wilt, either, but I couldn't help myself: I began to plan an experiment focusing on mosaic.

Here's how I went about it (if these details bore you, feel free to skip ahead): I didn't want to waste time duplicating the research of others, so I made several trips that summer to Penn State's main campus at University Park to extract from their excellent library everything that was known about all previous efforts to breed virus resistance into muskmelons. These trips were fun. For one thing, it pleased me a lot to be doing research again. For another, I did the trips in undrag, stopping at every highway rest area on the Pennsylvania Turnpike between Valley Forge and Harrisburg, to investigate men's rooms—and in fact simply to use them too, as this was, prosthesis and all, easier, quicker, and less grubby than using the ladies'.

It turned out that except for a man called Henry Munger, at Cornell, the breeders had never made much headway against virus disease in muskmelons. Munger's work had been left uncompleted at his death, and since the introduction of row covers and beetle traps the subject of virus resistance had generally been slighted. Commercial growers had been getting around the problem of pollination for quite a while by constructing great tents of Ultramay over their fields and putting a hive of honeybees inside with the melons. As this was hardly practical for the home gardener, the state agricultural extension services recommended several pesticides for use on the beetles (and aphids, another serious virus vector for cucurbits) during the two or three weeks when the plants would have to come out from under cover to be pollinated. Spraying at dusk was suggested, to spare the bees. But these were persistent toxins and I doubted that all the bees would be spared, though they might pollinate the vines before they died.

I also read up on the life cycle of the striped cucumber beetle, then built a clever cage in which to rear as many generations of virus-bearing beetles as necessary to carry the critters through the winter—they hibernate in garden trash, but I wanted to guarantee my supply. When the cage was ready I rigged a shelf-and-fluorescent-tube setup in which to raise a sequence of zucchini plants to feed the beetles—nothing grows faster or is easier to grow than a zucchini, and the beetles love them. As each plant in turn began to sicken I would transplant a new, healthy seedling into the soil on the bottom of the rearing cage, then cut through the stem of the sick zucchini, shake off the beetles, and remove the plant. The roots had to be left undisturbed because the soil around them contained eggs, feeding larvae, and pupae, but by the time the space was needed for a new transplant the roots would have died or been eaten up.

It worked beautifully. My quarter-inch black-and-yellow beetles spent that winter, and the next four winters, living the life of Riley.

Throughout that hard late winter of 2001 I spent all my spare time thinking out my project, its objectives and procedures, until I knew exactly what I wanted to do. By April a small ranked and labeled army of cantaloupe seedlings stood waiting in my basement, under fluorescent lights, for the day when they could safely be set out in their carefully prepared beds and tucked under Ultramay, some to grow without the risk of insect-borne disease until I sent in a few of my pampered beetles to infect them, some to be crossed with other varieties according to a scheme I'd worked out over the winter, some for controls. In this way I meant to produce exactly twenty-five hybrid cultivars never before tested for resistance to mosaic. Honey Dew and Honey Ball had shown some resistance in the field, so one or the other would be a parent of each new cultivar I hoped to breed. Harper Hybrid also looked promising and I planned to try crossing its parent Perfection with other varieties, notably with the parents of Hybrid Milky Way. I would then collect and save the seed and field test the M1 generation the following summer. At the same time I would be growing another group of open-pollinated melons and hybridizing *them*.

The plan called for an elaborate schedule of trials and controls, specifying exactly when each variety of melon would be cultivated and which others it would be crossed with. Assuming no spectacular early success, the plan would organize my summers for the next five years. Plant breeding is not an enterprise for impatient people. It *is* a gesture of faith in the (personal) future.

In early May, just as the azaleas were at their peak of bloom, a week before the last frost date in Delaware County, Jacob Lowenfels and his team of American and French researchers announced their discovery of the AIDS vaccine.

The announcement threw me, and the rest of the Company with me, into a profound funk. Except for us and several thousand dying people, the whole city seemed to rejoice around us; even the war news yielded pride of place. Thank God the spring quarter had ended, except for some finals I could grade with one hand tied behind me. Watering my cantaloupe seedlings before turning in on the night of May 15, I came within a hair of wrenching the table over and dumping the lot of them, *smash*, onto the concrete floor. Why should these frivolous *Cucurbita* live when so many innocents were dead?

I know, I know: the Lowenfels vaccine was of enormous importance even to us—even, for that matter, to those who had developed the disease but would not begin dying seriously for months or years; for overnight the fear of discovery and persecution ended. We were no longer lepers. People could acquire immunity to us now. Only those already in the final stages of dying from AIDS benefitted not at all, so that the AIDS wings of the hospitals lay for weeks beneath a blanket pall of sorrow.

And of course I knew all this really, even at the time. I carried out my trays of cantaloupes and honeydews on the fifteenth after all and planted them on schedule. The beds beneath their Ultramay covers looked so peculiar that I decided to fence the yard, discourage the neighbors' curiosity. I planted with a leaden heart that day, but the melons didn't seem to mind; in their growing medium of compost, peat moss, and vermiculite dug well into my heavy clay soil they soon sent out runners and began to produce male flowers. When the female flowers appeared about ten days later I pulled the Ultramay off of some beds just long enough to rub the anthers of the male flowers against the pistols of the female ones. At other beds I sent in the beetle troops. At the same time, I was growing a year's supply of vegetables in my kitchen garden. My computer kept daily records for both garden and field trials. In August I gave my control melons away by the carload to the Companions, ate tons of them myself, froze some, and saved the rest to rot peacefully till they could be blended with autumn leaves into a giant compost tower. (The vines that died of mosaic and the malformed fruit they produced, if any, went out with the trash.) And I preserved, packaged, labeled, and froze my hybrid seeds.

None of the varieties I'd inoculated with the virus that first year had resisted it worth a damn. I saved seed from only one mosaic-stunted hybrid cultiver, a *Cucumis melo* called ''Mi ting tang,'' which had shown good resistance to cucumber mosaic (plus gummy stem blight and downy mildew) in field trials in Japan. That one had managed to struggle to maturity and produce a crop despite its illness. The fruit, though dwarfed, had a fair flavor and good thick flesh, and I thought I might backcross and then cross it with other varieties after I saw the results of my hybridizing the following year. Resistance in the Ano strains of muskmelon appeared to vary according to the weather; I wanted to find out more about that too.

Between times I canned and froze and dried my garden pro-

108

duce as one after another the overlapping crops came in. Once I'd gotten over the shock of the vaccine it was a wonderful summer, the best of my life, full of pleasurable outdoor work; and the four that followed resembled it pretty closely.

Each fall and winter I would overhaul my records and revise my schedules; compost plant residues; treat the soil of the inoculated beds to kill any leftover beetles; care for the next year's beetle crop and manage their supply of zucchini plants; clean and oil my tools; consume my preserved stock of organically grown, squeaky-clean food; teach my classes and run my labs; put in my afternoon at the hospital every week; meet with the Company; and take my treatments. In a small way I'd also begun to write for gardening magazines, mainly Rodale's and *National Gardening*, though occasionally for *Horticulture* or even *Country Life*. I'd never been so busy or interested or free of anxiety, and I think now that unconsciously I'd come to believe that I was safe. "Magical thinking," sure—but it *was* a much healthier and better-rounded way of life, no question.

It was in the fifth year of the research, spring 2006, that two events occurred to shatter the even tenor of my days. The arrival of the ship from outer space was the big news; but the Hefn delegation was still in England, and in the daily headlines, when devastating news broke upon us in the Company: for our counselor Elizabeth had developed the bodily wasting and red-rimmed eyes of AIDS-Related Complex, and confessed at last that all this while she had been keeping a secret of her own.

One and all we were stricken anew with terror, my eight surviving Companions and myself. Elizabeth who had been our mother, our guardian, our stay against destruction, who had held us together and wedged the door shut against the world's cruelty, could not be dying—for if she were dying we could none of us feel safe. Our reaction was infantile and total: we were furious. Who would take care of us when she was dead? When an accountant who called himself Phil promptly developed skin lesions, we all blamed Elizabeth.

Phil's symptoms turned out to be hysterical; his apparent defeat had been the medium through which we had collectively expressed our reactivated panic and dread. After that episode we pulled ourselves together and stopped whining long enough to think a little of Elizabeth, and not so much about our miserable selves.

She had been admitted to Graduate Hospital, the one our psychoneuroimmunology team was affiliated with. I sat with her for a while one afternoon, a sulky, resentful child and her mortally ill mother. When I apologized for my behavior Elizabeth smiled tiredly. "Oh, I know how you all feel, you're reacting exactly like I thought you would. Listen, Sandy, this had to happen sometime. You folks have all been much too dependent and you know it. Now's your chance to stand on your own, ah, eighteen feet—but I'm sorry you feel let down." She grimaced. "I feel pretty bad about that myself."

Her generosity dissolved my fretful resentment; and love, shocking as the dream-love of Gregor Mendel, flooded into the vacancy. I choked and burst into wrenching tears; Elizabeth patted my arm, which made me cry harder; in a moment I was crouching beside her bed, my hot, wet face pressed against her shoulder, the first time in twenty years that I had touched another human being intimately. A surreal moment. It was glorious, to tell the truth, though I felt as if my chest would burst with grief.

When I forced myself to report this scene on Company time, the story was received in a glum silence tinged with embarrassment. Finally Larry, a balding, thickening physical therapist I'd known since he was a skinny teenager, puffed out a breath and said disgustedly, "Well, don't feel like the Lone Ranger, Sandy. I never touch anybody either, except on the job. Hell, we *all* love Elizabeth! But I never let myself know that, I haven't taken an emotional risk in so many years I literally can't remember when the last time was, and you people aren't any better than me."

"I've often thought," said Phil, "that it's funny we don't love each other. I mean, as much as we need each other, you'd think . . ."

He trailed off, and we glanced obliquely (and guiltily) at one another, except for the two couples present—who naturally couldn't help looking a little smug—and the one father who blurted defensively, "I love my kids!"

"Elizabeth knows we love her," said Sherry, over against the far wall.

"Maybe she does," Larry growled, "but *we* need to know it. That's my point, goddammit."

"Other groups do better. Some of them are really close," I

put in. "Maybe we fuss over ourselves so much we can't connect, except to spot weaknesses."

"Other groups don't have our survival rate either," Mitch reminded me.

Breaking the gloomy silence, Phil roused himself to say, "What about these spacemen, anything doing in that direction?"

When the Hefn first arrived, half the world's people had recoiled in panicky dismay; the other half had seemed to expect them to provide a magical cure for all our ills: war, cancer, pollution, overpopulation, famine, AIDS. So far they had shown no interest in us at all. The landing party was presently in London because the mummified corpse of one of their relations, stranded here hundreds of years ago, had been discovered in a Yorkshire bog; but suggestions that they set up some sort of cultural and scientific exchange with humanity had been politely ignored and I doubted there was any chance at all that Elizabeth's life was going to be saved by ET intervention. The AIDS Task Force in New York had already sent them a long, pleading letter but had received no reply. We were all aware of these facts. Nobody bothered to answer Phil, and after a while the hour was over and we broke up; and when the Hefn ship took off from the moon a few weeks later, having neither helped nor harmed us by their visit, we weren't surprised. It was what we'd expected.

Just as we expected Elizabeth to waste and decline, and finally die, and she did—leaving the Companions rudderless and demoralized. At least we'd rallied and borne up pretty well throughout the last weeks of her dying. We must have done her, and ourselves, a little good.

Surprisingly, despite even this trauma none of the rest of us became ill. Apparently we who were still alive were the hardiest of the lot, or at least the ones who had taken the best care of ourselves. But the emotional jolt of Elizabeth's death—the one death we had *not* protected ourselves from being badly hurt by—showed me, as the dream of Mendel had showed me all those years ago, that something was still wrong with my life. It was still a loveless life, and just when I seemed to need it least it now appeared that I was no longer willing to do without love. I'd failed to acknowledge Elizabeth alive; now that she was dead I wanted at least to keep alive the emotion—the capacity for

111

feeling and showing emotion—that she had released in me at the end.

It didn't have to be romantic love, in fact I rather thought that any other sort would probably be preferable, though I was still determined not to *teach* lovingly. It seems odd now that I never thought of getting a pet—or maybe the image of a dog wouldn't readily superimpose itself upon the image of a back yard carpeted with melon vines? And I'm allergic to cat dander . . . anyway, whatever the reasons, the idea never crossed my mind. The months glided by as before, and became years, before anything changed.

III

What happened was that I broke a small bone in my left ankle in a common type of running accident: one foot came down at the edge of a pothole and twisted beneath me as I fell. The X ray showed a hairline fracture. They put me in a cast and crutches and ordered me off the foot for a month, and this was May.

May 2010; year four of my second five-year plan. With the whole season's research at stake I had no choice but to hire some help.

A bright, possibly talented sophomore in my botany course took the job. His name was Eric Meredith, and he was the first person other than my unobservant parents, a dishwasher repairer, and the water meter reader to have entered my house in the ten years I had owned it. I bitterly resented the need that had brought him there; but I knew the source of this bitterness (apprehension: what other infirmities would interfere with my privacy in future summers?) and made a perfunctory effort not to work it out on Eric.

He seemed not to take my unfriendliness personally—I had a certain reputation at the college as a grump—and willingly did what I told him to without trying to chat me up. I showed him *once* how to handle the transplants, how big and how far apart to make the holes, how to work fertilizer and compost into the loose earth, dump in a liter of water, and firm the soil around the stem. He never forgot, never did it wrong, even beneath my jealous eye; he seemed to discover a knack for the work in the process of performing it that pleased him as much as it mollified me. He was scrupulously careful with the labeling and weighted the Ultramay at the beds' edges with earth, leaving no gaps for wandering bees or beetles to find. In a week the entire lot of transplants was in the ground. I recorded the data myself—I could sit at a keyboard, anyway—but Eric did everything else.

He grew so earnestly interested in the experiment, what's more, that after the second week he couldn't help asking questions; and I found his interest so irresistible that before I knew it I'd invited him to review the records.

For I did, finally, really appear to be getting someplace. Several hybrids of the Mi ting tang (Ano II) strain had done unusually well the previous year; I thought I knew now which of their parents to cross with Perfection and Honey Dew to produce at least one variety that would show exceptional tolerance to cucumber mosaic virus in the field. Immunity now looked impossible, resistance unlikely; but I felt I would be more than satisfied with a strain that could *tolerate* the presence of the virus in its system without being killed or crippled too much—that could go on about its business of making a pretty good crop of sweet, firm-fleshed melons in spite of the disease.

Eric sat for an hour while the screen scrolled through the records of a near-decade. I jumped when he spoke. "This whole thing is just *beautifully* conceived." His amazement was understandable; why expect anything good from a professor as mediocre in class as I? "You're just about there, aren't you?"

He had a plain, narrow face, much improved by enthusiasm. I felt my own face growing warm. "Mm-hm, I think so. One more summer. Of course, this isn't a very exciting experiment— not like what they do in the labs, genetic manipulation, that sort of thing."

"Well," said Eric, "but it's not so much the experiment itself as the experimental model. Heck, you could apply this model to any traits you were trying to select for. Did you work it out yourself?" I assumed this was doubt, but when I nodded he did too. "I thought so. I never came across this system of notation before and I bet everybody'll be using it after you publish."

I'd been working in isolation a long time, without admiration, and the traitorous balloon of gratitude that swelled my chest undid me. "Come have something cold to drink," I offered gruffly, and as I went before him into the kitchen the rubber tip of my crutch slipped on a wet patch of linoleum and I fell, whacking my head hard on the corner of a shelf on the way down.

113

For a few seconds the pain in both ankle and scalp was blinding. Then as I struggled to rise, embarrassed and angry, and as Eric leaned over me to help, I saw the drops of blood on the floor, brilliant against the pale tiles. "Get away!" I shouted, shoving him so hard he stumbled against the counter and I fell flat on my back. In rage I hauled myself upright, holding to the counter, and managed to rip off some paper toweling to blot my head with. Again Eric moved instinctively to help, and again I snapped, "No, get back I said, keep away from me. *Did you get any blood on yourself*?"

"Unh-unh," said Eric, looking at his hands and arms, bewildered and then—bright student—suddenly comprehending. "Oh, hey, it's okay—I'm vaccinated."

I froze and stared at him, my head singing. *"What did you say?"*

"I'm *vaccinated* against AIDS. A bone punch in the sixth grade, see?" He pulled down the neck of his T-shirt and showed me the little V-shaped scar on his collarbone.

Vaccinated. Immune. Of course he was. *Everybody* was vaccinated nowadays. Eric had been in no danger from me—but in my instinctive panic I'd given myself away. For exactly the third time that decade I burst into tears, and I couldn't have told you which of the two of us was the more embarrassed.

I don't remember how I got him out of the house. I spent that evening raging at myself, my situation, the plague that had blighted my life, aborted my career, turned me into a time bomb of thwarted need. So what if it came out that I was a carrier of the virus? Nobody gave a damn anymore. During the past few years, the deadly microorganisms that had built up strength in my system throughout the first ten had begun to decline. I might never die of AIDS now, might not even be infectious—nobody knew. Even if I were, the world had been immunized against me. Yet I *felt* infectious, consumed with longing for something that would certainly be destroyed if I tried to possess it. No amount of rational certainty that this was *not* so acted to defuse a conviction which had for so long been the central emotional truth, the virtual mainspring, of my life. For the past nine years I had abstained from sex for my own reasons of stress avoidance, not to protect others; I had known this and not-known it, both.

The truth was, I had lived as a leper too long to change my self-concept. Now here was this boy, who had guessed my guilty secret just like that and spoken it aloud without batting an eye. He would have to be replaced, possibly bribed . . . no, that was crazy thinking. Yet the thought of facing him was unendurable. I'd pay him off in the morning and dismiss him. The pain of this thought astonished me; yet I couldn't doubt it must be done.

I had not, however, factored in Eric's own attitudes and wishes. The next day he showed up at the usual time and went straight to work in the kitchen garden, spreading straw mulch on the tomato and pepper beds, whistling the noble theme from the second movement of Beethoven's Seventh. From the kitchen window I watched his tall, bony frame fold and unfold, gathering the straw from the cart in armfuls and heaping it carefully around the bases of the plants; and gradually I became aware that here was the only living being, not one of the Company, who knew The Truth. Gradually it even began to seem a wonderful thing that somebody knew. Eric dragged the empty cart across the yard for more straw bales, then back to the nightshade beds. I regarded his back in its sweat-soaked T-shirt, the play of the shoulder muscles, the stretching tendons at the sides of his knees as he folded and straightened—and something fluttered and turned over in my middle-aged insides. "Eric," I murmured in wonderment; and as if he had heard, he turned his head, saw me at the window, waved, and grinned. Then he stooped to gather another armful of straw and I fell back out of view.

That grin . . . I dropped onto a stool, hearing in my head the incongruous voice of my best high school friend: "He looked over at me from the other side of the class and it just really boinged me." Boinged—I'd been boinged! By Eric's cheerfulness, the wave of his long arm with its brown work glove at the end. I knew by then, I guess, that I wasn't going to fire him; but I couldn't see how to do anything else with him either.

At noon Eric came to the house to wash up under the spigot before leaving, in his khaki shorts and old running shoes. He had taken off his shirt, and dust and bits of straw had stuck to the sweaty skin of his chest and back, and in the curly golden hairs of his legs and the blond mop on his head. He was a very lanky guy, pretty well put together, not a bit handsome. I regarded his long body with awe.

"I'll be late tomorrow, got a dentist appointment," he said. "Listen, I wanted you to know I'm not going to say anything to anybody else about yesterday. In case you were worrying about it. I mean, I don't go in for gossip much anyway, and even if I did I wouldn't spread around stuff about you.''

I managed to reply, ''Thanks, I'd appreciate it if you wouldn't.''

Eric started to say something else but instead stuck his head under the faucet for a minute, dried himself on his shirt, and slipped away around the house. There was a paperback novel crammed into the back pocket of his shorts, its title *Sowbug!* scrawled diagonally across the cover in screaming colors, and water droplets spangled his bare shoulders.

And so we went on as before, but nothing was as it had been for me. Once again I became an actor, for I found myself against all sense and expectation carrying a blazing torch for a boy considerably less than half my age: a clever, nice, probably not terribly remarkable boy who (as the Companions agreed) was serving now as representative object of the pent-up love of half a lifetime. Eric, the wick for this deep reservoir of flammable fuel, became ''Lampwick'' in Company nomenclature: Lampwick, the boy who went to Pleasure Island with Pinnochio and turned into a braying jackass before the puppet's horrified eyes.

I felt like the jackass, let me tell you. *Knowing* the passion that so rocked me to be symbolic and categorical, hardly about Eric-the-singular-individual at all, made exactly zero difference to my experience of it. In the Company we'd been talking and thinking more about love since Elizabeth's death, and they all thought it was great. *All* loves are part personal, part associational, the more worldly among them assured me. Go for it! Get it out of your system. Wasn't your primary sexual involvement in the past with a teacher? Hey, the unconscious is a tidy bastard; naturally yours would think it fitting to pass the baton to the next generation by making you fall for a student of your own.

And I have to admit that even the hopeless misery of *this* passion was, in a weird way, kind of fun. It rejuvenated my libido, for one thing. It took me out of myself. I no longer feared the lethal effects of stress so much, and in any case this stress was salutary too.

I did take enormous care to protect myself from the humiliation of letting Eric catch me out, as he had caught me out about my antibody status. He never dreamed I seethed with lust for him, I feel quite sure of that. I think he did regret my aloofness—

he was a sociable boy, and truly admired my work—but not so much as to be pained by it; and in any event Eric had other fish to fry that summer.

My ankle had healed well enough by late July for me to take over the kitchen garden and, a bit later, the processing of its produce when that began to roll in; but I pretended a greater disability than I really had just to keep Eric around. And when my old mother in Denver had a stroke, making a visit unavoidable, I was happy to leave him in charge of both kitchen garden and melon plots. The special hybrids were looking great, but records on rainfall and hours of sunlight during this crucial month would have to be kept. I asked Eric to come live in the house while I was away, and promised him a bonus if he did a meticulous job of keeping the records.

I decided not to fly, and drove west in an erotically supercharged state of psyche, sleeping in the carbed, peeing in the men's rooms of seven states, feasting my eyes on hundreds of penises and fantasying that this or that one could be Eric's . . . I hadn't done much of this recently and suspect I made a less convincing man as I grew older but I had a terrific time for a while, although to tell the truth I rather wore out my imagination. My mother was feeling better and received my attentions with gratified complacency; but the five grandchildren had become her life, and we regarded one another, benignly enough, through a glaze of mutual incomprehension. It seemed likely that I would see her next when I flew out for the funeral.

All the same I stayed a week before returning by easy stages across the hot, dusty plains, eager to get back but pleased to think of Eric still holding the fort in my stead. No point in pretending I couldn't handle the work now, not after a drive like this. Anyway, the term would be starting soon. When I got back I'd have to let him go; and so I dawdled and fantasied across Kansas and Missouri, and late in the afternoon of August 30 was approaching Indianapolis when I told the radio to turn itself on and was informed that early that same morning there had been a meltdown at the nuclear power plant at Peach Bottom, on the Susquehanna River downstream from Three Mile Island.

Luckily traffic was light. I managed to pull off the road without smashing up and sat gripping the wheel while the radio filled me in. The disaster was unprecedented, making even Chernobyl look paltry. The Peach Bottom plant was fifty years old and overdue to be shut down for good. It *had* been shut down in the eighties, then reopened when improved decontamination technology had reduced its radioactivity to acceptable levels. Though the plant had a history of scandalously inept management, technicians asleep on duty and so on, it didn't appear that the meltdown had been caused by human error.

From the standpoint of damage to nearby populations the weather could not have been much worse, given that it was summer. A storm system with a strong south-southwesterly wind had pushed the enormous radioactive plume across the fertile Amish farmland of Lancaster County; then a westerly shift had carried the plume over the continuous urban sprawl of Wilmington, Philadelphia, and Trenton. Heavy rains had dumped the hot stuff on the ground across that whole area. The storm had also put out the fire at the plant; damage was therefore horrific but, so far, highly localized.

The plume had been washed to earth before it could enter the upper atmosphere . . . but in one of the most densely populated regions of the world. A very high death count from acute radiation poisoning was expected; the Amish farmers, working in the fields without radios to warn them, were especially at risk. *Eight million people*, more or less, had to be evacuated and relocated, probably permanently, for the Philadelphia-Wilmington area would be a wasteland for at least a decade to come, perhaps much longer.

Congressman Terry Carpenter's name was mentioned again and again. A moderate Republican from Delaware County, Carpenter was being touted by reporters as a miracle worker. His understanding and the speed of his response suggested that Carpenter had planned carefully for just this sort of emergency. Because of him the cost in human lives would be far less, though no one person could cope with every aspect of a disaster as great as this one. (I'd crossed over and voted for the guy myself last election. Good move.)

People who had not yet left their homes had been urged to keep doors and windows shut and air conditioners turned off, to reduce inhalation uptake, which would be reduced somewhat anyway by the rain, and to draw water in their bathtubs and sinks before the runoff from the storm could contaminate the supply. Each was to pack a small bag. . . .

The radio went on and on as I sat by the highway, shocked

beyond thought. My house, my garden, the campus, the hospital where I worked and the one where I had my monthly treatments, the Company, the experiment—all the carefully assembled infrastructure of my unnatural life—had melted down with the power plant. What in the world was I going to do? My trip had saved me from radiation poisoning and from being evacuated and stuck in a Red Cross camp someplace; my car and I were clean. But my life was in ruins.

And all the while, still in shock, I thought about Eric, whom I'd left to mind the store, who might be in my house right now with the doors and windows shut, waiting to be evacuated. Abruptly snapping out of it, I drove back onto the road and went off at the next exit, where I found a pay phone that worked and put the call through.

But the phone in my house rang and rang, and finally I hung up and stood shaking in the already-sweltering morning, unable to think what to do now, stranded. Impossible to go back to Denver. Impossible to go home. Impossible also to find Eric, at least until things settled down. Eric, of course, would go to his parents' house—only what if they lived in the evacuation zone? A lot of our students were local kids; it was that kind of college.

I knew not even that much about Eric's personal life, I realized with a furious rush of shame, and at this moment all my uncertainty and powerlessness fused into a desperate need to find him, see him, make sure he was all right. Of all the desperately threatened people I knew in the area of contamination, only this one boy mattered to me.

I got back in my car and started driving. I drove all night, stopped at a western Pennsylvania sleepyside for a nap the following morning, drove on again. The radio kept me posted on developments. All that way I thought about Eric. Half of my mind was sure he was fine, safe in his parents' (grandparents'?) home in Pittsburgh or Allentown; the other half played the Eric-tape over and over, his longness and leanness, the grownup way he'd handled my breaking down, his careful tenderness with the melon seedlings (like Mendel's!), his reliability, his frank, unstudied admiration of my trial model, his schlock horror novel *Sowbug!* Why hadn't I been *nicer* to him while I'd had the chance? Why had I played it safe? My house and garden were lost, my experimental records doubtless ruined by fallout, the work of the past decade all gone for nothing, yet worse by far was the fact that I had squandered my one God-given chance to come close to another person, thrown it away, out of fear. I beat on the steering wheel and sobbed. Eric, Eric, if only I hadn't been so scared.

Whatever happened now, I knew I would never again watch him fold that long body up like a folding ruler to tend the crops or sic the virus-loaded striped cucumber beetles onto a melon cultivar. That life was finished. There was nothing to connect us now, because I had wasted my one chance and would never get another. I was hardly thinking straight, of course; I was in shock. I'd heard my colleagues speak often enough, and wistfully enough, of promising former students from whom they rarely or never heard anymore. Students go away and teachers stay—that's the way it's always been, they'd say. Put not your faith in students. A card at Christmas for a year or two after they leave, then zip.

But I wasn't thinking of what Eric might or might not have done in some hypothetical future time; I was thinking of what I myself had failed to do and now could never do. I cried, off and on, for hours, being forced once by uncontrollable weeping to stop the car. I shed far more tears during that nightmarish trip than in my whole previous life since childhood. If I'd only put my arms around him, just one time, just held him for a minute, not even saying anything—if I'd just managed to do that. . . . As the hours and miles went by my grief became more and more inconsolable, as if all the tragedy of the meltdown, and even of my life, were consolidated into this one spurned chance to become human. It didn't matter whether Eric wanted to be befriended (let alone held) by me, diseased middle-aged spinsterish schoolmarm and part-time pervert that I had become; what mattered, beyond measure or expression, was that I'd been too cowardly even to consider the possibility of closeness with another person, and now it was too late.

I drove and wept, wept and drove. Gradually traffic going the opposite direction began to build up. Just west of Harrisburg a bunch of state troopers were turning back the eastbound cars. Beyond the roadblock only two lanes were open; the other two, and the four going west, were full of cars fleeing the contaminated zone. I pulled over, cleaned my blotchy face as best I could with a wet cloth, and got out. A trooper was directing

U-turns at the head of a line of creeping cars. I walked up to him. "Excuse me, do you know how I can find out where somebody is?"

The trooper turned, gray-faced with exhaustion. "You from Philadelphia?" I nodded. "I dunno, bud," he replied—reminding me that I was still in my traveling costume of undrag. "In a coupla days they'll know where everybody's at, but it's a madhouse back there right now, there's eight million people they're trying to evacuate. You had your radio on?"

"Yeah, but—"

"Maybe it's too far to pick it up out here." He took off his cap and rubbed his hand over his face. "Everybody that's got someplace to go, that has a car, is supposed to go there. Relatives, whatever. That's what all these people are doing. These are the ones from Lancaster and thereabouts—Philadelphia people were supposed to take the Northeast Extension or else head down into south Jersey or Delaware along with the Wilmington people. The ones that don't have noplace to go, they're all being sent to camps up in the Poconos or down around Baltimore. The army's bringing in tents and cots."

"For eight million people?"

"Naaah, most of 'em'll have somebody they can stay with for a while. They figure a million and a half, two million, tops. Still a hell of a lot of campers. Who ya looking for?"

"A student of mine, he was house-sitting for me."

"Local kid?"

"I don't know, actually."

The trooper looked me over, red swollen eyes and rumpled, slept-in clothes, and drew his own conclusions but was too tired to care. "Probably went home to his folks if they don't live around Philly. They're telling everybody to call in with the info of where they're at as soon as they get to wherever it is they're going. There's a phone number for every letter of the alphabet. A couple more days, if the kid does like he's supposed to, you'll be able to track him down."

"Sounds pretty well worked out," I said vaguely. A couple of days, *if* he was okay, and no way to find out if he wasn't.

"It's a goddamn miracle is what it is," said the trooper fervently. "That goddamn congressman, Terry Carpenter, that son of a bitch was just waiting for something like this to happen, I swear to God—must of been. He had everything all thought out

121

and ready to go. He commandeered the suburban trains in Philly, the busses, all the regular Amtrak trains and the freight trains too, that were anywheres around, and had 'em all rolling within a couple hours of the accident, got the hospitals and so forth emptied out, and look at this here''—he waved at the six lanes of cars contracting into four but moving along pretty well at about forty—"it's the same back in Philadelphia except at the ramps and like that.'' The trooper put his cap back on. "I got to get back to work here. Don't worry about your little pal, he'll be okay. You got someplace to go? I can give you directions to a refugee camp.''

"No thanks, I'm fine.'' It was stupid to resent the trooper for what he was thinking but I did all the same.

I edged my car into the stream of traffic being guided back the way it had come, but at the first exit I slid out of formation and onto a little road that headed off toward the mountains. I drove along for several miles, looking for a town with a phone; but when I finally found one, in front of a closed-up shop in a closed-up town, there was still no answer.

That was crisis time, there and then. I don't know how long I stood beside that phone kiosk while the battle raged. At one point several busloads of Amish families went by, probably headed for relatives in Ohio; they stared out, faces blank and stony; for them too it was the end of the world. The wind had only held south-southwest a little while, but that was long enough.

Finally I got back into the car, turned it around, reentered the turnpike by the eastbound ramp, drove back to the roadblock, and found my trooper. He stood still and watched me walk up to him, too beat to show surprise. "Look,'' I said, "I'd like to go in and help search for the people who got missed. They must need volunteers. I'm volunteering.''

Very slowly he nodded. "If that's what you want. Go on into Harrisburg and talk to somebody there. Get off at the capitol, there's a trooper station set up around there somewheres, you'll see it. Maybe they'll take you. I'll radio ahead so they know you're comin'.'' I thanked him and started to leave; he called after me, "Listen up a minute, bud. Later on it might be too late to change your mind. We might be moving people out of York and Harrisburg if the wind shifts again.''

"I understand," I called back, and felt him watch for a minute before moving to his car to use the radio.

In Harrisburg I talked fast and they took me—took me also, at face value, for a youthfully middle-aged man. They issued me a radiation suit and minimal instructions and flew me into the contaminated zone along with a batch of other volunteers, a few Quakers and some workers from Three Mile Island.

We were dropped off in Center City, fifteen miles from where I needed to be. They didn't like to spare any people for the suburbs, but emergency volunteers are hard to control and some of the others were looking for friends or relatives too. In the end they let each of us take a police vehicle with a loudspeaker and told us to make a mad dash for home, then drive back slowly into the city, keeping the siren on and picking up stragglers as we came.

I'd only made it a little more than halfway home when I ran out of gas. The damned van burned methanol and I'd been driving some kind of electric or solar car for thirteen years, but even so . . . I tore off on foot in my radiation suit to find a filling station, looking I'm sure exactly like a space invader in a B-grade flick, trying to run along the deserted street—not deserted enough, though: when I got back with a can of methanol half an hour later, streaming with sweat and nearly suffocated, the van was gone. Like an idiot I hadn't taken the keys. I heaved the can into a hedge and started walking.

I was seven miles from home, give or take half a mile. Just as I set off, the sun came out. I had to pee badly and didn't know how (or whether) to open the suit, and I was already terribly thirsty.

That walk was no fun at all. I had to rest a lot. I also had decided that wetting the suit was preferable to the consequences of any alternative I could think of, which made the hike even more unpleasant than it would have been in any case. It was more than three hours from the time I'd left the van when I finally got home. The key was in my pocket but I couldn't get to it; I ended up breaking my own basement window to get in.

Eric wasn't there.

I knew the house was empty the instant I got inside. In the basement I leaned against the cool wall, overcome with exhaustion and letdown. After a while I fumbled with the suit till something came unfastened and crawled out of it, drenched and

123

reeking; I left the suit in the basement with all my seed-starting equipment and insect cages and dragged myself on wobbling knees upstairs, shutting the door behind me.

The kitchen sink was full of water. So were both bathroom sinks and the tub. My feeling of letdown lifted; he'd followed instructions then, which probably meant he'd gotten safely away. Good old Eric. I drank a couple of liters of water from the sink before stripping off my vile clothes and plunging into the full, cool tub. Might as well die clean.

Almost instantly I went to sleep. When I woke an hour or so later with a stiff neck I took a thorough bath, got dressed again (this time in my ''own'' clothes, some shorts and a shirt), realized I was famished, and raided the refrigerator for a random sampling of Eric's abandoned provisions: cold chicken, super-market bread, a banana, a tomato from the garden. The power was off, but the doors had been kept shut and nothing had spoiled. I drank a can of Eric's Coke, my first in nearly thirty years. It was delicious. In a cabinet I found a bag of potato chips and ate them all with deliberate relish: exquisite! There were half a dozen boxes of baked beans in there, and pickled herring, and a box of cheese. . . . Irrationally I began to feel terrific, as if the lost chance with Eric were somehow being made up for by his unintended gifts, the last meals I expected ever to eat. I meant to enjoy them, and I did.

Sated at last, I wandered into my airless bedroom and fell across the bed. Strange as it may sound, I never thought to switch on the transistor, so wholly had I crossed over into a realm governed by the certainty of my own imminent death. I had been fleeing my death for so long that on one level I actually felt relief to believe I could give in to it now, stop twisting and doubling and trying to give it the slip. Nor, still stranger, did I even glance into the garden.

The house was stifling, must have been shut up for many hours. It had been many hours too since people had been told not to run any more water or flush their toilets, though both of mine were flushed and clean. These things confirmed the prob-ability of Eric's safe escape. I sank like stone into sleep. When I woke it was dark, and the house was being battered by the amazing racket of a helicopter landing in the little park a block away.

They'd caught the person who had pinched my van as he was

trying to cross the Commodore Barry Bridge into New Jersey. A police van is a conspicuous object to steal, but he'd been offered no alternatives and didn't mind being apprehended at all, so long as his captors took him out of danger. He'd seen me stop and leave the van, waited till I was gone, then poured fuel from some cans in his landlady's garage into the tank and taken off, while I'd still been hoofing it up the road. Inside the helmet I hadn't heard the engine start. It seemed less reasonable to steal the van outright than to beg a lift, but people act oddly when their lives are at stake and that was how he'd chosen to play it— a white man in his fifties, no family, a night-shift worker who had somehow slept through the evacuation. In fact, the very sort of person I'd been sent to pick up. All this I learned later.

It had taken time to trace the van, and everybody was plenty busy enough without coming to rescue the would-be rescuer, and they didn't even know my name. But I'd mentioned the name of my development to one of the other volunteers, and its general location near the campus, and eventually they sent the helicopter out to find me. It wasn't till I was out of my suit again that anybody realized the fellow they'd come to find had metamorphosed into a woman.

The rest is all aftermath, but I may as well set it down anyway.

I lived for a month in a refugee camp near Kutztown, Pennsylvania, on land owned by the Rodale Research Center; I chose it for that reason. By month's end it was obvious that Greater Philadelphia was going to be uninhabitable for years—maybe ten years, maybe twenty.

A month to the day after the accident they sighted the returning Hefn ship.

I took a pretty high dose of radiation. My chances of developing leukemia in fifteen or twenty years aren't bad at all. However, I don't expect to be around that long unless I accept the Hefn's offer (of which more later).

One day in the camp they paged me, and when I got to the admin tent, who should be standing there in pack, T-shirt, and shorts but Eric Meredith. I'd found out, quite quickly, that he had indeed gone to relatives in Erie with the first wave of the evacuation, and had sent him a letter saying how relieved I was that he'd gotten away safely. I'd mentioned that I would be staying at the the Rodale Camp for a while. Eric had come all that way not to collect his bonus (as I thought at first) but to deliver the contents of his backpack: a complete printout of the records of my experiment, this season's preliminary notes on disk, and six seriously overripe cantaloupes containing the seeds of *Cucumis melo reticulatus* var. Milky Tango, the hybrid melon I'd had the highest hopes for, saved by his quick thinking from the radioactive rain. "I didn't know how to get the tough disk out of the computer," he apologized.

I stared at the bagful of smelly spheres on the table before us with the oddest emotion. For part of a day not long before, I had surrendered, I'd given up my life. By purest luck my life had been restored to me; but I had crossed some psychic boundary that day and had never crossed back again. And Eric and the experiment both belonged to the time before the accident, when fighting viral diseases had been most of what I cared to do.

It only took one step to close the distance. I took it, put my arms around that bony, sinewy, beanpole torso and held myself against it for a moment out of time. Eric stood stiff as a tomato stake, and about as responsive, but I didn't mind. "Eric, do me a favor," I said, letting go of him and stepping back. "I'll take half of these, you keep the others. Plant them in your grandparents' back yard next summer. Finish the experiment for me."

A coughing fit made me break off, and Eric unstiffened enough to say, "Are you okay? That cough sounds terrible."

"I'm fine now. I had a cold, then bronchitis. Listen: the soil at my place will be contaminated for years, and God knows when I'll get another yard to grow things in. The college may reorganize, but it hasn't been decided whether or where. Not in Delaware County, though. Will you be going on down to University Park?"

He nodded. "Next week. They're letting us start late."

"Good, then you just have time to collect yourself a supply of cucumber beetles. You can expose them to mosaic later if they haven't already picked it up." The poor kid was staring, unable to believe what was happening. "I'm perfectly serious. Look: *you* saved the data and the seed. I was in the house for eight hours or so myself and it never crossed my mind to try to rescue either one." This was true. The only thing *I'd* thought to rescue, when the helicopter came, had been my fake penis. "You've earned the right to finish the work. But don't feel you

126

have to, either; the Rodale people will be glad to take over, or a seed company would.''

"Oh no, I *want* to! Really!'' he protested. "If *you* don't, that is—but you could make money from this. It isn't right.''

"Tell you what. For safety's sake, let's have another copy of these records made and print out the ones from this summer. I'll hang on to half the seed, as I said. If you don't produce salable results I'll see that somebody who might gets my copy and the seed; and if you do get results we'll split the money down the middle. How does that sound?''

The camp had several notaries. We wrote up an agreement and got one of them to notarize our signatures. I wasn't even sure it was legal—Eric was only nineteen or twenty—but never mind, I thought, never mind!

I walked him back to his car. Still bedazzled by the turn of events, he let the window down to say earnestly, "Nobody *ever* gave me anything this important before. I don't know what to say.''

"You gave me something important too.''

"*I* did? When? What was it?''

I thought of trying to tell him just what, thought better of it. "Cold chicken. Potato chips. Baked beans. Cokes.''

It took him a minute to realize what I was talking about, but then he objected, "That's different! That's not the same thing at all!''

"Less different than you know. Think about it, eh?'' And then, a bit rashly, "Think about *me* once in a while.''

Last month I attended Eric's graduation from Penn State: magna cum laude in biology and a graduate fellowship to Cornell. For a boy from the nether regions of academe, not bad at all. Maybe he'll do with his life what I'd have done with mine if things had been different. Eric's final proof of Milky Tango's tolerance to mosaic under a wide variety of growing conditions earned him his classy degree, though he gave me full credit for my own work, to which his was only the capstone—but a beautifully cut and polished capstone, every bit as good as the one I might have cut myself. I wore a long-sleeved shirt to the commencement, too warm for such a sunny day, to cover the Kaposi's lesions that have spread now over much of my body.

My own research has taken an unexpected turn.

Early last summer I donned a radiation suit and went back

127

home to see my abandoned garden and my field trial beds. Everything was a disheartening mess, but that wasn't what I'd come to see. Eric had ripped loose the Ultramay cover on the Milky Tango beds to harvest those six melons. Remnants of the stuff flapped around me as I knelt to look, imagining his haste and fright as he'd scrabbled frantically among the vines while behind him in the house the printer pipped and pinged. But such thoughts weren't what I'd come for either.

The rest of the Milky Tango seedcrop had eventually rotted where it lay, and the seeds had been directly exposed to the elements all these months. I'd been reading a lot about using fast neutrons, X rays, and gamma rays to induce desirable mutations in plants, including disease resistance, and had begun to wonder what effect the fallout might have had on my own already highly resistant muskmelons. I wanted to know whether any of the accidentally irradiated seed had made it through the winter and germinated, and so did my new bosses at Rodale Press, who were paying for this expedition. Our Hefn observer was interested too—enough to come along and help.

Sure enough, there were about two dozen volunteer seedlings growing in the Milky Tango plots. Some leaves showed signs of moderate beetle damage but not enough to set the plants back much. With Godfrey's help I transplanted each seedling, radioactive soil and all, into its own large peat pot brought along for the purpose. Back at the Research Center we planted the lot of them at a special site set apart from the other trials and waited to see what would happen.

While we were waiting I got sick. Before that, the eighteen months between the Peach Bottom accident and my illness were my happiest ever.

When Penn State made the decision to disband the Delaware County Campus, they offered to try to place the tenured faculty at other branches of the system; but by then the Rodale Press had offered me a job. I'd been writing for their magazines for years and knew a number of Rodale editors and writers through correspondence, so it was natural enough that they should think of me when an editorial slot opened up that September at *Backyard Researcher* magazine, the newest member of the Rodale family of publications.

I can remember when all this part of Pennsylvania was farmland and Kutztown was a tiny college town with one main street, one bad motel, and one decent restaurant. But high-tech industry like AT&T and Xerox had moved in with the new expressway, changing the character of the area completely. When I came here to live the Research Center had become a green island in a sea of development. I moved into one of the old farm buildings at the Center and commuted to my job in Emmaus, where the press was located. Living out at the Center made it easier to keep an eye on my new experimental garden. No more battling with diseases now; the project I devised had to do with increasing yields in several varieties of potatoes. No more hyperpure living, either: the potato chip and I were strangers no longer. No more Companions; we were scattered to the winds, but the new friends I made here knew about my condition. No more celibacy: for a while, one of these friends became my lover.

When the Hefn decided to take charge of us, they looked around for pockets of sanity and right action in the general balls-up we'd made of things, and so they were interested in the Rodale enterprise and in sustainable agriculture generally—enough to assign us a permanent observer/advisor, and that was Godfrey. He moved into the farmhouse with me. When I got sick he knew about it; when the lesions appeared he asked about them and the disease they meant I had. It's because of Godfrey that the search for a "cure"—fallen on very thin times since the numbers of still-living victims dropped below ten thousand—has taken off again.

It looks pretty promising, actually. They've found a way to paralyze the enzyme that the virus uses to replicate in the cell—not like zidovudine and its kindred, which only slowed the enzyme down, but a drug that stops it cold. There's no way I'd still be alive by the time they finish sanding the side effects off the stuff, not in the natural course of things. But Godfrey's had another idea.

You know that the Hefn hibernate and that their bodies use chemicals pretty much the same way ours do? Well, Godfrey figures it should be possible to synthesize a drug—using a chipmunk or woodchuck model in conjunction with a Hefn model—that would put the ninety-five-hundred-odd AIDS patients and HIV-positives to sleep for a couple of years, until the cure can be perfected. There's a problem about testing the stuff if we *all* take the cold sleep, because of course the bosses, the Gafr, won't let them use animals. So we might be asleep for quite a while—or forever—or be damaged by the procedure. But the Gafr have given the go-ahead, and I'm thinking seriously about it. The KS can be treated effectively only with radiation, and I've had much more than my fair share of that already. I'll die of cancer anyway, probably sooner than later; in a month I'll be forty-nine. But I'm thinking about it. I wish they'd come up with this before, is all.

I have to tell you something funny. One of my irradiated melon plants turned out to be one hundred percent *immune* to mosaic! It's peculiar in other ways that make it useless for commercial purposes at this point, but the Rodale breeders are sure to keep working on improvements. I mentioned before that like all cucurbits melons produce separate male and female flowers, the male flowers bearing the pollen-producing stamens, the female flowers the pistil and ovary. Ordinarily it's easy to tell which is which, because the ovary behind the female blossom is a large hairy structure and the male flower has nothing behind it but a slender stem.

Well, the immune melon bears male and female flowers that look exactly alike! You can't tell them apart, except by peering closely at the inner structures or tearing off the petals, because the ovary is tiny and concealed entirely within the flower. The fruit is correspondingly tiny, about the size of a small orange—much too small to appeal to growers, though I'd think home gardeners might raise it as a novelty.

I've given this new cultivar the official name of Tiny Tango, a name to please the seed catalogue writers. Privately, I think of it as Male Impersonator (or sometimes—a pun—Atomic Power Plant). Its rind is tan and thin, netted like the rind of an ordinary cantaloupe, and its flesh is a beautiful deep salmon-orange, as sweetly, intensely delicious as any I have ever tasted.

4

FINAL TOMTE

2011

They rode up the escalator from the subway and stepped blinking into the bright Nordic sunlight. Or rather, the young man blinked; his odd-looking companion opaqued the inner lid of his eyes against the glare.

"We could walk from here," Anders Eklund suggested uncertainly. "It's rather a pleasant walk, along a shady street and over the Field itself. Or, if you prefer, we can take a taxi most of the way." He addressed his companion by the formal Swedish word for "you"—*Ni*—which had recently come back into vogue after all but disappearing from the language during the late twentieth century. Anyone listening would have known at once that the two were mere acquaintances, not friends.

"Oh, a walk sounds fine," the Hefn replied in a deep, cheerful voice. The top of his head came even with Anders's shoulder. He wore trousers and shoes and a shirt, but all the parts of his body not concealed beneath clothing were covered with grayish hair, and his long gray beard hung below his belt.

The two set off together down the center of the busy, handsome thoroughfare called Valhallavägen, where a sandy footpath and an avenue of tall linden trees divided the two lanes of traffic. Between the lindens Anders walked stiffly, the Hefn energetically; he had no difficulty keeping up with the long-legged man. He looked about him with an air of intense and genial curiosity at the cars, the post office, the small shops, his fellow pedestrians. In the capital of any other country he would have created a sensation, but those Stockholmers who sighted and recognized the Hefn kept their composure and scarcely looked, let alone gawked, at him. Pomphrey, by contrast, peered from beneath shaggy brows at every person he passed. He appeared to be enjoying himself thoroughly, while Anders grew more miserably self-conscious with every block and regretted a dozen times the taxi they might have been concealed within.

Eventually the street opened upon an enormous sloping field carpeted with the tall brown grasses of late summer and dotted with huge gray glacial boulders. "Here we are. This is Gärdet," Anders said with relief, stating the obvious. "The Girl Scouts are camped in the trees near Kaknästornet—the radio tower, you know," pointing at a distant structure that soared above the broad horizontal like a bristly rocket. "We might have lunch up there later if you like—there are tremendous views of Djurgården and the canal, and the surrounding terrain."

His voice faltered suddenly as he thought, too late, of the lunchtime crowds of summer in the tower restaurant; but Pomphrey only said pleasantly, "I doubt there'll be time for lunch, and I've already seen the view. Let's wait and see what develops, shall we?"

Anders kicked himself mentally; what was he doing spouting off like a tourist guide, when he knew perfectly well that the Hefn had been in town for nearly two months already? He looked away to hide his hot face and led the way along a track beaten through the grass, one leading in the general direction of the tower.

After several weeks of stupifying heat, many Stockholmers were taking advantage of the wonderful weather to let their dogs or children run or to lie in the sun, disregarding their knowledge of the danger from ultraviolet radiation—even in Scandinavia—just as many of them also were disregarding what they knew about the dangers of tobacco. There appeared in fact to be a general engagement in denial; certainly, one would never guess to look at these people how profoundly events of the past year had affected the terms of their existence on the planet or their future lives. This denial could not last. But while it did, these Stockholmers would go doggedly on in pursuit of their customary pleasures.

In the distance several people moved on horseback along one or another of the tracks through the grass. Pomphrey gazed with great interest at these, and at the topless sunbathers and shrill, white-headed children; and even Anders relaxed somewhat in

132

the relative informality of the Field. More people stared openly at Pomphrey here than in the subway or the streets; several even said *"Hej!"* as he went by, and whenever that happened the Hefn returned the greeting cheerily. A number of others recoiled, averted their eyes, made inaudible comments to their companions; these he ignored.

Anders was sweating by the time they neared the shade of the birches at the top of the field. "Look over there," he couldn't help saying, pointing to a miniaturized palace to their left, partly screened by trees. "Did you know that the kings of Sweden used to review their troops from that vantage? Gärdet was a parade ground before it was a recreational resource for the citizens of Stockholm."

"Stockholm is a very nice city," said Pomphrey agreeably, without actually answering him. "Anywhere else, this whole tract of ground would have been developed long since, and then all these people would have no place to walk their dogs on a beautiful Sunday afternoon."

Anders regarded this as a self-evident truth requiring neither thanks nor reply. All the same, he was gratified. "The Scouts should be somewhere around here. It isn't usual for camping to be allowed. This group has special permission, and the protection of the American Embassy—I believe they send a couple of Marines up here to guard the site at night, and when the girls are away. Don't ask me why *these* girls get special treatment."

"I wasn't going to."

Anders glanced quickly at Pomphrey; was this a too-literal reading of his remark? Or was the Hefn being sarcastic, making fun of him? He flushed furiously again at this possibility; but at that moment Pomphrey said, "I think I smell wood smoke. Would they be permitted to build a fire up here?"

"I don't know. Perhaps. There's plenty of dead wood to pick up if they were."

Just after that they struck a jeep road through the birches and turned right, in the direction of the now-invisible tower. A few minutes' walking brought them to their goal: six wall tents, two Johnnys-on-the-Spot, a fire circle, and twenty or so American teenagers absorbed in making sandwiches, gathering firewood, or fussing with a pot set over the flames.

All these activities stopped when Anders and Pomphrey hove into view. Unlike the Swedes, these kids stared at the Hefn with

133

all their might; almost certainly, none of them had ever seen a Hefn before except on TV. Nobody said anything, but after a moment one of them went into a tent and came out again followed by a young woman—Anders guessed she might be several years older than himself, and he stood with as much height and dignity as he could, for he thought her attractive.

The woman approached the two visitors and addressed them in English: "Hello. You're from the Swedish Institute, right? I'm Brenda Hollis; I'm the one who called this morning."

"Anders Eklund," said Anders, offering his hand. "And this is, ah, Pomphrey. The Hefn Observer to the Swedish Government."

Brenda shook hands with Anders in a perfunctory way, but her eyes were all for the Hefn, who extended his own hand in an obvious show of courtesy—adopting the customs of the barbarians, Anders thought with irritation, observing that Brenda held onto Pomphrey's hairy-backed hand noticeably longer than she had held his own. "Your name is *Pomphrey*?" she asked. "It isn't really, is it?"

"It *is* really. Or as near as makes no difference," the Hefn replied, with that elusive *semblance* of smiling and twinkling that they all had, which was no true human expression at all if you looked carefully. "My real name, or part of it, actually is" and he made a noise which did in fact sound a lot like "Pomphrey."

"Come and sit down," said Brenda. "I'm afraid all I can offer are these big stones to sit on, but we find they do very well. Go on, kids, finish putting lunch together, and go ahead and eat it when it's ready if I'm still tied up," she added to the Girl Scouts, who were whispering to one another and watching the visitors with their tongues all but hanging out. As they began to move, reluctantly, Brenda explained, "They don't mean to be rude; it's quite a thrill for them to see a Hefn close-to. Please don't be offended."

Her directness made Anders cringe, but Pomphrey said, "I'm not a bit offended. It's a good thing for youngsters to be interested in what's strange to them. If they were afraid, instead of curious, that might make them dangerous, and *that* would be offensive perhaps." His English was much better than Anders's, and even better than his Swedish—which was very good—and

134

he had, of course, no "foreign" accent in either language. No Hefn did.

Brenda hoisted herself onto a granite boulder and waited for her visitors to seat themselves. She was as slender as one of her charges and dressed like them in jeans and running shoes and a green polo shirt with a gold trefoil on the left breast. "I'll tell you both what I told Mr. Hildeman on the phone, only in more detail, and let you decide whether it was worth your while to come all the way out here for the information."

Pomphrey had scrambled nimbly onto the rock of his choice, despite his short legs. He nodded, twinkling.

"We'll tape your story if you don't object." Anders produced a tiny, expensive tape recorder from his shoulder bag, set it on the rock beside him, pressed buttons. "The microphone is very sensitive; it will pick you up easily. Now. Begin."

"This is Brenda Hollis, speaking from my campsite on Gärdet near the Kaknäs radio tower, outside Stockholm, and the date is August 14, 2012. With me are Anders Eklund of Svenska institutet and the Hefn Observer Pomphrey.

"I'm the leader of a Cadette Girl Scout troop from Allentown, Pennsylvania. My brother, Victor Hollis, who is Cultural Attaché at the American Embassy, arranged for us to camp here for a week. Through the Swedish Institute he also arranged a number of excursions and entertainments for us, including an evening with the folklorist and storyteller Gunnar Lundqvist. Mr. Lundqvist came out to our campsite last evening with Elisabeth Hall of the Institute. The Scouts cooked dinner for themselves and the two guests, and then we all sat around the campfire while Mr. Lundqvist told stories for, oh, an hour and a half or thereabouts.

"I ought to say that Mr. Lundqvist had brought a bottle of *snaps*, from which he fortified himself from time to time throughout the evening. He was certainly a little drunk the whole time, though I doubt that any, or many, of the kids noticed—he was subtle about it and didn't slur his speech or drop things or stagger or anything like that."

Anders stopped his recorder. "This is a very serious accusation, Miss Hollis, that the Swedish Institute would send a drunken storyteller to a visiting group of American Girl Scouts," he said, looking severely at Brenda.

"I know. Elisabeth was very embarrassed, and apologized

afterwards before taking him away—she said he had proved 'unreliable' in that way before, but not for quite a while, and she certainly would recommend against his ever being employed by the Institute again. But drunk or sober he was a wonderful storyteller; the kids loved him. Shall I go on?''

Anders, looking sour as well as flushed, starting the recorder again.

"He was a very good storyteller," Brenda repeated. "He talked about trolls and water sprites as if he'd known them personally. He'd lived for some years in America as a young man, he said, and spoke excellent English, of a pretty unvarnished sort, and the kids just gobbled him up.

"The last story he told, while he was the drunkest he ever got, was about a *tomte*. Tome-teh, is that how you say it? Yes? Well, he told that one as if he actually *had* known a—a *tomte* as a boy on his father's farm in southern Sweden. I didn't think of it at the time—I was too absorbed in the story, and also too nervous that he would get just a little bit drunker and become obvious—but this morning I realized what he might have been saying, and that's why I called.''

From the gathered Scouts at that moment there suddenly arose the sound of singing:

> Back of the bread is the flour,
> And back of the flour is the mill,
> And back of the mill is the wind and the rain
> And the Fa-ther's will.

Brenda smiled. "Lunch must be ready, finally. It still takes them a solid hour to make three dozen sandwiches and heat a kettle of soup. Well, anyway: Mr. Lundqvist said that when he was a boy there was a *tomte* living on his father's farm. He lived in the barn and helped with the planting and harvesting and—and seed cleaning, and whatever else they used to do on the farms here, sixty or seventy years ago. He did all this during the night, so that nobody ever saw him at work. Mr. Lundqvist said his parents and uncles and the hired hands—all the adults there—knew perfectly well about the *tomte* but never spoke of him, and when *he* used to try to talk about him, as a very young child, he was always hushed right up, because it was believed to be dangerous to mention him, or bad luck, or something like that.

"He told how his father and uncles used to stew and debate about modernizing the barn, none of them ever mentioning the real issue, which wasn't sanitation or the expense but the fact that everyone knew a *tomte* wouldn't bring seed into a barn with a floor; he had to have bare earth or nothing, and in fact they put off modernizing year after year because of it, yet nobody ever came right out and said so! And how they kept horses instead of a tractor after all the other farms around had switched to tractors, and they treated the horses very, very well too, because everybody knew a *tomte* was partial to horses and worked extra hard where they were well cared for. Stuff like that. How they put out a bowl of porridge for him every weekend, and he had to have a spoon made out of wood or horn, never of iron— oh, and lots more. Tipsy or not, the old guy really was terribly good. He made us see exactly how it was.

"Well, so things went along like this until Mr. Lundqvist was fourteen or fifteen years old—about the age of my Scouts, actually—and he and the *tomte* were pretty good friends, even though it was kind of hard to be good friends with a *tomte* because they were so easily offended—'touchy,' he called it. But one day the *tomte* came to Mr. Lundqvist while he was doing chores after school and made a kind of declaration.

"Right out of the blue he told him: 'I'm the last of my kind. All my relatives are dead. It's high time I put myself away, but I'm going to need you to help me, Gunnar.' "

On the boulder next to his, Anders saw the Hefn stir and lean slightly forward.

Brenda glanced quickly at Pomphrey, then went on with her story. "Well, naturally Mr. Lundqvist was very perplexed and upset, and he said, 'Do you mean *all* the other *tomtes* in Sweden are dead?' and the *tomte* said, 'That's not really what I mean, but it's none of your affair. I need you to think now: where's the coldest place we can get to? And how can we get there? If you were ever my friend, you'll help me now. In fact, you'll have to, because I won't get far on my own.'

"Well, to make a long story short, Mr. Lundqvist was very worried and sad and all, but he cudgeled his wits and decided he and the *tomte* could take the train up north somewhere if he disguised Lexi, that was the *tomte*'s name, as a dwarf—"

Pomphrey's entire body seemed to shudder. "Lexi," he murmured heavily, and sliding down off the great stone he stepped

137

forward and laid his hairy hand upon Brenda's knee. "This *tomte*'s name was Lexi?"

Brenda stared at him. She shivered. "I should have said so right at the start. It was Lexi, or Alexi, or something pretty much like that."

"Lexi, short for Lexifrey," said Pomphrey. "Please go on, Miss Hollis. What *did* they do?" He did not remove his hand, which gave Anders the creeps, but there was no escaping anyway the terrible intensity of the Hefn's totally engaged regard.

Connie crawled into the tent and shook the figure in the sleeping bag gingerly by the shoulder, wrinkling her face at the terrible smell. "They're gone," she said. "Listen, uh, Granddad, you can't stay here, there's no way we can hide you. Every so often Brenda checks the tents—and anyway, you just can't stay here anymore." Her face was a study in uncomfortableness.

The person stretched and yawned—while Connie grimaced and held her breath—then blinked his bleary eyes at the girl. "Can't keep the old man, eh? Can't take care of your own granddaddy, is that it? Where'm I goin' to go, then?" His voice became wheedling. "Just a couple more days, eh? I won't be no trouble, I just got to keep out of sight for a little while."

"No," said Connie desperately, in over her head. "I *told* you, Brenda inspects the tents, and besides, the other kids don't like it. Here, you can eat this," thrusting a sandwich wrapped in a paper napkin at him, "and then you really have to go."

The old man eyed this object with indifference. Absently he rubbed his stubbly chin, making a scraping sound within the tent's little island of silence, and shook his head sadly. "I thought you'd be glad to see your old granddaddy. I guess family don't mean what it used to anymore."

"Come on, you ran away from home yourself when you were my age and didn't go back for twenty-five years!" said Connie with a flash of spirit. "You said so yourself. And anyway, I *was* glad to see you at first, but now . . ." she trailed off miserably.

"But now I'm just a smelly old drunk with a hangover," he finished for her. "Who said more than he should last night and got himself in Dutch. Ah, well. I'm off, then, but where I'll spend this night I wish I knew. Are you going to tell your mother how you ran me off so mean, when all I wanted was a place to sleep for a little while?"

Connie's face got red and she sat back on her haunches. "Hey, *you* left my mother and Granny and Uncle Bill when Mom was only fifteen. One year older than me. I doubt if she'll be very mad." But at this he looked so woebegone that another terrible rush of remorse and indecision came over Connie like a wave of dizziness. "Look, I'll give you some money for a hotel. You don't have to sleep on the Field or anything, but now, no kidding, you've got to get out of here."

The sounds the clean-up squad was making outside had been dropping off gradually and now were replaced by Brenda's voice calling the girls together. Connie jumped, rummaged hastily in her duffel bag, counted out some bills, put them down on her grandfather's knee inside the sleeping bag, and began to back out of the tent. "We're going on a hike. As soon as we're gone you have to clear out of here, I mean it." She paused on hands and knees in the tent door. "But I really loved the stories last night, I really did, we all did. And I'm really sorry about everything. 'Bye. I hope you'll be okay." She backed all the way out of the tent, pulled the zipper closed with a long screech that made her grandfather flinch, and let the outer flap fall to.

The old man sat a moment in the scented dimness. Outside he could hear a girl's grim voice: "So is he going, or what?" and his granddaughter's equally grim reply: "He's going." He shrugged, fumbled with the zipper of the sleeping bag, gave up, and struggled with difficulty out of its end, like a snake shedding its skin. He scrounged for the bills where they had been shaken off onto the tent floor by his struggles, counted them, shrugged again, then folded them and put them into his shirt pocket. Since he had not undressed, there was nothing else he needed to do.

He listened till the voices of the Scouts had faded in the distance, then crawled to the door and peered out. The coast looked clear. He pulled the zipper up cautiously and let himself out of the tent, glancing furtively about him for the Marines assigned to guard the campsite. But they were sitting on rocks way over by the jeep road, smoking and exchanging remarks about the rear ends of the girls, which were now receding across the Field. They weren't looking for intruders *within* the site at all, and never noticed the old man slipping off through the trees in the other direction.

* * *

"He stole all the money his parents had in the house," Anders said, consulting the screen of his NotePad. "He then bought two tickets on the overnight train to Lappland, smuggled the, ah, the *tomte* aboard—people would naturally not look too closely at a person with a physical deformity, so it must have been easier than it sounds—disembarked with him somewhere in the mountains, and left him there, presumably to freeze to death in a place of his own selection. Lundqvist did not suggest why Lexi should have chosen such a bizarre way to die, and seemed never to have felt much curiosity on the subject; at least the Scouts got that impression.

"He then bought a ticket to Göteborg with the rest of the money, persuaded a freighter to take him on—he must have looked some years older than his age—worked his way to America, where he wandered around, got a job someplace in the Middle West, married and settled down, and returned to Sweden twenty-six years after running away from home, as a journeyman carpenter whose hobby was Scandinavian folklore." Anders paused in his recitation of known facts to glance at Pomphrey; Pomphrey looked back at him without a trace of the pseudo-twinkle Anders had so disliked—as if, Anders thought, I were a bug or a stick. He suppressed a shiver.

Pomphrey, his voice just this side of menacing, now addressed Elisabeth Hall, who sat behind her desk wearing a frightened expression. "This *'tomte'* of Gunnar Lundqvist's was quite certainly a Hefn called Lexifrey. Evidently he was the last survivor of the group of thirteen Hefn that our ship marooned in Scandinavia a little more than 350 years ago, as I assume you both had deduced from my extreme interest in him. A very convivial fellow, Lexifrey, and, as it happens, a relative of mine. You must see, Miss Hall, why it's absolutely necessary that we locate Gunnar Lundqvist."

Elisabeth cleared her throat. "To find out from him where your relative's grave might be."

"His grave?" Pomphrey shot her a look like a knife blade, sharp and steely. "Don't be quick to say so. Haven't you wondered why Lexi insisted on going so far north? He hoped to find a—a cleft or fissure in the permafrost, inside which he might induce in himself a state of very deep hibernation. In that state, in the right place, it's possible for a Hefn to sleep for decades. Miss Hall, he may still be alive up there."

"But—are you suggesting that Lexi still might have expected to be rescued?"

"I'm suggesting," said Pomphrey, "that there's a very good chance that our time-window message, the one sent on our first visit, was received. We had difficulties with the terminal; a message could have got through without our being able to confirm it. I'm suggesting that Lexi *knew* the ship would be back and hoped to stay alive, by hibernating, until it returned. In that case, I believe he would have tried to leave clues to help us find him. Perhaps he told Gunnar Lundqvist rather more than Lundqvist told the Scouts. In any case we must certainly pick the man up and question him."

"But surely Lundqvist would have come forward in 2006 if he'd had anything to tell you," Elisabeth protested. "Assuming he realized then that Lexi was a Hefn."

"That's not an assumption we can afford to make, Miss Hall. It's possible, of course, that he tried to contact us and could not persuade the officials to let him through. In any case, whether or not he made the connection or the attempt, the fact remains that he did not come forward. We will have to ask him what he knows directly."

"But Lundqvist was just a boy," Anders blurted, "fourteen or fifteen at the time, and this was nearly sixty years ago—is it likely he'll be able to remember *what* Lexi said or *where* they went together? There's still a lot of wild country in the north of Sweden. Back then it would have been a great deal wilder."

The look Pomphrey sent him nearly made Anders bite his tongue. "Oh, we can help him remember," he said, almost blandly. "That's not our problem; our problem is to find him. You're going to have to help us, Miss Hall. You have an address, I suppose."

Elisabeth looked more flustered and frightened than ever. "We have one on record, but Lundqvist told me the other day—when he dropped by to ask if we had any work for him—that he'd moved out and was staying with a friend who had no phone, so we wouldn't be able to contact him quickly."

"You have the friend's address, though?"

"I'm afraid not. I paid Lundqvist by postgiro, at his request. He told me he no longer keeps an account at a bank."

"I see." Pomphrey stood abruptly on his short, strong legs. "Miss Hall, we are going to find that man, whether he wants to be found or not. If the Swedish Institute can't help us I'll have to try the police."

Anders said in agitation, "But what can the police do? They can hardly arrest him; it's not a crime to have helped your friend get himself into the mountains, or to be an alcoholic, or even to tell stories to little girls! All the *police* can do is make an appeal, perhaps over the television—and what if Lundqvist refuses to turn himself in? He seems to be leading a very secretive sort of life."

Pomphrey waited for Anders to finish, then treated them both to his impression of an icy smile. "It doesn't matter what he wants. It doesn't matter how he feels about it. He's got to be found and that's all there is to it. You two may as well understand this now, just as the police must be made to understand it—that Lundqvist's feelings in the matter are of no importance at all."

Sharon stood to one side of the tent door, chewing her lower lip. "He's back."

"Oh *no*!" Connie sagged, then pushed aside the netting and thrust herself past Sharon into the tent. "What are you *doing* here? I told you you can't stay, and that's what I meant!"

The old man looked at her pleadingly, sober now and rheumy-eyed. "I know you did, but honey, I didn't have nowhere else to go. They're trying to find me. Them Hefn are. There's announcements in the papers and on the TV and radio—that leader of yours told that Hefn that came out here yesterday, and now they're going right into people's houses looking for me."

"What for? What did you *do*?"

"Nothing! I didn't do nothing, but they think the *tomte* I told you all about, the one I knew on the farm when I was a boy, that I went up north with on the train—they think *he* was one of them Hefn they left here all that time ago, and they want to ask me where I took him."

"What for?" said Connie again.

The old man moaned. "Ah, they think he might still be alive up there, like some kind of frozen Rip Van Winkle!"

Connie's face lost some of it's tension; she sat back on her heels. "Really? Do *you* think Lexi could have been a Hefn?"

"Lexi was a *tomte*," the old man said fiercely. "He worked on the farm. He didn't come off no spaceship."

"Well . . . but why not just tell 'em where you went anyway? I mean, just to get 'em off your case."

"Because I don't *remember*," Gunnar Lundqvist wailed gently. "It was sixty years ago, pretty near! I don't even recollect the name of the town where we got off the train—someplace in the mountains, that's all I know!"

"So tell them that," said Connie reasonably.

"Think they'd settle for that? Ha! They'd get it out of me," her grandfather said, his voice full of fear even Connie could recognize. "They've got ways of digging out old memories— that's what the papers are saying. Just like they can take memories away, like they did with them poor Africans that cut down the jungle. I don't want nothing to do with it! I was a God damn fool to shoot my big mouth off the other night! I ain't never told about Lexi before, what did I want to go telling about him now for? I didn't do nothing wrong when I went up there with him— they got no right to go digging around in my mind if I don't want 'em to!"

Connie frowned. For once she agreed with the old man, and besides, she could tell he was frightened out of his wits. "Oh, okay. You can stay till we leave here—but that's only three more days, Granddad. And I'll have to tell Brenda, because there's no way we could hide you and keep her from finding out."

Lundqvist squeezed his eyes shut. "She'll tell," he wheezed. "She told before and she'll do it again."

Connie got up. "I don't think so, but anyway, that's a chance we'll have to take. I'm gonna go get her right now." She crouched through the netting and zipped it behind her, and he heard her tell her tentmate, still lurking outside, "I'm going to get Brenda."

While waiting for his immediate fate to be settled, the old man got the shakes and took a nip from a bottle in his inside coat pocket. He cursed himself again under his breath for several kinds of fool. Again he saw his hand on the brass plate of the door of *Systembolaget*, the government-controlled liquor store, his rumpled and grizzled image reflected in the glass, the fresh notice taped beside it: WANTED: good information leading to the whereabouts of GUNNAR LUNDQVIST, 73, height 1.8 meters, weight 74 kilos, hair gray, eyes blue, recently of Storskärsgatan 47, Stockholm. May be disheveled. This man is urgently wanted by the Hefn Observer and the police. Reward.

They *would* post their notices at *Systemet*—at every liquor store in the city, having deduced the likelihood of his spending the Institute honorarium on booze. He thought with dismay of his image in the glass. I look a hundred years old, he thought, and then: I always did look old for my age, the *H. C. Andersen* wouldn't have signed me on if I hadn't. What a big, husky fellow I was at fourteen, and what a mistake it's all turned out to be.

That young woman, Brenda, could not be trusted, whatever she said. She would betray him to the Marine guards, under whose noses he had crept back into the empty campsite, and collect the reward; and the guards would turn him over to the Hefn, and they would tie him down and put a silver helmet on his head and zap him with electrical charges and pry his memories out of him, and he would be helpless to protect himself. He shuddered and groaned with horror.

Connie was back. He heard low voices outside, and then the Scout leader crouched into the tent behind his granddaughter. "Hello, Mr. Lundqvist. Connie's explained your problem. The trouble is, we aren't very well equipped to hide a fugitive here, and I'm afraid you're putting us in a very awkward position."

"That's just where you've put me, young lady," Lundqvist answered her back with energy. "You didn't need to go telling the Hefn about me. It's your fault I'm in this predicament now."

"Yes, well," Brenda frowned unhappily, "it's true I had no idea they'd mount a house-to-house search for a person who hadn't committed a crime. And—well—I suppose I thought you'd be pleased to help out—since you'd helped Lexi, you know."

"Hell, I'd help 'em out if I could remember where we went, but I don't want no part of them mindreading machines," the old man fired back. "And if you think they'll let me refuse to let 'em *use* their contraptions on me, then you're a bigger fool than I am."

Brenda slumped back on her heels. Lundqvist was probably right: once they had him, what he'd done would be squeezed out of him by whatever means they possessed. Brenda doubted that these means would cause pain or disability, but the idea that the old man's feelings would be disregarded by the aliens upset her badly. Resentment gave a new color to Brenda's own view of the Hefn, for she was—had been—a thoroughgoing Hefn lover, one who regarded the alien ship as a deus ex machina, bringing humanity's last, best hope for averting self-destruction.

It was an awkward situation, one that Lundqvist had accused her—not unfairly—of having created herself.

"All right. We'll hide you till Saturday," she said. "But we leave on Saturday, and after that I'm afraid you'll have to take your chances." (Connie gave her an odd look, whether of approval or dismay she was unable to tell.) "It's a good thing it didn't occur to me to tell Pomphrey you were Connie's grandfather—if he knew that, he'd have been back here looking for you already." She glanced around at the girl. "You kids will sleep one each in the other tents. The whole troop will have to be in on this," she added to Lundqvist, "and I can't guarantee that one of them won't tell somebody before Saturday. I'll do my best to discourage it, that's all I can promise. And I hate to think what their parents are going to say."

"I'm obliged to you," said Lundqvist sourly.

Anders Eklund was just finishing his lunch in the restaurant atop Kaknästornet when two business types sat down at his table (all the others being full). The businessmen were having exactly the same lunch as Anders: thick yellow pea soup, and plate-sized, thin, rolled-up pancakes with lingonberry sauce. Every restaurant in Sweden would be serving this traditional Thursday repast; Anders hadn't needed to come all the way out to Gärdet just for the meal. He'd come because he very much liked being up in the tower, and had hoped the long, familiar vistas would soothe and lift his spirits.

The two men unloaded their trays onto Anders's table after asking and being granted permission (*"Är det ledigt här?"* *"Javisst."*). Anders lit a cigarette and sat morosely fiddling his fork in the smear of purple lingonberry juice left on his plate, while the men picked up their conversation. He smiled grimly to himself when he realized they were mimicking not only his lunch but also the argument that had been going on in his mind.

"They're saving the world, little friend. The one *we* damaged almost beyond repair and can't begin to fix; how can we ask them to respect our rights as free citizens when *we're* responsible for the mess *they've* got to get us out of?"

His companion replied, "I know, I know, I know everything you're going to say, but I still insist that when you undertake a house-to-house search for a person who is not a criminal, then the means simply fail to justify the end."

145

"Should the world-savers be expected to justify themselves to the world-wasters, do you think?"

The other man shook his head impatiently. "That's all very well, Sven-Erik, but don't you find yourself wondering what *else* we'll be forced to accept from the Hefn before they've finished with us?"

"Oh, a great many things I've no doubt, some very unpleasant ones too," Sven-Erik replied, steadily spooning his soup. "But if there were an easy, agreeable way to undo the damage, we wouldn't need the Hefn to show it to us, would we?" He jabbed his spoon at his friend. "You have to remember, Pelle: *we* are the criminals, and the Hefn are the judicial system now. They don't have to account to *us* for anything they do."

Pelle, turning bright red, threw his own spoon down with a clatter. "If you really mean that, then you're accepting the fact that we are at the mercy of tyrants! And this is just the beginning—today it's that poor old drunk, but we're all going to feel the force of the Directive soon enough, you know we are." He leaned across the table toward his friend and his voice rose angrily. "If a million people have starved or frozen to death a year or two from now because they couldn't get food or fuel under the new transport regulations, what will you say then?" Several heads turned, and he added more quietly: "Will it still be 'They don't have to account to *us criminals* for anything they do'?"

Anders stubbed out his half-smoked cigarette and scraped his chair back: *enough of this!* He stalked out and rode the elevator up one flight to the observation room, with its panoramic views of the city, the Field, the Nordic and Maritime Museums, the canal leading out between central Stockholm and the harbor, and the large island of Djurgården just across the water. The room was moderately crowded; Anders had to wait for a turn at the mounted field glasses. He leaned on the railing meantime and brooded through the dirty glass.

His turn finally came, just in time for Anders to be the first to spot the approaching police helicopter. He fished a fifty-crown coin out of his pants pocket, jammed it into the slot, and swiveled the binoculars to focus on the chopper in time to see it land close to the Americans' campsite.

He saw the two Marines and two policemen jump out, saw them duck under the spinning rotors and run into the birches, and swore. A few minutes later—long enough to cost Anders another fifty crowns—they emerged, supporting a gray-headed figure, one on each side. The people in the room behind Anders were questioning and exclaiming, sounding puzzled and uneasy or curious; none seemed to realize what was going on. Just before the timer clicked off he caught a good look at the old fellow who was obviously the fugitive Lundqvist—at his horrified face as he was boosted into the chopper. He swore again.

Seconds later the helicopter lifted off. Anders, having relinquished the binoculars, saw through the window glass a now-tiny figure he somehow knew to be Brenda Hollis walk out alone toward the spot where the chopper had set down. He bolted back to the elevators; when he left the tower he was running.

It was one of the Girl Scouts, not Brenda, who had told—a girl who'd been flirting with the guards all week and who finally had been unable to resist teasing them: *I know something you don't know!*

The two Marines on duty at the time had argued about what to do. One sympathized completely with the old man's position, declaring he had a right to refuse to cooperate. But the other wanted the manhunt called off. His leave had been canceled; he'd had to change plans that might be on again if he could get it back. The rights and wrongs of the situation interested him not at all.

Brenda said to Pomphrey, who had come along to make the "arrest": "I don't understand you. This old man turned his whole life upside down to help your friend; is this any way to reward him for that?"

The look Pomphrey presented to her then lacked any resemblance to a human expression. As the police hauled Gunnar Lundqvist out of the tent Pomphrey said, "Your values are not ours, Miss Hollis. This may be no reward, but neither is it the punishment you both appear to think."

"But Lexi was his *friend*," she protested, near tears.

"Lexi wasn't no friend to me," Lundqvist said bitterly. A uniformed policeman held each of his arms and he stood trapped and vulnerable between them in his stained clothes and stubble, a pathetic figure lent a certain dignity by his very bitterness. "*I* was *Lexi*'s friend, but hell, he didn't care nothing about me, didn't even like me much. He *used* me though, he didn't mind

147

doing that, moaning and shaking his head till I gave in—and I was too blame weak, I thought he'd be grateful. Grateful my eye! I wish to Christ I'd never raised my hand to help him."

"But you did, and so now we must find out where he is. Put him in the helicopter," Pomphrey said to the escort. Behind him clustered the Scouts, bewildered and upset; the girl who had "told" stood by herself, crying ostentatiously into a Kleenex.

"It isn't *right*," Brenda said fiercely, clenching her fists at her sides.

"It's necessary," Pomphrey replied. "Surely what's necessary is neither right nor wrong? Good-bye, Miss Hollis. I hope we'll meet again."

They watched the helicopter take off, the forlorn group of girls and a distraught Brenda. In a moment Connie came over and leaned against Brenda's shoulder. "Why didn't the Marines just refuse to help? And the Swedes too—the police?"

Brenda pulled a tissue out of her jeans pocket and blew her nose. She put her arm around Connie. "Nobody knows what would happen if we did that, honey. That's the trouble. Everybody's afraid to stand up to the Hefn when they want something as badly as they wanted to find Mr. Lundqvist. We're not sure what they'd do or who they'd do it to. We just know what they *could* do—blow up the world, or take our memories away." She smiled shakily at Connie.

"They didn't do anything to *us*, for hiding my granddad."

"No. But they found him almost right away; it might have been different if they'd gotten frustrated."

"I wonder," said Connie savagely, "what Marcia's going to spend that reward money on."

"A flak jacket, if she's got any sense." Brenda gave Connie a little squeeze. "The Hefn are going to show us how to clean the world up, sweetie, don't ever forget that."

"*Make* us clean it up. I know," Connie said dispiritedly. In a moment she added, "What'll they do to my grandfather now?"

"Probably just get him to remember where he went with Lexi and then let him go. I don't think they'll hurt him at all, if only because I doubt they'll need to."

"He was so *scared*." Connie sniffed a little.

Brenda hugged the girl again briefly, then let her go and walked away by herself, down through the birches to the place below the trees where the helicopter had landed. She stood on the spot,

148

breathing deeply. The Scouts, showing unusual sensitivity for them, left her alone. Ten minutes later Anders Eklund found her still there. "Miss Hollis, I must apologize," he gasped—he had been sprinting. "I saw what just happened. Please, please believe me, I myself had nothing whatsoever to do with this—it was that *förbaskade* Hefn—I wanted you to know—"

With some difficulty Brenda brought herself to focus on Anders. "I hadn't supposed it was any of your doing. If anybody's to blame it was me."

Anders still had not caught his breath but was trying anyway to adjust his expression to one of relative dignity and control. Abruptly he gave the effort up. "What's to become of us?" he broke out. "What will these Hefn have made us into before they're through."

Brenda shook her head. "I've just been trying to work that out," she said, and stared at the ground, and scuffed her running shoe in the grass.

The Hefn dealt firmly but gently with Gunnar Lundqvist and released him when they were through with him, undamaged in body or mind and richer by several thousand crowns. That same day a Swedish military plane loaded with three Hefn, a dozen young Swedes doing their compulsory stint of military service, and a time transceiver took off for the northern city of Östersund.

At the Östersund airport they transferred the personnel and equipment into two covered army trucks and headed in convoy over a twisting mountain road toward the town of Rågunda. Just southeast of the town, on the bank of a stream called Indalsälven, they made a camp and set up the time window at the base of Döda fället: the Dead Mountain.

This was the place where Lexi and the fourteen-year-old Lundqvist had parted company. No one in the whole world knew what Lexi had done then; the Hefn would try to pick him up via the time window in order to discover where, or whether, he had eventually gone to ground.

Nothing had turned up in the old man's memory that could be construed as a message from Lexi to his rescuers—nothing to indicate that the message they had sent six years before, in Skåne, had been received or that Lexi expected them to find him, unless his very effort to live a little longer by such desperate

149

means was a sign that he knew they would be coming. But in that case, why hadn't he told Lundqvist something to aid them more materially? How could he expect to be found if nobody knew where to look?

It seemed little less than a miracle that the time terminal, oscillating for weeks through a range of days and times (for young Lundqvist hadn't himself known the precise date of his journey), made contact with Sweden's final *tomte* just after he had sent his companion away and before he had succeeded in locating a place to sleep. There was mutual rejoicing. Yes (said Lexi), the Swedish exiles had caught enough of the garbled message sent in 2006 to know that the ship would finally return, but he alone was left to wait it out through the medium of sleep. He would have a tremendous lot to tell when they found him.

The Hefn reset the terminal for a couple of days later, to allow Lexi time to choose his spot, then reestablished contact so he could give them coordinates and directions.

The directions were concise. They found his body, partly decomposed and frozen solid, exactly where he had told them it would be.

5

GLASS AND CHINA DOGS

1990–2006

A week after our adventure in the park, Terry poked his head around the open door of my office. "Busy?"

"Not very. Come on in."

He slouched into the room, pulled off his coat, and dropped into the chair beside my desk, bundling the coat in his lap. "I've been thinking. It seems like we should talk over what we're going to do—decide together, or discuss it, anyway."

"I've been thinking about it too." (An understatement.) "I warn you now, I haven't got any sage advice to give you."

Terry shrugged this off; it appeared that he had dropped by to consult, not to be advised. "What *I* think is that the best thing would be to just, you know, go on with our lives without trying to change anything, and without trying to tell people what happened. Nobody but weirdos would believe us anyway, so what's the point? But *we* might want to make some decisions differently because of knowing about it now."

I agreed with him there. For instance, Matt and I had talked from time to time about moving up to Kutztown when Matt retired. Kutztown was pretty far from all of the nuclear power plants but Limerick, and off and on during the past week I had pondered the possibility of putting this plan into action *before* his retirement, though the thought of both of us having to commute so far was a daunting one. I wondered which of Terry's decisions might be affected by foreknowledge of the coming catastrophe, and decided to ask. "Like what?"

"Well, like my major." He flashed a grin.

"What *is* your major, by the way?" I realized I had no idea.

"Pre-law." I rolled my eyes; wasn't everyone's? "But now I'm thinking of beefing up my poli-sci minor into another major, and then, even if I do go to law school and end up practicing for a while, I think later I'll probably go into politics."

"How come? To stem the tide of events?"

"Something like that. At least I'd like to, you know, be in a position to influence events. I can see where a little bit of forethought could make a big difference. Like, a person who knew what was coming could do a lot to help people get ready. Calm people down, move them out of the danger zone. Have a *plan*. Do you realize that you and I will be the only ones in the *whole world* not taken completely by surprise when the meltdown happens? Did you think of that? Nobody else will be *ready*!"

I pushed my chair back and regarded his flushed, serious face with surprise. This was a Terry I hadn't seen before. "And you're not going to tell anybody?"

"No, I decided not to. You?"

"I guess not. As you say, who'd believe it? *I'm* still not more than, oh, ninety-eight percent convinced that the whole thing wasn't a coincidence." I grinned at myself and Terry laughed. "I told my husband, actually. He was concerned, but mostly because the experience had affected *me* so much; for such a romantic soul he's the least credulous person I've ever known. *He* isn't going to pass it around."

Terry looked dubious; Professor Franklin's image among the students was not that of a romantic soul. But he nodded slowly.

"How much time do you think we've got, incidentally?" I asked him then. "It can't be *too* soon, because for one thing there isn't any cousin yet—the cousin you saw through the time window hasn't even been born!"

"Do you mean how long before the aliens arrive? Or before the meltdown?"

"Oh, God, the meltdown I guess. Start with that: how much time?"

Terry ran his hands through his black hair, glossy and thick, and stared raptly out the window. "Well, the two I saw were thirty years ahead of us . . . it's just an impression, but I'd say we've got on the order of, like, fifteen years till the meltdown?"

"Oh." Then I wouldn't have to start trying to persuade Matt to sell the house just yet. "You know, what's been preying on *my* mind is this: are the events of the future set—the future you

152

saw in the time window—or does knowing about them in advance give us a chance to change them?"

"You mean, preventing a meltdown from happening would be a lot neater than mopping up afterwards?" I nodded. Terry sat forward in the chair, looking eager. "This is just my impression too, but I'd say the future I saw in the time window is set, that it's the only possible one. There was just something so totally true and . . . *actual* about those two, Lee and the alien . . . I don't know. *I* can't imagine any other future now that I've seen them—a future without them in it, I mean. Doing what they were doing, when they were doing it."

"So you think there wouldn't be any point in pushing to get all the power plants in the state more carefully monitored, or anything like that?"

Terry frowned thoughtfully. "Well, I guess that would always be worth doing. But I don't think it would keep the meltdown from happening—not that particular one. Because in some funny sense it already *did* happen, and all we can do about it is just be ready."

This was asserted with confidence. Terry seemed to have grown up phenomenally in the past week. The maturity was attractive. Just to keep things familiar and stable I told him, "By the way, you're going to have to make up that exam."

"Okay. When?"

"Monday?"

"That'll be fine. And, to answer your other question, I'd say the aliens will probably arrive within ten years after the meltdown."

"They'll almost have to," I said wryly, "if the plant does blow in plus-or-minus fifteen years, and if one of them intends to help make me a present for my seventieth birthday."

It wasn't difficult to go on with my life as if nothing had happened. Very little, in fact, had happened to *me*; it was almost entirely Terry's adventure, and for a long time the chief consequence of our shared afternoon in the park was just that he and I got to be friends. Over many years of teaching I had accumulated a handful of friendships with former students, though it was a rare former student who managed to sustain his or her side of such a friendship for more than a few years after graduating.

Terry proved to be something special in this line. Not only did his work improve so much that he finished up my course with an A, but he took to coming by my office even when he was no longer my student, and we discovered common interests besides the shared adventure with the mating deer. I got quite fond of Terry. Since Matt liked him too, we had him out to the house fairly often during what remained of his student career; and later, when he came up from Georgetown for the weekend, he sometimes stayed with us.

The event that had sparked our friendship in the first place was rarely referred to by any of us. But one beautiful spring Saturday in 1993 or 1994, when Terry was up visiting, he and I went for a walk in the park and found ourselves by common consent heading along the creek and up the White Trail toward the gigantic boulder where we had sat together during the strangest hour of our lives. We had been talking about the ardors of law school and of Terry's intention to specialize in environmental law, but as we approached the big rock we fell silent. The trail was narrow, I was in the lead; I slowed in front of the rock and raised my eyebrows at him.

Terry grinned. "Let's do it for auld lang syne." He crashed through the dry undergrowth and clambered up the rock face, nimble as an undergraduate, and hunkered on top in the same place he had sat that late afternoon years earlier. "Watch where you put your hands, there's poison ivy everywhere up here."

I climbed up more slowly and lowered myself beside him. For a few minutes we said nothing. I was trying to decide how I felt. Uneasy? Skeptical? Surrendered for the moment to the truth that was stranger than fiction? Suddenly, to my surprise, Terry reached over and took my hand. I looked sideways at him. He was gazing at me gravely. "Do you still believe it?" he said. "Tell me the truth: do you still think the power plant's going to blow and the aliens are coming?"

Do you still believe in *me*, I knew he meant, and I'm afraid I involuntarily glanced away from this intentness. "Well, I don't dwell on it, and I don't *want* to believe it, but most of the time I do, God help me." I added gently, "How about you?"

Terry faced forward again, but he kept hold of my hand. His voice shook a little as he said, "I believe it more than ever. I'm *sure*."

"Has something happened?" My grip tightened, and I realized again—with a fierce pang, and a desperate look around at the wooded slope—how much I didn't want his vision of the future to be true.

He shook his head. "No. But with every year that passes—every month, every week!—I feel more certain about it. Let me put it this way: I feel more certain every year that what happened to me, what I saw here, was real. And I'm ready now more than ever to plan my own future around that future, the one I'm positive is coming."

I found nothing to say to this, and soon after we climbed down and reentered the walk and the conversation interrupted by this side trip into the past.

The year he graduated from Georgetown Law, Terry married one of his classmates and moved back to Philadelphia. He and Anne found jobs without much trouble—both had finished well up in their class—and before long they bought a small house in Haverford, near the college, and gave up their apartment in Center City. By a pleasant coincidence, my favorite cousin Mark and his family lived only a block and a half away. We saw a good deal of Terry and Anne because of this, and because—despite a gap in their ages of ten or fifteen years—the two Main Line couples got along well and got together often.

Their friendship was strengthened when first Anne and then Mark's wife Phoebe became pregnant within a few months of one another. "This one's a boy, Feeb, I feel it in my bones," I told her the evening she called with the news.

"Then I hope your bones know their business," Phoebe replied. "We'd like a boy, and the girls would like a brother, and this is the last one. Three's enough."

Phoebe was a wonderful mother but I thought myself that three was at least one too many. All the same I was pleased at the news—pleased, and something more. "What will you call him?" I asked her, and held my breath.

"Mark William," she replied promptly. "We've been saving it for six years."

Mark William? Not Lee? I tried to think if either she or Mark had mentioned this name to me when Margy or Brett was born. If they had I didn't remember. Six years, she had said. Brett was six.

Disappointment on Terry's account left me momentarily at a

loss; but I pulled my wits together and said "What're you planning to call him, Mark Twain?"

"Ha ha," said Phoebe drily. "One Mark in this family is enough, thanks all the same. No, if it's a boy we'll call him Liam."

"Liam?"

"Mm-hm. My grandfather in Ireland was called Liam, it's the last four letters of 'William.' Don't you like it?"

I stammered that I liked it fine, I just hadn't been expecting it and had never known anybody named Liam before, and hung up the phone. I stared at it for several minutes, then picked the receiver up again and punched in Terry's number.

He answered on the third ring, sounding happy to hear my voice. "I was going to call *you*, tonight or tomorrow, to tell you I've made up my mind to run for the state legislature."

"Good for you!" But I had to force myself to sound delighted. First Phoebe, now Terry; things seemed to be beginning to move, queasily enough from my point of view, in the direction of a goal I would have preferred not to think about. I knew Terry had been active in local politics, but . . . "But won't it be hard, getting a campaign off the ground while Anne's pregnant, and while the baby's still so small?"

"Well, it won't be *easy*, but it feels like now's the time. Anyway, there's not all that much to do till Labor Day, if I get through the primary. Anne's all for it. I'll have to run as a Republican to get elected from this district, of course. Just as well you guys aren't able to vote over there."

I laughed. "A Republican environmentalist?"

Terry laughed too, though I heard a note of sharpness cut through the levity. "The country can't afford to keep environmental issues within party lines anymore. Anyway, there's precedent—remember Curt Weldon?"

I did. I remembered George Bush too, and other GOP noteworthies who had appropriated the name without playing the game; but I decided I had rained enough on his parade. "We can help you with the campaign, can't we, even if we're in the wrong district to vote for you? That's assuming there's anything we could do to be useful."

"Any number of things, you'll be sorry you offered." He sounded excited and happy again, the cloud dispersed.

"Well, let us know when you need us. We'll both pitch in."

"Thanks, I appreciate it. By the way, what were *you* calling about? I never gave you a chance to say."

I took a deep breath. "To tell you I just had a call from Phoebe. Have you heard their news yet?"

"I don't think so. What's up?"

"*She's* pregnant. Due in August."

There was silence on the line. When Terry spoke again his voice shook. "I wondered . . . you know, I've been wondering ever since we met them whether they might not be the ones, rather than those other cousins of yours in Cincinnati and Louisville, even though it looked like Mark and Phoebe weren't going to have any more kids. I mean, they were right *here*. God. It's starting to happen, then, isn't it? Starting to come true."

Reluctantly I said, "There's more, actually. I asked Phoebe what they meant to name the baby if it's a boy . . . you get three guesses."

Another silence. Sounding scared to death of what he might hear, Terry asked faintly, "What was it—what did she say?"

"She said Mark William."

There was a pause. "Mark William? But—"

"To be called Liam."

"Liam?"

"From the last four letters of William. After Phoebe's grandfather in Ireland."

"Liam?" he repeated incredulously, exactly as I had: the shock of hope restored following hard upon the shock of disappointment. "Liam," he marveled, "so that was it. Not Lee, but *Liam*! I must have heard it wrong. Back then I didn't even know there *was* any such name! I guess I thought—I must have just *assumed*—"

Then his voice broke, and I realized belatedly what this news, which virtually confirmed the truth of his bizarre experience, must mean to Terry. Made insensitive by my own anxieties and regrets, I saw only now that despite what he had said with such conviction that morning on the rocky outcrop in the park, Terry must have been living every day for years with a fundamental uncertainty about himself. Now he could stop wondering, stop running on pure faith. I listened to him trying to control his voice and felt contrite and sorry.

"Well, anyway," he finally said, "I guess it would be prudent

157

to wait and see if the baby's a boy before I get too carried away here. Not that I doubt it will be, but other people might."

Other people? There was a question I'd often wondered about. "Terry, I probably shouldn't ask you this, it's none of my business, but have you ever told Anne?"

"Oh, I told her, all right, before we were married. We don't discuss it, but she knows that's part of why I want to go to Harrisburg. When she hears Phoebe's pregnant . . ."

"Would you mind waiting and letting Phoebe tell her herself? I didn't ask if I could spread the word. I suppose I shouldn't have told you either, properly speaking, only I made a judgment about that, I thought you needed to know more than she needed to keep it to herself. But it ought to stop there."

If Anne had remained skeptical—and who could blame her?—that would have increased Terry's insecurity. It seemed to me that if the baby Phoebe was carrying should turn out to be a girl, it might be necessary to take special care of Terry for a while. For my part, I thought and felt that I did still believe him—and yet that extra 2 percent of doubt persisted, even in me.

Amniocentesis failed to settle any questions. Phoebe and Mark declined to be informed of the child's sex.

Fairly soon the pregnancy was general knowledge. I don't know how Anne reacted to this evidence that her husband's strange story was true; Terry didn't confide in me and I observed no signs of strain between the two of them, not then.

Their son Jeff was born the following March—Terry stopped collecting signatures on the petition to put his name on the primary ballot in order to rush Anne to the hospital—and on August 25 of that year I was at the same hospital myself, to be one of the first to meet Mark William O'Hara, eight pounds eleven and a half ounces, black hair, blue eyes, nineteen inches long. They let me hold him. I looked into those blue eyes, when they opened briefly, with the strangest possible feeling. I was forty-eight years old, and the infant in my arms was my expectation of living to be seventy at least. Twenty-two more years, guaranteed. Not even Terry had that assurance.

As for Terry, he stood rapt before the hospital nursery window, tears streaming down his cheeks. "Watch them try to stop me now," he said. "Look out, Harrisburg." Labor Day, by tradition the day candidates for the legislature kicked off their campaigns, was only a week away.

They didn't stop him. Terry was good looking, articulate, and sincere, the voters appreciated his handsome wife and adorable six-month-old baby, and he had his party's support. He won easily, despite a somewhat controversial stand on the AIDS riots that were rocking the country that winter. A lot of people who wouldn't break windows themselves were in sympathy with the sentiments of those who did; but against the advice of his party leaders Terry came out for law, order, and compassion—out-Democrating the Democratic candidate on compassion, in fact, and nearly out-Greening the Green—and they elected him anyway.

When Anne went back to work six months after Jeff's birth they tried a daytime sitter at home for a while, then a live-in nanny, but eventually the perfect solution to the child-care problem presented itself in the person of Phoebe, who was staying home anyway with her own baby and who had loved Jeff from the day he was born. Anne or Terry would drop him off at Phoebe and Mark's on their way to work and pick him up on their way home. Jeff was happy as a little lark at Phoebe's house. My two nieces, ages seven and ten, carried the babies around interchangeably, and the babies themselves played beautifully together from earliest infancy, gurgling and patting at each other in a way that sent the grownups into fond hysterics. All in all the arrangement suited everyone concerned. Anne and Terry, who had begun to think about moving into a larger house, gave the idea up; they didn't intend to have more children, and the surrogate sibling situation was so obviously wonderful for Jeff that they agreed it would be crazy to give up their convenient nearness to Mark and Phoebe in exchange for a little more room.

Terry did well as a state representative, and in 2002, the year the boys turned four, he made a successful run for the United States Congress. (This time we were able not only to work for Terry but to cross over and vote for him.) A bachelor pad in Georgetown was found and fitted out, and he took a leave of absence from his law firm and began a life of shuttling back and forth between Washington and Philadelphia. Usually he was able to be home on weekends, but he was very busy. Anne took to spending many of her evenings with Phoebe and Mark.

We saw a lot of them all while the boys were little. Jeff Carpenter was probably the only four-year-old scion of yuppies in the whole city who didn't go to nursery school—almost certainly the only U.S. congressman's child who didn't. They thought about it, but the attractions of leaving him with Phoebe were just too great. "Sesame Street" taught both boys to read; for the rest, they had the sort of old-fashioned unregimented early childhood I myself had enjoyed.

Matt and I were busy too. A dozen years earlier the English Department had taken leave of its senses, and of old-fashioned literary values, and had madly hired a stable of high-profile critical theorists, leaving us low-profile types to scrub the sinks and mind the shop. Classes kept getting larger and larger; the undergraduate student-teacher ratio was a scandal. Classes were large because so few were offered, and this was because the superstars constantly went on leave (and because the leave-replacement money from the dean never seemed to be spent on leave replacements). We were grading more papers and keeping more office hours and attending more committee meetings than ever before. We also complained a lot and talked of early retirement. Professionally it was not a happy time.

Evenings and weekends in Haverford were our chief recreation during those years, that and the park. A knee injury had forced me to trade in my running shoes and exercise bike, but I still managed to get to the park one afternoon or so a week; and starting with the summer that the Lyme-disease-carrying deer ticks had been bioengineered into harmlessness, when Jeff and Liam were four and almost four, I began to take them with me occasionally. En route we would stop off at the recycling center so the kids could pitch all our collections of glass containers—clear, green, brown—one by one into the gigantic dumpsters. They purely loved being allowed—even encouraged!—to smash all that glass, and would go through box after box of jars and bottles, squealing with delight, while I deposited the less gratifying metal, paper, and plastic trash where it belonged. We would then make one more stop, at the doughnut shop, before winding up at the park.

In my mental pictures of these park expeditions—formed before Liam had been born or even conceived—I had always visualized myself walking along the creek and up the White Trail with *one* little boy in tow. But now it seemed as natural to bring Jeff along with us as it had seemed natural to Anne and Terry not to take Jeff away from Liam by moving or by sending him to nursery school. Seeing those two together made all discussion vain. They were bonded phenomenally. I hadn't known many small children, knew little about the sorts of relationships they developed, but even to me it seemed that what we had here was something special. Certainly I remembered no such friendship from my own early childhood. You wanted instinctively to get out of the way of this one, to respect and support it, somehow recognizing that even in marriage life would seldom again grant such a boon.

Liam O'Hara at four and five and six was an adorable child with a round face and dark bangs, small and graceful and beautifully formed. I realized from the time he could talk that part of his special attractiveness to me was his oddness: he was given to locutions and observations so peculiar that we were always telling one another we ought to write them down. Nobody ever did, but this example—one of the few I can remember now—ought to convey the flavor:

On the Fourth of July just before Liam turned six, Matt and I had slathered all four kids in sun block and taken them to a parade in Center City. We arrived early and sat on the curb in a line, watching the floats and police bands go by and passing an enormous container of popcorn back and forth among the six of us.

Liam had broken his arm only the week before; the arm was in a cast, which he had not yet really gotten used to. But it was a beautiful day and everybody seemed to be having a good time.

After an hour or so Liam turned to me and announced solemnly, "I like my cast better than this parade."

Jeff had a sunnier disposition and was generally less of a "character" than Liam. Already, at six, his singing voice was strong and pure. There was talk of sending him to a choir school when he was older, he was that good, and when Terry went to Washington in 2002 he and Anne talked very seriously of moving the family down in three or four years, assuming Terry kept his seat, so that Jeff could sing in the Washington Cathedral Choir and go to St. Albans School. Anne would have had no problem finding a job down there; but when the moment of decision came it was crisis time for a while in that household, because it brought into focus for the first time a fundamental disagreement in point of view. Anne wanted Jeff to have his chance at being a Cathedral choirboy, even at the cost to herself of leaving a law firm where she was doing extraordinarily well.

Terry wanted Jeff to stay in Haverford and go to the Germantown Friends School with Liam, even more than he wanted to have the whole family together in Washington.

Knowing that Terry's parents had been divorced, and that he had missed his father dreadfully as a child, I found this preference surprising. What surprised me even more was the realization that he wanted not to separate the boys even at the cost of keeping Jeff in southeastern Pennsylvania, convinced though he was that the day of the meltdown could not be far away.

Perhaps, I thought, Terry believed that Jeff would be safe as long as he was with Liam.

Anne argued, at first with good humor and then with increasing anger, that Liam and Jeff could visit each other on alternate weekends and that it would do them both good to spend more time with other kids, but Terry would not see reason. The issue brought buried resentments to the surface; fond as Anne was of Phoebe, it now emerged that she resented the strength of Jeff's attachment to his long-time nanny, and of Terry's attachment to Phoebe's own boy as well. She felt left out of things, short-changed emotionally, and there was some basis to these feelings. No one meant to exclude her—or to exclude Mark, who was in somewhat the same position—but the plain truth was that Phoebe and Terry were more involved with both boys than was either of their spouses.

Most of this Terry told me several years after the fact. At the time I was aware of a coolness and shortness between him and Anne but had only a general idea of what the trouble was about.

They had temporized by arranging for Jeff to take voice lessons and to audition for the Philadelphia Boys' Choir.

One Saturday in October, a day when Jeff had a lesson and then a rehearsal—he had just started singing with the choir—I picked Liam up and took him to the park for a walk, just the two of us. Liam was then seven years old, small for his age, still graceful, still attractive (though his early beauty had been somewhat marred, at least temporarily, when his permanent front teeth came in), still grave and strange. Now that he and Jeff were older we did sometimes take Liam out by himself; and though Matt and I (as might be expected of a childless couple) were entranced with him, he didn't take advantage of this, for he was very fond of us both. These outings revealed a love of order and ritual in Liam that bordered on the obsessive, and I enjoyed

162

indulging it, knowing how difficult it would be for anyone to satisfy a craving for order in the relaxed, chaotic household run by Phoebe.

Accordingly we always took exactly the same walk, the very walk Terry and I had taken on that Halloween afternoon so many years before: from the parking lot along the road by the creek to the foot of the White Trail, and up the trail to the place Liam called the Ragged Rock. (The first time I heard him do this and asked why, he had grinned and quoted, "Round and round the ragged rock the rugged rascal ran." "*Rugged* rock," I had protested, "ragged *rascal*!" But the Rock thenceforth remained Ragged.) We would climb up, avoiding the poison ivy, and sit where Terry and I had sat, dangling our feet while Liam broke out the tea and doughnuts we always stopped to pick up on the way. (His choices never varied: one rainbow doughnut, one of some other kind.) After a while he would cap the thermos— always the same thermos, a huge old one with a glass liner— and reshoulder the backpack, and we would return to the car by way of the Blue Trail and the Red Trail, stopping to climb a particularly excellent climbing tree en route. I could still climb a tree quite creditably, though it made me puff, but Liam was sure-handed and -footed as a little monkey.

If we timed things right and ended the walk at dusk, we would often hear or see deer bounding through the trees, their tails' white undersides raised toward us in alarm. I had told both boys already, many times, of the day I had been sitting on this very rock and seen the mating deer: how the buck chased the doe up the slope and caught her just below me, both too intent on their own business to notice or be frightened. What I'd never mentioned was that Jeff's father had been with me that day.

On this afternoon I accepted my own doughnut and cup of tea from Liam and we munched in companionable silence for a time, enjoying the mild weather and our freedom from the sticky sun block that the damaged ozone layer made necessary in summer. "Are you and Jeff going out trick-or-treating?" I asked him finally.

"Probably," said Liam. "He has a rehearsal but he should get out in time."

"What are you going to be?"

"A spaceman. We're both going to be spacemen. We're making the costumes ourselves. Well, Mom's helping. But we're

163

doing most of it. I figured out how to do the helmets and Jeff figured out how to do the air tanks.''

A spaceman. I managed to say in an ordinary voice, ''An astronaut, you mean?''

''Nope. A man *from* outer space, an alien! We're both going to be the same kind of alien.''

''What kind would that be?''

''I'll show you when we get home. They come from a planet that has very strong gravity, so they feel like they don't weigh very much here on Earth. They have these great big feet, and real small faces, and no hair. They're *hideous*,'' he declared with satisfaction and took a big chomp of doughnut. ''But they're very nice,'' he added.

Watching the way he held the doughnut, I thought—not for the first time—that I had never seen a hand more beautifully attached to a wrist in my life. ''Sounds like a lot of work to go to, if you guys aren't even sure you're going out,'' I told him tenderly.

''It doesn't really matter,'' said Liam in a calm voice. ''We're having a Halloween party at school anyway and we need costumes for that. I'll show you when we get home, remind me.''

''Tell me, how does Jeff like singing in the choir?''

''He loves it, he loves that stuff they sing.'' He became still, and a minute went by before he added, ''I don't really like that kind of music too much, but I wish I could be with Jeff in the choir. Do you think I'd *learn* to like that music better, if I could sing it?''

He looked up at me then with such open sadness that my heart turned over. ''Sweetie, do you remember when you were five years old, and one time you were watching 'Sesame Street' at our house and they started singing 'Rockabye Baby'? You were playing on the floor, drawing a picture I think, happy as could be, but the minute you heard that song you burst into tears and ran and climbed into my lap, and you said over and over that the song made you *sad*. Remember that?''

''Unh-unh, I don't remember a thing about it! 'Rockabye *Baby*'?'' He laughed, tickled at the picture of this babyish self.

''Mm-hm. I've always thought, ever since that happened, that you were probably very sensitive to music, a very musical kid. Maybe you should try out a few instruments and see if there's one you'd like to learn to play. Singing's not the only way.''

"Yeah, that's a good idea. Hey, thanks, Carrie. I'll ask Mom about it tonight. And maybe Jeff would have a suggestion of an instrument—like, if I played the piano, I could play for him when he sings!" He grinned, plainly delighted at this prospect.

It hurt me to think of Liam struggling to make his ordinary musical tastes conform to Jeff's elevated ones. "What does Jeff think about going to St. Albans and singing in the Washington Cathedral Choir?" I asked, and could have bitten my tongue out at my tactlessness.

But Liam only frowned as he went on cramming paper cups and napkins into the bag. "He might like to go to a school like that, if there was one up here, but he doesn't want to move to Washington. He says he won't go even if they try to make him. His mom's real mad at his dad because his dad wants him to stay in Philadelphia, but even if his mom wins, Jeff says he won't go. He'll come and live with us. He says, anyway, if they try to make him go, he'll refuse to sing, so then there wouldn't be any point. He just wishes they'd stop fighting about it."

That was how I found out there was trouble between Terry and Anne. It wasn't clear whether either of them had asked Jeff what *he* wanted to do.

The conflict had not been resolved when, only five months later, the Hefn ship appeared in the solar system.

Terry was in Washington when the ship was sighted and the media broke the news. I had tried repeatedly to reach him by phone but had not yet succeeded when he turned up at my front door less than three hours after I'd heard on the radio of the ship's approach. He had driven straight to us from Washington. That he'd managed to get there in one piece was a wonder; I'd thought *I* was in a state, but Terry looked as if he could barely hold himself together. Giving thanks that I was home that day instead of at the university, I poured him a drink and settled him on the sofa in the living room—the same end of the same sofa, in fact, where he'd sat, a student in my American poetry course, and read with increasing confusion and distress the strangest exam I had ever encountered in my life. More than fifteen years ago.

"I *know* they're not supposed to get here before the power plant blows! What do you think, Carrie? Does it mean one of the plants is due for a meltdown any minute? Which one? Peach

165

Bottom? Limerick? Three Mile Island again? It's got to be one of them, don't you think? Not one of the new ones.'' He gulped down a mouthful of bourbon and grimaced. "I've had an evacuation plan ready to put into action for years, ever since I ran for the state legislature. I get it out nights, in my apartment down there, and update it and make little refinements; it's practically been my hobby, evacuating southeastern Pennsylvania! But all this time I expected the Hefn to help.''

I watched him in a daze. Even when Liam was born, I realized again, I had secretly withheld some last shred of conviction from Terry's glimpse of the future. Now it no longer seemed possible to doubt that this future had turned into the present and was rapidly becoming true. While Terry fretted over details, I sat overwhelmed. "We always meant to sell this place and move to Kutztown,'' I said, trying to take it in. "But somehow it never seemed . . . and the commute . . . and Matt didn't really . . .''

"*You* didn't ever really believe me either, did you?'' Terry said, more in sorrow than in bitterness. He drained his glass and plunked it down on the coffee table. "I came here, instead of going home, because I thought you were the one person in the world who did. I knew Matt didn't, and as for Anne—'' He broke off. "But none of that matters now. What matters is getting all of you out of here while there's still time and sounding the alert so the plan gets put into action the second the plant goes out. The Governor's got a copy, but there are other people who need to know where to put their hands on it right away.''

"Terry, believe me, I *wanted* to believe you,'' I said desperately. "And I'm positive Anne would have given anything to believe it, but maybe this is just one of those things that you *can't* believe unless it happened to *you*.''

He gave me a sharp look. "Did you and Anne ever discuss it?''

"No, never.'' Anne was a rather reserved person and not particularly fond of me, and I had never felt comfortable broaching the subject myself. "You know, right after that day in the park I think I was really convinced. But as time went by it all seemed so improbable! Though when Liam was born . . . but I must have had a fair degree of certainty about it, all the same, because Liam and Jeff have both heard the story of the mating deer just about every time I've taken them over there.''

It meant that the motive for making the birthday film had been

set in place. Terry's face relaxed. "That's something, I agree."
He leaned across and hugged me. "I'm sorry. It's been a long,
lonely wait, and I'm confused by having the ship turn up before
the meltdown." He flopped back onto his end of the sofa. "Want
to know something? Every time I see that little Liam he looks a
little bit more like the guy in the radiation suit. Till I started
losing my hair I used to wonder why *he*—the twenty-two-year-
old Liam—hadn't recognized *me* through the time window. I
mean, he'd known me all his life! Which of course is something
I couldn't have imagined back then . . . but I guess I don't look
much like a college kid anymore."

He didn't and it wasn't only that the beautiful thick black hair
was mostly gone. Without responding to that remark I said,
"You know what else it means? Unless he was acting very, very
well."

"That I won't have told him. Yeah, I thought of that. By the
time he lives that scene himself he'll be older than I was that
day, and I'll be an old crock with a scalp you can see your face
in." Terry shook his head. "What a thought."

"I'd like to collect our families and get out of here, till whatever happens happens," I told him, returning to the matter at
hand, "but how are we going to do that? How can Matt and I
cancel classes—on what pretext? Would Anne drop everything
at work and take Jeff out of school? I doubt Mark would let Liam
miss school . . . I don't see how we can do it, not straightfor-
wardly like that."

"I've thought about this, about a thousand times. I was going
to give you this anyway the next time I saw you." He took an
envelope out of his inside jacket pocket and laid it on the coffee
table. "This is the evacuation plan for us—you and Matt, Anne
and Jeff, Mark, Phoebe, and Liam. There's a copy for everybody. Memorize it. And pack some clothes. When the time
comes, head for our cabin in the Poconos. Unless it's Limerick;
in that case head for my place in Georgetown." He fished in his
pants pocket while he spoke and unclipped two keys from a
ring. "These are for the cabin and the apartment. I had a set
made for Mark and Phoebe, too; I better get over there right
now."

"Supplies?"

"Stocked like a bomb shelter, both of them, years ago. The

167

whole cellar of the cabin's crammed with canned goods and bottled water.''

A thought struck me. "Won't you be coming with us?"

Terry shook his head. "I'll have to get to Harrisburg, to mastermind the evacuation. Don't worry, I'll be okay." He got up to go.

I got up too. "Then I'll gas up the cars, and buy some fresh produce, and wait for a signal. And Terry—" He looked back, already barging through the door. "I'm sorry. I really am."

But there was no signal. I filled both cars' fuel tanks with methanol and their trunks with apples, potatoes, and root vegetables (good keepers all), and with sacks of flour and an assortment of grains, and packed suitcases for Matt and me. I memorized Terry's evacuation plans and made Matt memorize them too. For days I kept the radio on all the time. But the aliens parked their ship on the moon and brought their lander down to JFK, and still there had been no nuclear disaster.

April 2006

"I tried St. James' Court: no good. I tried Whitehall—I only had a couple of strings to pull there but I pulled all of them. No good *what*soever. Then I went up to Yorkshire and waved my identification around, and tried to explain to the UN people doing the Secret Service thing that I was a United States congressman with some important information for the Hefn. No good, in spades. Nobody believed me, they'd been arguing with flakes all week. As a desperate last resort I went to a newspaper office in York and said I was ready to tell *them* my story, in hopes that they'd publish it and word would filter through to the Hefn somehow. *They'd* been turning flakes away all week too; they were pretty rude."

Terry knocked back the rest of his drink, stood the glass on the floor, and stretched his arms above his head. He had come by taxi from the airport straight to Matt and me, and was rumpled and bleary-eyed with exhaustion, but his face glowed.

He certainly had his audience in the palm of his hand. I doubt that my eyes had left his face since the little flurry of his arrival at the door. "So what did you do then? Tried to waylay them in Sweden, I'll be bound."

Terry grinned happily at me from "his" end of the sofa. He bent over to untie his shoes, then stretched out his legs and crossed his feet, in their black socks, on the coffee table, a gesture that asserted his role as child of the house. "Tried to is right. Every last plane was booked solid. All the other nuts had been there ahead of me." He laughed, the secret joy breaking out once more at the memory. "God, was I frantic! Here I was, the one person on the planet who could tell the Hefn anything useful, absolutely unable to get their attention, however I jumped up and down and waved my arms and screamed! At least I thought *then* I was the only one."

"Where were you when the news broke about the body in the bog?" Matt roused himself to say. Ever since the sighting of that alien ship Matt had been uncharacteristically quiet. He had never believed a word of Terry's story, and now, a fair-minded man, he was abashed.

"On the train from York back to London. There was an announcement on the intercom that a Yorkshire farmer and an American woman had found a little alien corpse in a peat bog. I tell you, there was pandemonium on that train. Half the people aboard were Yorkshiremen."

I observed that some of them must have been Yorkshire-women, but Terry was too tired and too exhilarated to find this critique of his terminology very relevant and waved it aside. "Whatever! They'll never change over there, they all still think of men and women as two separate species. I'm not responsible for *them*!"

" 'For he *is* a York-shire-person!' " Matt sang, making me laugh. "Okay, okay, let it go. What happened then?"

"Well, I didn't think we'd ever get to London, but finally we did, and I barreled out of the station in search of the nearest pub. When I found one it turned out to be crammed with a lot of other people who'd had the same idea, but they had the sound turned way up on the viewscreen and they kept breaking into the regular programming with special announcements. The body had been taken by police helicopter from the grounds of the Early Warning System, up there on the moors, to Leeds, and then flown on to London, and the Hefn delegation was on its way to Heathrow from Stockholm right that minute. I roared back to my hotel in time to hear that they'd landed, and then a

169

little bit later they had positively identified the body as one of their crew. After 350 years, they actually knew which one!''

He glanced from me to Matt and back to me and grinned the joyous grin. ''Carrie, God, I can't begin to tell you how I felt when I heard that. I don't really know why, either, I still wasn't any closer to solving my own mystery at that point, but I felt so *glad* about it! Glad for them, maybe, who knows.''

''Maybe you're just one hell of a nice guy,'' I said, and patted him on the knee.

He put his own hand over mine and squeezed it. ''And guess what? It turned out that the American woman who'd found the body comes from around here. One of my own constituents!'' He laughed, delighted with the coincidence. ''So naturally I thought Aha, *here's* my chance to connect with the Hefn after all—I'll get at them through her.''

He picked his glass up off the floor and filled it from the bottle on the coffee table. He set the bottle back and drank from the glass. After a minute I prompted him: ''So did it work? Did you get to talk to them?''

Terry shook his head, swallowing. ''I talked to *her*, finally, after a lot of hassle, but she couldn't do anything about getting me in to see *them*. Security was tight like you wouldn't believe. She's coming back herself in a few days—she teaches in the History Department at Penn, had you heard that? She's a colleague of *yours*. Has to finish up the semester. You guys would probably like her, she's a forthright, down-to-earth sort of character. She reminded me of some of the Quaker teachers at Jeff's school. Anyway, I told her my story.'' He drained his glass, put it down, and settled deeper into the sofa cushions, fingers laced behind his head; he looked very much at home.

Matt and I spoke together. ''How'd she take it?'' was his question; mine was ''What's her name?''

Terry answered mine. ''Her name's Jenny Shepherd. Know her, either of you?''

I shook my head. ''Only the name. Matt was on a committee with her once, though, weren't you, honey?''

''The Personnel Committee. Yeah, I was. A long time ago, though, I don't remember much about her. Her field's something like the Scandinavian influence on the north of England.''

In my keyed-up state this struck me as terribly funny. ''*Vik-*

ings? Really? Hey, she's been specializing in alien invaders right along, then, hasn't she?"

The other two smiled and nodded to humor me. "What *did* she say, Terry?" Matt asked again.

"Not too much that cleared things up from my end. She was pretty interested in my story. She turned out to be fairly familiar with the park. Oh, and she did say that one Hefn she met on the moors, back in 1994, had mentioned time windows. Speaking of which, did you know the delegation's going to use something they're calling a 'time transceiver' to try to contact the crew?"

I had seen it in that morning's *Inquirer*. "They're bringing one down from the ship and taking it to the landing sites in Sweden and England." I leaned toward him, excited by a thought. "*Liam* told you that, remember? That the window has to be set up in the exact physical location, and something about haunted houses?"

"Absolutely!" Terry started to say something else, but Matt interrupted: "Was the Hefn—the one Shepherd met—the same one whose body she found?"

"Apparently not. It was somebody else. But listen, about this time business." Terry lifted his feet off the coffee table and sat up. Still watching him closely, I knew he was now about to reveal the source of the inward joy, and by some prescient impulse felt dismayed. "I was watching a news transmission during the flight back," he told us, "and they had on some famous physicist, a Nobel Prize winner. And this guy was just ridiculing everything the Hefn said about time, the nature of time, when they announced about using the transceiver."

"Which was what? I didn't catch that."

"Well, mainly they're contradicting all the accepted thinking—that at any given moment there are an infinite number of possible futures, and things are altered by being observed. You know?"

"Sort of," I said. Matt looked dubious.

"Yeah, well, I don't either, really. But even so—see, apparently the Hefn are saying that's wrong, that there's no such thing as an infinite number of possible futures—that in some sense everything that's ever going to happen already *has* happened. This physicist was practically apoplectic, he thought this was so outrageous. He kept insisting that the Hefn are lying for some reason."

171

"Wait a minute, wait a minute," Matt said unbelievingly. "What are they trying to sell us, Calvinists in Space?"

"No, the interviewer—it was Bryant Gumbel—he asked about that and the physicist said no, that just because events are knowable in advance, if you have a means of knowing them, doesn't make them predestined to happen. He wasn't objecting on those grounds and I'm not either."

"But you are objecting?"

"I've been thinking about it all the way back," Terry said with great intentness, "and it seems to me that our physicists might be right and the Hefn must be wrong. And you know why?"

Full of foreboding I said, "I'll bite. Why?"

"Because there has to be one time line where there's a power plant meltdown just before the Hefn come and another one where there isn't."

This was met by both of us with uncomfortable silence. Finally Matt asked cautiously, "Why does there 'have' to be?"

"To explain the inconsistencies between what I saw in 1990 in the park and what's happening now! It's the only explanation that fits all the facts." Again Terry looked from me to Matt and back to me, and sighed. "Okay, tell me what's wrong with it."

My foreboding now made gloomy sense. Here we were again, Terry needing me to believe something I felt a great deal less than completely convinced of. I sat silent. Matt said, very kindly, "Don't take this wrong, old son, but what you've been saying sounds an awful lot like something out of one of Jeff's fantasy novels."

"Not fantasy, dammit, Matt! Physics!"

"Theoretical physics. Up to now, so far as *I* know, theory has been turned into fact only on the quantum level. If you were right, it would be the first life-size proof ever that *Schrödinger* was right. Not so easy to swallow just like that."

"But that's the point," said Terry, half indignant, half pleading. "Before this happened we'd never had a chance to preview the future and compare what we saw with events as they actually occurred. It *is* the first life-size proof! The future I saw *isn't the one we're having*!"

I said carefully, "Terry, the future you saw through the time window was *years* from now. Liam was all grown up, I was about to turn seventy! Mightn't there be time and opportunity

172

for 'the future we're having' to conform to what you saw, between now and then? We're talking about something like fourteen years here.''

Leaning forward stubbornly, forearms on knees, Terry shook his head. "I don't see how. There's no confusion about it. First the power plant had the meltdown. Then the Hefn came. In the future I saw, that was the order of things. It just about *had* to be a different time line. Can *you* think of a better explanation for the discrepancies?" He frowned and banged his head with his fist. "I wish I could remember that physicist's name—he's another Penn faculty member."

"Wilson's our Nobel laureate," I told him tiredly. Poor Terry. I knew exactly how Matt would be silently answering his question: *A better explanation is that you're some kind of a nut case, my lad.*

"Wilson, that's the guy. Okay, the three of us may not understand this all that well, but he does, and he's not exactly a nitwit. And the Hefn can only use the time window to look into the past, and the past *is* fixed—did you think of that? Maybe the reason they can't look into the future is, the future's *not*!"

I cleared my throat. "Didn't *you* look into the future? Isn't that what we're talking about?"

"The future from *my* perspective, in *their* past, on *that* time line! See? They can't direct the time transceivers toward their own future from their present. It only works in reverse." He rubbed his hands over his face and over his scalp, shiny in the lamplight under the sparse hair. "Anyway, it doesn't necessarily follow that because the Hefn made a device that can tap into the past, they know everything there is to know about time. People are always inventing things that work, without understanding the principles behind their own inventions."

There was a short pause. "Well," Matt said finally, "it does suggest to me that they may know more about it than Phil Wilson does." *Or than you do,* he might as well have added. Terry flushed. All the eagerness and happiness had drained out of his face, leaving it merely exhausted. When the flush faded, his skin looked gray.

My heart misgave me. Treading carefully, I reminded Terry of how he had once told me he was more certain every day that everything he'd seen through the time window was set.

He nodded. "And that's how I felt, too, for years, but everything's different now."

Plus ça change . . . I nearly said, but refrained for fear it would sound ironic or, worse, condescending. *The more things change, the more they stay the same.* The Hefn had ushered in a future Terry had not foreseen, that was the "everything" that was different. But he still needed as desperately as ever to have his own experience confirmed. Nothing had changed there. He would never have any peace until he did, and I had let him down again.

So instead I said, "We shouldn't keep you up talking, you must be tired to death. Why not sleep here tonight? You won't be putting us out any."

He shook his head, not meeting my eye. "No thanks, I guess I'd better get on home. I haven't seen Anne and Jeff for a week."

"Give us a call tomorrow then, after you've slept it off?"

"Sure." He levered himself up and went off to use the phone and the bathroom.

The minute Terry was out of the room, Matt peered at me over the top of his glasses and murmured, "Whether Phil Wilson is or is not exactly a nitwit is a highly debatable question."

"Shush. I'll debate it with you later." Why, oh, why did Terry always require reassurance exactly where I found it impossible to reassure? Feeling truly terrible, and more to fend off Matt for a little while than for any other reason, I picked up the remote and clicked on the screen; they were five minutes into the evening news.

When Terry came back into the living room a few minutes later, the expressions on both our faces stopped him cold. "What's up?" he asked, instantly apprehensive. "What happened?"

Matt stood up. "The Hefn are leaving."

It happened that June that year was very rainy. The combination of daily downpour and the now-chronic high summer heat had made a steaming jungle of the park, and the expedition was planned and called three times on account of bad weather. But eventually an afternoon arrived of spectacular blue sky and air so clear that ordinary things, leaves and stones, seemed to glitter, and that day found Jenny Shepherd and me seated side by side on the rocky outcrop where, long ago, Terry and I had seen the mating deer.

I hadn't driven out to the park with Liam and Jeff in quite a while. Swamped by end-of-semester hassles and the possibility of needing to leave home at a moment's notice, I hadn't been there at all for weeks and weeks, either alone or with Matt. It was nice to be back, especially on a day of such rare beauty—rare enough in the past, all but unknown in June during the past dozen years of the greenhouse effect; and it had given me a surprising amount of relief and comfort to bestow upon this other person, a middle-aged female academic like myself, the troublesome secret at the center of my life.

Offering Jenny the last Dunkin' Donut, I wound up my story. "So this is where it happened. The time window opened *there*. The scrape was over there, and the buck and doe were *there*, right below us. And what has Terry in a swivet now is, how could what he saw through the window be so right, and at the same time so wrong? In the future he saw, the Hefn were an established presence here on Earth and this park had been made into a wasteland by a nuclear meltdown. In actual fact, there was no meltdown and the Hefn took off again. On the other hand, he *did* actually see my little second cousin Liam, who'll be nine this August, grown up to young manhood and trying to make a film of an event that actually did take place, as a present for my seventieth birthday. And a Hefn was helping him."

"And this happened before Liam was even born?"

"Before he was even conceived. Before I had any idea that my cousin Mark and his wife would decide to have another baby, or what they would name it if they had one. As a matter of fact, before Terry had even met either of them."

"And we're the only ones who know, even though the Hefn have come and gone? Why's that?"

"He says he doesn't want it told until he finds a convincing explanation for the discrepancies." Thinking about it made me groan. "He doesn't know any more about time than I do, but he's got this idea in his head, from seeing Phil Wilson on a talk show, if you'll believe that"—Jenny rolled her eyes—"that the future he saw here was on a separate time line from the one we're living on. A separate time line, as God is my witness!"

"Does he think his being here when the time window opened

changed the future?'' asked Jenny, more comfortable than I was with Terry's idée fixe.

"I don't think that's occurred to him or he would have mentioned it, and far be it from me to suggest anything that might fan the flames! He used to believe, intuitively I think, something along the lines of what the Hefn said—that everything that's ever going to happen has, in some sense, already happened. Now he's changed his mind.''

"And you're worried about him.''

"I'm very worried about him.'' How wonderful to discuss the subject with somebody who grasped the essential point at once! "Keeping that secret bottled up for all those years was bad for him—all that self-doubt, his wife frankly disbelieving, nobody but me to look to for support, and I've been a pretty frail reed. And now, in a funny way, having it come *partly* true is almost the worst thing that could have happened.''

"I can see that it might be,'' Jenny remarked thoughtfully.

"How did he strike *you* when he approached you in London?''

Jenny chuckled. "Beside himself, actually, but under the circumstances that doesn't seem too surprising. I was pretty beside myself, myself, come to that. He struck me as right on the edge, and seemed almost pitifully grateful when he heard my story.''

"Mm. It *would* have been a huge relief to hear about somebody else being hagridden for years, like he was, by a—a maddeningly inexplicable experience.''

"That's certainly how I felt when I found Frank. You're hagridden by another thing, too: the recurring fear that you're not quite sane.''

"Have you seen him or talked to him since you got back?''

"No.''

Two male robins were hopping and fluttering in the path below the Ragged Rock, a territorial squabble. The rain had caused an extraordinarily rapid growth of vegetation, as if a green bomb had gone off, and a light wind kept continually unraveling and reweaving the patterns of sun and shadow on the forest floor. Rain had created a population explosion of mosquitoes, too, but I had had the foresight to provide our expedition with repellent. I looked about me, marveling. "Jenny, you know—it's all still here! The Hefn came and went, and the park's still here. I can't get used to it, though before they arrived I couldn't bring myself to believe anything would ever happen to the place either.''

"It's a miracle all this open space wasn't swallowed up by condo developments years ago,'' said Jenny, also looking about admiringly. "I wish I'd gotten out here more often in recent years. I used to come out all the time; I remember I used to see an albino deer . . . that was back before the Lyme disease epidemic. When that got bad I stopped coming, and then I guess I just never re-formed the habit. I spent nearly all my summers in England anyway, sleuthing after Elphi.'' We had already discussed Elphi. I'd seen a PBS documentary about the hobs, in which Jenny and Frank had appeared, just the evening before.

"Not much point in re-forming the habit now, I guess.'' Jenny had explained that she was moving to England in a month to marry the Yorkshire farmer. "But you're right. Delaware County was pretty open when I first started teaching at Penn, lots of open space and no more traffic on these old roads than they could handle. There were even some farms in the western part. Now I don't suppose there's a building lot left in the county.''

"Wasn't there any effort to control development? I know for a fact that that kind of mess just couldn't happen in Sweden.''

"A few voices crying in the wilderness, but money kept changing hands, and all the decisions were made at the local level—no attempt at growth management *at* all till things were already ruined.'' I waved my arm, an inclusive gesture. "This all used to be a private estate. It would have been ruined right along with the rest of the county if the whole 2500 acres hadn't been given to the state as parkland, back in the sixties or whenever it was. A very lucky break for us, and we never forgot it. The quality's declined some, acid rain has killed off a lot of the conifers and a lot more people use the place than when we first moved out here, but it's still a pretty phenomenal resource.''

"Here's a funny thought,'' Jenny said. "If this estate hadn't been set aside for parkland, where would Terry have had his vision of the future?''

"That's right! No park, no deer; no deer, no birthday movie; and so on.'' This woman's shrewdness was as confidence-inspiring as her sympathy. "You know,'' I found myself telling her impulsively, "I never seem able either to believe in Terry completely *or* disbelieve him. It was true before the Hefn came and, God help me, it's still true.''

177

Jenny said nothing for a minute, long enough for me to wonder if I'd made a mistake. Then she gave me a searching look. "I think I'd better tell you something Frank and I kept out of our public report. Are you willing to be burdened with one more secret?"

"Why not?" I said, relieved and also curious. "No, wait— don't tell me anything I'd have to keep from Terry. I couldn't do that at this stage of things. Especially if it's something that would help him feel any better, or clearer."

"Terry can know, I'd thought about telling him myself. And I guess you can tell your husband; but nobody else, okay?"

"Okay."

"Okay then. Here it is: the Hefn aren't the only aliens aboard that ship. They're not even in command. The commanders are a different species of alien called the Gafr, and *they* decide what's what, then they send the Hefn around to do their dirty work for them. Elphi and his chums were rebelling against the Gafr, not against the other Hefn."

Startling as it was, this news left me at a loss. I wondered whether Jenny had told it as a means of changing the subject, for it seemed to have no bearing on my problem. Purely to be courteous I asked, "Why didn't they show themselves, then? Why stay hidden?"

"Not sure. Maybe they're too refined for contact with humans, maybe they're too hideous, or too unimpressive looking, I don't know. We didn't ask. The point is, though, they're the ones in charge."

I said uncertainly, "Well . . . that's a whole new angle, but—"

"The Hefn delegation told us, in the only private meeting we had with them, that some of the Gafr wanted to stay and save the world for us, but the ones in command of the ship weren't interested in that."

"So they left." I still didn't get it. "But in Terry's version of the future, they stayed."

Jenny pulled up her legs, in their brown twill pants from England, and clasped her arms around her knees. "Isn't there another possibility? What if they took off, and then developed more engine trouble or something, and turned the ship around and came back?"

I sat in the car in front of the Germantown Friends School, re-reading a letter from Jenny Shepherd, now Jenny Flintoft (imagine using your husband's name! but that was England). She didn't write often, we had known each other too briefly to become close friends, and the farm work—which Jenny apparently thrived on—seemed to absorb nearly all of her time and energy. But neither of us wanted to let the connection drop, either, so every so often a piece of e-mail would cross the Atlantic.

Regular classes at Germantown Friends had been over at three, but on Tuesdays and Thursdays the fifth through eighth graders had a meditation class from three o'clock to four. Twice a week the school brought in a psychoneuroimmunologist from the Hospital of the University of Pennsylvania, who was training the students in meditation techniques for the purpose of building up their immune systems. This was to help protect them from the many chemical carcinogens they ate and breathed and otherwise came in contact with every day. It was even hoped that meditating would provide the kids with some resistance to skin cancer caused by ultraviolet radiation.

The public schools were watching this with interest and were talking about starting a program of their own, but so far the Quaker schools were the only ones to have actually added meditation to the official curriculum. It was just the sort of thing they *would* do: a little countercultural, flaky in a nice, or at any rate harmless, way.

It was still far too early to tell whether children who meditated regularly were less likely to get cancer than those who didn't. I suspected that the experiment might never produce clear results, since carrying it out scientifically was impossible. But I thought it couldn't hurt, which is what most of the parents thought. Understandably enough the kids themselves, for the most part, were pretty unenthusiastic.

I had spread Jenny's letter flat across the steering wheel. She wrote:

We saw Terry last month, as I'm sure he told you, when he was up here with a group of MPs and the Minister of Defence to officially close the Early Warning System on Flyingdales Moor. A great day for us. We're hoping they take down the radomes after they've been switched off or whatever's done to deactivate the beastly things. They've been a blot on the landscape for as long as I've been coming up here—three enormous golf balls, right in the wildest part of the moor! The North York Moors National Park is still holding its own against developers, by the way; hope the same can be said of Ridley Creek State Park.

Frank and I both thought Terry looked tired. I suppose politicians, the conscientious ones, work awfully hard. If you ask me, though, this politician badly needs a break. You can tell him I said so.

We've been lambing for a fortnight and are bottle-feeding eight little fellows—five orphans, and three others who had the bad luck to be odd lamb out of triplets. The mothers can feed only two. We did manage to get several ewes that had lost their own lambs to accept an orphan by skinning the dead lamb and dressing the live one up in the skin, like a little wooly jacket, but we haven't enough bereaved mothers to go round! So we, and the two hired men, are on bottle duty round the clock.

You must be wondering how it happens that I'm writing this during one of our busiest times of the year. The fact is, you've been on my mind a good bit just lately. I've got something to tell you. Not in a letter, though, or on the phone. I thought of sending a message through Terry—seeing him is what put me onto this line of thought, actually—but he looked so done in that I couldn't make up my mind to broach the subject. So. . . .

I wonder whether you and Matt mightn't enjoy a farm holiday this summer. Yorkshire makes quite a change from Delaware County. Do think about it; I'm sure you'd like this country and *quite* sure you would be very interested indeed in what I have to tell you.

Frank has been—

The doors of the shabby old building suddenly erupted with children. I folded up the letter, tossed it into the glove compartment, and got out to stand beside the car.

Jeff and Liam burst through the doorway in the middle of the pack. They spotted me at once and raced each other toward the car, open jackets flapping in the chilly April air. Jeff was then

180

half a head taller, a slim boy with wavy dark hair; he had turned twelve the previous month. Jeff had grown up handsome; Liam, who had been beautiful as a small child, was much less so at eleven and a half, though he had kept all his grace of movement. He won the race by a stride and bashed into the front fender, catching himself by his hands. "Wow, what a car! Look at that, Jeff, Carrie's got a brand new solar car! What is it, a Saab? How fast does it go?"

Jeff was less excited; cars didn't interest him so much, and anyway, his mother drove a solar car. "How *far* does it go without recharging, Carrie? What kind of a backup power system have you guys got?"

But Liam was knocked out. "Look at these photowhaddya-callums, all over the hood! Hey, your mom's car only has 'em on the roof!"

"Photovoltaic cells," Jeff told him before I could.

I let them exclaim over the car for a while, supplying information on request both to Jeff and Liam and to the crowd of other kids the car had attracted. Solar cars were still a novelty then, more because of their relative inconvenience than their price—our model could go only about eighty miles before the batteries had to be charged up again—but increasingly they were being called the car of the future. Methanol-burning engines had cleaned up the air in the cities, but they emitted as much carbon dioxide as a gasoline engine and, as Jeff was explaining to Liam, carbon dioxide was a greenhouse gas. Anne's car was an older model, one of the first, with cells on the roof only instead of on the roof and hood both. Terry had bought it for her birthday, thereby making a political statement at the same time. He had recently sold his own methanol guzzler and had been commuting by train, to dramatize his support of mass transit—again, two birds with one stone.

"Okay, guys," I said finally, "we'd better hit the road if we're going to the park."

Liam looked as if he had suddenly remembered something unpleasant. "Listen, Carrie, would you care if instead of the park we went to the zoo?"

Taken aback, I stared at him across the car's twinkling top. "The zoo? How come?"

"Well, there's a new baby rhino. But if you'd rather take us to the park . . ."

181

Ugh. Embarrassment made me duck into the driver's seat and busy myself with my seat belt. I'd been expecting this; the boys were getting too big to think doughnuts in the park with old Cousin Carrie much of a treat. But anticipating it didn't seem to have made much difference. It was still a jolt, and it still hurt, and the really embarrassing thing was, Liam had obviously known it would hurt. He was sensitive that way.

But I drew in a deep breath and said gamely, "The zoo it is. Come on, pile in."

"Loser has to sit in back." He and Jeff threw in their book bags and buckled their seat belts. Neither looked at me directly. I started the car and pulled into the Germantown Avenue traffic. Nobody spoke. After a few silent blocks Liam looked at me askance: "Is it really okay about the zoo?" Jeff said nothing. I was Liam's relative; it was Liam's job to deal with me.

To my relief, inspiration struck. "Did I ever tell you guys that when I was about your age I used to spend part of every summer with my grandmother, out in Lancaster? That's your dad's mother's mother, Liam. Your great-grandmother. Her name was Lillie Proctor and she was a lot of fun. She'd grown up in a big Mennonite family on a farm, and she used to tell me stories about that after we'd gone to bed—I slept with her in a double bed with feather bolsters. We always went to town for a day during each of my visits, and we'd go shopping in all the dime stores, mostly for little glass and china dogs—she had a collection of them, all arranged on a little three-tiered table with legs made of wooden spools glued together, and she'd made a dog table like hers for me and started me collecting too. And we'd have lunch at a nice restaurant called the Blue Boar, in one of the downtown hotels. It was a big deal for me and a pretty big deal for her. And then one day, out of the blue, when she was visiting us in Philadelphia and talking about next summer and how we'd go to town together, all of a sudden I realized it didn't really sound like a whole lot of fun anymore."

I glanced over at Liam and smiled. "I must have said something halfhearted—I don't remember what. But the awful thing was, she could *tell* I wasn't really interested, and it hurt her feelings. She was disappointed. It was our special thing we did together, see, and here I didn't care about doing it anymore. And I felt bad, I really did, but what could I do? People grow up, that's just the way things are. It wasn't anybody's fault."

In my rearview mirror Jeff smiled and nodded as the point struck home. Liam sent me a dazzling grin. "How come you *always* understand everything?"

Returning the grin I allowed myself a moment of self-congratulation. "Anyway, baby rhinos are some of my favorite things." Then, so as to quit while I was ahead, I changed the subject. "How's the meditation coming along?"

"Well, nobody in our school has cancer yet," said Liam grumpily; he was not very good at the kind of concentrating required.

"I'm kind of getting into it," Jeff surprisingly said. "Today my hands got completely numb. They felt like they didn't even belong to me, like they were made of wood or something, and sometimes my face gets numb, or it tingles. It feels good in a weird way. Dr. Feinman even told us that there's a team of guys like him—psycho, neuro, immunologists—at Graduate Hospital in Center City, that's been teaching people with AIDS how to meditate since a long time back. There's this one group of AIDS patients that have been meditating for, like, twenty-five years, and some of them are still alive!"

"They aren't actually AIDS patients, they're asymptomatic HIV-positives," Liam corrected him.

"Yeah, I guess that's right. But anyway, they're doing a lot of other stuff too, exercising and eating all this pure food and everything, but Dr. Feinman thinks the meditation is probably a big part of it."

"I'm just not any *good* at it," Liam complained. "My mind keeps wandering. The public school kids laugh their heads off when they hear what we do in there, you should hear 'em."

"They do, do they?" I could well imagine.

"Yeah, you know what they call us? *Flakers*," said Jeff. "But who cares, if it works? Listen, Liam, I think I know how you could learn to stay with the mantra better. Want to come over Saturday after rehearsal? We can do it together and I'll show you what I mean. Or I could come over to your place."

"Won't your mom mind?" Liam asked. That surprised me; why should Anne object if Jeff wanted to help Liam with his schoolwork?

I glanced at Jeff's face in the mirror and was startled by the look of fury that flashed across it. "I don't know, I'll see about it," he said. "Dad'll be home, but this shouldn't take very long . . . I'll have to see."

"I've got baseball practice in the morning but that's all. When do you get out?"

"At four-thirty. It's two to four this week because of the concert, and then I have to stay after and work on my solo."

"Hey," said Liam brightly, "sing your solo for Carrie!"

"Right now?"

"Sure!" said Liam and to me: "Jeff's going to be the star of the spring concert. Come on, Jeff, sing it."

I smiled at him in the mirror. "Sure, go ahead if you wouldn't mind. Please. I'd love to hear it."

"Well," he said, "but I'll have to sing the treble line of the whole piece *and* the alto and tenor solos. My part kind of comes and goes. It's going to sound a little weird."

"That's okay, sing the whole thing. We won't mind the weird bits, will we, Liam?"

"Well, okay. This is 'Alma Dei Creatoris,' by Mozart." And sitting up as straight as his seat belt would allow, Jeff began to sing:

> Alma Dei Creatoris
> sedet rei peccatoris
> mater, mater clementissima. . . .

That's when I got my second jolt of the afternoon.

I'd heard Jeff sing before, of course. At twelve he was still the choir's best treble and had been given solos regularly for the past couple of years—a fact that had done much to reconcile Anne to his not being a Washington Cathedral chorister, by the way—and we always went to the Philadelphia performances. But with very few exceptions I'd heard him sing in concert, never from the back seat of my own car, nothing so intimate or . . . inevitable in its effect. In that setting, on that afternoon, it seemed an uncanny and astonishing thing that this young person, known to me since birth, should be capable of transforming himself effortlessly from a scruffy twelve-year-old schoolboy into a musical instrument of unearthly purity and beauty, merely by using his voice.

My eyes watered and stung. Blinking, I glanced over at Liam

and saw that he sat facing forward, his whole body radiating pride and happiness.

Poor Liam could still scarcely sing a note, and though he had been taking piano lessons for several years and had turned out to be remarkably talented, he never, after all, had tried to accompany Jeff; it still just wasn't his kind of music. But, for Jeff's sake apparently, he had managed to learn how to listen to it all the same. Seeing his face, I didn't doubt for a moment that Jeff would be able to teach him to meditate as well.

We had watched the two boys develop in different directions as they'd grown older. Both were Scouts, and loved to go camping, but that was pretty nearly the only keen interest they shared, and *Dungeons and Dragons* was about the only pastime. Jeff had his singing, and his best subject in school was history. He also owned a thriving tankful of tropical fish and an elaborate electric train set. The animated cartoons he made, using the computer-graphics camera Terry had given him on his tenth birthday, were elaborate and wildly fanciful. And he took being a Young Friend seriously, much more so than Liam did.

Liam liked cars and jazz and had begun to bring home astonishingly high aptitude scores in math. Both boys were readers, but of different kinds of books: sports stories and *Games Magazine* for Liam, fantasy for Jeff. Liam owned a large collection of computer games, which he played with ferocious and dazzling skill. He loved baseball and soccer and was good at them; Jeff wasn't at all athletic, nor was he even remotely interested in the Phillies or the Sixers.

But for all their differences—even the last, which at that age I would have thought insurmountable—the bond forged in infancy endured. The two boys now spent much less time together, but each was still more important to the other than anybody else was, parents and siblings (and cousins) included.

It was still true that none of us had ever seen the like.

The strength of their bond had begun to make my cousin Mark, Liam's father, uncomfortable. I don't think he was aware of that—the possibility of having produced a homosexual son would have filled him with such horrified panic that I doubt he ever allowed himself to consider it—but it was noticeable in the way his attitude toward Jeff had altered.

I didn't, myself, believe theirs to be a sexual bond; but I also believed that if by chance I turned out to be wrong, the boys would still be luckier than most. You thought of David and Jonathan when you were with them. They never quarreled, they scarcely disagreed. They accommodated, with an easy grace that many a married couple might envy, to each other's differences. They admired and supported and stuck up for each other, all without fuss or smarm. I thought their friendship a wonder, and felt privileged to know both it and them.

I was curious to know how aware the boys themselves were that the bond they shared was extraordinary. I wondered whether the other kids ever made cracks about it. Occasionally I tried to imagine how girlfriends, or in due course wives, were going to fit into the scenario. That sort of speculation was premature, of course; a lot could happen by the time they were ready to be seriously interested in girls. Still, it was the kind of thing I used to wonder.

They did, in fact, have other cronies noiw—Liam on the baseball and soccer teams, Jeff in the Young Friends and the choir—but these friendships were conducted separately from their own central friendship. There never, even among the Scouts, seemed to be a gang made up of Liam and Jeff and a bunch of other guys.

Reflecting on all this, I drove; Jeff sang, natural as a skylark; Liam sat beside me, motionless and alert as a pointing setter. I remember that we stopped for the light at the intersection of Hunting Park Avenue and Thirty-third Street, snarled in traffic, most of it, fortunately, headed the other way: north, out of the city. A few other futuristic-looking solar cars could be seen glinting in the pack, but most were methanol burners, busily pumping CO_2 into the upper atmosphere. While we sat waiting for the light to change, the world was getting warmer.

Beyond us, through the windshield, both sides of the street were lined with seedy-looking shops and businesses that represented, at that moment, the paved-over, built-over world in which I would have to finish living my life, in which the boys would have to grow up: an overcrowded, dirty, dangerous place. Behind my head, framed in the mirror, unperturbed by any such considerations, Jeff continued to wend his way surefootedly through Mozart's glorious piece of liturgical music, composed 250 years earlier and sung in a dead language: *Tu fac clemens quod rogamus, fortes ad certamina!*

I knew that Mozart's life had been short, and as difficult in its way as that of any twenty-first-century genius; but the world that had shaped him, for all its hardship, pestilence, and injustice, had made more sense to him than my world made to me. I wasn't romanticizing eighteenth-century Europe, far from it. I had read my Jonathan Swift. But I remember thinking then that such music could not be written now by anybody but a hermit in a tower or cave, communing only with himself and his muse—that there was no seedbed anywhere in the world, anymore, for a beauty that innocent or confident or pure.

The light changed, the moment ended, we drove on through. *Alma Dei Creatoris* continued to fill the car. The neighborhoods got worse and worse. Presently I pulled into the parking lot at the Philadelphia Zoo, killed the engine, and waited peacefully beside Liam, leaning back, eyes closed, till Jeff stopped singing and turned back into a boy.

When the music ended, on impulse I unclipped my seat belt and stretched my arm around between the front seats till I could tousel Jeff's dark, curly hair, so much like his father's had been when he was younger. "You're a wonderful singer, Jeff, you know that? It crossed my mind while I was listening to you just now that I don't know whether I ever told you I love you—not since you were a tiny boy anyhow—so I'm going to tell you now, just to make sure. I do really love you, I always did and I always will. You're a terrific singer, but I think you're an even more terrific kid.''

My good angel was with me that day. I'm not a gushing sort of person; it's never been my style to announce to people—blat!—how I feel about them. I can't explain why I felt the need (and found the courage) to say to Terry's son a thing I might very well have said, but in fact never had said, to Terry himself.

Embarrassment could have swallowed us both. But in fact I stayed pretty cool, and Jeff seemed to take the avowal right in stride. He looked me in the eye and replied calmly, "I don't remember if you ever told me that before, but I knew it anyway, Carrie.''

"Did you? Good enough. Let's go see the baby rhino.''

Jeff was splendid in the spring concert, though the public performance, all wine-colored blazers and black ties, struck both Liam and me as second-rate. (During the applause Liam leaned over to say directly into my ear, "I like it better in the car, didn't you?" I nodded, smiling to myself at a suddenly revived memory: Liam asserting, on the Fourth of July when he was six: "I like my cast better than this parade." *Plus ça change!*)

Anne was simply radiant that evening, and Terry—less musical than she, less able to measure or appreciate Jeff's gift—was relaxed and happy because she was happy. Things were going well for him in Washington, with a liberal Republican in the White House and a Green heading up the EPA. This year he was chair of the House Interior Subcommittee on General Oversight and Investigations, an important and useful position, and I knew he planned to make a serious run for the Senate in the coming election. He seemed as unshadowed by his demons as he'd been in quite a while.

That summer Matt and I accepted the Flintoff's invitation to spend a few weeks in the moors of North Yorkshire. It had been another rough academic year, for Matt especially, so we decided just that once to take a proper vacation. We flew over in mid-June, traveled around in France and Holland, and in southwestern England, and then in August went on up to Yorkshire by rail to escape the heat, catch the heather in bloom—and to hear Jenny's mysterious (and fascinating) confidence. And so, after all Terry's detailed strategies and maps and scrupulous duplicating of keys, we were in Yorkshire with Jenny and Frank, and not in southeastern Pennsylvania, when news reached us of the meltdown at the Peach Bottom Nuclear Facility.

For days it was impossible to get information about individuals, and in the general chaos nobody thought to call us. A desperate week dragged by before we finally learned what fates had befallen our relatives and friends.

Mark and Phoebe, with Liam, had followed Terry's evacuation plans precisely. They had driven to the cabin in the Poconos and were still there, safe and sound. Brett had been visiting friends in Michigan, far from the danger zone, at the time of the catastrophe, and Margy had been at work in New York City.

When the accident occurred, Anne was in Washington with Terry. She was able to be there because Jeff was away on tour for a week with the Philadelphia Boys' Choir. On the morning of August 30 the choir had been traveling by chartered bus from Baltimore, where it had given a concert the previous evening, toward Lancaster, where it was to have given one the following day. There was no hurry and they had all voted to take the more attractive, slower route, over I-95 as far as the Susquehanna River, then north along the river to Lancaster over U.S. 222.

The bus had been only a few miles east of the plant at the time of the meltdown. Everybody aboard had taken a lethal dose of radiation—far more than even a very gifted meditator could possibly defend himself against. By the time we in England got the word, Jeff was already two days dead of radiation poisoning.

6

ELPHI

Over a period of several months Frank Flintoft had been sur-
veying some minor Bronze Age sites between Nab Farm and
Blakey Topping, just outside the southern boundary of the four-
square-mile still-forbidden zone of the Early Warning System
on Fylingdales Moor.

Private land within the North York Moors National Park was
thickly strewn with these ancient sites, mostly cairns and field
systems. Many still had not been officially identified, and quite
a few of the landowners were unaware of their existence. The
Park Committee were only too happy to accept Frank's skilled,
and free, assistance with the mapping and recording of the less
important sites, and Frank enjoyed the work.

But the painstaking patience it required was more in his line
than in his wife's; Jenny preferred to poke about in the bogland
of Nab Farm and nearby May Moss.

One morning in early summer the two of them—as they fre-
quently did—took the Land Rover and hamper of sandwiches
up to the tops for a spell of archeology and botanizing. The
prospect of a day to be spent alone in the sloping gray-green
wind-harshened landscape filled Jenny with the same buoyant
joy as it had when she was young, and a visitor, instead of a
year-round resident farmwife with arthritis and hair more gray
than brown. She left Frank setting up his equipment under a
gray ceiling of cloud and, taking half the sandwiches, hiked off,
purposefully through a narrow spur of pine plantation to see
whether the lesser twayblade had yet produced its small green
flowers in the peat bog on the other side.

For the rest of the morning Jenny stalked and crouched about the bogland, her eyes filled with mucky peat and rare plants, her ears with the wind and the despairing bleats of sheep, her heart with perfect contentment. Toward midday she was peering through the viewfinder of her camera at a bog rosemary in bloom when one of the Herdwicks grazing nearby ambled still nearer and said, "I should like a few words with you, my dear."

She looked up, already thunderstuck by the knowledge of what she would see: a shaggy moor ewe with dead, flat eyes and legs too thick to be quite sheeplike. The hairs rose on the back of Jenny's neck. With a small groan she carefully stood upright and let her camera swing by its strap. As she straightened up, the sheep also stood on two legs and threw back the upper part of its fleece.

"Elphi," she said with careful joy, "hello."

The hob peered mildly up at her out of the straggly gray hair of his face, looking—to her eyes, precisely as he had looked eighteen years before; Jenny herself had aged far more apparently.

For a long moment they confronted each other while the wind blew. Jenny had so hungered for another look at Elphi for so long that she hardly knew how to do justice to the moment, now that it had come. For the past six years, except in hard winter, the evidence of Elphi's active presence had been part of her daily life. But to feast her eyes upon him, to talk with him again—

The hob spoke first: "You did remember, of course. As soon as ever you clapped eyes on those Hefn you remembered *me*, and our day together, and all about it—isn't that so, my dear?"

She managed to nod. "And it was the same with Frank, exactly the same." She drew the moor wind into her lungs and held it there, then burst out "Elphi—this is wonderful, it's *wonderful* to see you! How—how *are* you? Are you all right?"

The conventional phrases sounded ridiculous, but she was too flustered to do better, and Elphi didn't seem to mind. "I'm well enough, my dear, I thank you, and very happy to be able to say how much I regretted having to deal with you so roughly at our first meeting. 'Twas no pleasure to me to take you prisoner, no indeed. Nor to steal away your memories, come to that."

"It doesn't matter now," said Jenny. "Anyway, you've paid me back in service, many times over."

"We'd wondered whether there mightn't have been others who

remembered us—besides the two of you. We did know about you, of course."

"Of course—from the radio."

"Just so. A little black transistor it was, that a neglectful walker left behind atop the Face Stone, over on Urra Moor. A cunning thing, that plays compact tapes in addition to bringing us the news—we'd picked up a few tapes now and again, and a rare treat they are, some of them, though they do run the batteries down . . . but perhaps, when the ship finally came, nobody else who had ever seen us was left alive."

"The friend who was with Frank on the Lyke Wake Walk was dead, I know that," Jenny offered. "But, you know, there might well have been some others who couldn't get anybody to take them seriously. We were listened to because we found Woof Howe."

"Aye, *that* was a clever bit of work and no mistake." Elphi glanced toward the three lowering radomes of the Early Warning System—dead now but yet to be dismantled—in the direction of May Moss. He shook his head. "Such a time I had, getting him over the fence. None of the others woke for days. I'd begun to feel rather desperate, I can tell you."

Jenny, beginning to get over the first shock of the encounter, reflected that in the old days it was unusual but not unknown for hobs to accost humans on the open moor and have speech with them. The question was, if he wasn't ill or hurt, what could have caused this hob to break his concealment now?

At this thought, uneasiness intruded between Jenny and her joy, but she thrust it away. No doubt he would explain when he was ready. Meanwhile—"There's something we've never been able to figure out. We've talked about it a lot, Frank and I—why in the world you all stayed hidden when the ship came back the first time. Unless you just didn't know they were looking for you."

"We knew, all right. Oh aye, we knew," said Elphi, still mildly, "what with the wireless and the loudspeaking lorries and I don't know what all, how could we help knowing? But, you see, by then we were only two. All the rest were dead—all but Broxa and me; *we* hung on. Now Broxa's gone as well . . . but when the two of us woke that April to discover Hodge Hob and Tarn Hole and Hasty Bank cold as three stones, and the wireless full of the news about the ship, well! for a time we swung backwards and forwards between grief and delight. To live so long and then die at the very brink of rescue! Well, well . . . but even then our delight was greater than our grief. If one of those blaring lorries had driven by, that first day, I daresay we'd have bolted out of hiding quick enough.''

He paused so long that Jenny's curiosity got the better of her patience. ''So why didn't you, when they *did* come?''

''Have you guessed, I wonder? You and Frank Flintoft between you?''

Jenny looked into his ancient face and said, ''You were so thoroughly at home on the moors, we both had such a strong sense of that, that we wondered whether you hadn't just got too old to give them up, finally—in spite of the tourists and their dogs, and the grouse shooting, and all that bother.''

Elphi beamed, or at least he seemed to. ''A very good guess and a good part of the truth! The rest, though, was that at first we weren't able to agree on a way of making our presence known. Think of it, my dear. After hiding for so long, to walk up to a farmhouse and knock at the door—or frighten a farmer out of his wits in his own barn? Or flag down a car on one of the moor roads? Or perhaps stroll into one of the shops in Danby or Castleton? We couldn't think how to go about it . . . and, to speak plainly, we were afraid. Stopping a stranger in a car, for example: anything might happen! I wanted to try one of the farmers and Broxa favored Danby Village, but no way seemed truly right, or safe.

''And then, *just* then, came the news that you and your man—we remembered you both, oh, very well!—had dug Woof Howe Hob out of a bog on Fylingdales Moor. They said on the newscast that Frank Flintoft was a farmer in Westerdale, over at the edge of the park. And I don't now recollect which of us was the first to say, Suppose we were go to and live *there*? To work on a dales farm again, you see—that was something we'd never dreamt could happen, and yet why not? Why not, if the farmer knew of us already—always supposing he could be trusted to keep quiet about us? He'd not spoken of the Gafr, we knew that, for there was nothing about them in the news; and if the two of you could keep *that* secret. . . .''

Here Jenny looked at the ground a bit guiltily, for there *were* several people she had told that secret to; but Elphi didn't seem to notice.

"It was something to think about; and the longer we thought, the more we understood how little we cared to pass the rest of our lives among shipmates who would now be young while we were old, or to live on board ship again at all, whether serving the Gafr or no.

"And the long and the short of it was, that by the time the lorries arrived, neither Broxa nor I would willingly leave the moors."

"Rescue came too late," said Jenny.

"It came too late. That it did. We lay low, buried our dead—not in the same bog you found Woof Howe in—and let the ship leave without us. We spoke constantly then of moving to Moor View Farm that summer. And yet, we never quite brought ourselves to the point somehow. How were we to be *sure* of Frank Flintoft, that was the problem. We debated, and hung round the farm a good deal, looking things over, but in the end we went to earth the next autumn without having made up our minds; and when I woke again, Broxa was dead."

Jenny tried not to imagine too vividly the moment when Elphi had realized his absolute aloneness. "And that decided you?"

He shook his shaggy head. "Not at once, no, no. What decided me finally, my dear, was the news that you and Frank Flintoft had married and were living at the farm together. When I heard *that* on the wireless I took to skulking round the eaves of the house of an evening, listening to your talk; and after a while I says to myself, I'll risk it. You'd mentioned, more than once, how you meant to muck out the henhouse. Well, one night I slipped in and did the job myself, and the next night a jug of cream was waiting on the back doorstep . . . and the rest you know."

"And you still felt the same when the ship came back the second time."

"More than ever, my dear. More than ever."

They had been standing all this while, pitching their voices above the keening of the wind. Now Jenny felt cold. "Will you share some bread and cheese with me? And some tea, in memory of our long day underground?"

She picked up her daypack by one strap and pushed her way up through the heather to a drier spot. There she pulled out her battered old foam pad and sat on it. Elphi settled himself beside her, accepted a cheese sandwich with equanimity—his first in more than a century—and let Jenny pour him some tea into the thermos cap. "The Hefn say their time window wasn't working right in 2006, and that's why the message didn't get through," Jenny said. "But what if it had? Do you suppose you'd have gone with the ship?"

"If we'd been certain of rescue through all the long years of waiting, d'you mean? It's possible. Oh, aye, it's possible."

"Then it's hard to say whether the story has a sad ending or a happy one," she mused. "Something of both, really."

"A good deal of both, I believe, and the story's not over. But," and he held Jenny's gaze, "for myself, I've no regrets."

Alarmed, Jenny sat up straighter. "Why isn't the story over?"

Elphi groaned faintly and swung his head a little, in a mild version of the frantic gesture Jenny remembered. "*They* won't let it be over, I fear. Seeing as how they sent our Pomphrey to call on you."

"We *wondered* if you knew about that! But of course you would," thinking of the helicopter's racket and the fact that she and Frank had talked chiefly of this visit every evening for a week. She wrinkled her nose now at the memory. "He was one of that delegation we met with, after we dug up Woof Howe Hob—I don't mean the big public hearing, when we made the tape, but the private interview. Last week he just turned up at the farm, without warning—do you mean to say you actually saw him yourself, while he was there?"

"I did, as a matter of fact—heard the helicopter, put two and two together, and did a spot of eavesdropping."

Jenny stared at Elphi; how could he sound so indifferent? After nearly four centuries, to behold one of his own people in the flesh again, so near that a couple of steps would have closed the distance between them, and not reveal himself! More than anything else it confirmed the force of the choice he had made, to stay in Yorkshire.

"Well," she said, "then you know all about it. It took the Gafr a while to remember that Frank and I *knew* about them, but once they'd remembered—even though we'd already had a year and a half to go public and hadn't done it—they got uneasy. Pomphrey didn't exactly threaten us, though I must say we didn't think much of his manners." She glanced speculatively at Elphi, hunkered in the heather. "Were you worried we might tell him about you?"

Elphi met this glance and Jenny felt herself grow warm. "Forgive me, my dear. I ought to have known you could be trusted to the end, for you've proved it time and again. Our Pomphrey wasn't to know that, but *I* might have known—but he needn't have shown his teeth at you, even so."

"No, because Frank and I both—especially Frank—feel that your people just might manage to do a better job of saving the world than ours seem able to. So we'd already decided not to add to the general hysteria by spilling the beans about the Gafr—not for the time being anyway. More tea?"

Elphi held out the thermos cap and Jenny refilled it and put in some whole-milk crystals and sugar with a spoon. Watching her stirring hand, he said thoughtfully, "All the same, it's what *I* mean to do."

"What is?"

"Spill the beans, my dear—all of them."

"It began when we got the news of Lexifrey," Elphi explained after he and Jenny had walked back through the pine plantation to find Frank, and Frank, absorbed in his screening, had glanced up to see his wife approaching, hours earlier than the agreed-upon time, with a sheep moving beside her like a dog at heel. "You asked me a little while ago whether Broxa and I mightn't have chosen to go with the ship, if we'd *known* . . . Lexi and the others in Sweden, *they* knew. When they made contact with him last year through the time terminal, they said he was still desperately hoping to be found, trying his best to stay alive till the ship should come—that he'd never stopped expecting to be rescued. *He* would have come skipping out when the loudspeaking lorries went by, no doubt of that. Well, well," said Elphi, swinging his woolly head gently from side to side, "I felt somehow that I ought to do it for Lexi. He was a good sort. And then, he was the last of the Swedish Hefn, just as I'm the last of us in England."

He was quiet for several minutes. Frank had finished hauling his tools and boxes back to the car—left parked at the road's edge, to spare the fragile ground—and now he turned toward Elphi, hands stuck inside his anorak, thick white hair blowing in the wind. "But you didn't."

"No, I didn't. No." Elphi stirred and stood upright; he had been crouching low in the heather, for all the world like a resting sheep. "I was happy, you see. I had two fine masters that knew how to hold their tongues, and a fine farm to serve. Danby Dale might have suited me better than Westerdale—I only say might!—but there wasn't another blessed thing I wanted in the world, anymore, than I hadn't got already. It's not to be given up lightly, that sort of happiness. I'd had it once before, you know, and lost it, and had a good long while to mourn the loss."

"Then why give it up now?" said Jenny in distress. "And what's it got to do with Pomphrey's visit, anyway?"

"I'll tell you, my dear, indeed I must, but I'd rather tell you at home. Let's go home." Elphi dropped down and scrambled on four legs over the moor toward the Land Rover, hesitating only a moment before climbing nimbly over the front seats and into the back. Frank and Jenny, who had trailed behind, looked at each other across the car's square top. Frank's eyebrows waggled and frowned: *What's going on?* Jenny shrugged and shook her head: *Search me!*

They got in, and Frank started the engine. As they pulled onto the road Elphi's voice came from behind their heads: "Am I much changed, d'you think my dear? Since last you saw me?"

Jenny twisted in her seat to crane back at the old fellow, too worried to feel like laughing when she saw that following their example he had buckled his seat belt around himself; he looked like a law-abiding ewe. "No," she assured him soberly, "you haven't changed a bit, that I can see."

Frank had built a fire in the grate and fastened the shutters. He and Jenny, wearing long faces, sat on opposite ends of the sitting room couch facing Elphi, who lay on the hearth rug with every appearance of perfect comfort. He'd been given his dinner—a bowl of porridge, a jug of cream—and they'd had theirs, and the three of them had settled down to plan a strategy for breaking both long-kept secrets at once: the secret of Elphi's continued existence, and the secret of the Gafr.

Elphi wore only his long body hair; he would never need the fleece again. His eyes, for the moment, were closed. "You haven't changed a bit," Jenny had said, yet what he had decided to do made him feel desperately changed. Not since the knowledge that the ship would not be back had closed upon his heart, four centuries before, had he felt so strange to himself.

In his mind's eye he watched again through the window as

197

the Hefn Pomphrey, still young, still sleek and smooth, his body bent into the unnatural position required for chair-sitting, sat in the big armchair and said, with his American-accented semblance of sincerity: "You've behaved wisely, keeping your knowledge of our lords the Gafr to yourselves. Take my advice: go on being wise. People are upset enough. What's the point of stirring up a hornet's nest when the hornets have nobody to sting but each other?"

Frank had looked disgusted. Jenny had said, "Have *you* ever seen a hornet's nest?"

The Hefn shook his head and hardened his voice ever so slightly. "You lost your memory, didn't you, Mrs. Flintoft? And struggled for many years to get it back, and still it took the sight of us to do the trick? Yes? Well then, please believe me: no good can come of telling tales, not one bit of good to anybody."

The Hefn's I'm-telling-you-this-for-your-own-good earnestness had fooled the humans no more than it fooled Elphi; they knew whose good Pomphrey didn't have in mind as well as Elphi did, and they also knew what had been done to the old Swede, Gunnar Lundqvist. It struck Elphi that he had never much cared for Pomphrey, and that if anybody had brought this unpleasant sort of pressure to bear on his own farmer in the old days, back in Danby Dale, it would have been a job for t'hob right enough. All his old protective instincts flared up; but what was he to do? Strange, strange, how entirely he found himself ranged on the side of Jenny and Frank, ready to defend them against his own former would-be rescuer!

Pomphrey had been one of the obedient Hefn, of course, and Elphi one of the renegades; perhaps that accounted for it.

The hob had retreated to his cubby in the hayloft to ponder the turn of events. The more he thought, the uneasier he grew. As the days passed he gradually became convinced that the Gafr would come to see Jenny and Frank as an intolerable threat. He knew them, he knew how it would be. The sense of threat would grow and grow, and in the end Pomphrey would be sent to call again.

And afterwards, neither of the humans would remember that they had ever met or conversed with hobs on the moors.

It was general knowledge, of course. A documentary film had been made of Jenny and Frank in 2006, when they had dug up Woof Howe Hob together. Millions of people knew about their experiences with the hobs, so the Flintofts would inevitably repossess that public information in any case. But they would lose their personal memories of what had happened—meaning that unless they had made a written record, they would never remember having been told by the hobs about the Gafr.

Pomphrey could remove the memories with surgical care—excise all references to the Gafr and leave the rest intact, instead of the crude way Elphi himself had done the same thing to each of them—but he probably wouldn't bother to be that careful. He would probably be rough but thorough. He would see to it that this time, nothing would ever again trigger those memories back.

And whichever way he did it—a deep groan burst out of Elphi and he swung his head furiously as the realization struck home—whether Pomphrey was casual or precise, went searching for any reference to Elphi or only to the Gafr, he would discover the other secret. He would discover that Elphi was still alive.

Either way, then, this life as Moor View Hob was finished.

All that rainy night, the night of the day he traced the implications of Pomphrey's visit to this conclusion, Elphi had ranged inconsolably across the moors, lowing like a heifer. He splashed through becks and scattered sheep. Passing close by the den he had emerged from only a couple of months before, at the end of the previous winter's sleep, he heaved aside the stone and clambered down the ladder; but the place felt more like a prison than a refuge to him now and he charged back up into the rain and wind with a great roar.

Toward morning, his tremendous strength exhausted, he began to calm down. As he made his way back to the farm he reflected that he had two choices, and only two. When the helicopter came again he could resume his life on the moor, with its fleeces and its raw grouse dinners, scavenging a living from the tourists' leavings. Elphi doubted the Hefn could catch him, try though they might. Since Frank and Jenny had never known the location of the den, that was information the mind search would be unable to extract from them.

But the thought of going back to that life now, all by himself—of undergoing yet a third exile—was intolerable. Faced with the choice, he understood that—rather than endure that bleak solitude—he preferred to let himself be ''rescued'' and be taken back among his own kind.

How soon? The Gafr came to their decisions by slow deliberation; he might reckon on one last bittersweet summer of service on the farm.

Elphi slipped into the barn, a gray shadow in the gray dawn, shaking off the rain. Several pairs of swallows, nesting on the rafters, swooped above his head, fetching and carrying strands of dry grass and beaksful of mud. The two Ayrshires, mother and daughter, had come in for milking. It wouldn't be long till Frank appeared.

In the corner of the loft, behind the last bales of last year's hay, Elphi settled down for a short rest before setting about his few daylight chores. After a bit he heard Frank speaking fondly but firmly, in the Yorkshire dialect of his childhood, to Truth and Beauty below. Then came the clang as he shut the stanchions, and the dry swish of loose hay being forked. Then came the rattle of milk streaming forcibly against the sides of a metal pail.

A thought, unbidden and unwelcome, came into Elphi's mind as he lay and listened to these familiar, homely sounds. He tried without success to push it away. Soon he began groaning rhythmically (but quietly, so that Frank wouldn't hear).

He could wait for Pomphrey to return, savoring each day, knowing the days were numbered.

Or instead he could do one last hobbish deed, and cut the days to zero.

He lay and thought about it. Gradually his moaning ceased. A while later Jenny's voice and Frank's drifted up to him. They were going out for a day on the tops; he'd heard Jenny telling the hired man, Peter, about it yesterday. Frank wanted to finish mapping a field system not far from Nab Farm, she to explore the nearby bogs for rare wildflowers. The car came to life, drove up to the house. Its doors clashed with that abrupt metallic finality they had and it drove away. Silence descended on the farm, except for the swallows' twittering.

Presently Elphi roused himself and dusted the hay out of his pelt. He scaled a rafter and unwedged a fleece he had stored up there, which he had scarcely worn during his years on the farm. Though a bit moth-eaten it was still serviceable. He dropped it onto the barn floor and in a flash was down the ladder after it. He had made up his mind.

And now the choice was taken, the die cast. Moor View Hob

had vanished, never again to sow a field of turnips nor assist at lambing time. Instead—

The fire blazed hot at his back. The room had filled with a gamy, wet-animal smell. Elphi opened his eyes and sat up. "Come, let's put our heads together. How is it to be done? I must say I rather like the notion of using the wireless, that's been my friend so long."

Jenny appealed to Frank: "Where's the nearest radio station? Whitby?"

"Middlesbrough, I think." He brought the telephone directory and his reading specs to the dining room table, paged back and forth, and presently announced, "Middlesbrough." He peered at Elphi over his glasses. "I'll ring them if you like—if you're absolutely fixed on doing this."

While Frank was phoning, Jenny got up and went to sit on the floor, close to Elphi. "*Why* are you doing this, that's what I want to know. There's no telling how people will take the news. And what about you—won't you be punished when the Gafr get their hands on you?"

"The Gafr have no hands, my dear. The Hefn are their hands, and their feet as well." By neither word nor expression did he reveal distress, but as he looked into her face the wave of his own sadness broke upon her. "They'll punish this little rebellion of mine as they did the other—by separating the rebel from his masters. They'll find out all about it, oh aye. Read my memories they will." He looked away. "But I must act now, before they've had time to think it through, for if I don't they'll surely send young Pomphrey back to punish *you*, for knowing what you know."

Jenny blinked. " 'Punish' how? Wipe our memories, you mean?" Elphi nodded. "But that's what Pomphrey said—implied, anyway—would happen if we talked. We're not going to talk."

"*I* believe that, for you've proved many a time that you could be trusted. But the Gafr will doubt it, and as time goes on they'll doubt it more and more, and one day they'll decide the risk isn't worth running. I know them." It was much too hot there by the fire; Elphi got up and walked on all fours to the front window, the one at whose eaves he had listened during so many long, pleasant, half-lit summer evenings.

Behind him Jenny sputtered, "But—do you mean you're going to leave the farm, give yourself up, maybe create a global incident—just to keep Frank and me from being mindwiped?" She shook her head. "That *can't* be the only reason, I don't believe it."

"Don't you, my dear?"

He turned from the window to meet her eye, and Jenny got up in her agitation and began to walk up and down the room. "No, because you told me yourself—I remember this very well—you said the hobs were perfectly able to up and leave a farm where they'd lived for a hundred years without a backward glance! You said they had no friends among the humans, that their bond was to the service, and they could always find somebody else to serve!" Frank came in from the kitchen and stood in the doorway. Jenny crossed to him and said shrilly, "Elphi claims he's doing this to keep *us* from getting our memories wiped!"

Her voice was so full of accusation that Frank threw back his head and laughed, not very happily. "Well, if he is, then you ought to thank him, not berate him! But whatever you do, do it fast—there's a helicopter full of reporters and paparazzi already on their way from Middlesbrough."

"Oh, no!" Jenny whirled away from him to Elphi, then back to Frank. "But—he can't change his mind then! We can't try to talk him out of it!"

Frank shook his head and put his arms around Jenny, pulling her tense body against him. "Not now, love. I had to tell them too much to get them to believe me. It's done."

"You could not have talked me out of it, my dear," Elphi put in. "Quickly now, while there's still time, let me make the situation plain."

Frank steered Jenny to the chair where Pomphrey had sat while delivering his thinly veiled threat, and she sank into it, twisting her fingers together. Frank lowered himself to sit cross-legged on the floor beside the chair and looked resignedly at the hob. "Calm yourselves now, do," said Elphi. " 'Tis not so very great a sacrifice after all, considering that when they came for you—and that would have been before very long—they'd have learnt about me in any event. Sooner than live out my time on the high moors, alone, I'd let them have me again."

Frank said, "Ah, but you *have* sacrificed something, all the same. You've given up the chance that they might never come back—and maybe that was a pretty slim chance, but still it seems to me to be one. And you've given up your last bit of time on the farm. Jenny's right, you know. According to what you told her, you should not be doing any sacrificing at all on our account.''

"Aye, aye, it's true enough, I won't deny it!'' Elphi looked from one to the other and then, instead of imitating some human gesture, lifted his arms in an eloquent alien way. "I daresay the Gafr will have it out of me, they'll work out what makes me do it, but for the life of me I can't tell you myself and that's the truth.'' He dropped suddenly to all fours, a movement which had the effect of shoulder-slumping in a human. "I'm the last, you know—perhaps it's that that makes the difference. We Hefn are never, never alone. There is always a crowd of us, and there are always the Gafr.''

Frank started to say something, but at that moment they all heard the helicopter. Jenny threw Elphi a desperate, beseeching look. "I'm sorry I was angry, that was stupid. I just wanted it to go on and on, exactly the same, forever!''

"So did I, my dear, so did I. But perhaps it's for the best. At least, it will be good to see my own Gafr again before I die, and to hear my own language and my own name spoken.''

The chopper had landed in the pasture below the house. Frank got up and moved toward the door; Jenny stood also. "What *is* your Hefn name? I'd like to know.''

Elphi gave her his impression of a smile. "Belfrey, my dear. Yes. Belfrey. An awkward name for England, don't you agree? It was as well the Yorkshiremen gave me another.''

He was really going. Certain of the answer but unable to help herself, Jenny wailed, "Will we ever see you again?''

He hesitated and half turned back toward her. "It isn't very likely, is it, my dear? And yet, who can tell? But in any event you *have* seen me, and shan't be made to forget.''

Now Frank was swinging the door wide, drawing a fragrant swirl of night air over the three of them. He looked back at Elphi. "And will they take away your memories of us?''

"No indeed. No, no fear of that.'' With an effect of squaring his shoulders, Elphi walked upright through the door. The reporters caught sight of him and broke into a run. The hob glanced back one last time at Jenny's woebegone face. "The memories will make the punishment, you see.''

7

THE RAGGED ROCK

2010

For the longest time Liam couldn't seem to get it through his head that Jeff was dead. The power plant meltdown that had killed his friend had also, by making his part of the world uninhabitable, completely disrupted his life. "Disrupted" was really much too mild a word; the life he had been living and taking for granted was finished forever, irrecoverable. Liam's school, due to open a few days after the accident, was closed for keeps. He and his mother and father were living in Jeff's family's vacation place in the Poconos. Liam had spent parts of a number of happy summers there, but he couldn't get the idea of being at the cabin on Lake Wallenpaupack, and the idea of Jeff being dead of radiation poisoning, to fit together in his mind; it just didn't make sense that he could be alive and Jeff not be somewhere in the world.

Liam's older sisters were there with them for a while, but then Margy went back to the guy she was living with in New York and Brett went back to college at Penn State, where she was starting her sophomore year, and it was just the three of them again.

His parents were worried about him, he knew that in a dazed, abstracted way, but they had a lot of other things to worry about as well. Their house and all of its contents—books, clothes, furniture, china, photograph albums, videos, pictures, carpets, knickknacks, the piano, Liam's baseball glove, his computer, everything—were so contaminated with radioactive fallout that they would never be able to go back there again. They had some clothes and papers with them, and his cousin

Carrie's solar car, and that was it. His father's job, as a systems analyst for a firm called SmithKline Beecham in Center City, was suspended for nobody knew how long. His parents didn't know where they were going to live when they left the cabin. They were waiting for the government and the electric company to sort things out between them, which seemed to be taking quite a while. So mostly they left him alone.

That was fine with Liam. He sat on the dock for hours and hours, staring at the water. On rainy days he sat on the porch and stared at the rain, or pretended to read. If he held himself very, very still, inside and out, he could keep the fact of Jeff's death at bay.

The only time he allowed this program to be altered was the day Terry showed up at the cabin. Liam hadn't known he was coming, and when Terry came walking down to the dock and Liam looked up and saw him, the most horrible feeling he had ever felt in his life rammed through him like a sword; he actually screamed. Without deciding to at all he had jumped up and shoved past Terry and was running as fast as he could along the lake shore, away from the cabin. He sprinted for a whole mile before the pain in his lungs forced him to slow down. All afternoon he hung around the far side of the lake, and when he finally worked his way back to the cabin, because it was getting dark, Terry had left.

That evening he could feel more of his parents' anxiety than usual turned toward him, and his mother cried again. But they didn't reproach him or try to make him talk about it, and in a numb way he was grateful.

Weeks passed. It got colder, then really cold.

From something he overheard his father say to his mother one day, he learned that Jeff's parents were getting a divorce. Liam wasn't surprised, he knew they hadn't been happy together; there was some basic friction or disagreement there that used to rasp on Jeff. Anne was going back to California. That was okay by Liam. Anne didn't much like him anymore, and hadn't liked him and Jeff being together all the time. When Liam was little she seemed to like him fine, but something had changed that after Jeff's father refused to move his family down to Washington. Jeff hadn't wanted to live there anyway, even for the chance of being a chorister in the Washington Cathedral Choir. But

Anne had never been the same after that, nor had she behaved the same toward Liam.

Terry was in Washington now. His bid for the Senate was likely to succeed because of the stunning way he had masterminded the evacuation of Philadelphia after the meltdown, and maybe also because of the fact that he had lost his only child in the disaster. Liam's parents told him one morning at breakfast that they were going to live outside Washington, D.C., too, in an urburb in Maryland called College Park, near the city. Terry was helping arrange things. Liam found that the thought of seeing Terry in Washington didn't upset him. He found that he didn't mind the idea of moving to Maryland. He didn't care at all what they did. He simply didn't care.

The day they finished packing and were cleaning up the cabin, the day before they were to leave, was the day the alien ship returned.

2013

The interview wasn't going very well, but Julie didn't seem easily discouraged. She smiled a lot, and she was smiling now. "And you've been living in College Park how long—two and a half years now, more or less?"

"About that. We moved down here from Philadelphia right after Peach Bottom."

"Why did your parents decide to come here?"

Liam shrugged. "My father's company had an opening in the Washington office, and we had a good family friend here, and he offered to help us find someplace to live and get settled in.

"I see." She made a note. "Is this family friend someone you're close to?"

He shrugged again, then wondered if he was being rude. He didn't want to go that far. "His name's Terry Carpenter. You've probably heard of him."

"The senator?" Liam nodded; Julie made another note. She was sort of nice looking, shoulder-length black hair and no makeup and a big-nosed, good-natured face. She was wearing a black skirt and vest and a long-sleeved white blouse of some silky fabric, and her shoes were plain black pumps with an inch or so of heel. Liam forgave her for the heel; she was shorter than he was, and he was certainly no giant.

206

Julie looked up. "How does your family happen to know Senator Carpenter?"

"My father's cousin used to be his English professor at Penn, and then he and his wife moved a couple of blocks away from us in Philadelphia—well, Haverford, really—before we—before I was born."

He tensed, expecting her to pick up on the slip, but she only said, "It must have been a terrible experience, losing your home and being uprooted without warning from your whole life."

Liam looked at her, his face a mask. Then he looked at his watch.

Julie said in a pleasant, neutral voice, "Tell me about the accident. What did you do?"

"I was in the middle of a ball game. My mother heard it on the radio and came and got me, and we drove up to the Poconos—the Carpenters used to have a cabin up there."

"Could you tell me how you felt and what you were thinking about as you were driving up to the Poconos?"

Liam sat up straighter in the director's chair and said, "Look, I know what you're trying to get me to say. You want me to say I was thinking about Jeff, but I wasn't. I didn't know anything about where the bus was at the time and we all just assumed he would be okay. We didn't find out till the next day that the whole choir'd been taken to the hospital."

Julie's face and body became very still, as if each separate muscle were under control. "Jeff is your friend who died?"

"I don't want to talk about it," said Liam firmly.

A line appeared between Julie's eyebrows. "What about your school—would you feel like talking about that?"

"What about it?"

"I was just wondering whether you liked it."

"It's okay. Quaker schools are all the same, really. They're tough and they leave you alone."

"And you like people to leave you alone."

"Yeah." This came out as a tired sigh.

"Why's that?"

"It's just easier that way."

Julie moved again, smiled and crossed her legs, briefly flashing the tops of knee-high stockings under the black skirt. "I think you're saying you'd rather *I* left you alone."

Liam managed to smile weakly back at her. "I'm sorry, it's

207

nothing personal. The thing is, this wasn't my idea. My parents are making me do this."

"And you consider it . . . unnecessary? Boring?"

"It's a bother. I don't want a shrink, I really just want to be left alone."

Julie wrote what seemed to be several sentences on her yellow pad. While she was writing she asked, "What do you do when you're being left alone?"

"Play the piano. Read. Do math problems." Jerk off, he thought to himself, but I'm not telling *you* about *that*.

Julie unclipped the pad and flipped through several pages of white paper that had been secured beneath. "According to this you're something of a math prodigy—taking a course in calculus here at the university this term, is that right? That's very impressive."

Liam shrugged again before he could stop himself. "Math's always been easy for me." He checked his watch again. "Time's up," he said with audible relief and popped out of the chair.

Julie laid the clipboard in her lap and gave him a steady, attentive look. "Yes it is, but Liam—sit down again a minute, please—before we stop I want to make something clear. Nothing will happen here that you don't want to happen. I promise not to put pressure on you to answer questions you don't want to answer, or say things you don't want to say. All right?" This time he stopped the shrug in time and merely nodded. "All right. Then I have one last question for you today, which you can answer or not, just as you please. Are you happy?"

He was startled, not just by her having asked it but by the question itself. He hesitated, then said guardedly, "Well . . . not really."

"Wouldn't you like to be?"

Frustration and outrage swelled his chest tight, an aerosol-bomb feeling, very destructive to his balance, his careful control. "That's just not *possible*!" he blurted. "You don't know what you're talking about—you don't know anything *about* it!"

Julie stood up. "I see. Well, maybe next time you could try to explain it to me."

When Liam got home from the Counseling Center he went straight to the piano, throwing his books in the corner and his coat on the floor. He settled on the bench with a grunt of relief.

For the next hour he disappeared, first into Scott Joplin and then into some improvisations of his own.

When he came to the surface again his mother and Matt were in the kitchen fixing dinner, his father's study door was closed, and Carrie and Terry had cleared the flotsam off two chairs and were talking quietly in the living room. They looked up and smiled when Liam came in, but their identical expressions of badly masked apprehension irritated him, he was so heartily sick and tired of being the focus of everybody's concern. He lifted a hand to them, grabbed his book bag by the strap, and went up the stairs two at a time to his own room on the second floor.

Liam was a tidy boy; he had always kept his private space neat. The books were straight on the shelves, the bed made, the desk and floor clear of clutter. Except for a small bulletin board with a few cards and pieces of paper thumb-tacked to it, the blue walls were bare. Shut into this refuge of clarity and order, Liam worked methodically at his desk—calculus, then a little English—until his father called him down for dinner.

Talk around the table was general. Terry, as head of the Senate Committee on Alien Affairs, was heavily involved with the Bureau of Temporal Physics set up by the Hefn and spent a lot of time with the one particular Hefn, whose name was Humphrey, assigned by the Gafr to direct the project. Humphrey had been on the job more than a year and would soon have to return to the ship for a hibernation break; he was taking special drugs now to counteract the sleepiness that was the normal Hefn response to cold weather. Terry would miss him; they worked well together and had in fact become friends—something that wasn't (Terry had learned from Humphrey) even supposed to be possible.

Liam's whole extended family—except for Liam himself—was fascinated by all this. His father and Carrie thought the Hefn takeover more a blessing than a curse; his mother and Matt were less enthusiastic; but they all loved hearing the latest about Humphrey and the other Hefn. Terry was always more than welcome whenever he could manage to get out to College Park for dinner.

After the divorce, after Anne had remarried out in California, Terry had become a semipermanent member of the household. He even had his own small room now across from Liam's, where he kept a few spare articles of clothing and toiletries and pajamas, so he could sleep over on the spur of the moment when he liked. There was a picture of Jeff and Liam on the wall, enlarged from a slide Terry had taken on a camping trip when the boys were nine and ten. They were both hunkered down, cooking something on a backpacking stove set on the ground, and grinning up at the camera. Both of them looked like their hair hadn't been combed in days.

Liam never went into Terry's room. When Terry wasn't there, Liam kept the door closed.

It was Terry who had found this big house with the wraparound porch, on a street that dead-ended at the College Park Metro Station, and inviting Carrie and Matt to move into the third floor had been his idea originally. Those two, vacationing in England at the time of the accident, had just stayed on in Cambridge doing research for the whole next academic year, since their house, like Liam's family's house, would never be habitable again and since the University of Pennsylvania, where they both taught, was closed. Then Terry had made inquiries and pulled a string or two, and the next thing Liam knew Carrie had a job at the University of Maryland, Matt was retired, and the two of them had come back and were settled in upstairs.

The arrangement worked fine. Matt was a very good cook, which was a big help to Liam's mother, and Carrie and his father had always been good friends, the way cousins sometimes are. As far as Liam was concerned, whether they lived in the house or in an igloo in Antarctica was all the same to him. It was strange to remember, and he seldom did, that his cousin Carrie had once been one of his favorite people in the world.

When Terry had been pumped dry of Humphrey gossip and lore, Carrie entertained them all with a sample of wacky mistakes that had turned up on student papers over the years: "we had a hare's breath escape," "it's a doggy-dog world," "deep-seeded guilt," "for all intensive purposes," "give it undo attention," "she had five brothers, all tolled," and so on. Matt added a few from his own collection. When everybody got through laughing about that, Liam's mother spoke about his sister Brett, who had just heard unofficially that she'd landed a research assistantship to Cornell. Brett was especially delighted and relieved because it meant that next year she would be up in Ithaca with her boyfriend, who had gone there on some fantastic scholarship the year before, instead of off by herself in Santa Barbara or wherever. The boyfriend's name was Eric Meredith.

He was supposed to be some kind of whiz kid in biology. Liam's parents liked him, though his mother thought him much too thin.

Nobody asked how the counseling session had gone, but Liam could feel the curiosity just streaming off of the four adults all the time they were speaking of other things. For a minute he felt sorry for them, they all cared so much and wanted to help so badly, when there was nothing in the world anybody could do. Then this feeling was replaced by the more familiar one of aggravation at the burdensome pressure of their love. He had agreed to start seeing a counselor in hopes that some of this pressure would thereby be relieved, but so far it seemed to have merely changed in nature without diminishing at all. He cleaned his plate and drained his glass without really noticing what either had contained. As soon as he could, he excused himself and went back up to his room.

After a while he was not surprised to hear footsteps on the stairs, followed by a deferential knock. Liam made a hideous face, but he got up from his desk resignedly and opened the door. Terry and Carrie were standing in the hallway. "Mind if we come in?" Carrie said, and Liam stood aside to let them pass, hoping the grilling would be short.

But it appeared that his parents hadn't sent them up to pump him about the counseling session. Carrie sat on the bed; Terry took the easy chair and Liam sat back down at his desk, and even before he hit the seat of the chair Terry was saying, "The two of us have been putting our heads together, and we've decided there's something you ought to know."

They were waiting for him to respond, both wearing very sober expressions. Liam thought *Big fucking deal*, but all he said was "Well, okay. What?"

Terry shot a glance at Carrie. Carrie leaned her elbows on her knees and said, "Sweetie, you remember the story about the mating deer, don't you?"

"Sure."

"What exactly *do* you remember about it?"

"Just that a long time ago, when Terry was in college, you guys were sitting on the Ragged Rock one Halloween Day and two deer ran up the hill and got it on, right down below you. You used to tell us—tell about that all the time, on those tea and doughnut hikes."

211

Another slip. He could see Carrie carefully not letting her face show that she had picked up on it, and suppressed another flash of irritation. "Well," she said, "did you ever wonder what Terry and I were doing together in the park that day?"

For a second Liam's face, though he didn't know it, lost its polite-robot look. "No, now that you mention it. I guess I just assumed you were going for a walk. And that you were friends, like you are now."

Terry shook his head. "We hardly knew each other. I was just a so-so student in Professor Sharpless's modern poetry class, before that day. We were there because during an exam I'd had a kind of hallucination of having seen something very strange in the park. When Carrie graded my paper she realized something was wrong. We were up on the White Trail trying to reconstruct what might have happened to me when I'd been out there the previous Sunday morning, before the exam. Are you following this? I'm trying to summarize."

"I guess so."

"To make a long story short, it turned out that while I was sitting up on the Ragged Rock that Sunday morning, trying to think of something to write a paper about, all of a sudden a time window opened, right up the hill behind the rock."

"You mean . . . transmitting, like, from when *after* the Hefn came?"

"From the year 2020. We know that for sure. I was looking up the hill, and suddenly there was a place that looked like summer in the middle of the fall landscape, and two figures in radiation suits were looking out at *me*—and one of them was a Hefn."

Liam felt a little wakening of interest within himself, a sensation so unusual that he absentmindedly took note of it while he was still talking. "What year was this—what year were *you* in, I mean?"

"1990. It was my junior year. They wiped my memory; if I hadn't written that exam just when I did, I doubt I'd ever have remembered it—I'd have been like Jenny and Frank Flintoft over in England, you know; they saw some of the stranded Hefn on the moors years ago but didn't remember what they'd seen till the ship came back the first time and they saw the landing party on TV."

Liam nodded; he knew who the Flintofts were. The hob people. Carrie and Matt had been over visiting them when the accident occurred at Peach Bottom.

"Actually," Terry was saying, "*I* might not have remembered even then. The Hefn in the time window was wearing a radiation rig—I never actually saw what he looked like, so I'm not sure whether or not the memory would have been triggered like Jenny's and Frank's were, just by seeing the Hefn delegation. Unless one of them had put on a rig just like it."

"How come the *exam* made you remember?" Liam asked, and after Carrie explained he said, "My gosh, how come I never heard about this before?"

"Nobody's heard about it except Matt—and Anne, who never believed a word of it—and Jenny and Frank." He paused. "I never told Jeff."

Liam blinked. "And not Mom or Dad?"

"No, not them either. Anne might have said something to Phoebe, I guess, but I never did."

"Oh," said Liam, "because they wouldn't have believed you, and everybody would think you were crazy."

"That's exactly it. The worst time of all, though, was in 2006, when the ship came and then took off again. I'd been told that day in the park that there would be a power plant accident *before* the Hefn got here. So when they did come—but there still hadn't been any accident—I didn't know what to think. It just never occurred to me that they might leave and then turn around and come back."

"Funnily enough," said Carrie, "it did occur to Jenny. She mentioned it just before she went back to England to marry Frank, one day when we went out to the park together. But only as a solution to the conundrum, mind you. A theoretical solution; none of us had the remotest idea that the Hefn really might turn up a second time. Well—third time, really."

Almost to himself Liam said, "Twenty-twenty and radiation suits. So it was after the meltdown. So that's how come you had the evacuation all planned out." Terry nodded, waiting tensely.

Slowly Liam went pale. He stared at Terry. "*You knew* there was going to be a meltdown."

Terry, now very pale himself, locked his eyes with Liam. In a tight voice he said, "You want to know why I didn't bring Jeff and Anne down to Washington with me, like Anne wanted to— why I insisted on keeping Jeff at Germantown Friends with you."

Liam nodded. "God knows I wish, more than I could ever tell you, that I'd let Anne have her way about it. You know Jeff didn't want to leave Philadelphia, but of course if I'd put my foot down he wouldn't have had much choice. The truth is . . . the real reason I kept him up there is that I wanted him to be with you—and that I was positive he'd be safe with you."

Still staring, breathing rapidly, Liam said, "What made you think he'd be safe with *me*?" Was it his fault then in some terrible way that Jeff was dead? This was very dangerous ground. Liam could feel the cords by which he held himself together threatening seriously to snap, but he had to know the answer to that question.

"Because," said Terry, "the other figure in a radiation suit, that I saw in the time window with the Hefn, *was* you."

Liam hardly ever dreamed about Jeff. Sometimes he would be jolted awake, as if someone had dropped him from about four feet above the mattress, but he hardly ever could remember what it was, what images or voices, that had jerked him out of sleep in such an alarming way.

But that night, the night Terry told him he had known of Liam's existence years before he was born, and known of Liam's identity from the time of his conception, he dreamed that he and Jeff were back with Carrie in the park. They were climbing the White Trail toward the massive boulder they called the Ragged Rock, atop which they would drink their tea and eat their Dunkin' Donuts. Always the same doughnuts: one rainbow doughnut for Liam and one with something else on top, chocolate or coconut, and for Jeff one sugary jelly doughnut and one fat glazed one that always got a little squashed in Carrie's backpack. The dream trail, like the real one, was narrow and they climbed in single file, Carrie in the lead wearing the backpack, Liam following Carrie, and Jeff—puffing noisily—bringing up the rear. Liam was himself, but was also younger, perhaps nine or ten.

It was a sparkling fall day. The sky was a deep, brilliant blue, and brown and yellow leaves curved like seashells had drifted deep in the path, so that Liam kept stubbing his toe on hidden tree roots. Despite his stumbling progress the happiness he felt seemed a substance palpable as water or the sun's warmth, one which completely filled him and through which he blissfully

214

moved. As they ascended the trail together Liam shaped the words to himself: *This is the happiest I ever was in my whole life.*

But even as he climbed brim full of the strangest joy, he noticed that Carrie was getting much too far ahead of him. *Wait*, he tried to call, but she vanished around a curve. Anxiety flowed into Liam, polluting the liquid joy. He tried to go faster up the hill but was quickly winded and tripping worse than ever. *Hurry up, Jeff, it's getting dangerous!* he cried, turning his head as he toiled to urge his friend to keep up; but now behind him the White Trail was empty.

Sobbing, filled with foreboding, he turned again and ran with great effort around the curve in the trail. To his immense relief he saw Carrie now, far ahead, red backpack bobbing as she strode. It seemed to be getting dark. *Wait!* he tried to call again. His voice came out in a husky croak, but she seemed to hear him at last, and stopped and turned at the very foot of the Ragged Rock. But as Liam labored closer, fighting to catch his breath, the sense grew on him that something was still wrong. Carrie's short gray-brown hair had grown very gray and very long, straggling past her shoulders; her face was covered with gray hair; she had broadened and thickened; she was no taller than a ten-year-old, than himself. With sudden icy horror Liam realized that Carrie had turned into a Hefn, and with a shout of fear he woke.

He lay still till his heart had stopped racing. *God, what a nightmare. One for the books.* All that Hefn talk this evening must have brought it on—Terry's anecdotes at dinner and his weird tale about the time window afterwards. Maybe also the things he had told Liam after that: one, that his pal Humphrey, the Hefn in charge of the Bureau of Temporal Physics, was looking for mathematically gifted kids to intern in the Bureau, and wanted to interview Liam; and two, in 2020 Liam had been/would be working for the Bureau, according to what he'd told Terry back in 1990. Terry and Carrie had talked it over and decided it wasn't fair to Liam to keep Terry's preview of 2020 a secret from him any longer, since the information bore so directly on his future.

"When you saw me in the time window, did I know you?" Liam had asked, and Terry had said, "You sure didn't let on that you did. But the Hefn say 'Time is One, and fixed,' meaning that everything that's ever *going* to happen, in some sense already *has*. So if that's true, since I'll telling you about it now, I guess you must have known and were just pretending not to know."

"In that case I don't see why you couldn't have told me before now," he had said a bit peevishly, and Terry had replied, "It was always possible to tell you. It wasn't possible to *un*tell you. I wanted to be sure. But I consulted Humphrey about it yesterday—Humphrey knows the whole story, by the way—and *he* said that since Time is One, et cetera, and what will be will be, and indeed has been already, telling you couldn't possibly damage the fabric of the universe. So then it was up to Carrie and me, and we decided it would be a good idea for you to know how it all turns out. We think what Humphrey's offering you is a shot at something pretty terrific—being taken on as a trainee at the BTP ought to just about guarantee you a career, whatever you decide to do later, stay on or do something else. One way or the other it'll make a big difference to your future."

"You mean 'later' as in *after* 2020, because in 2020 I'm *going* to be working at the BTP?"

"So it seems."

"So was *Humphrey* the Hefn in the time window with me?"

Terry had looked thoughtful. "Hm. I hadn't thought about that. Maybe. Probably, even. Whoever it was, you told me he was your boss at the Bureau."

Liam had said, not very politely, "Well, it looks to me like you guys and Humphrey have got my future all sewed up between you."

He got up now and went to the bathroom in the dark. Then he climbed back into bed and lay on his back with his arms under his head and his eyes open, staring into the blackness. The nightmare had shaken him up, brought home to him the tremendous contrast between the force of the feelings he used to feel all the time, like happiness and fear, and the emotional blankness of his present life.

What were his strongest feelings nowadays? Annoyance. Resentment. Irritation. Relief. Nothing that was any fun and nothing that was too upsetting. That shrink today, that Dr. Hightower who'd told him to call her Julie, *she* was partly to blame for the nightmare too. She had made him feel more bad feelings than he'd felt in ages by poking her innocent-sounding question at

216

him, like some kind of a pointed stick. *Are you happy?* Liam made a disgusted noise. He'd be damned if he was going back for any more of that. Feelings were mostly trouble, he didn't need a shrink trying to tell him different. If they were good ones, like at the beginning of the nightmare, it just set you up for a worse fall later on. Being happy wasn't worth shit if you couldn't count on staying happy, and you couldn't, that was one thing he knew for sure.

Terry had said that working with the Hefn at the Bureau of Temporal Physics would make a big difference to his future. Until he and Carrie had brought the subject up, Liam hadn't thought at all, himself, about his future; but now that the question had been raised it was perfectly clear to him all at once, lying there in the dark, that he, Liam O'Hara, didn't want to have any future, thank you very much. No future at all, by God, despite the Hefn and their "Time is One" *garbazh* that implied he was as good as apprenticed to the Bureau of Temporal Physics already. No future at *all*—not even one that might have fascinated him once, working with the aliens in some sane, orderly, mathematical realm, helping to put things right on Earth.

What are you going to be when you grow up, little boy? he asked himself in somebody's else's voice—was it Carrie's or Julie's?—and then answered himself: I'm not *going* to grow up. I'll be nothing. The word lifted him on a wave of pure relief, beyond despair. For some reason it felt like getting even with everybody for everything. *No future at all!*

Smiling, something he rarely did these days, Liam rolled over and closed his eyes again.

The next day after school Liam caught the Metro at the College Park Station a block from his house and rode into the city to see Terry in Georgetown. The arrangement had been that Terry was supposed to tell him in more detail, over dinner, about working with the Hefn—what would be expected of a trainee at the Bureau. Since he had already decided not to become a trainee, Liam could have cried off the dinner by phone. But the thought of an evening away from his mother's chronic worrying was agreeable, and the relief that had followed his middle-of-the-night decision was with him still. He killed some time at the Smithsonian, then hailed a taxi and rang the front doorbell of Terry's basement apartment at six o'clock sharp.

Terry opened the door, a pot holder in one hand and a big slotted spoon in the other, like a parody of the harried bachelor chef in a sitcom. He was wearing an apron. Cooking smells and ozone rock music poured through the door in one dense commingled wave. "Come on in," Terry shouted above the music. "*You're* right on the button, but you're going to have to watch the box or something for half an hour, because *I* got held up at the office."

"No problem," Liam shouted back out of his new bland peacefulness. "I bought a *Sports Illustrated* on my way over."

"Perfect. Go and make yourself at home in the den. I'll bring you a Coke in a minute."

Liam took off his jacket and hunt it up in the closet. He extracted the magazine from his book bag and went into the cluttered, book-lined den that Terry had superimposed upon what had been a bedroom, automatically averting his eyes from the dozen or so pictures of Jeff—Jeff and himself at various ages, most of them—arranged in a shrinelike display in the hall. He settled down in Terry's beat-up old armchair, kicked off his shoes, put his feet in their socks on the hassock, and opened the magazine.

A few minutes went peacefully by. Suddenly Liam gasped, jerked upright, and dropped *Sports Illustrated* on the floor. In the living room the tape of ozone rock had ended and now a single voice, clear and pure, soared like a skylark above an accompanying orchestra: *Alma Dei Creatoris, sedet rei peccatoris. . . .*

It was Jeff's solo from the spring concert, the last hometown performance the Philadelphia Boys' Choir had given before the meltdown delivered a fatal dose of radiation to every last chorister, as well as to the director and the driver aboard the chartered bus rolling between Baltimore and Lancaster.

Mater, mater clementissima! Liam knew the performance had been recorded but he'd never before heard the tape. Blindly he kicked the hassock out of his way and made for the door. Remembering then, he dived back for his shoes. As he sat on the floor shoving his feet into them, he heard Terry curse and the tape end with a squawk just as the full choir came in behind the solo.

Liam lurched to his feet, his shoes untied. He collided with Terry in the doorway to the den and fought to push past him, just as he'd done on the dock at Lake Wallenpaupack two and a half years before; but this time Terry blocked his way, grabbing him around the chest while Liam flailed at him snarling, "Let me go, let me go, I have to *go!*"

"Liam, goddamn it, Liam! Stop this! Cut it out! Stop fighting me! I'm not *going* to let you go, so you might as well stop." Terry, still in his apron, fringe of hair on end, finally got a grip on Liam's arms that effectively immobilized the boy. "Now listen to me—listen!" he panted. "I'm sorry as I can be that you heard that tape—I got home late and forgot to think about what was loaded in the stereo. It absolutely was not my intention to force you to face the fact of Jeff's death in that way. If I'd wanted to do that, I swear to you, I wouldn't have chosen that way of going about it."

Liam hadn't supposed Terry had played the tape on purpose. *Why* didn't matter. What mattered was that hearing it was unendurable, and hearing it unexpectedly today, after his dream of the night before, had shocked him terribly. Head down, he stood shaking with fury and breathing between gritted teeth in Terry's determined embrace.

Terry now loosened his grip on Liam a little, drew in a deep breath, and said, more calmly, "I'll tell you the truth, though. I've been wondering whether somebody *shouldn't* force you to face it—not me, necessarily, but somebody, your mother or Carrie, or maybe this psychologist you're seeing now—but Liam, somebody's got to! You're hurting yourself so badly by not allowing yourself to grieve for Jeff. You can't get over a loss that terrible without feeling it, you poison yourself inside. God knows—God knows it hurts. Don't you think I know that? And there's a sense in which you and I, and Anne, and your mother, never will get over it; but Liam, Jeff's dead. He's dead. You're not. You've got a whole long life ahead of you, and it can be a very good life, but unless you can accept the fact that Jeff's dead and move beyond that, you might as well be dead yourself. Do you understand what I'm trying to tell you?"

As he spoke, Terry's restraining grip on Liam had turned into a loose hug, and then relaxed. Liam watched his chance, and now he made his break, shoving Terry off balance and grabbing his coat from the closet on his dash through the hallway and out the door.

A couple of blocks away, when he saw that no one was chasing him, he stopped to put on his coat and tie his shoes. He decided to walk to the station. He had begun to recover from the first shock of hearing his dead friend's voice, and his head felt very clear.

You might as well be dead yourself was no more than the exact truth. Everything Terry had said made perfect sense to him; but since Liam knew he wasn't going to be able to stand facing the fact of Jeff's being dead, no matter who helped or forced him, not now and not ever, he would simply arrange not to have a 'whole long life' ahead of him, or any life at all. Just as he had decided the night before. He would simply foreclose his future— not at some convenient, vague moment in the coming weeks or months, but now, immediately. He knew exactly how he wanted to go about it, as if he'd been planning this without realizing it for a long time, as carefully as Terry had planned the evacuation of Philadelphia.

He had left his book bag at Terry's place. That didn't actually matter; he wouldn't be going to school tomorrow anyway, or ever again. But his mother didn't know that, and it would make a perfect excuse for getting out of the house early in the morning. Terry certainly would have called his parents to report on what had happened. Liam would go home and stonewall—he knew how to keep them from pressuring him too hard for information, he knew without thinking about it that they were all a little afraid of him right now—and then he would go up to his room and start his preparations.

He sat on the Metro thinking through what he would have to do, his face more lively and interested in the planning of his own death than at any time since the death of his friend. Not once did he remember consciously that the next day, March 3, would have been Jeff's fifteenth birthday.

Liam woke with a start as the train pulled into Baltimore. Disoriented, he hauled his backpack down from the overhead rack and hurried up the aisle to the exit, then doubled back to the baggage car to retrieve his solarcycle. Getting ready had taken a big part of the night, he'd had to sneak around assembling the camping gear and provisions without waking anybody up. His room was right under Matt's and Carrie's bedroom. Even so, he could hardly believe he had fallen asleep.

The elements of Liam's departure had fallen into place as

smoothly as if he actually *had* planned it with the same pains-taking care as Terry had planned the evacuation. Last night, after stuffing everything in a big cellulose trash bag, he had waited for a freight train to go by on the Camden Line tracks, opened his bedroom window under cover of the racket it made, and lowered the bag to the ground by the rope he had tied it shut with. It had then been a simple matter to climb down after the bag via the chestnut tree growing right outside the same window (he'd done that plenty of times in broad daylight), haul the bag to the station—closed at that hour—and stash it in the dumpster with the rope trailing over the side. That done, he had gone back for his bike, wheeling it in perfect silence out of its storage niche under the porch.

It was now after ten. He had left the house at seven, saying he had to get into the city and back before school to get his books from Terry's house. The solarcycle was waiting at the Metro station exactly where he had triple-locked it. A few people saw him hauling the bag of gear out of the trash bin by the rope, but this was Washington and nobody looked twice.

Liam had clipped and strapped his equipment onto the bike and carried the whole rig down the stairs into the station, walking it onto the Metro as if he had no idea a permit to do this was required. But the station, like the train, was fully automated and no one stopped him. He'd gotten off at Union Station, bought a one-way ticket on the Camden Line—the one that went right past his house—to Baltimore from a machine, and taken the next train north. And here he was.

Baltimore was as far as he could get by train; the Camden Line trains terminated here, and after Baltimore the Amtrak trains would be sealed and pressurized like jet planes to cross the contaminated zone that included Wilmington, Philadelphia, and Trenton. They wouldn't stop again till Newark. Before Newark each train would pass through a special tunnel, where water would spray it from all sides to remove the radioactive dust. That was why he'd brought the bike.

At the information booth he asked directions to the Army-Navy store he remembered from being here a couple of years ago. He knew it was somewhere in the spruced-up area around Camden Station and had gambled that it would still have some-thing in stock that he'd seen there before, and he was in luck.

"We've got a few left from the scare after Peach Bottom,"

221

said the salesman, a middle-aged black man. "Everybody wanted their own radiation suit for a while there, then they all got used to it like. We haven't sold one of these since I can't remember when. Don't know if any of 'em are gonna be small enough to fit a little fella like you, but we'll sure see." As he spoke he was leading Liam through aisles crowded with piles of khaki pants and nylon raincoats and tents and sleeping bags, and down a flight of stairs, and there they were: three white radiation suits hanging up on hooks, with booties and gauntlets and visored helmets. "Think you can manage one of these?"

"It's not for me," said Liam, "but I can tell if it'll fit the person it's for by how it fits me."

"Try this one," said the storekeeper kindly. "This one's probably meant to fit a woman but it don't make no difference really, they're all made the same."

The suit was still a mile too big for Liam, even over his down jacket, but it was the smallest one they had. "How much?" he asked, and gave the man his TEEN card and waited for him to check the account. This purchase was going to clean him out, just about, but so what? He had to have some protection or he wouldn't get anywhere close to the park; the radiation would get him before he even got across the river. He wanted to die in the right place.

One right place might be on Route 222, near the plant—the spot where Jeff's choir bus had encountered the radioactive plume. That was closer and easier, but that place had, as a place, no meaning at all for Liam. Better would be to try to get all the way back to the park, as he had already done in his nightmare. He might not make it all the way to the Ragged Rock, but the idea of dying while trying to get there suited his sense of fitness.

There was a calendar on the counter, one of those thick pads with each day's date on a separate page. As the storekeeper handed back his card and receipt and his bulky purchase crammed into a big paper bag, Liam's eyes fell on the large red 3, and he realized, like a confirmation of his plan, that unwittingly he had chosen Jeff's birthday for beginning to end his own life.

He had included in his equipment a road map of the country he must try to cross, from before the disaster. Studying this last night, he'd decided that the best idea would be to follow U.S. Route 1, the old Baltimore Pike, which ran directly from this city to within a couple of miles of Ridley Creek State Park, and which crossed the Susquehanna, the major physical barrier of the trip, at Conowingo Dam by a bridge Liam was pretty sure was still standing, even though the dam's sluices had been opened and electricity was no longer generated there. He knew that at the edge of the forbidden zone the road itself had been broken up into rubble to prevent cars from driving in, but the broken up part wasn't supposed to be all that long.

He regretted now not listening more closely when Terry had talked about this, but probably it wouldn't matter. He was planning to bike up to where Route 1 ended, at its intersection with Pennsylvania Route 152, check out the situation, somehow figure out a way to get around the stretch of rubble with the loaded bike (preferably letting the bike's solar cells recharge while he did this figuring), pick up the road again beyond the point where it had been broken, and manage all of this without being detected from the ground or the air.

The worst immediate flaw in this scheme was the cloudy day. His batteries were on the low side already; he would not get very far under power unless the sun came out again or he stopped at a charging station first, before starting up Route 1. He could always pedal the bike himself, of course, but it didn't take much imagination to realize how difficult that would be once he'd put on the too-large protective rig.

He hated to take the time, but prudence won over impatience and he biked slowly along Calvert Street till he found a service station with a small sign saying SOLARCYCLES CHARGED. He was lucky; solarcycles hadn't caught on yet to the extent that very many stations were equipped to service them, though Terry thought they would be like solar cars, ubiquitous in a couple of years. It was like with clotheslines replacing electric dryers; usually you could just wait for a sunny day. But emergencies did arise, with bikes as with cars, and probably not that many people would have bought either if there a hadn't been another way to charge them up besides the built-in photovoltaic cells.

Nobody was ahead of him. "I'm not sure how much credit I have left," he told the attendant, a bored-looking blond woman, "but please find out and juice me up for all but fifty dollars' worth of my balance." No problem about emptying out his account. Fifty dollars would buy him lunch and some more provisions for the road, and by tonight he would be where money

223

could do him no good anyway. While he was waiting he walked half a block up the street to a McDonald's and ordered a McMonstro and fries and a chocolate shake, and when he had eaten his way through all of that he crossed the street to a supermarket and bought half a dozen assorted sandwiches, already made up, a bag of apples, and a three-liter carton of Swill.

Seventy-nine percent charged, one hundred percent broke, Liam remounted his overloaded bike and glided with the faintest possible whir into the street. At the intersection of Broadway and Straight (which had been called Gay before the residents had renamed it during the riots at the time of the AIDS Terror), he turned right. The street *was* straight, and wide, but hilly; Liam used the motor on the steep parts and switched it off to coast downhill. He passed a lot of brick row houses, each with a short flight of marble steps in front, and Johns Hopkins University, and a cluster of old hospital buildings and some small, crummy shops. Rails ran along the street on both sides of a central island planted in rows of huge locust trees. A trolley passed him, going the other way, toward town.

Soon the houses got even more run down and ratty-looking and only black people were on the streets. To his right Liam saw the castellated ramparts of Baltimore Cemetery, and shortly after that Route 1 swept in from the left to join Straight Street.

The street was poorly maintained and full of potholes and loose stones from temporary patches in the macadam. Two sets of trolley tracks were set into the paving, but this far out there was no longer any service; the rails dated from when private cars had become less common in neighborhoods like this one, around the turn of the century.

Several miles of grubby commercial lots and buildings later, the traffic thinned down to nothing. After Peach Bottom, people had moved out of the northwest quadrant of Baltimore's suburbs and urburbs, and nobody much was driving up that way. Liam crossed 695, the old Beltway, and rode under several sets of derelict power lines that he guessed must run from the Peach Bottom plant. He went by some empty townhouses, wrecked and looted looking, and then began to pass between small meadows of winter-pale dried grasses and weeds and small bare trees that, two years before, had been people's front lawns.

It was all pretty grim, and the gray day and penetrating wind did nothing to alleviate the grimness, but Liam found it all agreeably in keeping with his mood. A line from a poem came into his head, one Carrie must have planted there a long time ago: something like *The world is dying, let him die.* He stopped to pull a wool cap over his aching ears, then rode on into the wasteland.

North of the ghost town of Perry Hall, Liam entered an area of expensive-looking houses that must have been abandoned while still quite new; you could tell that until recently the surrounding countryside had been farmland. Here and there were patches of forest, the first he had encountered in twenty miles. He passed ghost service stations, modest single-family houses, a posh retirement village which had obviously been there only a very short while before Peach Bottom emptied it out.

And here he was. Less than two hours from the moment when Liam had thrown his McMonstro container and cup into the recycler in Baltimore, he had reached the end of the passable part of Route 1.

He had wondered if the road would be guarded, or obstructed physically, or both. There were no guards, human, canine, or (as far as Liam could tell) electronic; but a high chain-link fence blocked the road and ran away out of view to either side, and a huge sign displayed the radiation symbol and warned DANGER KEEP OUT RADIATION HAZARD BEYOND THIS POINT in thick red letters a foot high. The metal fenceposts were bent out at the tops and strung with three strands of barbed wire, and on Liam's side of the fence a ditch deep enough to stop a tank had been gouged clear across the road.

Liam got off, holding the bike by the handlebars, and sighted through the mesh. For as far as he could see ahead, the surface of the road had been turned into chunks of concrete rubble.

The fence was a poser. How far did it actually run either way?—and supposing he could get through, which way would it be easier to maneuver the loaded bike overland? Unless he could find a good-size break in the fence *and* a way to move his bike over rough and/or wooded ground, he was going to have to abandon the solarcycle and strike off on foot, with something more than a hundred miles still to cover. He would never make it.

Liam glanced at his watch and snapped out of this brief reverie of indecision. School would be out soon, he would be expected home. He had to get himself and the bike undercover before he was missed, and to accomplish that he had to try to find a way past the fence.

The sign pointing left said UPPER CROSSROADS 9, MADONNA 17, SHANE 30; the sign pointing right said JOPPA 10. For no better reason than that Shane was the name of a movie he had liked, Liam wheeled the bike left, restarted it, and swung aboard.

The road, 152, went up and down through mostly open, hilly country bare of distinguishing features. On both sides were modest-looking houses set in rough meadows of abandoned lawn. The fence hugged the verge of the road to Liam's right and rose and fell with the landscape, a tight barrier between the road and the houses, impossible to burrow under without a jack-hammer. At some of the intersections more ditches had been gouged across the northbound tributary roads, some of which had also been broken to rubble.

Liam rode along, anxiously searching for a break in the fence. After a mile or so he shut down the power to conserve it and began to pedal; but he was getting tired and there were a lot of hills. Most of the houses he could see through the wire mesh looked pretty old, and some were burned-out hulls, but the fence was almost new and in excellent repair. Liam searched for weak places or gaps as he rode with all the intense personal interest of a fence-riding cowboy, but there were none.

Cars passed him occasionally, and motorbikes. Somebody might remember seeing a boy by himself on a solarcycle at the edge of the forbidden zone. It made him anxious, but there was nothing he could do about that. At a turnoff called Pocock Road he checked his odometer. He had come eight miles from Route 1, and the fence flowed smoothly on ahead; there was nothing to do but go back and try the other way.

But the other way was no different: same houses, same rolling hills, same tight chain-link barrier snugged to the very edge of the road. Liam biked all the way to where Route 152 crossed on a bridge over I-95, five miles west of Route 1, before admitting to himself that the fence was not going to let him over or under or through.

He turned back toward Baltimore Pike because he didn't know what else to do. At a place where a wooded gully with a little stream at the bottom separated two houses on the north side of the road, he stopped. He leaned the bike against the fence and got out his packet of sandwiches; then he braced his own back

226

against the fence and sat down on the hard black surface, eating chicken salad on rye and drinking from time to time out of the carton of Swill, too bushed to think what to do next. The wind blew harder; he would be chilled soon, even in his down jacket. Through his pants the surface of the road was cold. He stuck the hand not holding the sandwich into his pocket. When he had finished eating he continued to sit, mind blank of everything but discouragement and fatigue.

Half an hour may have passed before the racket of the little stream in the gully below caught Liam's attention; but when it did he twisted around and got up on his knees to peer down at the water clattering over stones above thirty feet below. He was not on a bridge; the creek and its little valley were too small to require one. Into the weary vacancy in his mind intruded a thought: Where was the water coming from? It emerged directly below the spot where he was kneeling; there was no sign of a stream bed to the right or the left. Where else, then, but from the other side of the road?

Liam waited for a car to go by, then darted across the road and down a steep slope into what had once been somebody's big back yard. He could see the flash of flowing water in the long, flattened, dead grass below and the lines of paved drains slicing through—and there, Eureka! under a heavy brow of earth, covered thickly with dry weeds and shrubs and little trees, was a round concrete culvert. The concrete was several inches thick and full of gritstone; it must have been laid there decades ago, because culverts nowadays were made of recycled PVC pipe or fired clay. Heart thumping with the charge of adrenaline, Liam skidded down to the very rim of the culvert, directly above where the water disappeared. Even before he reached it he could tell the concrete tunnel was at least thirty-six inches in diameter. Big enough to let him through. Big enough to admit the bike, if he stripped it down and took off the wheels.

Liam slid down on the seat of his pants to the bottom of the slope and sighted through the culvert, holding his breath lest the way be blocked by more of the fencing, or by some obstacle he wouldn't be able to move. He could see the round eye of light in the distance, but from where he crouched it was impossible to tell whether the far end was blocked by metal mesh. He debated going back for a flashlight, looked at his watch instead, and plunged into the echoing darkness.

He tried at first to straddle the water, keep his feet dry, but the tunnel was too cramped and heavy rains had carried brush and silt partway through. Before long not only his shoes but his pants and even the sleeves of his jacket were soaked. For once in his life Liam felt grateful to be small; a larger boy would have had to crawl the whole way on his knees. He managed a kind of crouching walk for most of the distance, but his back and legs ached by the time he pushed out the other end and saw that he was indeed behind the fence. He could see the solarcycle on the other side, silhouetted high above his head.

It was the hardest work Liam had ever done in his life, but by six o'clock that evening he stood in deep twilight at the edge of the woods he had picnicked beside, having moved his bike and all of his camping equipment through the tunnel, carried them piecemeal, staggering, up the side of the ravine, and put the whole rig back together. To accomplish all this he had made five arduous trips back and forth through the culvert and four up the steep, slippery side of the gully. He was soaked and filthy and more exhausted than he could ever remember being before, and he ached everywhere.

At the same time he was aware of another feeling, one as unfamiliar as this extreme physical exhaustion. It was glee. He had tackled a really difficult problem and solved it, as successfully as he might have solved a problem in chess or calculus, and the resulting glee had something to do with the effort having required not only his mental but his muscular "personal best." The success had brought him that much nearer to his death, but that didn't seem to matter. Tired as he was, he felt whole.

But he could do no more that day. The air was freezing, and while Liam stood reconnoitering, a few flakes of snow drifted out of the rapidly darkening sky. Liam left the bike where it was, concealed among the trees from anybody driving past on the road. He hauled on his backpack one last time, shouldered his saddlebags, gripped his sleeping bag in his arms, and made his way clumsily across the overgrown yard to the back door of the house.

He was prepared to break in, but the door was unlocked; Liam simply turned the knob and went in. He felt his way through to a carpeted room and dumped his burden. It was as dark and cold inside the house as out, a dead, stale, penetrating cold, but Liam was grateful enough just to be out of the wind and snow.

Quick as he could he unrolled his sleeping bag on the relative softness of the carpeting. He identified the sweat suit in his pack by feel, shucked his wet clothes, pulled on the sweatpants and sweatshirt (which was hard to do because he was shaking so badly) and some thick dry socks, and crawled into the sleeping bag. Before his fingers had found and closed the zipper he was asleep.

My Gafr secured the coupling and inquired, what was my understanding of the nexus between the boy Jeff Carpenter and the boy Liam O'Hara. Was it like the connection between us two? Was it like that between Hefn and Hefn? Or between human parent and child, or between siblings, or like a sexual pairbond? Or was it a connection of another sort entirely? What was the nature of this bond, that—if Jeff's father's fears were well grounded, and I felt certain they were—Liam would choose to die because Jeff had died?

My reply was not very coherent. I conveyed my impression, based on observation and some knowledge of the background supplied by Jeff's father, Terry Carpenter, that the boys had been extraordinarily interdependent virtually from birth, and moreover that humans not infrequently form attachments which cannot be correctly understood as ties of blood or sexual attraction. Even such a phenomenon as a soccer team can evoke very powerful feelings of bondedness in certain humans. Those bonded to one team have been known to kill those bonded to a different team. I said that the link between Jeff and Liam seemed to me, simply, one of a wide range of possible links between human and human. The word love, *commonly used to designate these ties, had therefore such wide application as to be almost useless in defining the connection between the two boys, whereas the word* friendship, *while accurate, and applicable, appeared in some ways to be too weak.*

That the link was very strong was obvious from the probability that Liam had decided to die, and in the same way Jeff had died. This would be a clear act of desperation, like that of a Hefn separated by death from his Gafr. I reminded my lord of Belfrey's report, that some of the mutinous Hefn in England had died of a similar despair when they believed the ship would not return and they might well be separated from their Gafr forever.

My Gafr responded that she had not forgotten any of this, that

229

that was why she had inquired whether the tie between the boys was like that between herself and me. I accepted the rebuke, affirming that the two cases do appear to be alike in this respect. But in this respect only, for among humans the relationship of servant and master does not commonly appear to give rise to a mutual devotion. Examples of such devotion do occur in their literature and folklore; Belfrey had found it between the English aristocrat Lord Peter Wimsey and his manservant Bunter and between the hobbit Frodo and his servant Sam Gamgee, and in the religious myth of the Good and Faithful Servant.

But in all of these cases devotion seems entirely unrelated to sexual pleasure or procreation. Indeed, in cases where the master and servant form a sexual union, the offspring are subject to great suffering, and the relationships seem universally to be fraught with difficulties and often to end in despair and death. Whether the phenomenon is peculiar to certain countries and cultures Belfrey did not know.

He had also picked up references to slaves of whom sexual services were required. It would seem, however, that a bond of devotion between human master and sexual slave is virtually unknown and all but impossible, psychologically speaking. Paradoxically, however, I myself also have observed, and I said so, that within the typical marriage bond there is a degree of mastery on the part of the husband and a degree of service-rendering on the part of the wife, even at times when the bond is exceptionally strong. Exactly how the cases of slavery and marriage differ, except in degree, I have been unable to explain.

At all events, Jeff and Liam were paired equals; and Liam, at least, is heterosexual.

My lord said impatiently that she wanted from me not facts—and these facts were already familiar to her in any case—but judgment. For instance, how in my judgment could it have come about that Belfrey and the other rebels had transferred the service they owed their Gafr to several generations of primitive farmers.

I indicated my belief that Belfrey and the others had done their best in the absence of their Gafr to preserve their sanity and health. But I correctly anticipated what she would say next. That this was well enough, but that Belfrey and Saxifrey remained in concealment during our first landfall and attempt to locate them. Then, having in effect rebelled a second time, Bel-

frey transferred his bond of service to Frank Flintoft and Jenny Shepherd Flintoft. Worse, he remained in concealment after the second landfall, and later utterly violated his duty to the Gafr by revealing their presence to the humans. Worse still, it was clear that he had done this to protect Frank and Jenny Flintoft, surmising correctly that we could not have allowed them to remain in possession of what they knew concerning us. What was my view of all this?

I was becoming very uncomfortable, as she well knew. I reminded my Gafr that it was Belfrey who had spearheaded the rebellion and therefore must be presumed unstable and eccentric in his bonding functions.

She asked, What then of Godfrey's behavior toward the woman Nancy Sandford, an AIDS patient, now in hibernation? I could answer honestly that I knew nothing of this, but the direction her questions were tending was now plain and my discomfort began to be fear.

My Gafr increased the power of the coupling until it was very difficult for me to concentrate. What then, she asked, of your own connection to this Terry Carpenter, who as a very young man saw a Hefn who was all but certainly you, together with Liam O'Hara, eight revolutions from now, by means of a time terminal?

My Gafr knows perfectly how emotional a thing it is to have been seen in a time window. She understands perfectly that I must now be bonded both to the seer and to the one seen in the window with me, assuming as I think we must that the Hefn in the protective coverall, seen by Terry, was me. It was not a true question; yet at the risk of telling her again what she already knew I gave a true response: that I feel a fascination for Liam, both because he seems to have appeared with me in the time window, and because like her I am intrigued by the nature of his connection with the other boy and wish to understand it better.

In fact, my Gafr told me, you wish to experience it, as you partly comprehend already.

I felt weak and sick, for I recognized the truth of this and did not know what it meant or what she would do. Certainly I had no wish for Belfrey's fate to become mine.

She thought, and while thinking contracted about me until between pleasure and fear I was in a sorry way. Finally she

231

*said, I will not prevent this, nor will Godfrey's Gafr prevent him
from trying to save the life of Nancy Sandford, so long as you
both do the work we require of you and report everything you
learn. We must understand this better; your susceptibility to
bonding with the humans is therefore useful.*

*But attend me, Humphrey Gavnl. I remind you of a fact you
know already: that Belfrey saw neither his Gafr nor his Flintofts
again after he was brought back to the ship. If you do not wish
to lose me—or lose the chance of procreation for us both—take
care to avoid the traitorous example of Belfrey, for if you do not
I believe I will kill you myself.*

*Then she completed the conjunction, and when I came to
myself again I was aboard the lander on my way back to the
planet surface.*

Liam woke to the sound of a helicopter beating back and forth
above the house. The sound of it faded and grew, and he realized
that he had been aware of it for some time before coming completely awake. His watch, to his astonishment, said 9:52; he had
slept fifteen hours! He sat up, hurting everywhere and absolutely
famished.

It was still very cold in the room, but bright. As expected, it
was a living room. Liam extracted himself from his sleeping
bag and limpingly padded to the picture window in his boot
socks. The clouds had cleared off during the night and there was
no snow at all on the ground. Only now did it occur to Liam
that if the few flakes that had fallen on him the evening before
had developed into the kind of heavy spring snowstorm that
often struck this part of the country in March, his trip would
have been over.

What he had to do now was get dressed, get out to the bike,
put it in full sun, and open the solar panels. While the battery
charged he could be scouting a route to the nearest road that
might put him back on Route 1 above the broken section. He
also had to pee and eat, but the second of these could wait till
he'd taken care of the bike.

Getting dressed, however, turned out not to be so easy. The
clothes he had worn the day before, including his down jacket,
were still soaking wet. He had a spare pair of pants and two
sweaters besides the sweat suit he had slept in—an experienced
camper always takes extra clothes—but sometime while Liam

had been struggling back and forth through the culvert, his light cycling shoes, not designed for such rough treatment or for that much wetting, had split along the seams. The only other shoes he had brought were hiking boots, on the assumption that if the bike broke down or ran out of juice or if the roads were impassable on wheels, he might have to walk a long way. In their present state the cycling shoes were useless for walking, and the boots were clumsy for cycling, yet it seemed likely that at least today he would have to do a fair amount of getting on and off the bike, walking wherever he couldn't ride or where he needed to scout the terrain.

The parka was a much worse problem. The insulating value of wet down, as Liam well knew, is zero. At home he would have tossed the coat in the dryer, which would have dried and fluffed it nicely in an hour or so, but even if this house had a dryer, and even if by some chance it happened to be a solar one, and not dependent on nonexistent power from Conowingo or Peach Bottom, he doubted that after two and a half years of neglect the panels would still be working. Most likely there would be no dryer at all.

This proved to be correct. Here at the very edge of the danger zone, people had been given time to move out in an orderly way, taking all their belongings with them. The living room where Liam had spent the night was furnished with a green carpet, a fireplace with empty built-in bookcases on both sides, and open drapes at the picture window, and nothing else. The only sign that this had been anything other than an ordinary move was the amount of trash lying about. Liam found a laundry room off the kitchen, but all that was left of the appliances were some wires and cables sticking out of the wall.

He should have taken off the coat and carried it through the culvert dry, as he had carried the sleeping bag, also down; but there was no pint in thinking about that now. Liam shrugged, put both sweaters on over the sweatshirt, changed the sweatpants for dry corduroys, laced up his boots, and went out the same door he had come in, which opened off the kitchen.

It was *cold*, colder than yesterday; the wind cut straight through his layered wool sweaters. Liam stayed out only long enough to pee, then went back inside and rummaged in his saddlebags for gloves and the woolen watch cap he had worn the day before. Out in the wind again, he had to hunt for the bike he had hidden in the dark, and then force his stiff muscles to haul it up the last part of the hill and, after listening to be sure no cars were coming, run with it across the back yard to the house.

He had positioned the bike in a sunny spot where it couldn't possibly be seen from the road and had just opened the solar panels, which folded out like stumpy wings from the crossbar, when he heard the helicopter again and realized with a jolt of alarm that it might well be looking for him.

Heart in his throat, Liam clipped the wings flat again and hurried the bike up the back steps and into the house. The racket grew deafening. Could they have electronic sensors aboard the thing? Did they already know he was here? Despite the dead chill of the house Liam broke into a sweat; but instead of landing, the chopper flew over and past and the noise began to lessen.

When it was gone altogether and Liam's heart had slowed down, he was seized with a sense of urgency. He had to get going, he had to figure out how to proceed. His head pounded with anxiety—also, he realized, with hunger. He was absolutely ravenous. Sitting down cross-legged on the dusty carpeting, in the patch of sunlight under the window, he gobbled three sandwiches and three apples without stopping and drank at least a pint of Swill, as well as he could judge by peering critically into the carton's spout with one eye. Briefly he regretted not having bought two cartons while he'd had the chance; but there was a full canteen of water in one of the saddlebags for when this was gone.

Sunlight was streaming over him through the picture window, which faced south, toward the creek and the ravine. The drapes had been left open and the carpet beneath the window was faded. Some dead plants in pots on the sill cast their shadows on the faded spot. Staring at these while cramming bread and cheese into his mouth, Liam suddenly had an idea, his second really bright idea in as many days. He obviously couldn't risk charging the battery outside. With the panels' light cells flashing and twinkling in the sun, the bike would be plain as a pikestaff from the air no matter where he put it. But he *could* leave it in the deep pool of sunshine under the window, inside the house! The tomato and broccoli seedlings his mother set on the windowsill at home every spring grew leggy, but they grew. The battery wouldn't charge as well as it would in full sun outdoors, but it was something.

Liam got up from the floor and brought the bike over to the window. He fussed with it till he was satisfied that the solar wings would have the maximum exposure to the sun for the longest time; then, encouraged by having found a creative solution to yet another problem, he started opening closet doors. Maybe the people who lived here had left behind some old clothes that weren't worth taking along. The coat closet in the entry hall was empty, but Liam worked his way through the bedrooms and was finally rewarded with a moth-chewed lumberjack shirt in a red and black plaid, with an L. L. Bean label inside the collar, and an ancient trenchcoat. Both of these garments were much too big for him, but he was not in a position to be choosy; he hacked the tail off the trenchcoat (which otherwise could have gotten tangled in his spokes) and put both of them on. His wet clothes, including the useless down jacket, he let lie in soggy heaps, just as they were. He took his compass out of an outside saddlebag pocket, and he was ready.

The helicopter had not returned. Liam let himself out the back door again, walked perpendicular to Route 152 until he was among trees, then struck directly westward on a compass bearing, heading away from the gully. His map showed that the only road connecting 152 and the one farther north leading into Bel Air, where he was sure to be able to get back onto Route 1, was not far away to the east at all; but he had noticed the day before that that was one of the broken-up roads with a ditch. So heading east would be pointless.

He had gone only a couple of hundred yards through the woods when he broke out into back yards again, and houses, and walked down a driveway onto a road running northeast and southwest, meaning it ran parallel to Route 1. To Liam's joy, this road's surface was intact. Maybe that meant it didn't lead anywhere much, or maybe they hadn't bothered to wreck the distinctly secondary indirect routes. This one wasn't on his road map; but, whatever that meant, he would follow it for a while to see if it would take him where he needed to go. If it would, if his luck held, it would not be too hard to carry the bike and his gear this far, and *then* he could load up again and ride.

Soon the road alarmed him by jogging southeast in a wide curve, but then it straightened out again and went in the right direction for nearly a mile, between abandoned houses like the one where he had spent the night. Liam passed several side roads, most of them with signs saying NO OUTLET. When the road he was following forked he stayed with the northernmost fork, which continued to bear the same name as before: Reckord Road. He began to feel quite hopeful; but just as he was starting to think of turning back and taking his chances with the bike he saw something like a roadblock up ahead.

When he got closer his spirits suffered a terrible blow. Improbable as it seemed, the obstacle ahead was *another* chainlink fence turned out at the top and strung with three strands of barbed wire, and it ran right across the road and as far as he could see in both directions. For a wild few minutes as he approached this new obstacle Liam wondered if he could somehow have gotten turned around, despite the compass, and come back to the original fence again. Anxiously he hurried forward.

There was a double gate in this fence the same width as the road. On the gate was a large sign. Liam broke into a clumsy run until he got close enough to be able to see that the sign read: ATKISSON RESERVOIR (ARMY CHEMICAL CENTER) NO ADMITTANCE. The gate was chained shut and locked with three enormous padlocks. On the other side the road ran straight on.

Liam stood in his ragbag clothes and admitted to himself that, even in the unlikely event that he could find a similar way of getting under it, he would not be able to cope with one of these fences a second time. His strength and resolve had already been expended to their limits in that direction. He would have to go back and take the one sideroad on the north side of Reckord Road that hadn't been signposted NO OUTLET.

Wearily he turned around and trudged back the way he had come. At the turning he hesitated, but there was no point in scouting the only route available. If this road led nowhere, then nowhere was where Liam would be going, at least on wheels and under power.

On the way back the wind blew into his face. The sky was now full of large fluffy cumuli that kept covering the sun. Liam pulled the sawed-off trenchcoat tighter around himself and bent forward into the wind; at least it would be a tail wind, once he was mounted, which would help conserve power.

And then above the wind he heard again the clatter of an approaching helicopter.

Liam sprinted across the front yard of a derelict house and squeezed into the space between its brick wall and a hugely overgrown rhododendron. Twigs poked into his eyes and raked off his cap. The helicopter passed so close above him that the whacking of the rotors filled the world, and he could plainly see the two figures inside.

When the outrageous noise had dwindled, Liam plucked his cap out of the shrub, pulled it back on his head, and set off again at the fastest pace he could manage in the heavy boots. Soon, despite the cold wind, he was sweating with effort and anxiety. Almost back to the house, a fresh anxiety struck him: which yard had he come through to reach Reckord Road? He failed absolutely to recognize the place and wasted time in trial and error; but in fact there were only half a dozen houses whose driveways he could have come down, and finally he found the right one.

Back inside "his" house the sun had moved and the bike stood in partial shade. But the charge on the battery was up eleven percent, and Liam's spirits lifted for the first time since he'd sighted the gate blocking Reckord Road. Quickly now he prepared to abandon his refuge. He decided to leave behind all his wet clothes except the down jacket, which he might have a chance to dry (and whose warmth he would miss badly tonight if he couldn't). Standing, he ate another sandwich—the last of those he had bought—and drained the carton of Swill.

It went against Liam's grain to leave stuff lying around messily, like the astronauts leaving waste and trash on the moon; at the last minute he put all of his wrappers and the crushed Swill carton into the sandwich bag and left the bag by the kitchen door. He also squandered a couple of minutes hanging his pants on a hook, his socks on doorknobs, and the shirt on the hanger he'd found the lumberjack shirt on, but it made him feel better. He carried the rest of his things outside and closed the door securely.

First, the bike. The wheels came off again with two quick twists; then, with an ear tuned to the possible return of the helicopter, Liam shouldered the frame, light but awkward, and carried it through the trees and yards and down the driveway to Reckord Road. He stashed it there on the porch of a house and went back for the rest of his gear. Another half hour and the bike had been reassembled and loaded, and Liam was cruising along looking out for his left turn.

Again luck was with him. After an anxious hour of backing and filling among the unexplored roads he hit the Army Chemical Center fence again and almost despaired. But this time he could see houses to his left through the bare trees, and a short scouting expedition on foot showed that the fence angled abruptly north only a few hundred yards beyond the road. He circled around through the woods, between the fence and the houses built on the ridge above it, and struck the same road he had just left, now exiting the Chemical Center from the opposite side by way of another gate. By pressing himself against the gate on this far side and squinting back along this road, he could see all the way across the long, narrow space enclosed by the fence, back to where the other gate had stopped him. He and his bike were almost at one tip of this space; he would simply strip the bike again, carry everything around, reassemble and reload, and be back in business.

He heard the helicopter again shortly after he had accomplished these labors and was back in the saddle, riding briefly under power as a reward. This time, to Liam's great relief, the chopper never came into view. He was getting very tired. It would have taken all his strength to leap off the bike and run it off the road into the trees or behind some houses; in fact, it would have taken all his strength to do anything that had to be done quickly. He had used up a week's adrenaline humping the bike and everything else around the fence through the woods. Lucky for me, he thought, that it's still so early in the year. The new growing season's berry canes would have ripped his clothes and skin to pieces; the brittle old ones could be trampled down.

After that things went more smoothly. The first time a left turn led back to Route 1, he followed it only to find the highway still in chunks. But the next left was Pennsylvania Route 24, which ran straight into Bel Air and intersected with Route 1; and this far into the danger zone the authorities had suspended their efforts to prevent people from exposing themselves to radiation. The road was whole. Liam had made it through.

It was late and he was tired and chilled clear to the bone. Best to hole up here in town for the night. Tomorrow he would have to start wearing the radiation suit; from now on he would risk exposure to radiation every time he ate or drank anything or relieved himself but—always assuming the bridge over the dam at Conowingo to be passable—he thought that the chief logistical difficulties were behind him now and it would mostly be a question of not getting too sick till he'd covered the rest of the distance to the Ragged Rock. If he started queasing out this side of the Susquehanna, there was still the option of heading up 222, as Jeff's bus had done. But, having gotten this far, he felt pretty confident of making it all the way.

Liam steered the solarcycle through a few back streets, chose a house at random, and tried the door. That one was locked, but he went along the street trying doors until the latch of one clicked under his hand. People had been evacuated more unceremoniously from Bel Air. The house he entered was as cold as last night's house, but it still had furniture and smelled powerfully of mildew—or perhaps Liam wasn't quite as tired as he'd been last night and noticed the smelliness more. The front door was at ground level; he walked the bike inside with all his gear still loaded.

There was a windowless room off the kitchen, a kind of pantry-cum-storage-room-cum-spare-bedroom, with a cot and a thin mattress, and a lot of boxes and cans and things stacked against the walls. Thinking an inner room might be less contaminated with radioactive dust, Liam decided to camp in there for the night. He brought the bike in too. Sitting on the cot in almost total darkness he unpacked and opened a can of beans, then another can, then chomped his way through several apples. Finally he unscrewed the cap of his canteen and took a long drink of the stale tap water inside, brought all the way from home.

The tap at which he had filled that canteen felt a million miles away, though in real miles Liam actually hadn't come all that far. Almost for the first time since leaving home he thought of his parents, and Carrie and Matt, and Terry, and what they must all be feeling and saying about him. For the very first time he thought of the note he had left: "This is something I had to do. Try not to feel too bad." Not enough to give his plan away in time for them to stop him, but enough to tell them what he wanted them to know, after they found out what he'd done.

The bare mattress was smelly but seemed free of mouse nests as far as he could tell. Probably radiation had killed all the mice. Thoughtfully, feeling oddly old, Liam unstrapped the sleeping bag from his bike and rolled it out on top of the cot. He stripped and put on the sweat suit again. His down jacket, not much dryer after a day spent strapped across his saddlebags, was beginning to reek; he tossed it onto the kitchen floor, deciding with a shrug to leave it behind tomorrow. Another forty-eight hours or so and things like being cold and hungry and tired, and worse things, weren't going to matter anymore.

Liam woke the next morning from a complicated dream about Jeff which dissolved the instant he opened his eyes. He lay still, trying to make it come back, but all he could get were a sense of confusion and distress, and Jeff's voice saying "Didn't you even *try* to—" something or other. Try to what? He wanted desperately to know, but nothing would come and after a while he gave it up and wriggled out of the bag. This was the day he would cross the Susquehanna.

By eleven o'clock Liam, wearing his brand-new too-big radiation coverall, including gauntlets and booties and visored helmet, and the respirator with a mouthpiece like the sort you wore skindiving, was riding his recharged solarcycle along Route 1, north of Bel Air. He rode slowly, partly to conserve power, partly because shortly after leaving the town the road had entered a wooded area for the first time since leaving Baltimore, and dead branches littered the road. A branch could snag his spokes and dump both him and the bike onto the pavement if he wasn't careful. From inside the helmet, unfortunately, it was a little hard to see.

He had been lucky again; the morning had begun brightly, and his battery had been able to breakfast on sunlight while he spent an hour and a half figuring out how to put the suit on. Without the puffy down jacket to pad it out the thing was huger than ever on him and the lead lining made it drag awkwardly. *Pedaling* the bike would obviously be impossible; he would have to nurse it along as far as he could and then walk until he dropped. Maybe Route 222 would be the better choice after all— but he would wait till he got to Conowingo and see.

Now that there were no more problems to be solved or decisions to be made for a while—now that he could simply balance his body in its baggy leaded long johns on the solarcycle, steer around tree limbs, and endure the suit's discomfort—Liam found himself doing something he had assiduously and consistently avoided doing for a very long time: he found himself thinking about Jeff. Thinking about him directly, not flinching or freezing

240

at the first whiff of Jeff-thought but letting the memories come, letting the flavor of this morning's lost dream, and the whole pushed-under *sense* of his friend, fill up his mind. Jeff would have loved this trip, he knew. Jeff's being along would have made an exciting adventure of it, instead of the dreary, uncomfortable struggle it had mostly been. Somehow it felt right— safe—to remember Jeff now, to invoke his personality and presence, knowing that in a few more days these things as he had known them would be gone forever from the world.

It did seem safe at first. Vivid pictures came to him: Jeff beside him in meditation class, sitting straight with his eyes closed and his right hand palm upward on his left, still as a statue while Liam chafed and squirmed and sneaked looks at the clock; Jeff in his wine-colored Philadelphia Boys' Choir blazer and black tie, his thick hair neatly parted and combed, stepping to the front of the bright stage to begin his solo; Jeff at the cabin, racing him up Mount Pocono, racing to see who could pick the most blueberries, optimistically racing (in the tent together that last summer, at twelve and almost-twelve) to see who would finally be the first to actually come; Jeff in a fury in his own back yard in Haverford, saying "Why won't she leave me the hell *alone* about it? What's she got against you, anyway?" Saying, "I don't care what she says or what she does, I'm going to be with you as much as I want. Dad'll make her let me."

But these memories had been dammed up for more than two years—and unlike at Conowingo, the sluices had stayed clamped shut. To open them now was to risk carrying the dam itself away in a flood of backed-up feeling. Liam had just started to feel a little funny when he was struck, as by an enormous fist, with more anguish than he had known a human body could contain. He cried out. Behind the helmet's visor his face went out of control, stretching and flexing as if it too were a fist, and from his eyes, tightly clenched though they were, came a literal outburst of tears.

With some part of his mind still able to observe and think he tried to make himself turn the bike off and stop, but—unable to breathe or see—instead felt the front tire hit something, the handlebars jerk sideways in his hands, and himself be hurled to the ground; but he could scarcely tell whether he had fallen off the solarcycle or whether the appalling pain of remembering Jeff had left him sprawled in the road like this, crying so hard he

241

was just about screaming, unable to use the respirator right, unable to stop, unable to stand it. It was in order not to have to stand feeling these things that he had decided to die, and gone to all this trouble, and here he was feeling them anyway! It wasn't fair. He felt as if he were dying *now*.

In all of Liam's first twelve years, there never was a time when his life and Jeff Carpenter's hadn't been tangled together, when Jeff hadn't in fact been the most important person *in* his life—more important than his parents or his sisters or Carrie or Jeff's father, the one most necessary individual he knew. The one Liam had most needed not to die, and the one who, for some reason he didn't understand, he could not face the rest of his life without.

When he finally sat up, a long time later, it was because he had heard the helicopter. The suit impaired his directional hearing, but wherever the whack-whack-whack of the chopper was coming from, it didn't sound too close. This was just as well; Liam was in no shape to take evasive action. His visor was so steamed up he couldn't see out at all, and his face felt completely covered with guck. He couldn't blow his nose or defog the faceplate without risk; this close to Peach Bottom everything was bound to be pretty hot, and if he was going to make it all the way to the Ragged Rock he should open the suit only when he absolutely had to.

But he couldn't see a thing, and there was finally nothing to do but loosen the fastenings, remove one gauntlet, and reach his bare hand up inside the helmet to wipe the visor and his own face with a sleeve of the sweatshirt from his saddlebag. As soon as he fastened the helmet again the visor steamed up some, but not quite so badly; at least he could just about see to pick up the bike, check it over for damages, secure the saddlebags and sleeping bag. All the time he was doing this the chopper faded in and out of range, but it never came close and after a while Liam realized he wasn't hearing it anymore.

The bike seemed undamaged—a very good thing, because repairing anything broken would have been impossible. As soon as he could Liam remounted and set off again, badly shaken, his brain throbbing and swollen-feeling. The experience of being slapped to the ground by grief had changed his thinking and stiffened his resolve. He had made a mistake. Less than ever, now, could he afford to think about Jeff.

242

But thoughts and images of Jeff, released from their long bondage, invaded and plagued him and refused to be bound again. It was awful. Not even when they got the news that Jeff had died in the hospital had Liam felt so bad. After a while he began to wonder if the degree of his wretchedness might mean that the radiation sickness had already begun, and felt a thrill of fear that surprised him: how should he fear the thing he had come so far and endured so much to find? Confused and miserable, he rode on through the windy, cloud-fraught afternoon.

At last, after an endless time of steep hills and swooping valleys, and one more ghost town, called Hickory, where he saw the big pale bones of cattle half-hidden among the tall dead weeds of a pasture, Liam came in sight of a sign saying CONOWINGO 4. If the dam and bridge were still there, if he got across the river, he would now certainly achieve the lesser of his goals at a minimum; and if it were not he could stop now on this side and remove the protective clothing, knowing he had come as close as he could. The last major logistical question about the trip was about to be settled, and when it was, then he wouldn't have to think anymore at all.

The bridge *was* there, and looked solid; Liam swooped around a wide curve and there it was below him, a long straight line ruled across the broad river. Before the meltdown at the Peach Bottom Nuclear Facility—which was now very near, only a few miles away—the dam had held the water on the upstream side of the bridge at a much higher level than the water on the downstream side, which used to be quite shallow and full of rocks. Now the river was about equally deep on both sides, and the bridge merely a terrifically massive bridge, not a functional dam that cars could cross on top of.

How much longer it would be there probably depended on how important the people in charge thought it was to have a bridge at Conowingo. The one at 95, near the mouth of the Susquehanna, the bridge Jeff's bus had crossed to get here, was regularly maintained, as was the Amtrak bridge, but this one was closer to the plant and probably very hot. The river water itself was not especially radioactive now, because the intakes at Peach Bottom had been sealed off with concrete when the plant itself had been contained. They had had to do that, otherwise the whole Chesapeake Bay area, including Baltimore, would have been as uninhabitable as Philadelphia. Liam had heard

Terry bring all these matters up from time to time but had paid little attention, not imagining then that he would ever have occasion to take a personal interest in any of them.

Well, after tomorrow, he wouldn't. Anyway, all he really needed to know he now did know: the bridge still spanned the river.

He coasted down the curve of the hill and approached the dam. The Susquehanna, very wide, gleamed pale blue under the blue sky in that washed-out late-winter landscape. Liam switched on the power, which was getting pretty low again, and started across the bridge. Once well and truly across, he would stop for a while to let the battery charge up between drifts of cloud.

At first there was a rusty metal wall to his right, part of the housing for the machinery that used to operate the dam, and he couldn't see downstream. Then the wall ended and he had a full view in both directions. The wind blowing at the bridge's midpoint had teeth in it, and the helmet restricted his vision, but his spirits soared unexpectedly at the prospect from the middle of the river—followed instantly by the sort of thought that had been tormenting him all afternoon, like a carving knife twisting in his stomach: *Wow, I sure wish Jeff could see this!* He sobbed once and struggled fiercely against tears, teeth clamped on the respirator mouthpiece, knowing his visor would steam up again if he gave way.

The bridge ended in an uphill curve of road. To the right an extension of railroad bridge struck off at an angle to the road; and smack in the middle of the span, dressed in a radiation suit very much like Liam's, sat a small stumpy figure.

Liam was so astonished that instead of gunning his bike and fleeing up the hill he stopped dead. The little figure hopped down and came toward him, and then Liam did gear down and start to ride away, but he was too slow. Before he had collected his wits the dwarf, straddling the front wheel, had seized the solarcycle's handlebars with both gloved hands, and Liam discovered that small or not it was a much stronger being than himself. He yanked and wrenched, but the bike wouldn't budge.

At close range it was also obvious that the dwarf's suit was of a much higher quality than his own, probably custom-made, definitely not scrounged on the cheap from an Army-Navy store. The suit had a built-in microphone, into which its wearer now spoke. "I'm not here to try to stop you," was the first thing it

244

said. "I've a pretty fair idea of what you're up to, and as a matter of fact I think you have a perfect right to carry out your plan, though your family wouldn't thank me for saying so. Nor would Terry, and he's the main reason I've been tracking you. He's a good friend of mine. My name is Humphrey."

Still dumbfounded, Liam's mind worked sluggishly to take this in. Humphrey? Terry's pal Humphrey the Hefn, from the Bureau of Temporal Physics—the one that had offered to interview him for an internship at the Bureau? Finally he did manage to mumble, "Tracking me?"

"Most of the way from Baltimore. You're quite an enterprising fellow, Liam O'Hara. We would very much like to have you on our staff at the BTP."

Light dawned, or rather struck. "That was *you* in that helicopter! Shit! You had heat sensors, didn't you? You knew where I was the whole time," he said bitterly. "How come you let me get so far?"

"I've already told you," Humphrey replied calmly, "and you can believe me, that I have no intention of preventing you from following your plan. I'll even help you carry it out, if that's what you want—the chopper is at your service—though I'll understand perfectly if you prefer to complete the trip under your own steam. I doubt you'd make it all the way, quite frankly, but I suppose honor would be served in any case. It's entirely up to you. By the way, were you making for your friend's house in Haverford or for the park in Delaware County?"

This was too much. "How did you *know*?" Liam cried, really furious.

"I—deduced it from the available information," said Humphrey placidly, "or rather I should say that Terry did. Consider the facts. Your friend's death had depressed you deeply. You drifted, you withdrew. More than two years went by. Finally you left a note and disappeared. You took your bike. A boy matching your description bought a radiation suit in Baltimore. A boy on a solarcycle, boy and bike both matching the police descriptions, was seen by several people riding along the edge of the contaminated area. Terry could think of only one or two reasons why you might have done those things, and all of them boded ill."

"Oh." Liam's fury drained away. He *had* left a trail a yard wide. "Well, I still don't see what it's got to do with you."

"I offered to undertake the search as a favor to my friend Terry, who is nearly frantic, by the way. He keeps saying, 'I can't lose them both. I just can't.' " (Liam winced.) "You're aware that he saw you in the time transceiver, quite grown up and evidently in excellent health? Yes? *I'd* have said that ought to give him confidence, but this development is testing his faith."

"What's that supposed to mean? Confidence in what?"

"In your survival and safe return."

Who the hell did this little guy think he was? "Are you trying to tell me that because Terry saw me in the time window, there's no way I can *possibly* not die until after 2020?"

"According to our understanding of time, if he saw you, then you're definitely still going to be alive seven and two-thirds years from now, yes. Nevertheless, my offer stands."

Liam said, outraged, "Yeah, well, what if I just take off this radiation suit *right this minute*?"

Humphrey pirouetted suddenly and let go of the bike; Liam staggered, thrown off balance. Humphrey dropped to all fours. "Then you won't be alive seven and two-thirds *days* from now. But you're not seriously thinking of doing that?" He stood upright again and came forward until he could lay one hand on the bike again. "What we never know beforehand, you see, is *how*. By what means will you be alive in the year 2020, so that Terry can have seen you in the transceiver? I myself feel certain of the outcome; but it's perfectly possible that your survival could be achieved somehow by my flying you back to Philadelphia in the helicopter, or even by stepping aside and letting you proceed on your own. Either of those ways might be *how*. We won't know the answer till events have revealed it. We never do."

Liam stared, then shook his head, confused. "I thought it was the police looking for me," he mumbled.

"The police have been told to keep out of this," Humphrey said, shocking Liam with this evidence, so seldom pushed down people's throats, of how completely the Hefn were in charge here now—so completely they could tell governments and police forces to butt out when they liked. In the face of such authority and power, what should he do? He was just a kid. Was it really true that his tremendous effort had been doomed to failure from the start? Was he sorry or glad? He didn't know; he couldn't tell what he felt about any of it, except that he still didn't know any better than before how to go on living without Jeff.

"Let me be entirely honest with you," remarked Humphrey in his tinny microphone-processed voice. "I also offered to help Terry because I was curious. Why would a boy with his whole life ahead of him want to die, only because his friend had died? Other youngsters lose friends or parents or other people important to them, and they're naturally distressed, but after a while they . . . adjust. You haven't even begun to get over this loss of yours. It's unusual. The relationship was unusual. I'm interested in humans and in human connections, and this connection of yours with Jeff is something I wish to understand better."

"It's none of your business," said Liam shakily. "It's nobody's business now but mine."

"I agree in a sense," said Humphrey. "And, as I promised, I'll do precisely as you instruct me. Leave you here if you like. Fly you the rest of the way. But I do have a third suggestion, and it isn't simply to take you home."

Liam's mind felt muddled. Things were taking a peculiar turn. Evidently he really would not be rescued against his will; his wishes, even his self-destructive wishes, were to be respected by this alien as they could not possibly be respected by his family or by Terry.

If he chose to go on, what would Humphrey do? Tell his parents and Terry that the search had been unsuccessful? Wait till he died, then bring his body back to be buried in a lead-lined coffin? One thing was sure, he certainly wouldn't tell them he had allowed Liam to refuse to be brought home.

But the Hefn had said he wasn't going to die.

But if he said no, if he went on, how could he *not* die? What other escape could there be? In frustration, in bewilderment, Liam waited head down to hear the Hefn's third suggestion.

Humphrey said, "I can remove your memories of Jeff."

Liam's head jerked up. *"What?"*

"Remove your memories. Wipe your mind." And when the boy still stared at him: "You know, of course, what happened to your cousin's friend Jenny Flintoft, in England?"

Liam nodded. After Jenny had seen a Hefn in Yorkshire, she had been made to forget all about the encounter for years and years.

"And you also know, don't you, what happened to the Swede, Gunnar Lundqvist, who had forgotten some essential information relating to one of our exiles in Sweden? We looked into his

247

mind and found his memories of the event in question. I imagine you have also heard about the Tanzanian farmers who destroyed several hectares of rainforest, and about the miners in Brazil. And I know you know what happened to Jeff's father, as a young man just a few years older than you. We Hefn can do these things with memory, Liam O'Hara—dig up events you've forgotten completely, bury others so deep you'll never get them back. We can do this, and we do do it, with or without the agreement and cooperation of the rememberer; but it's not my intention to remove your memories of your friend without your consent.

"However . . . if having them removed would make you able to continue living your life, and if you wish it, I can cover those memories so well you would never again remember that you knew a boy called Jeff Carpenter, if other people didn't tell you."

Liam felt spacey; he leaned on the bike to steady himself. Lose all his memories of Jeff, as if he had never known him? That would be to lose the most important thing in his life so far—and right away, without knowing how he knew, Liam understood that he could decide to die more easily than he could ever consent to that.

But—lose them for a while? Till he grew up some more, got his life in some kind of order, formed some goals and made some other friends without the specter of Jeff standing always in between? *That* could be the biggest favor anybody had ever done him, an enormous time-release tranquilizer to help him through the next couple of years.

"You can still die if you like," Humphrey repeated placidly. "Or I suppose I should say, if you can."

Liam looked at Humphrey now, straight into the Hefn's large eyes surrounded by hair, like an animal's eyes, behind the faceplate of his helmet. It wasn't—he understood this now—it wasn't that he had ever *wanted* to die! If there turned out to be some other way of escaping the anguish of Jeff's death without dying himself, he would be glad enough to take it. He just hadn't imagined that there *was* any other way. All the same—"You could really dig the memories up again, when I was ready?"

"Certainly. Anytime you say."

At that moment an image flashed into Liam's mind, a scene from one of the classic "Star Trek" episodes that he must have watched fifteen or twenty times with Jeff, who had been crazy about them. In this one Captain Kirk had once again fallen in love with some space bimbo he had had to leave behind. At the end Kirk had gone to sleep in his quarters, mumbling that if only he could forget . . . and Dr. McCoy had then seized the opportunity to treat Spock to one of his "humanism" lectures, saying how sorry he was for Spock because Spock, being unable to feel emotions, would never know the glories of love. "Really, doctor?" Spock had intoned. McCoy left the room. Spock leaned over the sleeping Kirk, arranged his long fingers about Kirk's head in a miniversion of the Vulcan mind meld, and murmured: "Forget."

This image of the Vulcan with his hand spread across Kirk's head, giving the lie to everything McCoy had said, was what flashed into Liam's mind. His last resistance collapsed. Sagging against the bike he said, "Could you do it now?"

"Now? Do you mean—right here?" Liam nodded. "Well—it *would* be considerably easier if we weren't both wearing those pestiferous coveralls . . ."

"I want you to do it *now*," said Liam. "Unless it's impossible."

"Not impossible, just harder. Very well. I'll make a rough-and-ready job of it now and do the more delicate work when we're back in Washington, where I'll have access to the equipment we used on old Lundqvist."

"I don't want to forget he ever existed," Liam said.

"You won't. You won't. You'll remember that you had a friend who died, and that the blanks in your memory represent thoughts about that friend, but the details will be unavailable until you want them again. Will that do?"

Liam laughed raggedly. "It's kind of like a lobotomy, isn't it?"

"Yes it is, in a way. But reversible."

"Will it hurt?"

"Not even a little, as Jenny Flintoft could tell you."

Liam thought of something else. "When you said you wanted to understand the connection between us better—will wiping my mind help you do that? I mean, will you know everything *I* ever knew about Jeff, when you're done?"

Humphrey nodded, his helmet bobbing. "I can't explain the process so you'll understand it, but yes, after I treat you in Washington I'll be in possession of whatever memories I will have removed—concealed, rather—from you. And I'll know a very great deal more than I do now about human bonding."

Liam thought, And a very great deal more about human pain than you bargained for, I bet. "Okay," he said, biting down hard on his respirator mouthpiece, "let's get it over with. Where's the chopper? And then I guess you can take me home."

"By way of the Ragged Rock," I think," said Humphrey. "So we'll know how to find it again. When the time comes."

8

TWENTY TWENTY

On the morning of my seventieth birthday, I woke up feeling sad.

I lay in the dark and thought about a dream I'd had many years ago, shortly after my adventure with Terry in the park. In the dream I had entered a room which was in total blackness but for a single shaft of light falling across the face of a feeble, sad old woman seated in a rocking chair. She was wearing a black dress and holding a piece of paper up for me to see. On the paper was written, in blue ink, in an unfamiliar but very legible hand: "It's so easy to go after seventy." In the dream, aware of her sadness and helplessness, I had gone to her, leaned over, and kissed the poor old soul on both cheeks.

And now, amazingly, *I* had become the poor old soul; and the life insurance policy that Terry's experience had bought for me expired today.

This rather queasy-making dream had been on my mind a good deal during the past few months. *It* wasn't the main reason I felt sad, however. Seventy is a ripe age; anything more is gravy, though I wanted more. No, mostly I felt sad that neither my husband Matt nor my cousin Mark had lived to celebrate this day with me. Matt had been carried off suddenly by a stroke the year before, at seventy-seven: a good age, and a good way to go; but I missed him all the time. Mark, less lucky, had fought off cancer for a painfully long while, but it got him in the end.

(I didn't think, that morning, of the third person who had not lived to attend my party: Terry's son Jeff, dead more than ten years now. I suppose I had finally grown used to his not being around, but still it seems strange).

251

Now Phoebe and I, we two geriatric widows, kept thinking we ought to sell the house. Neither of us wanted to, and all the space was nice when any of Phoebe's three children came to stay, but the place was getting to be too much for us to keep up. Phoebe, though a youngster of fifty-nine, was overweight and chronically short of breath; and we knew it was poor management of our limited joint resources to hold onto the place. Something would have to be decided about it soon, and that made me sad too.

But I pulled myself together and thrust these gloomy matters out of mind. By early afternoon I had to have the ingredients of a party put together: my own party, thrown mostly by me for myself, with help from assorted friends and relations.

I rolled out of bed and raised the blind: a dull, gray day. Oh, dear. *Not* helpful. At least it wasn't raining: nothing quite so dismal as a cold November rain, unless it might be a cold February rain.

And actually, that was about as bad as it got. While I was still scowling up at the cloud cover, Phoebe came puffing up the stairs with breakfast on a tray; and while I was still drinking my tea the doorbell rang, and when Phoebe puffed down to open the door it was the florist with a big arrangement of chrysanthemums, bronze and yellow, with many happy returns of the day and love from Phoebe's older daughter. Margy, an editor for a publishing house in New York, had to be at a conference in Dallas today, so she wouldn't be able to make it to the party either. Too bad. But neither would she be bringing Rika, so there was a silver lining to that cloud. Margy had been five months pregnant at the time of the Broadcast that brought the pandemic of infertility upon the world; her little girl was one of the very last children born. Phoebe, who had loved being a mother and looked forward passionately to having at least half a dozen kids calling her Granny, had instead to make do with just Rika.

Naturally it was very hard not to spoil the last generation of children to be born for nobody knew how long, but in my opinion the seven-year-old Rika was a beautiful little monster.

But I was very fond of Margy, whom I had known all her life, and the mums were perfectly gorgeous.

The bell went again just as I'd finished dressing and was spreading up my bed. This time I went down myself to admit Frank and Jenny Flintoft, who'd flown over from England specially for the occasion. Jenny and I had gotten close during the year Matt and I fretted away at Darwin College in Cambridge, after the meltdown. I particularly wanted her here today, both for my sake and for hers. She and her husband had been the first humans ever befriended by a Hefn. A Hefn was coming with his human friend to my party, and I had a hunch it might do them all good to meet.

Jenny looked wonderful. I'd rarely seen her looking anything else—the life on Frank's farm had suited her right from the start—but her beautiful pink complexion under a cap of gray curls was a sight for sore eyes on that gloomy day. In back of her stood a grinning Frank, with his flyaway white hair and blue eyes of a deceptive innocence, that had made me underestimate him at first. Seeing them together framed in the doorway I realized that over the years Jenny had come to look like Frank, while Frank simply looked more himself than ever.

Their married solidarity triggered a tremendous pang of missing Matt—I couldn't help it—but I mastered this and welcomed them both with genuine pleasure. We'd kept up a much more regular correspondence after the year in England, and phoned each other every three or four months, but I'd seen them only once in the nine years since our return: last year, at Matt's funeral.

Jenny embraced me warmly. Letting go, she said—to get it out of the way—"I do so much wish Matt could be here too."

"So do I, love," said Frank then, hugging me a little stiffly.

"And so do I," I echoed them, "and so would he be sorry not to see you both, but let's be glad there are still three of us left to enjoy the occasion."

"Amen to that." Frank took off his coat and helped Jenny out of hers. "We've come round early to be put to work. We've both been awake for hours and straining at the traces, so I hope you've got something lined up for us to do."

"We'll need to consult with Phoebe about that," I told him, "since she's the brains behind the kitchen work, and that's about all that's left to do." And I led the way into the kitchen, where Phoebe was beating a huge mixing bowl of strawberry cake batter by hand, the bowl tucked at her side and the spoon whirling."

Phoebe had met the Flintofts at Matt's memorial service, but they had spoken only briefly. Now Jenny said, with a big smile,

"You're the mother of the famous Liam, that I've been hearing about from Carrie since he was seven or eight!"

Phoebe laughed; she was pleased. "Carrie's had a soft spot for that boy from the day he was born. You'll get a chance to form your own opinion when he gets here."

"How old is he now?"

"Twenty-two. Hard to believe, isn't it, Carrie? You folks probably know he's on the staff at the Bureau of Temporal Physics here in Washington."

"We did know that," Frank said. "Did he go to college, or did the Hefn take over his education when he joined the staff?"

"No, he didn't go to college," said Carrie. "That's a bone of contention, actually; Liam's educated way beyond his age in math and physics but he's way behind in everything else. But he loves the Bureau and they're very happy with him, so I suppose we ought to count our blessings."

Frank said, "I take it, then, that he's finally managed to accept his friend's death? Carrie told us what a difficult time he had about that."

Phoebe, who could tear up at the drop of a hat, did so now. "Yes, he's come to terms with it, finally. He saw a counselor for several years, and he had some special help from one of the Hefn at the BTP."

Knowing of their own experience with Hefn-induced amnesia, I had made a point of keeping the Flintofts up to date about this "special help." There was an awkward moment, caused by their uncertainty about how much Phoebe knew they knew.

Phoebe rescued us by failing to notice. "Jeff was like my own son," she explained. "I raised him myself till he started to school, and he was in and out of our house almost every day of his life. He was a lovely boy and sang like an angel. We'll never get over his death, any of us, not Carrie nor his father nor Liam nor me, nor his mother out in California, but I'd say Liam has come to terms with it about as much as the rest of us have—that is, pretty well."

"I heard from Anne, by the way, Feeb," I put in. "I forgot to tell you. She called last night while you were out, to wish me a happy birthday—she wasn't sure exactly which was the right day, but of course she did remember it was just a few days after Halloween."

Phoebe nodded. "Terry must have told her that."

254

Jenny brightened: "Oh! because of the time you and Terry were in the park—"

"Right. You got it. As a matter of fact, she was very nice. Anne never really took to me," I explained to Frank and Jenny, "but she and Phoebe were pretty good friends for a while, when the boys were little."

"As good friends as she ever let herself get with anybody," said Phoebe. "She was a bit of a cold fish, but we got along."

"Well, she sounded less cold and less fishy on the phone last night, and I must say she looked pretty good. Maybe she primped a bit for the call, so I could tell Terry . . . no, I'm being unkind and there's no need. She says she's well and happy, and asked to be remembered to you. She had a baby the year after she remarried, did you know that? She showed me a picture. A little girl, named Gillian, who'd be about eight now I suppose— and guess what? Gillian sings like a lark."

"Another singer, what do you know!" This from Jenny.

"And not so surprising at that," I observed. "The musical genes were Anne's, they certainly weren't Terry's."

Phoebe laughed and said, "No, poor soul, they certainly weren't," in a funny echo of my early-morning lament.

By two o'clock we were ready for the hordes to descend. The invitations said three. Jenny and Frank went back to their motel, and I decided to lie down for half an hour to compose my thoughts.

Ten minutes later, having discovered that I didn't much care for these thoughts, I was back downstairs in time to let in the first two guests: Terry and his second wife Pat, leaning on her cane.

"We're early," Terry said, giving me a long, hard hug and a kiss.

"But we had a reason," Pat added. She and I pecked each other's cheeks in a gingerly way. I liked Pat all right, quite apart from sympathizing with her, for fate had dealt her a fearful blow. Pat had been one of the first-diagnosed victims of Lyme disease, which she'd contracted while working as a CIT at a summer camp. She'd had no early symptoms at all, being one of the minority whose first sign of infection was swelling and pain in her knees, hips, and ankles, and she was only fifteen. This was Lyme arthritis. She was treated, but the arthritis became chronic

255

and considerable damage had been done to the large joints before they found a way to arrest its progress. I admired her persistent cheerfulness in the face of this unfair youthful crippling.

The problem was, I was jealous of her too, on account of Terry. There was an aspect of our own relationship, Terry's and mine, that had never been worked out or through. As long as Matt was alive I had kept the question closed, though I could feel it being asked in Terry's demeanor toward me even before Anne had left him, and more insistently thereafter.

But no sooner had Matt died and removed the obstacle on my side, than Terry had turned up with Pat. He had even married her, despite the fact that marriage had gone so decidedly out of fashion after the Broadcast. I couldn't see the point, when even the tax laws no longer distinguished between married and single filing status for marriages taking place after June 6, 2013. But Terry declared himself too old to change; and Pat, whose first marriage at forty-plus this was, insisted that she wanted to find out what being married *felt* like.

I granted her that right. My resentment wasn't personal—I'd have borne a grudge against any woman Terry took up with, in or out of wedlock—and I had hopes that my feelings would moderate with time and familiarity; but I still felt grumpy whenever I saw or thought of this person who stood, leaning bravely on her cane, right in the way of something I wanted.

Well, when one turned seventy it was time to grow up. Pat was a teacher of the hearing impaired, a thoroughly admirable person. She was also a children's book illustrator, and quite talented. No two ways about it, I was going to have to get my head straight on the subject of Pat. Terry had accommodated handsomely to Matt for many years; I was going to have to try and be as handsome in my turn.

Beginning now. "You know you're both welcome here any time of the day or night. We don't see nearly enough of you, now that Terry's got so famous."

Terry looked pleased. "As a matter of fact, that has something to do with our reason for beating the crowd."

"Your getting so famous?"

"Our not seeing nearly enough of each other." He took his coat and Pat's and hung them, out of long habit, on pegs in the closet, though he knew perfectly well that we always piled the coats on the bed in his old room on the second floor when we had a lot of guests. "We've got something to say to you both, before anybody else gets here."

Phoebe joined us in time to hear this last bit. "Come and sit down, then," she said after greetings had been exchanged. "Coffee?"

"No time. In twenty minutes people will be banging the door down, and Pat and I want to give Carrie our present before they do."

Somewhat self-consciously I led the way into the living room. "It's a business proposition," said Terry when we were all seated. "Carrie, you and Phoebe will have to talk this over between you, but here's what we'd like to do. I know you've been fretting about what to do with the house. Well, Pat and I would like to buy it and live in it, and we would *both* like *very much* for both of you to stay on here. There's plenty of room. It would need some reshuffling and redesigning of the space, but there's no reason four adults couldn't fit comfortably with everybody's privacy protected."

He stopped and waited expectantly. I was dumbfounded; the scheme he had outlined was one that had never once occurred to me—nor to Phoebe either, who looked as astonished as I felt. Involuntarily I glanced at Pat and found her looking frankly at me. When our eyes met, she colored and nodded. "Terry's speaking on behalf of us both. That's the absolute truth, Carrie. I'd like to live here, and I'd like the two of you to stay on. We'd keep the place in Georgetown and sell my house, and then Terry would have to get out here much more often than he does these days, which would suit everybody."

"But why?" I was finally able to say. "Why would you want to saddle yourselves with the responsibility for two elderly housemates, either of whom could turn into an invalid between one day and the next?"

Terry grinned. "I already *have* the responsibility, you dimwit! I worry about you all the time! This way I could be sure you were both all right. I'd want to put in an elevator and get somebody in to help with the housekeeping and shopping."

"And the nursing?" said Phoebe, beginning to get the picture.

"If that becomes necessary."

"I'll be goddamned if I'll see myself as your responsibility, Terry Carpenter!" I burst out now, suddenly so indignant I could

257

hardly keep my voice from shaking. "I may be seventy but I'm not senile yet! Who the hell put *you* in charge of *us*?"

Terry opened his mouth, but before he could say anything his wife spoke up with energy. "You're being foolish, Carrie," she said, flushed but firm. "You *are* Terry's responsibility. He loves you. You love him. There's half a lifetime of responsibility between you, so don't waste your strength being proud and independent, and lying to yourself about how things are. That's one lesson my disability taught me a long time ago."

"That's the God's truth anyway, Carrie," Phoebe chimed in. "How would you feel if Terry were in trouble and tried to tell you *he* wasn't *your* responsibility?"

My eyes filled up; my indignation collapsed. "That's exactly what he *did* try to tell me, thirty years ago!"

"And did *you* listen? Not much!" We all laughed shakily. Terry reached across the space between our seats and took my hand. "You started it; now finish what you started. What Pat said is the truth. You know it is, you old curmudgeon. I found this house, I always loved it. Let me buy it, and take care of you and Phoebe—it suits me, and it suits Pat. The elevator and housekeeper would be for her sake too, you know. Hell, if we take a long enough view, they'll probably be for mine!"

At that moment the front door banged open; Brett's voice called, "Hello! Where is everybody? Where's the birthday girl?" Phoebe levered herself out of her chair, passed me the Kleenex box from the end table, and hurried out to greet her younger daughter. While I blotted my eyes and blew my nose, Terry stood up and came and laid his cheek on the top of my head. "Think about it, okay?" He pulled me up by both hands, kissed me again, and stood back to let me pass.

My first thoughts on the subject were not the sort I felt able to tell either of them, of course. Such as: what about the tensions that would be generated by all of us living in the same house, with me constantly being drawn toward one of you and gnawed by resentment of the other? What about Pat's feelings? What about Terry's, juggling his commitments to Pat and me in such confined quarters? It sounded like a terrible idea—and yet, in some ways, it was plainly a very good one. It solved as many problems as it raised, I had to admit that. "Okay," I told him. "I will, but you two had better think about it some more too before we decide anything."

When I reached the door Phoebe's heavy arms were still im-mobilizing Brett, while behind the tableau they made stood a very tall, very thin, awkward-looking young man. "You must be Eric," I said, and he grinned with relief. "*I'm* the birthday girl. Come on in, let me take your coat. Hello, sweetie," I added to Brett over Phoebe's shoulder. "My, don't you look wonder-ful! When I was in my last year of graduate school I looked like death, and there are pictures to prove it. What's your secret?"

Phoebe released Brett, who came and gave me a kiss. "Happy Birthday! It's not a secret, Carrie, it's Eric. He just makes me happy. I'm not surprised it shows." She gave Eric a devoted look that pierced me—again—with a sharp pang, the loss of paired-ness. "Here's your present, by the way. Many happy returns of the day, and we hope you don't already have one."

I thanked them both and laid the box on the table by the door. "Don't you have any luggage? Surely you're not going all the way back up to Ithaca tonight."

Eric said, "We couldn't if we wanted to, there aren't any decent connections. We're staying at the BTP. Liam got a room for Brett, and my mentor from college got one for me. Her name's Nancy Sandford; she's the one who did all the basic work on my virus-resistant cantaloupe."

"Eric's invented a new cantaloupe," Brett put in, linking her arm through his. "Milky Tango hybrid."

"I beg your pardon?"

"Milky Tango, that's the cantaloupe's name. Hybrid plants are named like race horses, for their antecedents—in this case, Milky Way and Mi ting tang."

"It's very resistant to cucumber mosaic virus. Practically im-mune," said Eric, "but they may be splicing virus resistance into muskmelons pretty soon, like they've already done with just about everything else of any commercial value, so all my research *and* all of Nancy's may turn out to be sort of pointless."

"Except it got you a Ph.D.," I said. "And a post-doc for this year if I remember right."

He nodded and grinned. "Yeah, that's true. Lucky for me they held off on the vine crops till now."

Brett added, "*And* it gave him an excuse to hang around Ith-aca waiting for me to finish, so we could both go on the job market the same year."

"This year?" They nodded. "Well, I wish you both luck.

When *I* went on the job market, let's see, that must have been back in 1977, there were *no* jobs to be had in English anywhere a sane person would have the slightest wish to go. I ended up, I'm sorry to say, at Penn State's branch campus in Erie. I don't mean to be tactless, Eric—Brett's mother told me you come from Erie—but that was a *very* dismal teaching situation, the worst I ever had to do with. Soul-destroying. I only stuck it for two years, by which time I'd been able to pay off my Ph.D. debts and buy a car, and then I quit.''

"You'd have found my branch of the system just as dismal, I bet, but I wasn't such a hot-shot student my first couple of years and I knew I'd be going out to the main campus to finish up. And then I got lucky—I got a chance to work for Nancy, helping her with a plant-breeding experiment.''

"We've actually got a different problem, but just as hard to solve in another way,'' said Brett.

"Two of you needing to find jobs in the same department, you mean?''

"Or at least the same general area. Yeah, well, that too; but the real problem is that twenty years from now there won't be anybody to teach, and no telling how soon after that—if ever—''

"Oh, God, that's right! I'd thought about that, of course, but being retired has put me out of things a bit. Yes, I see what you mean: why go into teaching at all, if teaching is going to collapse on you in mid-career? Except, of course, that the kids growing up for the next twenty years *are* going to need teachers, they'll have to be instructed by somebody . . .''

"From a career perspective,'' Eric said, "as opposed to a purely service perspective, there's a lot to be said in favor of sticking to straight research, if you're any good at getting funded.''

Brett put her arms around his thin middle. "Eric's a genius at getting funded,'' she said; but the radiance had gone out of her and I suddenly realized that the subject had a delicate side. Scientist or not, Ph.D. or not, Brett was her mother's daughter and had grown up to whatever age she had been when the Broadcast happened—twenty-one or twenty-two—in the expectation of having a family if she chose, just as Phoebe had lived in the sure and certain hope of many grandchildren. I had never heard

Brett comment on the subject, but the relationship with Eric must have had an effect.

Now Eric gave her a solicitous look and put his arm around her. "When it comes to funding, it's a big help to have a Hefn connection. The reason I've got one is that my mentor has a Hefn friend. She's coming to your party later," he told me across Brett's bent head. "It was Mrs. O'Hara's idea. I hope that's okay with you."

"I'm going to get some punch," Brett announced abruptly, breaking loose. "We'll talk some more later, Carrie, okay?"

Eric watched her cross the room with a slight frown. "I'm afraid that talk about the Broadcast upset her," I said. "I'm sorry."

Eric shook his head. "No reason to apologize, but it *is* kind of a ticklish subject. She wants kids a whole lot, is the thing. And then, she and Nancy get along fine, but Nancy's got this very close Hefn friend, Godfrey, that I mentioned, and Brett just can't stand the Hefn."

"You know, I'm ashamed to say I hadn't realized that. She was in college when they came back. Has she always felt that way?"

"Just since she started, you know, thinking about wanting kids and not being able to have them. The past few years. It got worse after her father died."

Childless myself, my sympathy with this might have been more theoretical than real, except that I could clearly remember struggling in the grip of desire for a child for several years when I was right around Brett's age. The Biological Imperative, without a doubt. It wore off later, but that wasn't going to help Brett now.

Later on, of course, I had compensated by "borrowing" Brett and her brother and sister whenever I liked—an option which would not be available to Brett.

"This Hefn of Nancy's," Eric went on, "he saved her life. He's the one who initiated the research on AIDS, the hibernation project, you know about that? Nancy had AIDS. She was asleep from 2012, the year I graduated from University Park, till just last year when they developed the cure. Seven years."

"Good Lord. Really?"

"Yeah. And the main reason Mrs. O'Hara asked me to invite her is, she wanted Nancy to invite Godfrey. That's why Brett

261

and I came earlier instead of bringing Nancy with us. Brett's pretty upset with her mother."

"And Godfrey's coming?"

"Yeah, he is. Nancy's bringing him in a while."

It was turning out to be an unexpectedly emotional party, what with one thing and another. "Does Brett know Liam will be bringing Humphrey?"

"Yeah, and she kind of makes an exception for Humphrey—but she's still allergic to the general idea of the Hefn."

Brett was standing by the refreshments table, laughing at something Terry had said to her. "Funny. I'd have thought being a biologist would make her sympathetic with their goals. I hadn't taken the personal angle into account. Stupid of me . . . but I wonder why Phoebe invited Godfrey, then—didn't she know how Brett felt about it?"

"Maybe not how strongly. I think her mother just felt it would be good for the people from England to meet, you know, *two* Hefn who'd had close human friends. She's so grateful to Humphrey, you know—because of Liam."

At that moment "the people from England" entered, a piece of synchronicity that allowed me to introduce Eric to them and slip away with an admonition not to let the other guests eat all the goodies before they got their share.

I went over now and poured myself a cut-glass cup of Phoebe's punch. It was my favorite party drink, based on nonalcoholic champagne and gooseberry sorbet, pleasantly sweet and tart at once, a sophisticated child's idea of the perfect punch, though we had provided some real champagne as well. At the table Brett and Pat were chatting and munching petit fours. When I came up to them Pat said, "These are delicious, but I haven't eaten this much sugar in the whole past year. I hope my system is up to the assault."

"Carrie always starts with dessert on her birthday," Brett explained. "The courses go: first dessert, cheese-and-cracker-and-crudites, little sandwiches, second dessert. It was something she always got to do on her birthday when she was little."

"And it's still how I know I'm at a party," I said, "even if it grosses the rest of you out. As far as I know, though, no diabetics or hypoglycemics are coming, and anyway, whoever wants to can skip the first course."

"Not me," said Brett. "I've been to so many of your birthday

parties my pancreas understands perfectly what's going on."
There was a little bustle at the door; she glanced that way and
remarked, with a calm I now understood cost her something to
hang on to, "Here's Little Brother."

Hastily I put my cup down on the table and went to the door.
Liam saw me coming and grinned with so much unfeigned pleasure that the backs of my eyeballs prickled. He had a big brown
grocery bag in one arm, and in his hand a small, flat, gift-
wrapped package. He wished me a happy birthday and hugged
me with his free arm, then held out the gift. "This is the best
present I ever gave anybody in my life. It's from Humphrey and
me, and you have to open it before the party's over so everybody
else can see what it is."

My reaction was a little slow because my mind was bust with
two thoughts, neither of which I intended to express just then.
The first was that the *best* present he had ever given anybody
was his safe return from an attempted suicide seven years before. And the second thought—my eyes met Humphrey's comprehending look as I thought it—was that I knew exactly what
this present was, and that Liam didn't know I knew. He didn't
know because Humphrey, in lifting the memories of Jeff out of
his mind, had also lifted one more thing: the memory of a story
Terry and I had told him seven years ago, just before he had
vanished into the forbidden zone around the Peach Bottom
Nuclear Facility, intending to die.

"I'm planning to open everything before the cake and coffee," I assured him.

"Great." He set the bag on the floor and peeled off his over-
coat to reveal a dark suit and tie, an outfit I hadn't known he
possessed. When I remarked upon it he said with satisfaction,
"Bought for the occasion. This is a *great occasion*, Carrie,"
and gave me another hug with the arm not holding the coat.
"Pam's very sorry she couldn't come, by the way. She's in the
middle of a research project that's at a crucial stage, out in
California, and just couldn't break away."

Pam was Liam's . . . "crony" might be the word. They had
met as fellow Apprentices at the BTP. She was not his girlfriend
in any ordinary sense but was as close to him as we were, as
close as Humphrey, and I thought her an extraordinary person.
I was sorry not to see her, and said so. "She's going to write to
you," Liam said. "Where's Mom?"

"In the kitchen, I think. Isn't she always?"

He chuckled. "Will you look after Humphrey? Something I need to ask her about."

"Of course," I agreed, though Humphrey's look said plainly that he could look after himself; and Liam picked up his bag and went off toward the kitchen, leaving us alone together.

Everyone in the room was acutely aware of the arrival of the Hefn; there were not so many of them around that the presence of one could fail to stir interest. They were all watching as the chief of the Bureau of Temporal Physics astonished and flattered me by stepping forward and reaching his short arms up to bestow upon me a ceremonial embrace. When the gesture had been completed he stepped back a pace and explained, "I'm working on the semblance now, and not the substance only."

"Semblance and substance of what? Oh—of human bonding! I see."

"Yes." The Hefn on Earth had given up dressing like humans after a couple of years and now went about in their own long gray pelts. Peering up through his own hairiness Humphrey said, "I asked Liam about the protocol. He assured me you would be pleased. I hope he was correct."

"I am pleased. Was it your idea or Liam's?"

"Mine entirely. You're the first I've practiced on, after Terry and Liam. I am, you know, extremely bonded to them both, but lately I've begun to notice the beginnings of similar feelings toward you."

"Well, thank you, Humphrey," I said, feeling both amused and touched. "I'm very fond of you too."

"Yes, that's what I've been realizing," he stated serenely. "I've been realizing that a third bond can spring into being because of two separate bonds which have nothing to do with each other. A fascinating thing. For instance, you and I are separately linked to Liam and to Terry. Then, in some way, your feeling for them speaks to my own. I begin to feel a connection to *you* on account of your feeling for *them*, and vice versa. The same thing happened with Pam Pruitt, when she and Liam grew so close; Pam has now become important to *me*." Humphrey beamed. "This appears to be my discovery. Belfrey said nothing about it, and Godfrey seems not to have noticed it either. So I'm the first. It's a kind of breakthrough! I'm very pleased to have been invited to this party."

264

"I can cite you another example. My very strong feelings about Jeff began because he was Terry's son and Liam's soul mate. Later I cared about him for his own sake, but it started because I cared for them and they cared for him."

"Yes, yes, I see," murmured Humphrey, eyes glinting.

"By the way," I said, "I want to tell him."

He knew at once what I meant, despite the abrupt shift in subject. "Yes, I agree to that. He has repossessed all his memories of Jeff now; there's nothing left to be worked through. He should have this last memory back as well; there will be less disappointment at the lost surprise than pleasure at how amazingly the pattern has resolved itself. I take it that's your own opinion."

"It is." And it was, but my chief reason for wanting him to know was simply that I didn't want to go on concealing anything from him any longer. I'd nearly slipped a dozen times during the years since Terry and I had told him our story, and Terry had had some close calls too. For all our sakes, it was time to come clean.

"Tell me," I said now, "have you learned all you hoped to from your study of Liam and Jeff?"

"Indeed I have," Humphrey said with great feeling. "Do you know, Carrie, I believe I am perhaps as close to Liam now as Jeff used to be. And he is perhaps as close to me as he was to Jeff, though one cannot know this, of course. But I believe it to be true. This is fascinatingly different from the Gafr-bond. I still serve my Gafr, as you know; but the bond with Liam doesn't depend on service. I can tell you this much: Godfrey and I are determined to serve the Gafr by saving the Earth, but it's hard for us to see the people suffering. That girl over there, for instance, Liam's sister—"

"Brett."

"Yes, Brett. Liam has told me about her. She is a young woman who wants to marry her young man and raise a family. We can't let her do that. The ship says she deserves to pay the price for what humanity's excesses have done to its planet; they feel no sympathy for her individual situation. But Godfrey and I—we can no longer be indifferent. Bonding with humans has changed us. We are being criticized increasingly. But the two of us are all they have to gather this particular information; they

265

have to give us more freedom than they like. They have no choice.''

"Will you be all right?'' I asked with alarm, thinking that the last thing Liam needed now was to lose Humphrey too.

"Oh, I think so,'' he replied. "As long as we avoid repeating Belfrey's mistake, of putting our priorities in the wrong order. Not that I'd wish to disparage Belfrey. He made his choice and was content with it.''

Belfrey, I knew, was Jenny's Elphi. "Speaking of whom, there are some people here who want very much to meet you.'' And I ushered him over to the table—where I saw that the first dessert course was over and Phoebe had laid on the crackers and cheese and plates of veggies and dip—to introduce him to Jenny Flintoft, who was talking with Liam.

Belfrey had not survived very long as a Hefn after ceasing to be a hob. I left the three discussing his last months as a virtual prisoner aboard the ship—I knew Humphrey would tell Jenny the exact truth, though it would upset her and Frank—and went again to answer the door.

"You must be Eric's friend,'' I said to the person waiting on the porch. It took no special insight to recognize her, since standing beside her was another Hefn. "And you must be Godfrey. Please come in, both of you. Welcome to the party. I'm Brett's cousin Carrie.''

"Happy Birthday,'' said the thin woman, walking before me into the house. "My name's Nancy Sandford.''

"Happy Birthday,'' Godfrey echoed in a deeper voice than Humphrey's. "Many happy returns of the day.''

I thanked him and took Nancy's coat. She reached into a carry bag and handed me a large box wrapped in silver paper. I said, flustered, "Oh, you shouldn't have brought me a present! Brett's mother wanted you to meet our friends from England, who knew the Hefn Belfrey while he was living as a hob in Yorkshire. The birthday was just a pretext; Phoebe should have made that clear!''

"It's nothing much, not worth being embarrassed about,'' she replied easily. "I'd open it right away, though, if I were you. It's perishable.''

I unstuck the tape from the silver paper with care—it had probably been used before, and would be again if I could get it off without tearing it—and lifted the lid of the cardboard box. A heavenly aroma rose like a cloud. Inside, nested in straw in three

266

rows of four each, were a dozen round, rough-skinned, light tan fruits the size of oranges. I had never seen anything like them in my life. "What in the world—"

Eric, seeing that his former teacher had arrived, crossed the floor to greet her, calling, "Hi! Come and have some punch and veggies—they're organic, I already asked Brett's mother. Hi, Godfrey, good to see you."

"Hi," said Godfrey in his deep voice. The word sounded so odd in his mouth that I wondered whether I had ever heard a Hefn use it before.

When he caught sight of the box of fruit in my hands, Eric grinned delightedly. "Hey, great, Nancy, you brought some Tiny Tangos! Carrie, this is a really special present. Wait'll you taste one of these babies."

"They certainly *smell* special," I said, "but what are they?"

"Can't you tell from the fragrance? They're cantaloupes," Nancy explained. "Too little for growers to bother with, but they do make a nice gift. They were an accidental consequence of the Peach Bottom meltdown."

"Where on earth did you get cantaloupes in November?"

Eric said proudly, "She *grew* them! Nancy's got a whole greenhouse of her own to manage, up in Maxatawny."

"These won't be quite as good as a summer crop, grown outdoors in the sunshine, but they're surprisingly flavorful for hothouse fruit," his teacher admitted.

I thanked her, truly pleased and flattered by the gift. "Eric," I said, handing the box to him, "would you take these in to Phoebe and ask her to cut a few in slices, so we can sample them now?"

"That's a great idea. I'll fix them myself, if I can find a knife and a plate."

"Phoebe'll show you. Thanks." And to the other two, "Please come and have some punch, and meet my cousin Liam."

At the table Liam was tending bar. I introduced him to Nancy and Godfrey as Brett's brother, and he ladled out cups of punch for them both. Though the three had never met, they knew a great deal about one another. Liam handed Nancy her cup and said, "Congratulations on a successful recovery. Humphrey told me all about it. Peptide T, right?"

He addressed this last to Godfrey, who accepted his gooseberry punch with a nod. "Right. Humphrey told you how it works?"

"Prevents the AIDS virus from binding to a vasoactive intestinal peptide by filling up all the receptor sites," said Liam, a touch self-consciously; he was being Humphrey's bright pupil.

"Indeed," said Godfrey with a little smile. He lowered his voice. "AIDS was the Earth's way of fighting back, you know. One way. We've outwitted her for the moment, but she would certainly have tried something else had we not forced the population to stop growing. Of course, she may try anyway—there will be too many people here for a long time to come."

World population figures were dropping dramatically, after peaking at about eight billion, but apparently the Gafr were far from satisfied. I glanced about uneasily for Brett; this wasn't the sort of thing I wanted her to hear. Godfrey, picking up on this, did his imitation of a smile. "I won't spoil the party by lecturing," he said; and to Nancy: "I'll just go and say hello to Humphrey now, my dear."

When he had wandered away Liam said, "You're from Philadelphia too, aren't you, Nancy? When Eric told us how you staved off the acute form of the disease for such an incredibly long time, I realized you must have been part of that study they were doing at Graduate Hospital, that our meditation teacher Dr. Feinman used to talk about. Remember, Carrie? We used to have meditation class after school—I went to Germantown Friends through the sixth grade."

Nancy said, "Yes, I was part of that study. Feinman was at HUP, but he kept tabs on us. And yes, I'm from Philadelphia—but from Delaware County. I lived in an older development near Media called High Meadow."

"Good Lord," I said, "so did we! We had a house on Meadowvale Lane."

"Mine was on Meadow*park*. Well, it's a small world. Eric worked for me there that last summer, 2010, but of course that was before he went to University Park and met Brett, so he never made the connection."

The coincidence struck us both as remarkable, but Liam was more interested in Nancy herself. "What are you doing now?"

Nancy picked up a floret of cauliflower and squinted at it critically before popping it into her mouth. "I work for Rodale Press and do a little plant breeding on the side," she said. "Or rather, I'll get back to the plant breeding full time this spring. They woke me up too late for last year's growing season.''

"Forgive me if this is an intrusive question," I said, "but what's it like to be Rip Van Winkle? How much have things changed in seven years?''

Nancy smiled. "All of us in the project get asked that constantly. It's not intrusive, I'm just getting tired of talking about it! The short answer is: a whole lot less than in any recent period of equal length. The Gafr have brought things to a screeching halt. The world seems shabbier, I guess, and people generally act less confident—though I think a lot of their former confidence was based on denial. The main thing I notice is, no babies. The psychological blow of *that* development probably hasn't been fully felt yet; everybody's still kind of waiting for the ban on babies to be lifted, I think, as preferable to accepting that a whole generation may be doomed to childlessness. I was doomed to childlessness myself, of course,'' she added, a little sardonically I thought, "but that was only me, not society at large.''

Taken aback by the woman's bluntness, I was unsure how to respond to this speech. Still, she had set the tone herself. "I have a hard time imagining how you must feel, after everything you've been through. What's it like to live in daily fear of death for thirty years, and then lose seven years out of your life? It must have made you . . . well, what? Bitter? Resentful of the rest of us?''

Nancy gave me a keen look. "I was angry without knowing it for a long time, before Peach Bottom. But I'm not anymore, and not bitter either, not now. Isolated though. And pretty cynical. I'd made some friends before I got the disease, the first good friends I'd had since college. Not surprisingly, I guess, most of them moved away or got divorced, or just changed, while I was in hibernation. Seven years is a long time.''

"So it's like the message is, sorry, you don't get to *have* any friends?''

"Unh-hunh, and that's hard. No kids, okay. You never had kids yourself, right? No man, okay. But to *lose* friends, after going without them for so long . . .''

From being unable to imagine how Nancy felt, I was beginning to imagine rather too well. Surrounded by a whole roomful of friends, in a voice that in my own ears sounded falsely hearty,

I said, "Well, you can always start over from scratch, can't you?"

She shrugged lightly. "Oh, sure. The thing is, you get tired of having to, and you start to doubt that it's worth the trouble."

Liam said, "Yeah, but when you woke up, Godfrey was there."

Nancy's expression altered. "True. Godfrey was there." A look passed between her and Liam, and for a moment I was the one who felt left out, despite Humphrey's pronouncement of his growing fondness for me.

"And Eric too," Liam reminded her.

She nodded. "Eric too. *Two* eggs in the basket. It could certainly be worse."

At that moment, as if on cue, Eric himself appeared from the kitchen carrying a platter heaped with bright, thin wedges of the miniature cantaloupes. We each took one of the pretty things. Mine was as sweet as candy; I nibbled it to the rind and snagged another in each hand before Eric walked on to offer the platter around to my other guests.

When he had gone, Liam—to my relief—changed the subject. "I know what I wanted to ask—do you still meditate?"

"Mm-hm," said Nancy. "Every day, twice a day, for half an hour each time. It was while I'd given it up, after Peach Bottom, that I finally developed symptoms. The AIDS is probably cured for good, but I took a very high dose of radiation at the time of the meltdown and now I'm trying not to get leukemia." She picked up a piece of carrot and poked just the very tip of it into the dip. "How about you?"

"I was never any good at it—actually, I was *terrible* at it," Liam said ruefully. "My best friend was much better. He tried to teach me, and I actually improved a little, but not that much. But I took a lot of radiation too, a couple of years later . . . so do you think I better start again?"

"Well, it can't hurt," said Nancy. "Nobody's sure whether it was the meditating or the exercise or the squeaky-clean diet or *what* the hell it was that kept *us* alive so long—maybe nothing but luck, though actually I doubt that—but I plan to stick to it this time. After seven years in cold storage, I'm interested in living as long as I can."

"Me too," said Liam, sending me a private look. Again I felt

270

my eyes sting, it was so good, even after all this time, to hear him say so.

"Maybe your friend could try coaching you again, now that you've got more motivation," Nancy was saying. "Are the two of you still in touch?"

Liam shook his head. "He died in the meltdown."

I had hardly ever heard Liam mention Jeff, though I knew he now remembered everything about him, and about the friendship. This was turning out to be an *extraordinarily* emotional day. I excused myself and went to find a safer conversation, intrigued to hear Nancy—as I slipped away—hesitantly offer to coach Liam herself, if he was interested.

Phoebe had been placing trays of little sandwiches with the crusts cut off around the living and dining rooms; I saw both Hefn standing by one of these with Jenny and Frank and went to join them. When I came up, Jenny smiled at me shakily. "We've been hearing about Elphi," she said, "and wishing he could have been here today."

"Elphi, Matt, Mark, and Jeff," I listed. "And Margy. That would be everyone"; and looking around the room I realized it was true. Everyone else I wanted here to celebrate my seventieth birthday with me *was* here.

At that moment the doorbell rang yet again. Wondering who could possibly be arriving when the gathering already seemed so complete, I went and opened the door to a short middle-aged woman in a huge fuzzy coat. "I'm Julie Hightower," she said with a wide, pleasant smile. "Liam's counselor. He asked me to drop by; he wanted me to be here when you opened his present. I hope I'm not too late; I had a little emergency in my practice this morning and it's held me up all day."

So this was the Julie who had proved so helpful while Liam was coming to terms with his memories of Jeff. "No, you're just in time for the sandwich course. I was just thinking that everybody I wanted to be with me today was here already, but now that you've come that's even truer than it was before. I'm Carrie."

Liam spotted his counselor right away and left his punch-serving to hurry over and greet her. "Hurray, Julie's here! We can open the presents!"

"It's Carrie's birthday," Phoebe admonished from the chair

271

where she was talking with Terry and Pat. "She gets to say when the presents should be opened. Can't you wait?"

Liam looked so pleadingly at me that I said, "Let Julie get herself a cup and plate, and then we'll open them."

"Ours first," he said, and I agreed: "Yours first."

They gathered round to watch: Terry and Pat, Eric and Brett, Jenny and Frank, Nancy and Godfrey, Phoebe, Humphrey, Julie, and Liam. I picked the flat package off the top of the pile and removed the paper. It was, of course, a film cassette. Liam said, "I got Mom to help me find the big viewscreen, so we can show it now."

"Not before Carrie opens the other presents!" Phoebe protested.

But I overruled her. "No, we'll show it now. Set up the viewscreen, sweetie. Somebody get the blinds."

While everyone else found something to sit on, Liam rushed around excitedly, yanking curtains closed and shutting venetian blinds. He slipped the cassette into the slot himself. Then he disappeared into the kitchen and returned immediately with two plates heaped high with cut-up pieces of something it took me a moment to recognize. They were quartered Dunkin' Donuts: rainbow doughnuts, chocolate-peanut doughnuts, jelly doughnuts, glazed doughnuts, all jumbled up together. He handed one plate to Godfrey on one side of the room, and one to Pat on the other. "Pass 'em around," he said, and came and sat on the floor beside me, hugging his knees.

My eyes swam. I leaned over and kissed him, too touched to speak. The plates passed from hand to hand around the room, and even those who had no idea what was going on quietly chose a piece of doughnut, understanding that they were being included in some sort of Communion service.

The plate came to me. The piece I took oozed red jelly, and when I gave the plate to Liam he took a piece with jelly too, not looking to see what kind I had picked. Jelly had been Jeff's favorite.

The room was quiet. Liam said, "I'm very glad you're all here today to see this tape." He added, "Eat up, now, everybody," and we did as he said.

Then: "Terry, come sit by me," I was finally able to say; and he came readily and, when the room was darkened, tucked my sticky hand into his. Humphrey crouched nearby, watching Liam.

The rest of us watched the screen:

. . . a gray day, a duplicate of this very day: gray sky crossed with thin lines of branches, dull-colored earth. When the camera wobbled into focus, "The Ragged Rock!" I exclaimed, as moved as if I hadn't known perfectly what I was about to see. The Ragged Rock. Beside me Terry's breathing deepened and he gripped my hand tight. The camera panned slowly back and forth across that once-familiar stretch of the White Trail. "When did you film this?" I asked Liam.

"Last summer," he answered joyfully. "Wait'll you see, Carrie, just wait!"

And I did see. Suddenly the view was no longer blank except for rock and ground and sky. Uphill from the giant boulder there was movement, which resolved into a buck so large he filled the screen, so wild his eyes rolled and foam flew off his muzzle, so intent on making the scrape I had seen in that very spot thirty years before that he never noticed the hidden filmmakers or the boy crouching out of sight of the camera, on top of the boulder. His forelegs pawed and plunged, his full rack of antlers hooked at the bare branches above him. Vapor smoked from his nostrils. He was a marvel.

My feelings were too complicated to describe, even now. For five minutes or so the film ran. Then the buck stood over his scrape for a moment, puffing and nodding, before bounding away, and it was over.

The tears that had been threatening all day now streamed helplessly down my face; and beside me Terry was crying just as helplessly. Somebody opened the curtains and blinds. Liam's shining face gradually took on a look of puzzlement as both Terry and I wept uncontrollably. Obviously he had expected me to be moved; but *this* moved? And why was Terry . . . ? After a bit he came to sit beside Terry on the sofa and said tentatively, "Does it remind you of Jeff—is that why?"

Terry mopped his face with his handkerchief but couldn't speak. "That's only part of it," I said for him, "and not really the biggest part." The rest of the group, less disconcerted than I'd have expected by these fountains of tears, sat or stood quietly and watched the drama unfold. "Would you hand me that book

273

on the coffee table?" I asked Julie Hightower, who was standing in the most convenient place.

The book was the University of Pennsylvania yearbook for 1992, exhumed against this very need and left where I could get it when I wanted it. I'd marked the page with an envelope so it could be opened to the right place at once. "Did you ever see this, sweetie?" I asked. "No, I didn't think so," and passed the book to Liam, who looked down at the picture of Terry as a college senior and then in astonished wonder up at the bald man of fifty, still weeping into his handkerchief as if his heart would break.

Understanding broke over his face. "Terry," he said. "You," he said. "It was you. It was *you*. All this time—*all this time— it was you!*"

Absolutely vindicated, completely verified at last, Terry could only nod and weep. Yes. All this time. It was me.

I felt Humphrey's eyes upon me and met his look with a nod: That takes care of that.

Phoebe carried in the cake. Everybody started to sing.

When I think of my seventieth birthday party, that's what I think of: that moment, which I had in a sense been living for for three decades, when the final pieces of the pattern connected, snapped and fell together, and the oneness of time was complete.

Appendix

TIMETABLE

1623	Gafr ship lands two groups of Hefn mutineers in Sweden and England.
1941	Gunnar Lundqvist born January 12 in Skåne, Sweden.
1942	Matthew Franklin born February 17 in Louisville.
1950	Carrie Sharpless born November 3 in Philadelphia.
1955	Hefn Lexifrey leaves Lundqvist farm with Gunnar.
1956	Frank Flintoft born May 11 in Whitley, North Yorkshire, England.
1958	Jenny Shepherd born August 29 in Miami.
1963	Nancy Sandford (Sandy) born April 19 in Denver.
1970	Terry Carpenter born July 3 in New York.
1975	Pat Butler born October 12 in Stamford, Connecticut.
1978	Frank Flintoft rescued from a spring snowstorm by hobs.
1981	Brenda Hollis born February 5 in Emmaus, Pennsylvania; Gunnar Lundqvist returns to Sweden.
1985	Blood test confirms that Sandy is HIV-positive for AIDS.
1989	Margaret O'Hara born January 29 in Philadelphia.
1990	Carrie and Terry see the mating deer, October 31; Eric Meredith born September 20 in Erie, Pennsylvania.
1991	Brett O'Hara born September 11 in Philadelphia.
1992	Terry graduates from college, enters Georgetown University Law School.
1993	Sandy completes her Ph.D. and takes a job at Delaware County Community College outside Philadelphia.

1994	Jenny kidnapped by Hefn Elphi in Yorkshire; National Health chartered by Congress.
1995	Terry graduates from law school, marries Anne Redfern.
1998	Jeff Carpenter born March 3 in Philadelphia; Liam O'Hara born August 25 in Philadelphia; Terry elected to Pennsylvania State Legislature.
1998–99	AIDS riots (the Terror) in America.
1999	Sandy gets tenure, buys house, begins midlife crisis.
2000	Sandy's retreat in the Poconos.
2001	Lowenfels vaccine discovered.
2002	Terry elected to the U.S. Congress.
2006	Hefn ship returns (March 5) and leaves (April 30); Jenny meets Frank, they dig up Woof Howe Hob.
2007	Jenny and Frank marry; Elphi begins helping on the farm.
2010	Peach Bottom power plant meltdown in August; Eric works for Sandy, then goes to University Park; Hefn ship returns to stay in October; Carrie and Matt spend academic year 2010–11 in England at Darwin College, Cambridge; Liam's family moves to College Park, Maryland; Terry and Anne are divorced.
2011	Gafr (through Hefn) issue the Directive and impose the Deadline; Pomphrey orders manhunt for Gunnar Lundqvist (late summer); Lexi's body found in northern Sweden; Carrie and Matt move into College Park house with Liam's family.
2012	Sandy developes acute form of AIDS (January); Eric graduates from Penn State (May); Elphi decides to come forward, reveals existence of Gafr (June); Sandy enters hibernation (August); Elphi dies aboard Gafr ship.
2013	Liam runs away (March); the Broadcast revokes the Deadline, imposes moratorium on human reproduction (June 6).
2019	AIDS cure discovered; Sandy is brought out of hibernation.
2020	Deadline Year; Liam and Hefn Humphrey bring deer film to Carrie's seventieth birthday party.

About the Author

Judith Moffett published her first novel, *Pennterra*, in 1987 to great critical acclaim. In addition to her fiction, she has published two volumes of poetry, numerous translations from Swedish, and a volume of criticism on James Merrill. She is currently an adjunct associate professor of English at the University of Pennsylvania and lives in Rose Valley, Pennsylvania.